TIER 1000

ANSPACH   SPEARS

※   ※   ※

Ragnar Beck only wanted one thing out of a life—the chance to soldier. In a war for the survival of the last continent untouched by the invader, he finally gets his shot to prove he's a combat warrior. And like the soldier he was raised to be—when the only choice is to fight to the bitter end—he leaves no enemy standing on the last battleground he'll ever see. Or is it? Resurrected into an afterlife where he must prove his worth to join the ranks of an ultra-elite tasked with becoming the greatest warriors to ever exist, he asks himself the only question a real soldier can—who's gonna stop me?

This soldier's struggle to make the grade is as important as his quest to discover who he fights for and why. Part mystery, part alternate history, all thriller, Tier 1000 is the story of a determined fighter and the battlefields from the past to the far-flung future that forge him into the Ultimate soldier.

※   ※   ※

PROLOGUE

So, you want to join my army and fight for me?

Sorry. It doesn't work like that. I don't take volunteers. I don't care how perfect a soldier you are, how many you've killed, how many battles you've won. There are many worthy warriors. Maybe you are one of them. That doesn't mean you've got what I'm looking for.

You must be chosen by me and me alone before you can even attend selection. That's right, I'm a committee of one, so not a committee at all. More like, I hold the seat of divine authority. And all that talk about a god-complex? You can stuff it where the sun don't shine.

Because around here—I. Am. In. Charge.

It's good to be the king.

Say I call you take the challenge—and by some miracle you make it. That still doesn't mean you're here to stay. Every day is selection around here, not just the first day. Every day. And that's for eternity.

There's a quote by Heraclitus that out of every hundred men they send him, there are ten who shouldn't be there, eighty who are only targets, nine who are real fighters—who he's grateful to have—and then the one. The true warrior. And it's he who brings the others back. I like that saying, but Heraclitus didn't say it, not that it matters. It gets to the truth of the matter, except he was way off. By several of orders of magnitude.

It's one in a million who has the right stuff.

There's another saying I like. It's about not looking for the best guy but rather the *right* guy. No attribution on that one because I can recall it being said in a hundred similar ways by at least that many generals over the ages. But the essence of the saying is true. I'm only looking for the *right* warriors. They're marked in a way that I can spot them because they'll do whatever it takes to win. And once I give them the chance to be in the greatest army that ever will be, they keep doing just that. Whatever it takes to win. They don't care about the cause. Because it's enough to be doing a warrior's work. It's the ultimate profession waiting for the ultimate practitioner. Because without war, the universe itself would stop.

Don't believe me?

You don't have to. Just like you don't have to believe in gravity to be affected by it. But that's my job; to make sure that the universe keeps turning. Even a king has responsibilities. And if you make the cut to be one of my Ultimates, yours will be to turn the millstone that grinds the grist that powers the churn of all existence. And you'll most likely die doing it. But you'll get used to that. After all, what is death?

Think you still want to be part of the most badass unit in the universe? Well first you've gotta die in glorious combat to even get the chance. So, there's that. All sounds pretty serious, doesn't it? And you might be wondering who I am, to be in charge of such important matters. When the time's right, I'll tell you. Your first day here you'd be too stunned to believe it. But it's all real.

I'm king of the war gods, son. And you're trying out for my army.

Mars's Ultimates.

01

"Rag, we ain't walking out of this one, are we?"

I checked myself one last time before we went down the stairs and retreated from the last night sky I'd ever see. What at first had been a vaguely different tint to the skin between my uniform sleeves and gloves, a little darker than the usual grime of sweat and jungle mud, had broken out into thin purple spider veins. Nothing good about that. Skin only turned purple where blood pooled after death. Only we weren't dead. Not okay.

"No, Danny. We're not walking out of here." That was the truth. "But we're gonna hurt 'em before we go. You got enough hate in you to see it through?"

Danny Stokes made a wet, gurgling cough. "We walk with death." Our motto.

I made the rejoinder. "And he is our ally."

You know how many "death" mottos there are in the military? Death from above. Death before dishonor. Swift death. Death dealers. At least, there used to be. Before everything got so wussified. But then, mottos like ours are all chest-thumping bullshit. We know that. And yet when the good-idea fairies emasculated our military like they'd done to the rest of the country, getting rid of mottos like that, as shallow as they are, only pissed us off even more. The do-gooders always think they know what's best for you, especially when it concerns stuff they know nothing about.

Regaining a unit motto that sounded grim and warlike was one of the tiny things that hinted at the country shrugging off the "fair think" way of doing things. It was too little, too late though.

I'll save that maddening tale for later.

It was a tough slog to get across the lake and to the dam. You can't fight the jungle. You can't change it. But you can make it work for you. The same jungle that made it hard for us to move fast—to our very last target forever and always—also made it hard for the Han to find us.

The Lotus mob could've flat-out nuked the peninsula, but that would deprive them of the prize that was the canal. So instead, they checked us by releasing some kind of bioweapon. As if the nerve agent they'd already used wasn't bad enough. This bug had to be killing the Han, same as it was us. Screw their own troops, I guess. No way the hordes were immunized, if such a thing were even possible. Plus, people were the most disposable commodity they had. The analysts said they could lose a half a billion and probably come out better for it in the end.

"You in pain, Rag?" Stokes coughed again. There wasn't any blood. Yet.

"Just the normal amount."

"The normal amount is zero." It was a running joke. Being a grunt meant there was always pain. And yes, I was lying. I was having more than the normal amount. But my hate was stronger. It squelched the constant assault from the burning waves of pins, needles, and ice that throbbed like the beat of a bad techno song from deep in my bones, through my muscles, and ended up as the rot of my spider-webbed skin.

I had to over grip my rifle to make sure it was still in my numb hands, squeezing until I shook, then relaxing a bit so I didn't fatigue too quickly. I took a quick glance down my shirt and wiped at my chest. Even under NODs, I could see that if this kept up, the branching webs would slowly turn me blue. The Lotus Hegemony had done the unthinkable to us.

Now, it was our turn to do something back.

I spit into my hand. No blood. I had time to see this through. For a while I'd really thought this virus-thing, or whatever it was, wouldn't do us in, as fit as we were. It's true about hope springing eternal, or ignorance being bliss, or what we learned about a positive mental attitude being most important in a fight. But when it started killing us one by one, I knew not even my accomplish-the-mission-at-all-costs ethos would let me shake this off like a case of food poisoning. Dammit.

So all there was left to do was bring the hate.

Stokes grimaced as I helped him to his feet. He looked like I felt. I said the only thing that came to mind. It was stupid, but sometimes even stupid helps. "We get there, we can take a break."

"The biggest break of our lives, you mean." Stokes wasn't ready to let them get away with this BS either. "Screw rest. I'll rest when I'm dead. If they want Panama, they can have it. We're not getting our security deposit back on this rental, I'll tell you that much."

I tried to laugh but what came out instead was a moist hack. "Damn straight." If we couldn't beat them, then spoiling their victory was a kind of win all its own. My grandpa told me about how in his first war, the bad guys had done just that. The old US had trounced an army that was touted as one of the biggest and most dangerous in the world, and done it in a few days. And out of spite, the losers wrecked the place on their retreat back to their own cesspool.

It was a different time then. A better one in which to be a soldier. We're still the good guys of our own story, of that I'm convinced. But the rest of the world sees us as, I don't know, fighting a hopeless war? So, if we have to adopt the tactics of our old enemies, so be it. There's something to learn from the victor and the loser of every battle, grandpa used to say. What would he think of us now? I'm glad he's not alive to see how far we've fallen.

Today, I'm going to make him proud.

The Lotus mob threw everything at us. We knew they would. They'd done it a time or two before. The Hegemony were inhuman creeps, but they knew how to send a message. They had that going for them. They hit their first victim, Taiwan, hard and fast. Then Japan. Subsequently, the other Asian countries folded into the Hegemony without hardly firing a shot in their own defense. The New Russian Confederacy held them off better—and are still fighting—but the nukes have made a real mess of things. The politicians gutted our nuclear arsenal so long ago we couldn't do the same even if we wanted to.

This is our hemisphere! And the invasion brought the NorthAm Union together for the first time like never before. Our combined air forces clobbered the Lotus Navy, especially in the Caribbean. Most of it's sitting at the bottom of both oceans. Not a single bomber got off the decks of one of their carriers. I think we used some of our orbital kinetics too. But that's just a guess. You don't see much from deep in the jungle, and that's where we've been.

Yup. They're trying to take Panama, then sweep north and drive us into the Arctic, but the NorthAm is throwing everything we've got into holding them here. And like everyone before us who's fought the Hegemony, we're getting stretched thin. The Lotus mob have the numbers. We're simply running out of bombs, bullets, and people. And when it comes to people, they have more. They sent a second, and a third, and even a fourth wave, and that's what it took for them to finally get their foothold here.

We obliterated the first divisions they tried to land. Cannon fodder. Meaning we spent valuable assets against their worst troops. It takes just as many bombs and bullets to kill drugged-up, psycho-conditioned conscripts as it does professional soldiers. They used the bodies of their own troops like stepping-stones to move through the mangroves and onto land. And unlike their first, second, and third waves, some of these latest troops are real hard-hitters.

Even so, the tactics they used all over Asia and Eastern Europe don't work so well in the jungle. With no air cover for their troops, our artillery and air support are devastating them. On the Caribbean side, we beat them like they owed us money. It's a shame a peninsula has two sides.

We couldn't shut down everything coming from the Pacific, so we're losing. And things are in chaos. What's left of my team is going to stick it to them but good. We're not going to die trying. We're going to screw them right back. And then die. And I don't care.

The Lotus mob wants the canal. Had we been getting support from allies elsewhere on the globe, they would've just nuked the locks. But we're not. We've been on our own for some time now. Asia is one giant block under the Hegemony. The Aussies are doing their best to survive alone, just like the NorthAm. In exchange for a promise of coexistence from the Hegemony, western Europe turned their backs on us. I'm not sure why the European Crescent Union thinks they're going to be safe once the NorthAm falls, not after what the Lotus mob did to their Muslims back at home. Wishful thinking at its worst. Well, screw them too. Their turn is coming, and we won't be there to help them.

It seems my team is just an angry allegory for the North American Coalition. All alone and fighting to the last.

✳   ✳   ✳

"Airborne assault by the Han! Over Balboa," someone yelled just as we walked into the TOC. I have a knack for being close to the action. Does that make me lucky? Guess so, if you think being set up to be in the greatest suicide stand since Gunga Din qualifies as lucky.

"We're out of contact with second of the thirty-second." General Shinsen repeated back like a statement, but it was also a question. The 2nd Battalion of the 32nd Infantry Regiment, 2nd Brigade, 7th Division, the Buccaneers, had been holding the ground around the Gatun and Agua Clara locks. Now they were silent. When your two-star sounds worried, you get worried too. My team hadn't been back to the division but an hour, apparently arriving just in time to see it all go to hell. I hate being a witness to history.

We'd had a very successful week of ambushing Han patrols and walking artillery and air strikes on their 19th Division. To tell the truth, I've never been happier. To finally be in the right unit, at the right time, doing what I was put on this earth to do, was as satisfying as anything

I could've imagined. After nine years in the army, I was finally at war.

I said I'd tell you about how our army went from being a laughable social experiment back into a fighting force. As they say, it was the devil's needs that got us back to being an army instead of a bunch of politically correct burdens on the taxpayer. See, our army hasn't been in a real fight in decades. After the Long War, the country turned pacifist. That was grandpa's take. No crisis was desperate enough, no threat so grave, no loss so pressing, as to drive our politicians to exercise force against our foes. At first, the national sentiment was that it represented a new "wisdom" in foreign policy. Praised by the pundits as mature statesmanship. Let diplomacy reign in a new era of peace, they said. But at what cost? That's the question Gramps always had. Were American lives and interests not worth defending?

The Han swept across the globe.

The day finally came when it was clear we were the Lotus Hegemony's next target. Not even the current crop of politicians tried the same tired argument that diplomacy was going to win the day. More likely, they wanted to keep themselves from a Han firing squad. So suddenly, the army was supposed to be the big stick again. We were at war.

Deep in the Darien was the thickest jungle on earth. Like I said, the Hegemony army got their foothold when the Pacific side defenses failed. If you ask me, it was a bad break for the Lotus mob. The jungle's so dense, not even the locals live there. It made the Han easy pickings for us. We'd trained in reconnaissance and calling in airstrikes aplenty. Getting to do it for real? Awesome. We destroyed an entire battalion. Not in one sortie, or course. We did our job—brilliantly, I might add. We found them under the triple canopy when the drones and snoopers failed to, and directed five-hundred pounders and incendiaries on them for the better part of a day. Our BDA was the stuff of legend. Thousands dead. It was going to be the start of our revenge.

Another week of ambushing small patrols and collecting intel, and I was looking forward to at least a single day off my feet and letting them get dry. I didn't wear socks anymore. Or underwear. They just hold sweat and jungle water and rub you raw. That dream got squelched. Lieutenant Hokkanen, our platoon leader, Master Sergeant Bud Sydnor, our platoon sergeant, and I were checking in to the operations center. The LT and Top were reporting directly to the G-3. As the division's sole special operations team, we were run directly by the division command element. Eyes, ears, kinetics. You name it. If it was tough, we got the job.

I was tagging along to get the score on how the war was going from my best source. Major Hawkins in G-2 and I were on the division judo squad. The major was new to judo. He was a good student and an old-school thinker to boot. The "modern army" nonsense he'd had to endure as a lieutenant and captain had rubbed him raw like it did the rest of us. He enjoyed the new attitude we were cultivating, now that a warrior ethos including personal combatives was encouraged again. One of the many reasons we hit it off. He'd wrestled in school and had a good feel for judo once I showed him how to take out some of the unnecessary motions that ruined his attempts at throwing. Timing in three steps never worked. Two was better. One was best. We cleaned up at the last inter-division tournament, and I gave him his black belt. I don't really have the rank to do it, but who does? I'd wrestled and done judo since I was a kid, so I ended up as coach and head trainer. Fighting got me where I am today, so to speak.

"Major Jack," I said in greeting—same as I called him during mat time. He believed in what my platoon was doing. Providing intel for us was his job, but it was more than that. I know he wished he was in the platoon with us. We made sure to make him feel like one of the team. And he was. He was just a warrior saddled with too much rank, and the timing of our war left him out of the thick of the action. If he were lucky, he'd get a battalion soon. With the number of casualties we were taking, my bet was he'd get a chance to command soon. I made it to his station just as the commotion started.

"The Han are dropping south of Limon bay," Jack said from his console to the whole TOC. "I just got the confirmation from the Buccaneers when we lost contact. We can't raise them again."

General Shinsen frowned. One of the operations NCOs sounded off. "Sir, more troops are dropping across Colon, old Sherman, and over Gatun."

Holy hell! If that was the case, a step outside of the ops center and we should be able to see their aircraft. How had the ADA not engaged them? I'd seen F-99 fighters on the airfield. Why weren't the crews up in the air? Did the Han actually have some kind of cloaking tech like the rumors said?

Then it happened. Can you feel electromagnetic radiation? It truly felt like an invisible wave surging through me. Maybe that was just my way of making sense of it. The power died. Even in the dark, I recognized the next voice.

It was the G-3, Colonel Harms. "Their final push to take the locks is here."

Maybe it was me who mumbled it. If not, I at least thought it at the same time it was said.

"It's brilliance like that that makes this unit what it is today."

02

"Where the hell did they launch from?" I'm sure I hadn't said that. It was another voice in the dark, a good question, but it didn't matter now. We all knew what had caused all the lights to extinguish and the screens to die, leaving us blind and stupid.

"Airburst. Right over top of us," Major Jack said next to me.

An EMP had exploded somewhere overhead. Not a full blown nuke because the death of all our electronics would've come with a shock wave. Plus, we'd all be dead. No, this was something high altitude and aimed at us for the purpose of hog-tying us. But you can't really disable a light infantry division that way. Not like you could avionics and computers. A grunt doesn't care about any of that stuff. We were a whole division of cavemen, just much better armed and trained. And the Han were here to challenge us to a fight for our tribal hunting grounds. Our war switch just got flipped from all-out warfare to the last setting. Die-in-place.

Action beat reaction. Chemsticks cracked and glowing light returned our vision. The LT and Top were corralled by the G-3 and the commanding general himself. I was close enough to hear. "Get to the spillway. If it's still standing, make sure the dam comes down. That's your mission.

Don't let it fall intact to the Han. Do what you need to. Take what you need to in my name. Understood?"

They both popped to attention in front of General Shinsen and spoke as one. "Yes, sir."

As much as I knew I should've been scared, my internal generator revved, charging me to 110 percent. It was time to go to work.

We double-timed back to find the platoon already jocked up and waiting. Double-timed? We sprinted a four-minute mile. By the way I'm describing things, you're probably imagining a conventional infantry platoon standing around. That takes a little explanation.

When the Armed Forces Equality Act passed, all special units were disbanded. Well, not THAT one, but all the rest. And even they got messed with by the fairness police to make sure they looked "right."

It didn't happen overnight. The erosion of our armed forces took some time, just like wet ground under a leaking faucet that ended up as a pond seeping through our cracked and crumbling foundation. Our military had been all volunteer for generations. When the numbers got so low that hardly anyone was serving, the draft was reinstated. There's only so much you can do with a conscript to make them a soldier. I was a volunteer, like all the generations of Becks before me. To most of my peers, service was something to be avoided, not pursued. Grandpa said not even the army could take the current generation of spoiled and lazy children and make them into soldiers. The new generation of conscripts would bring with them their culture of entitlement, and that would change the army for the worse. My dad didn't agree. He always said the army reflected the society, and they both changed and that it was normal. I didn't know. I just knew I wanted to try my best to be like the two men who'd taught me everything I knew that was of value.

"Keep sharpening that knife, Rag," Grandpa would tell me. He'd learned the saying early in his career from an old Green Beret legend who still taught at the special warfare center. He didn't mean literally honing an edge to a blade, though that was a thing he taught me. He meant preparing for war—mentally and physically. I don't mean to sound like I was some kind of prodigy because of my upbringing, because I wasn't. I spent a lot of time in the woods and enjoyed sports, but I was as much a gamer as anyone from my generation.

I played lots of VR games, but instead of stealing cars or robbing banks, I played war. Gramps liked games too, but his generation was all about the first person shooter stuff. Me, I preferred the full immersion of the tank. Gramps saw nothing wrong with it and ran interference for me with Dad when I caught flack about spending too much time under. A lot of the sims are pretty realistic and have a good historical base, and Gramps used my interest to get me to read about the actual conflicts and their participants that so many of the games were based on.

Gramps taught me there were other ways to sharpen the knife besides just studying war. He taught me to like puzzles. He bought me every puzzle and trick he could find. "A warrior's greatest weapon is his mind," he'd always tell me. My dad's corollary was, "No soldier ever won a war without sweat and blood. Get off your butt and get some exercise." He was right, too. Dad worked me out most days, and Gramps made sure that most nights I read something or played some kind of game outside of the tank to keep my mind sharp. Between them, they got me ready for the service.

I always knew I was going to join up after school, and I felt at least a little prepared, maybe even secretly a little cocky. I was sure my upbringing would put me ahead of the conscripts when I finally got to basic training. I got a shock all right, but maybe not the kind you're thinking of. The cocky kid found out he wasn't as prepared as he thought, is that what you're thinking? I wish that was the case. Instead, it turned out that Grandpa was right. Our society's new generation of soldiers accomplished something never before done in history. They didn't change to adapt to the military. The conscripts changed the army.

Here's how it happened.

It wasn't but a generation after the Long War ended before conscripts outnumbered volunteers. It wasn't too long after that before too many complaints to too many non-vet congressmen and senators finally found an ear. Gripes about inequality and unfairness were taken seriously by a government and a society that thought the military was an anachronism. The press was more anti-military than ever. They led the chant that the military should reflect the same advancements our society had embraced. Chief among those: equal outcome, regardless of effort. Everything was a right, not a privilege. Besides, with a new era of diplomacy, war would permanently be a thing of the past. There were serious talks about disbanding the military all together.

In a generation, military training was nothing but another youth soccer league where everyone got a trophy just for showing up. So basic training and infantry school—not quite the baptism of fire I'd grown up thinking it would be.

I thought when I got to my unit things would improve. An infantry unit had to have standards. Its purpose was to ready for war. And because the enemy gets a vote in how a war is fought, it meant that you always trained for the worst scenario, right? Wrong. Training couldn't be realistic or have any element of potential danger. If training had the potential to "emotionally traumatize," it was forbidden. Since shooting, blowing things up, and generally practicing the arts of mayhem were just that, we didn't do a lot. We marched a lot, got inspected a lot, cleaned a lot. But training for war? Nope.

It wasn't the army I'd dreamed of serving in.

When I looked into volunteering for one of the select combat units like those my whole family had served in, I was in for another shock. A few years before I joined, those units were chosen for special attention by the so-called reformers. It was noticed that the volunteers and the few conscripts who embraced the warrior life inevitably ended up gravitating to the same units. The warriors flocked together. And even though service in those select units was voluntary, it was found that "elite units" bred jealousies and discontent. This furthered the disparity in military social status and reduced the esprit de corps of the regular units, who couldn't stand knowing they weren't considered quite as good. To lessen the supposed gulf between the professional military and the conscript military, a new law was enacted.

The Armed Forces Equality Act.

The solution to not everyone being the best was to guarantee that everyone was given the opportunity to feel special. Almost overnight, the army mirrored our public schools. No one was allowed to fail. Everyone got a badge or a tab. Attendance at a school was a guarantee of passing. Units couldn't reprimand someone for poor performance. The act also mandated a union, with stewards at company level to register complaints and investigate any reported violations of the AFEA. Standards were lowered, then dismissed altogether.

Soon, there were so many awards and insignias for any skill, no matter how common, that in no time a PFC could look like the most decorated veteran from the Long War. No one was special—because everyone was special. When I look at pictures from that time, it was hard to tell what army a soldier was even in. There were berets of every color, sashes and cords of every variety, badges for every MOS. Heck, there was a unit that started wearing kepis like the old movies about the French Foreign Legion!

It didn't work. Seemed the same disparities and jealousies about some people being more capable than others hadn't been solved by giving everyone more jewelry and hats to wear. The new solution? Everyone needed to be the same. This was about the time I'd joined up. An old paradigm was revived, one that dated back centuries and was used as the rationale to prevent elite units from being organized. Specialized units drained valuable resources of manpower and equipment from other organizations. By mandate, now the whole force was elite. Which meant it was unnecessary to have elites within elites. Oh, there's still an airborne division, but no more jump wings or maroon berets. No more jump pay, either. If you were there, it was because it was your duty, and true duty doesn't require special recognition. The armed forces union was made even stronger and added the SECs—sensitivity and equality counselors—to enforce the new mediocrity.

Everyone. Was. The. Same.

Achievement unlocked.

Now today in my army, except for the patch on someone's shoulder, you can't tell a tanker from a clerk, an airborne infantryman from an EOD tech, a cook from a sapper. There's only rank and division insignia on any uniform. What happened to my dad and grandpa's old units? Special Forces and the Ranger Regiment? Dissolved. And the opposite of what was intended happened. Rather than experienced guys bringing their knowledge back from those elite units to the "conventional" army, professionals left the service in droves.

I'm glad Gramps had already passed. If he'd lived to see this, the broken heart would've been what did him in.

The bright spot? At a division commander's discretion, special units could be formed for temporary purposes. Despite attempts to legislate away "elites" within the armed forces, reality dictated that there would still be difficult missions, and that special capabilities were necessary to perform such. Which meant soldiers with special training, skills, and equipment. Without any special insignia or uniform changes, of course.

Luckily, when the spin-up to prepare for the inevitable Lotus Hegemony aggression was happening, my division commander decided enough was enough. Most all divisions now had a Special Activities Platoon. Get that? The SAPs are called a platoon. No teams. No squadrons. Just squads and platoons and companies. It's got to be done under the "sameness" doctrine. Regardless of what you call us, we're organized as close to the model of an old Special Forces A-team as we could get away with. Duplicated specialties. All we train for is war fighting. Time spent in human interpersonal dynamics, social sensitivity, and emotional conditioning classes—ended. They just fudge the paperwork. It's a secret in the open. Or was. By the time the buildup to war was happening, the Pentagon and the civilians at the DoD were too busy worrying about survival to care what we were doing on the ground.

There was a selection. It was tough. Hundreds of us in the 7th applied. The first day, just the PT test alone sent over half the applicants back to their units. And it was nothing extraordinary. Just the regular yearly test. The difference? Instead of it being a self-assessment tool for fitness, this time, there was a standard to pass. That was new. People who failed to meet the standard were dismissed. There were a lot of hurt feelings and complaints that went up the line from the unit equality monitors. But the commander held firm.

After a month of testing, training, and evaluation, there were fifteen of us left standing. Finally, this was the army of my granddad! I felt great. Like I'd accomplished something. I knew I was going to become dangerous. A warfighter. The Lotus Hegemony was coming for the North American continent. And we were going to stop them.

We trained. Hard. We got to go to all the new schools that had been stood up again. The first school was to train us how to operate at the tempo of a real war. They couldn't call it Ranger school anymore, but that's what it was. I met soldiers from other divisions who were doing the same— building back skills that had been quashed from our army for a decade. A lot of knowledge had been lost and existed only in manuals and memories. In some of the courses, the instructors were still finding their way, unsure that what they were teaching us was right or best. We didn't have combat vets anymore.

They brought in some of those retired vets to supplement the cadres, teaching the instructors while they also taught us. Sometimes the training was just cruel and didn't seem to have any learning objective other than to make us miserable. There's always someone who thinks that's a kind of training in and of itself. But we didn't care. We were testing ourselves in combat conditions. No more mandated rest or sleep periods. No more choosing when you'd reached your limit and could call a "time-out." Patrol after patrol, planning, rehearsing, moving, shooting, communicating, destroying. If you couldn't keep up? You were out.

Had the sensitivity coaches been there, they would've put a stop to it. But with the war coming, they'd been silently phased out. Someone, somewhere, understood that the army was no longer a playground for social experimentation. We had one purpose. To win our war at all costs. And if you didn't have what it took to be that kind of soldier—the one who wouldn't quit no matter what—then we didn't want you standing with us.

My platoon did well. Of the fifteen who'd made it through our division selection, twelve of us were back with the 7th, ready to go to war. Captain Danforth broke his leg in airborne training. Not his fault. Staff Sergeant Hernandez caught some kind of flesh-eating bug during jungle training in Guatemala. Again, not her fault. Only Lieutenant Kim quit. That's what I'd call it. After working so hard and coming so far, I still don't understand, but one day in the middle of mountain training, he got a faraway look, walked to the edge of a steep rock face, and jumped.

Better now than when we were in combat and we had to rely on him.

When we finally got back from more than a year of training, the division had changed as well. Everyone had the look of pride and aggression. Live-fire training was back on the menu. So were full divisional exercises, with artillery, air support, movements to contact. Everything. People got hurt in training. Some got killed, even. Grandpa told me as far back as I can remember, "you have to train the way you want to fight."

After that year spent all over, doing all kinds of mayhem, we didn't return with any kind of badges or tabs. Those days were gone. But everyone knew who we were, and when I looked at myself in the mirror, staring back at me I saw the warrior I'd always wanted to be.

So, when I took in the platoon just then, jocked up and ready to roll against the Han paratroopers, I saw the same before me. Soldiers. Real soldiers. Not a group of pretend soldiers, elevated by some kind of social program who were told they were the best—even when they weren't—and not some kind of interchangeable drone, the same as everyone else, no better, no worse. These were warriors.

The LT paused just long enough to strap on his ruck. "Here's your OPORD. We're beating it to the airfield, and we're hijacking anything that survived the EMP and making for the dam. Our job is to make sure it's destroyed. We're going to deny the Han the Panama Canal."

"Sir?" Jess asked. "Do we know why the engineers haven't blown it already?" She was the sharpest on the team.

"No. The Buccaneers are silent, and the Lotus mob's dropping all over. If I had to guess, they prepped the battlefield with some kind of mass casualty weapon before they

EMP'd us, then jumped in. It's our job to go in and make sure the Han don't get to keep the canal intact."

Bud had his ruck on now. "No more questions. You know as much as we do. We're running out of time. Let's move."

We found an Osprey crew towing their aircraft out of a hanger. The old birds were supposedly hardened against EMP, but what did that mean exactly? No one had ever tested them. This one seemed to have enough of its systems working to get airborne, but when Bud and the LT tried to task the crew to get us to the fight ASAP, even dropping the general's name didn't have the desired effect.

"No can do, Army," the pilot said with hands on hips. "We've been ordered to retrieve replacement parts to get more aircraft up and running."

That's when Bud's pistol came out. "After you deliver us, you can fly to Dayton, Ohio for all we care. The war is that way." Bud thumbed over his shoulder. "You think about flying in any other direction, I have the authority to shoot you for cowardice in the face of the enemy. And your union steward, too." The captain flying the tilt-rotor wonder found his patriotism, and we were airborne in a minute.

Radios were still out, and so were the nav systems. I strained my eyes, squinting through a port window. Nothing to see. There was no moon. I caught the occasional glimpse of muzzle flashes here and there through the darkness. The internal comms worked, and the LT and the pilots were arguing.

"I'm not flying over Gatun. It's crawling with Han." The pilot had risked some altitude to get eyes on the locks and beyond. FLIR showed hundreds of troops on the ground.

A missile nearly hit us before we got off countermeasures and dove for the cover of the treetops.

"Get us on the other side of the lake," Lieutenant Hokkanen ordered.

"No can do, Army. Nowhere to land that isn't hot. It's no good for your mission if we get blown out of the sky. I'm putting you down on Davis. We're on the ground in one minute. Get your troops ready." We'd barely been in the air five minutes.

"Grrr!" The LT growled loud enough for us to hear over the rotor whine as he made his way back from the cockpit. "They're dropping us on old Fort Davis. Close as they'll get us. Cowards. Let's go."

I held on as the plane transitioned and we dropped. Fast. The ramp was down and my NODs were in front of my face before I stood. I followed the rest of the team off, ready to light up an ocean of Han. No sooner had I taken a short run and dropped prone than the Osprey lifted away, the rotor wash gone, the air still again as our ride disappeared over the treetops. Where were we?

We'd been deposited in a clearing. If I had to guess, it was the golf course. The LT and Bud were conferring in the center of our perimeter when automatic fire hit us from behind me. The team opened up. I sprang up and made a hunched-over dash to the other side of our circle, threw myself down and crawled forward faster than a pig to the trough, got on line, and let loose.

"Multiple gun positions, two hundred meters, in and around that cluster of buildings," Parker yelled next to me.

After some quick shots, I pulled out an airburst AP grenade, dropped it in the launcher, and let fly from on a knee. I dropped prone again and was behind my gun in time to see the flash. Now I knew exactly where we were. The gold-foil painted insignia of the police headquarters stood out in my night vision. The sandbagged machine gun position and the razor wire around it exploded in a very satisfying manner. Someone launched another one, and it landed on the shorter roof next to it. Troops somersaulted off the parapet, rifles flying wide, just like the movies. Others collapsed just like we'd hit their off switch. They didn't get back up.

"Those aren't Han shooting at us, those are Panahooches." Melgar identified the Panamanian police forces correctly.

"Dammit," I said out loud. "They're supposed to be on our side. They confused us for the Han." It was Green on Blue at its worst. I was waiting for Top or the LT to get us moving. "Top, what's the move? Assault through or move out?"

Stokes yelled, "Melgar! Top and the LT are down!" Melgar was our primary medic. I was alternate, but my primary was ops and intel. I stayed on my gun and let Melly check them.

"Shit. Shit. Shit."

"Melly, what is it?" Jess asked.

"They're both dead."

It was all on me now.

03

"You're sure?" I asked Melgar.

"I'm sure," he said. "They hit the ground dead."

"Damn Panamanians," Burris yelled into the dark. "We're going to clean out the lot of you!" Was it really an accident they'd fired on us? The Panamanians weren't bad folks. Quite the opposite. I'd gotten to know the people and their history. Like a lot of small countries with something someone else wanted, they always came down on the side of the winner. Whoever held the biggest stick had their loyalty. It's how they survived. Their government worked with China for decades, so the prospect of being absorbed by the Hegemony didn't really seem to upset the average local. Had they swapped sides?

This wasn't intentional, I was sure. It was a mistake. The so-called fog of war. Somewhere on the other side of the manicured golf course, a bunch of cops had been hunkered down, thinking they were defending their homeland from the Han horde. In reality, all they'd done was kill the good guys who were trying to keep their country from turning into a Chinese gulag.

"Forget it," I yelled. "We have to stay on mission." I knelt and took the key off the LT's neck and put it on my own. "Our job's to make it to the dam. We have to move. Follow me." I took a quick count. Ten of us. "Henderson, lead us out. Make for the hardball up Tower Hill." I had a plan. It wasn't much of one, and I gave everyone the essence of it as we moved.

"We get to the docks and we grab a boat and make it across Gatun. The Han don't have the lake locked down yet if all they have are airborne troops. We make our way to the far shore and get to the spillway. That's it. If we don't get across the lake, we can't do anything. Questions? Move out."

"If only the bird had put us closer!" JR fumed. He was my friend and teammate. Sometimes he was a little too vocal when things didn't go according to plan. This was one of those times. His mouth had almost gotten him bounced from selection over his peer reviews. I saw the best in him. He never quit. He never stopped. He never failed to step up. He was just young. Only twenty. I remember being the same. Learning to keep your thoughts inside took time for most of us.

"All true, JR, but there's nothing we can do about it now."

"Sorry, Rag. You're right. Let's get some."

We didn't get fired on by any surviving police as we moved out. Thank God for small favors. We moved as fast as we could off the greens and found the hardball road winding into the jungle. The road led to the top of the hill and wound back down as steeply to dead-end into the docks sitting on Gatun Lake—which practically looked right at the locks about a mile across the lake. We'd run the steep route before. It was a killer. Straight up, then straight down to the water, about a three-miler, then back. Watching the giant container ships glide across the lake in and out of the locks was a marvel. Once we were done, that everyday wonder would cease.

I thought about trying to find a vehicle along the way, but the EMP had probably canked any of the civilian cars and trucks we saw parked outside of the family quarters. Waste of time to even try. The good news? If there were Han on this side of the lake, they wouldn't have motor transport either.

"Best pace, two columns. Keep some space between us. Head out." If we did run in to a Han patrol, it would be time for ambush battle drill, speed and violence all the way. Assault into the ambush with everything we had, then regroup and keep pushing. There wasn't another option. Not if we wanted to get to the objective before the Han had the whole place firmly locked down. In the distance, the exchange of fire we could hear gave me hope the Buccaneers were still out there doing their best. My heart was pounding out of my chest as we humped. Anywhere the road leveled out, Henderson and JR broke into a trot to make better time. Under the distorted colors of our NODs we looked like of a herd of grunting elephants, rucks on our backs instead of Indian princes out on a tiger hunt, top-heavy loads swaying as we galloped.

At the crest of the hill was the satellite tower, the marker that as good as meant that the downhill route waited. Once in the woods I put us into a perimeter and took a security halt. "Good job, Henderson," I whispered in his ear as I made my way around the circle.

"We gotta bring the hate. LT and Top are dead 'cause of them."

"That we will," I promised him as I eased over between Stokes and JR. "Guys, if I buy it, you gotta make this happen. I'm wearing the key. Make sure someone gets it."

"We're all buying it on this one," JR said. "But we'll do it together."

Stokes grunted. "What's the plan?"

Doing a leader's recon of the dock was going to take too much time. "We occupy by force. We take the jungle route to the backside, come out on the railroad tracks, and approach the dock that way. Any resistance, we assault through. No other choice I can see."

Stokes's NODs made his affirmative clear, the dual tubes like antlers on his head. "Better than taking the road. That's where any Han would be posted up."

"That was my thinking. Glad you agree." I moved around the perimeter and passed the word. I would lead us through the bush. Wherever we came out of the jungle, we'd end up on the tracks following the lakeshore. From memory I dead-reckoned a course, flipped the compass on my chest down, and checked an azimuth.

The jungle hides a lot of the noise of movement—if you can go slow—but if we weren't deliberate about it the sound of ten pack mules stumbling their way through the black would broadcast our coming better than a flashing movie marquee. We'd gotten a lot of experience in this jungle in preparation for the final Lotus assault. We couldn't botch this. It was time to change tempo. We'd busted ass— balls to the wall—humping up the hill. Now it was time to slow down, move carefully and quietly, and hope we could surprise any Han that might be waiting below.

That was my plan. No sooner had I started down than it went to hell. I crested the hill and found what seemed like a smooth contour to descend along that eased down to the lake. My NODs were useless. They still worked despite the EMP, but it was so dark that without my short-wave infrared illuminator, I might as well have been wearing a blindfold. If the Chinese had NODs that could see in our IR wavelength, using my illuminator would be like shining a white light ahead of me. Time to go old-school. I flipped them up and used my God-given mod-one-mark-one eyeballs.

I'd just reached out to steady myself against a tree, hoping it wasn't a thorn-covered black palm, when the hillside gave way, and I went with it. Down, down, down. Just like I was on some kind of water-park slide. I don't think I yelled. Last time it had happened to us, it was Jess in the lead, and we'd all laughed at her comical screech as she careened down a ridgeline. There was nothing funny about this.

I laid back and tried to keep my feet in front of me, knees locked together, picturing getting my family jewels skewered on a tree. I broke through the last of the bush, and the night sky was back again. "Oooff!" The exhale escaped like I'd been gut-punched as I came to an abrupt halt, mud and brush and small trees with me. Things happened quickly. Movement to my left on the tracks! I flipped my NODs down and brought my M-7 up. Two shapes that screamed Han raised rifles in my direction, and I let loose. All our time on the range kept paying off for me. I ran a box drill as fast as I'd ever done it and the two dropped. My suppressed bullpup had no flash and so little sound that I could hear the brush cracking where my teammates were sliding down the loose ridge behind me. To everyone's credit, they didn't utter a peep.

After a quick check to make sure I was in one piece and that everything was still attached—limbs and gear—I checked the team. Bodies and guns had spread out in both directions along the embankment leading up to the track. I took a better look around. Past the bend to our left, the dock would be waiting. "Stay low," I whispered to JR for him to pass along. It was a stupid thing to say, but I didn't want anyone up on the tracks yet. Sometimes aggression got the better of my team. I wouldn't have put it past Burris or Henderson to charge down the tracks, ready to take on a whole platoon of Han by themselves.

Staying in the thankfully dry ditch—thankfully, because it kept us quiet—a path let me peer just over the railbed as we patrolled ahead. I expected to see the Lotus horde any second.

I raised a fist and nudged JR to join me. We crawled on hands and knees up to the railbed. "You make quite an entrance," he whispered as we got face-to-face with the bodies.

"I do my best." Mongols or Han, I couldn't tell which. Their XS-40s lay on the gravel of the railbed. The telescoping stocks were the confirmation that these were airborne troops. Their uniforms were soaking wet. I thumbed behind us, and we eased back to the team.

"Lotus airborne," I said. "There'll be more ahead."

We crept ahead until about two hundred yards away I could see the dock. It was hard to miss. There was an old landing craft beached on the ramp. It was ancient and being cut up for scrap, one section at a time. A billowing parachute canopy was draped across the superstructure, fluttering in the wind. I momentarily winced, thinking about whoever must've landed there. If someone hit that metal monstrosity in the dark, it broke something or probably killed them. In the water were a few bobbing craft of different sizes. More important to our immediate problem, a dozen troops stood around. Some were messing around in the boats, some on the dock itself. Two stood sentry in the middle of the parking lot, guarding the road.

I sank below the line of sight and huddled with the ones closest to me. I whispered, my throat mic turning my subvocalizations into an audible transmission in everyone's earpiece. A lot of our gear was still working despite the tech-ravaging blast by the Han. "There's about a dozen troops in the open around the dock just milling about. They've got no idea I greased their buddies on the tracks. My bet's they missed their DZ and landed on this side of the lake. I don't see any NODs on them."

We'd seen pictures of the Lotus night vision. It looked too much like ours—a knock-off copy for sure—but we'd been told most of those were for propaganda purposes. A lot of the supposed peer-level tech and weapons in their photos were mock-ups and props, all for disinformation. The guys ahead had bare helmets, so it didn't matter if the Lotus mob had night vision gear for anyone but their propaganda models or not.

"We're going to hit 'em from here. Everyone, low crawl up on line. Slow. Make this a turkey shoot. JR and Jess, you get the two guarding the road. We'll wait for you to initiate." They had Mk-10s. I wanted to make sure the Han with the light machine gun overlooking the road, probably a PK-51, got knocked out for sure. "If we can do this without grenades, I'd like to." There were grins all around.

"Get some, babe," Stokes said, meant for Jess.

"You know it, killer. You ready to pay these mongols back?" It was funny, Jess calling the Han mongols—her personal name for all of the Hegemony. The Han made it clear they were superior to all other Asians, much less all other people. Jess was part Han herself. Her Asian heritage made her the butt of a lot of our jokes. We kidded her that she could be our decoy once we ran into the People's Hegemony Army. She would be the stuff of wet dreams for one of those brain-washed goons. I couldn't tell the difference between them and didn't have to feel like I was being insensitive—or that an equality monitor would report me—as Jess confirmed it for us. It supported the rumor that they were clones.

"You and JR show us how," Stokes said. "We'll be right with you."

Stokes and Jess were in love. She was tough. Deadly. Playful at a times, but a killer. Since they'd come out about their relationship with the rest of the team, I'd never seen Stokes happier. Not that they'd successfully hidden their feelings for each other from us.

Everyone was happy for them. Maybe a little jealous. Their relationship was never an issue on the team, and they were always soldiers first. Only once in a while did a "babe" or a "sweetie" slip from either one of their lips, like now. When it did, they got ribbed about it mercilessly.

"Hand me that internal door charge, babe?" Bud, our team sergeant, would tease. He never harshly rebuked them but made their slip in discipline a joke. Without missing a beat, someone, usually Melgar, would run with it.

"Sure, sweetie. Do you need more shock tube to go with it, honey?"

They took it in stride. I knew I didn't have to worry about either of them. It was time to do this. "Low and slow," I whispered. "Move out."

Jess and JR moved left of me. I stayed back a moment to guide the rest of the team into position, then followed up at a crawl. I squeezed between Melgar and Mac, and rose on my elbows to settle behind my optic just as I heard Jess and JR both say, "ready," in my ear.

"Stand by. Rest of us, work from the left and right from your own side into the center. Kill everyone on the docks." There was a single voice over the water. I didn't speak the language, but if I had to guess, it was an officer cursing at the man bent over the outboard engine as he struggled to make the pull-start engine turn over.

"Send it."

The Mk-10s were suppressed too, but enough louder than our M-7s that I knew it was Jess and JR who'd fired, just as I commanded. I put the tiny red circle on the chest of the Han standing in the bobbing boat with hands on hips, lecturing away. I imagined where the heart was and hammered it with three shots—one each time the sight settled—until he was gone. They had body armor, but we'd already learned it wasn't capable of defeating multiple hits. I only got a single shot on one more falling body before it was all over. I took a quick scan and changed mags before I stood.

"Assault through," I said, loud enough for everyone to hear even without comms. I ran left behind my friends rising from prone, hopped over to the railbed, and when I saw someone in my peripheral come on line with me, moved out at a run-walk hybrid, ready to kill anything that moved.

It was Stokes on my right. I mashed on my IR weapon light. He did the same. We flooded everything ahead as we rolled, searching the dark shadows around the sides of the boat houses and into the mouth of the winding road, expecting to see the rest of the Lotus mob spring out at us. When nothing moved, I broke into a real trot and the thundering footfalls of the team let me know they were with me.

Bodies lay where they'd dropped. They hadn't gotten a shot off! Not one! So far, so good. There was nothing as thrilling as shooting at an enemy and not getting return fire. It charged me up as I thought about doing the same to whoever was waiting at the dam.

"Stokes, take Melgar and Jess and find us a ride." Stokes knew boats. He'd grown up in Seattle and had been a Sea Scout as a kid. He'd wowed me with his sailing ability one weekend on the Carolina coast in a little two-person dinghy, too small in my opinion to be fit for use on anything but a small pond. I'd never doubted my own courage until that day, but afterward, I knew I never had to doubt his. It was not my idea of fun. If there was something that could ferry us to the other side of the lake, Stokes would find it.

Two hours later, it was just me and him left.

04

"Same trouble the Han were having when we dropped
'em," Stokes said in our huddle on the concrete boat ramp.
"Everything's fried. But I found us rides." He pointed to a
pair of dugout canoes tied off on a short fishing dock.

JR cocked his head. "Cayucas?" The dugout canoes
were common fishing vessels, but not exactly the tactical
speedboat I'd hoped he'd find for us. Beggars can't be choosers.
"Let's hope there're enough paddles to go around."

I checked my chrono. Just after midnight. "Start looking.
Time to go." Across the dark lake, an even darker shore
awaited. There'd been less of the gunfire we'd heard earlier
from that direction. That could only mean the Buccaneers'
resistance was fading. Where was the big explosion that
meant they'd blown the dam?

We paddled. I aimed us for the opposite shore. One of
the monster container ships floated in the middle of the
lake, dark and dead in the water. I saw a tiny white light on
the deck for a brief flash, but it disappeared almost immediately.
Someone with some sense killed it, knowing that it
was a bullet magnet. It's a bad thing to stick out as the only
sign of life in the middle of an invasion.

The bottom of the canoe was wet. We were swamping
it, five of us with rucks and weapons crammed like sardines
into the narrow burned out log. I was in this one with
Stokes, Melgar, Jess, and Burris. JR, Henderson, Kottle,

Cortes, and Parker were in the other. We were about halfway across when we heard the roar of jets. Some people could identify aircraft by their sound. I thought I was one of those people, but not this time. It was thunder and rumble and tremor, over us, past, then fading before I could guess. It sounded like they were coming around again.

"What took them so long?" Burris said aloud. The engine noise was building to deafening again.

"Better late than never," Melgar scoffed. If the Air Force had finally gotten a few birds airworthy, maybe this would be over soon.

"Get some," Jess urged. "Bomb it so we don't have to."

I was wishing the same. If they could blast the dam apart, it would save us a lot of trouble. Small arms fire broke out from the ground.

"That never works." Burris laughed. He was right. Trying to intercept a fast-mover with ground fire was useless.

"NO!" Stokes said, just as I saw it too. Yellow streaks raced upward like a dozen bottle rockets from backyards on Independence Day, and our hopes were crushed a millisecond later as the blossom of explosions and fires showered over the peninsula from above.

"Shit." I wasn't alone in the shock and disappointment. Two, maybe three, aircraft had been shot down, the wreckage making terrible soul-crushing sounds, flames from fuel and secondary explosions from ordnance rising above the horizon briefly before fading. The extra illumination made everything daylight in my night vision. The tops of the jungle trees were clear, and over in the direction of the locks, the stacks and superstructures of ships trapped high above the lake surface told me traffic going through them had been operating right up until the moment of the attack.

"Keep paddling," I said over the team comms. "It's up to us. JR, break right. We're going left. See you on the objective."

"See you there, Ragnar," JR said with bravado. The sound of their paddles in the water disappeared. We'd decided to split, for each of us to find our own way as best we could onto the wooded shore from either side of the dam. The long strip of jungle swamp and twisted mangrove roots made observation from the land near impossible. We could do this. We could get to the spillway and to the charges on the dam and bring it down and kill the whole canal. We would.

Just then, the whine of artillery screamed above. The rumbling rush of the flying shells ended with more explosions ringing out. Airburst. Rounds came in a volley, one after another, diffuse flashes over the peninsula rained in a storm of fury, then stopped.

"Bring more rain, guys," Jess pleaded. "Don't stop now."

"That's not ours," Burris said with doubt. "Those airbursts weren't just over the locks. I was checking our six when it happened. Davis and the Division TOC got hit. The airfield, too," he said. "Not even the worst FDC would drop rounds there. It was Han arty."

"It didn't come from our lines," I added. "You're right, Burris. That's gotta be from their navy. But no ground impacts. I wonder…" I thought about it another second, and my heart seized. "Gas, gas, gas. Get your masks on." I hit the buckle on my helmet chin strap and grabbed for mine as I stopped breathing and pulled the hood over my head. I had enough breath to purge and checked the seal, then got my helmet back on and my NODs lit again.

"Rag." Stokes muffled voice was panicked. "You think they dropped the funky chicken on us?" A nerve agent was my fear, and a good reason for anxiety. I wish I'd been right.

"Everyone, get your injectors out and dose up. Now." I pulled mine out and jabbed it into my thigh. Hard. The bite told me the needle found meat. I held it there for a second, then tossed the empty stick into the water and massaged the area. If I was wrong, the meds wouldn't hurt us. If I was right, then this was a bad day made even worse.

For the first time, I was scared.

"Everyone okay?" I asked.

"Shit just got serious," Jess said, deadpan. I laughed.

"Let's get back on it." I picked up my paddle.

"Wonder if the rest of the team did the same?" Burris asked. The inter-team comms were only good for about twenty meters. JR and the rest of the team had to be hundreds of meters away from us by now.

"I'm sure they did," I tried to console, not sure myself if I'd even read the situation correctly. Maybe I was wrong and we hadn't just been exposed to some kind of chemical agent, and all I did was succeed in making a hard job even harder. "Dig in and let's get off the lake."

We paddled harder. Sucking air strained through my pro-mask, sweat fogging my eyepieces, the cloud cover and the fading fires all combined to make everything black again. We kept at it. Suddenly, the canoe crashed into a wall of vegetation and I fell forward.

We flipped the cayuca getting out. The rucks floated, and we spent an eternity getting our act together, blind and winded. The water was only knee deep, but the muck at the bottom of it was trying to pull my boots off as I lifted one foot at a time to get out of it and onto firmer ground deeper in the swamp. I felt my way through a narrow lane between roots and followed the blessed path of least resistance, not caring where it led. Just as long as it was out of this.

It was Jess who noticed it first.

"My skin's crawling. Anyone else feel it?"

Melgar heaved deeply. "It wasn't nerve agent. Nerve agent doesn't do this. Look."

Melly was right behind me. He rolled up a sleeve and held his forearm under my face. My lenses had cleared a little, but it was still hard to see. It looked like someone had tattooed a spider web on his skin. He tore off his pro-mask.

"Melly, no." I put out a hand to restrain him.

"It's the same stuff they used against the Japanese," he said. I knew then that he was right and took my mask off too. The fetid swamp air was welcome in my nose, and I took a deep breath.

"What is it?" Burris asked, his mask still on.

"The docs think it's some kind of virus. Fast acting. Attacks DNA," Melgar answered. "The Lotus mob haven't used it since the Hegemony invasion of Japan three years ago. If anyone's figured it out what it is, they've never let us grunts know."

"But it didn't kill everyone, did it?" I offered, knowing full well it had killed a huge number of its victims. "The JDF fought for months. We can too."

"That right, Melly?" Stokes asked, looking for confirmation. Somehow, hearing it from the primary medic carried more weight than if it was coming from me, just the backup doc.

"So they tell us. Other than a little itching, I feel fine. How about you guys?"

"Let's get out of this mangrove," Jess said.

Burris took his mask off and tossed it, the last to do so. It bounced off something solid, then made a lazy splash. "Never thought swamp air would be so sweet. Screw it. I'm fine."

It was good to be rid of the masks. I could see and I could breathe again. "Move out." After another half-hour of work, the water was only ankle deep and the mangroves thinned out. I was exhausted from tripping over the complex networks of roots, banging my shins and ankles on every one of them. It was still muck beneath our feet, but it was getting easier. I took a bearing, made a comparison from memory to where I thought we were on a map view, and gave a best guess as to our next direction. If I headed us east, we should come out somewhere in view of the spillway. If we could bust out of this so we could see the power lines, a building, or the winding road near the dam and power station, we'd be home free. We trudged on.

Automatic fire—first a single gun, soon joined by several—broke out ahead. Voices yelled out. Not American. I heard what could only be rounds from an M-7 grenade launcher, the "bloop" of 40 mm HE rounds landing in the familiar "crump" that I loved so much. I cradled my own M-7, making sure it was still with me. It was hard to feel things, like wearing mittens made of coarse steel wool.

"JR and the crew must be hitting the spillway. We've got to get there."

We finally reached a clearing. It was there we learned what had happened to the Buccaneers. Tents and sand-bagged fighting positions were filled with dead. What I saw

hurt. I'd come from the Bucks before I made selection for
Division Special Ops.

"Don't touch anything," Melgar said as he bent to look
at the first body. "They used something different on them
than what we got." The dead sergeant was contorted and
angular. In his rictus the frozen violence of the convulsions
gave witness to his fate.

"That didn't save him," Burris said, pointing to the pro-
mask sitting correctly over the dead man's head.

"Something nasty, all right," I whispered. "If it was still
around, we'd already be dead. Let's go." The firefight was
still going on but was dying off. I imagined JR and the crew
got spotted in the killing zone of knee-high grass and the
little else that bordered the plain beneath the dam.

"Push," I grunted. "Push hard." We trotted through the
wet thigh-high grass, ignoring the many dead around us
except when we tripped over them, their bodies splayed
in horrific poses in the grass and draped over vehicles and
sandbagged walls. A complex of fighting positions had
been constructed around the dam and spillway, layers of
concertina wire with more of the sandbag-hardened check-
points left to mark our way through the maze.

On top of the dam, Han occupied the machine gun
positions of the Buccaneers. I could be wrong, but there
were only a couple of squads of them. Their backs were to
us, their attention on the fight with JR's team coming from
the jungle on the other side of us. My heart soared just
then as I realized we weren't up against a massive horde of
Lotus drones. But where were the multitude of troops that
had dropped from the air? On the other side of the canal I
supposed, on the locks. I slowed us, crouched, then took a
knee as we came to the first checkpoint.

"Check it out," Jess said beside me. There were as many Han laying on the ground as our own troops. The magenta camo-pattern of their fatigues were a strange choice for the jungle environment. The colors were even more out of place in the jungle when reconstructed by our NODs into the full visible spectrum. But the same bluish spider webs were there too. Our enemy had been the victim of the same ghastly fate that killed our friends.

"They dropped too soon and right into the thick of their own poison," Melly said. "There was some fighting, but this was a disaster for the Han. They blew it."

"Still some left fighting," I reminded him. "We've got to use the break JR's giving us. Get out the burner." This was an ideal time to use it. So the Han liked to use weapons of mass destruction like biological and chemical warfare? They were about to get a taste of their own medicine. The gloves were coming off slowly for the NorthAm, and we'd been given one of the first of the new toys.

The Han on the dam still hadn't spotted us. Short bursts of machine gun and rifle fire continued, aimed down at the water and the jungle from on top of the dam. JR and the guys were still bringing the hate. My heart thumped in my chest. At first, I thought it was the normal excitement and exertion. Then, I felt dizzy. Before I could think more of it, Burris wheezed, then dropped like a rock next to me. Melly was on him. I kept on task. "Stokes, you and Jess get the burner set up." I pointed to where an M-100 machine gun sat, its barrel aimed in our direction, the machinegunner's body next to it. "Get it where it'll have a wide burst."

"What about JR and the rest of the team?" Jess asked.

"They're still blocked and below line of sight," I replied. "As long as we don't wait too long and they break out onto the plain. So hurry."

They moved through the maze of wire and wilting sandbag walls as I sank lower to where Melgar was working. "How is he?"

I heard my answer before he could speak. It wasn't just Burris. Melgar was wheezing now too. His skin was turning black. I spoke softly as I forced him to sit next to where he'd placed Burris, back against a stack of sandbags. "Stay here, Melly. I'm putting your shield down." I tilted his NODs up and dropped the full visor down over his face, then did the same for Burris, though I don't think he was breathing anymore. "We'll be back for you, Melly."

I knew we wouldn't be.

I made my way to where Stokes and Jess waited, to find a similar scene. Stokes knelt over Jess, struggling to pull her into a sitting position. "It's okay, Jess. It's okay."

She pulled her visor down. Just before she did, a big smile spread across her face. "Hit 'em hard, babe. Do it."

The burst-effect laser from Jess's ruck now sat on its tripod. The BEL was about the size of a cinder block and was covered with reddish lenses like some kind of faceted bug's eye. The huge charge cell that Stokes had carried in his ruck all this way was attached to it. It was aimed at the dam. It was fitting that their partnership had brought together the essential components for our revenge.

"Stokes, get your visor down. I'm going to make sure everyone's looking this way before I touch it off." We'd been told it wasn't essential for its effect, but a part of me just wanted to do it this way. I stood up and yelled as loud as I could. "NorthAm's for Americans!" I fired a burst from my M-7, dropped as I put my visor down, and hit the remote.

Even through the black face shield, I knew the BEL had fired. I'd had my eyes squeezed tight but the red burst still made it through to my visual cortex for a split second. I opened my eyes. It was all black. Then I remembered to lift my visor. "Stokes, you with me?"

He was mumbling to Jess. I could tell she wasn't with us anymore. I tried not to think about the life they were supposed to have with each other. They'd both planned to leave the army after this tour. Jess would stop the hormonal augment. They say about half of the Petronio program women who took the boost treatments were able to eventually conceive once they stopped the treatment. Stokes and Jess would've been fantastic parents.

None of us were going to be parents now.

"Stokes, we've got to go." I stood and dropped my NODs back down. On the dam, the firing had stopped. What Han were still standing stumbled around. Blind.

"Stokes, we have to finish this. You with me?"

He was. His NODs came down, and his carbine came up. "We're almost there, Rag. She wanted to go all the way. Let's do this for her. For all of us."

Some of the dead Han we passed had the same dark spider webs that we had crawling up their necks and faces. What had the sequence of events been to the Han assault? The Hegemony released some kind of nerve agent over Balboa to take out the Buccaneers before the drop, but their own airborne troops were nailed by it too. My bet was that wasn't their plan. Bad timing? Poor coordination? I'd likely never learn. Some Han officer's efficiency report was going to reflect poorly. If that wasn't enough, then they'd airbursted a bioweapon against everyone to take out any relief forces. Namely, us. The Han would gladly kill their own troops to keep us from blowing the dam and killing the whole canal.

There could still be combat-effective Han, but so far we'd only run into well-blinded ones. A cursing and flailing Han stood in front of us. "Not expecting that, were you? We can be pricks too," Stokes said as the surprised soldier tried to bring his weapon to bear. We shot him. The sound of our suppressed M-7s confused the others. On top of the dam one fired a wild burst, causing us to duck, but instead accidently hit two of his comrades, making their screams all the more satisfying to me. We'd made them suffer. I shot the wild gunman, and we moved on.

I knew what to look for. I hadn't been here personally, but it looked just like the vid Major Jack used to brief us. A remote-detonation site existed about a mile away, but if it had been found and disabled by the Han, a trip there would've been wasted time. It was probably knocked out by the EMP anyway. The failsafe was deep inside. I tossed a grenade through the access door framed by the stonework of the dam and counted. Before I reached five, it detonated.

"Let's do it, Stokes." He wasn't looking good at all. I supposed I was no better.

"Rag, we ain't walking out of this one, are we?"

"No. Time to hurt 'em before we go."

I turned on my white light, and we moved in. Down the stairs, past sweating and seeping concrete walls, through channels of giant gears and machines, we passed contorted bodies with Asian faces and those of every color and shape of my own countrymen and -women, until we reached the end. I took the key out and opened the lid of the box.

Crude. Plain. Unimpressive. Inside, two redundant deto-
nating systems sat side by side. One was an old-fashioned
electric cap generator. The other was a primer-fired initia-
tor with shock tube, not much different than what we used
for explosive breaching. There were branching highways of
wires and tubes leading to knots of detcord, in turn leading off to the stacks of explosives we'd passed along the
way—cones of shaped C-4 tamped by more piles of the
familiar sandbags stacked against the wet walls. I chose the
non-electric detonator.

"Think I'll rest here, Rag," Stokes said as he collapsed
next to the body of an engineer officer, twisted and grizzly
like his partners. The stranger had died a horrible death,
long before the order to blow the dam could even have
been issued. I wanted to tell the man that he didn't fail
his duty, that we were here to finish this act of honor for
him, but I was straining just to breathe. I decided to go out
standing.

"See you on the other side, Stokes." I pulled the safety
pin and cocked the hammer.
Stokes reached up and put his hand on the back of mine.

"I'm not scared, brother. Death's not the end. I'll see
you on the other side." He grinned. "I sure wish we could
see their stupid faces when this whole thing drains like a
bathtub."

"We did it, Stokes."

"That we did, Rag."

I closed my eyes and hit the button. My world turned
white, then black again.

An angry voice filled my ears.

"Before man was, war waited for him."

I opened my eyes. I wasn't underneath the dam anymore. I wasn't dead.

A flaming sword over his head, the speaker raised a shield. "And unto eternity, those who would call themselves warriors must always prove themselves worthy."

He swung at me.

05

A sword was in my hand. I brought it up just in time to deflect the blow and took some fast retreating steps. Was I dreaming? Was this heaven? If so, it wasn't what Sunday School made it out to be. There was no time for more of my existential ponderings. Hands pushed me, and I stumbled forward. One of the bare-chested warriors in the circle around us tossed a shield at me. I caught it and found the forearm straps just as the madman with the flaming sword made his next attack.

Prove yourself worthy, echoed in my head as the fiery weapon made another slash at my cranium. Flames danced off my shield with the clash of metal, and the heat made me wince. I slashed at his head to get some breathing space as he brought his own shield up. I'd played with knives and sticks but never a sword! I made some distance by circling away, keeping my shield arm to him.

He looked like the personification of an ancient statue. Golden curls and bronze skin that matched the metal of his shield. He grinned, then leaped, sword tip tracing a large arc to reach over my shield. Magnificent, I had to admit. But a mistake.

I didn't retreat. With shield a little higher to deflect his blade, I entered, lowered my center, got some contact, then turned and threw. My thigh found his groin as I raised him off his feet and dropped my shield. I wasn't going to let go. I ended up on top of him. Uchi-mata was my favorite throw. I pinned his sword arm, my own blade laid across his throat. I hesitated, ready to draw it deeply across the corded muscles of his neck to find the pipelines of red beneath.

"ENOUGH. Ragnar Beck! Enough. Stay your hand."

I didn't take my eyes off Mister Goldilocks, who wasn't grinning now. The flames of his sword flared, and he released the grip on the hilt. Hands were on my shoulders. The same voice that had called me by name was close behind me. "Stay your hand, I say." I allowed the hands to pull me off Gorgeous George and stood. Around me crowded a collection of characters I couldn't reason into clarity. Men of every earthly variety, dressed in strange, loose kilts and tunics. Scars raised under oiled skin.

I'd lost my mind. I was in a padded room somewhere, on enough meds to send me on a trip that would make Samuel Taylor Coleridge envious. I'd read Kubla Khan. Well, it was an assignment, so I skimmed it. It was supposedly written while he was high out of his mind. The Han had stopped me from blowing the dam, and I was under the influence of some kind of hallucinogen they'd sprayed to slow us down. Maybe I'd imagined the whole fight at the spillway. Maybe everything after the airburst was all a mad dream.

English was not the speaker's native tongue. He spoke it well but had an accent I couldn't place. "You can stand easy, Ragnar Beck. You've passed the first challenge." I turned to face my referee. He was dressed like a guy in charge, iridescent armor chest plates and helmet. I checked myself. My body was my body again. None of the fungus that'd been eating away my skin was there anymore. I suddenly felt ill and bent over and heaved my stomach onto the sand.

A voice with a familiar accent was in my ear. It was pure midwest US of A. "Maybe I'd better take it from here, Michael." I spit, waiting for another wave of nausea. A firm hand patted my back.

"It gets better," the owner of the cornhusking voice said. "Take a few deep breaths."

I did as my nurse commanded, hands on knees, and after a few breaths the dizziness eased back. I rose to see the crowd breaking up. My opponent was on his feet, the flames extinguishing as he sheathed his sword. He nodded at me curtly and turned away to join the others.

"That was a sight! I bet Gabriel hasn't had someone knock him on his keister like that in a long time," my Kansas-accented friend said. I could pick out a Sooner in a chorus, but right now I wasn't going to hold that against him. "But make no mistake, he was taking it easy on you. He telegraphed that attack to see what you'd do. I'd say that surprised him a bit."

"Where the hell am I?" I finally managed to blurt out. Above the walls, golden spires pierced the distant heights into a purple canvas sky.

"Let's find a place to sit down. It's going to take some explaining, but what I can tell you is, you're here to join us in becoming Ultimates. Or die trying."

※　※　※

"I was in the American Expeditionary Forces under Pershing." My midwestern friend passed me a canteen. I still had the taste of bile and rinsed my mouth before I took a long pull. "Eighteen was the big year for us Doughboys. When we watched you make your way through the trenches to the dam, it kind of reminded me of the Meuse. The Boche liked to use gas against us too, but those godless heathens you fought were worse."

He'd seen our battle with the Han? How? He'd said he was a Doughboy. He was talking about himself like he'd been in World War One. "Double-u double-u one?" I asked, not believing him. This was all too much to take in.

"We called it the Great War. Back then, we didn't know it was the first big one for the US. That there'd be a bigger one. It was supposed to be the war to end all wars. I didn't know then that war was eternal for some of us. I was an All-American. It made me proud to see how the 82nd was brought back for number two. I got to try an airborne assault in one of my little tests. Maybe you will too."

"Tests? What tests?"

"There'll be time to talk about that later." He stuck his hand out. "I'm Will. Will Jensen."

"Ragnar. You can call me Rag." If this was some mad dream, I might as well go along. His grip felt real enough. "Will, I'm crazy, aren't I? This is…" I couldn't find the words.

"I know. It takes some getting used to. But this is real, cousin. As real as real can be. And you're in the thick of it."

"In the thick of what?" Around us, the crowd had broken up into pairs to spar and wrestle. I picked the sword off the ground from where I'd dropped it next to the bench. I ran a finger along the edge. Dull.

"Oh, you wouldn't have been turned loose on Gabriel with a sharp blade," Will said as he noticed me check the edge of my weapon. "Not that you could've hurt him. And he wouldn't have done anything too damaging to you. It was just a test to see if you had the right stuff."

"Did I make the grade?" I asked, curious.

"If you'd turned yellow and ran or refused to fight, you'd be gone already."

"Gone where?"

He ignored my question and instead gestured to the training going on around us. "We start everyday with physical training. And by that I mean combatives. Hand to hand. It always comes down to what a soldier can do with his own two hands when someone's trying to do the same for him, doesn't it? You're good, but you're going to get better in ways you can't imagine."

I'd had enough. "Will, this doesn't make any sense. I'm dead. I know I died. I lit off enough explosive to kill everyone within a half-mile of me. This isn't what I pictured heaven was going to look like. But it doesn't look like the hell I was told to expect either."

He grinned, like I'd just said something funny. "Nope, cousin. It sure doesn't."

"So? Where am I?"

He put a hand on my shoulder again. "The simple answer is, it's not your calling to sit on some cloud plucking a harp. You're a warrior. Like the rest of us. And if you can keep proving it, you'll be preparing yourself to join us for the biggest fight there ever will be. The one we've been selected to soldier in. And the fight that's coming is one that's going to need soldiers like us. It'll be the war of all wars. The *real* war to end all wars. And if we fail, it'll be the end of everything."

I threw up again. "Will, are we angels?"

He laughed. "I'm no angel." He talked as he guided me across the courtyard. "My pappy was with TR in Cuba. My granddad was in the Army of the Grand Republic. I got family fought in the war for independence, too. Every generation of the Jensens have been soldiers. Just like your family, Rag."

We made our way inside through one of the arches that ringed the sunken training arena. "It's not all Spartacus and Ben-Hur here in the Cradle. I know what you're thinking. I thought the same when I first got here."

"The Cradle?"

"That's what we call the compound. It's the wellspring for our growth into Ultimates."

We passed armories full of weapons of every variety, the kind of stuff out on the training grounds now. Spears, swords, maces, hammers, halberds, armor of every type. The deeper we walked, the more advanced the armaments became, like a display of the history of arms itself. Black powder rifles gave way to the arms of Will's time.

I reached out to touch a pristine BAR, the blue so bright it glowed, only to be rebuffed by an invisible barrier, clearer than glass, firmer than steel.

Will smiled. "You have an eye for beauty, but the racks are locked. They get unlocked by Gabriel as needed. Let me show you the rest."

As we traveled deeper, we came to more and more modern weapons and gear, until the walls were lined with M-7s, M-100 medium machine guns, mortars, anti-tank rockets, and more. We stopped at the intersection leading to the next chamber, an armory within the armory. This one was protected by a barrier at the entrance. Beyond it were things I couldn't recognize. Stuff from science fiction movies and books, stuff from the games I'd played in the tank since I was a kid.

"We've got a lot of toys, that's for sure." Will saw my wonder at it all. "Time for that soon enough. First let's get you settled. You'll bunk with me. You're the first American in the unit in a while. We try and get the new guys a buddy from the same neighborhood when we can to help get 'em acclimated. I'm about as close as you're going to get to a schoolmate. We'll get you kitted out and go from there. Ready to get something on that stomach to replace what you lost? No? Don't feel bad. Happens to us all. Maybe later. Hey, just remember, the one thing to get used to around here is that you won't get used to a thing. Welcome to Valhalla."

"Valhalla, huh?"

Will shook his head. "Well, not really Valhalla. Magnus assures me of that much. He's a Viking. Anyway, that's just our slang for it. The demis you met like Michael call it Aricia. The city beyond is Capitoline."

"Demis?" I asked.

"Sorry. Demigods." To me, demigod implied there had to also be gods. But before I could press that issue, Will moved us along. "Forget about it for now. Come on. We've got to get you settled."

Will had taken me around and gotten me in-processed, just like joining any other unit. I was issued uniforms, bedding, field gear—all of it quite familiar, but all of it strange in the weight and texture of the materials. Will left me in a cubicle and told me he'd be back. "Just follow the directions."

Before I could ask, he was gone. A hologram with a new face appeared. It was unlike the demigods Michael or

Gabriel's in that it wasn't perfect or beautiful in a classical way and immediately made me think of the first supply clerk I'd ever met in the army. With the disinterest of a lab technician sorting through samples of fecal matter, he spoke. "Lie on the palate." A table slid out from the wall. A silver band the size of my head rested at one end. "Place the Diadem of Minerva on your head and repose on your back. Don't move."

The next thing I knew, Will was back beside me. "All set?" It felt like I'd lost time, but not as though I'd slept. The light outside was dimming. He helped me sit up and eased the silver crown off my head. I felt a little dizzy, and suddenly very sleepy. "Grab your diadem and let's get you to your bunk." He grabbed my things and escorted me out of the cubicle, across the sandy training ground, and down a short ramp into the barracks area. We went by room after room of men retiring for the night. The day had passed me by while I lay in the cubicle.

"Will, how old are you? How long have you been here?" Will eased me onto my bunk and took the one opposite.

"Time doesn't pass here like you're used to, Rag. Enough questions for one day. Tomorrow's going to be here sooner than you think, and you need to rest." He took the silver ring off the shelf next to him and placed it on his head.

I was still fuzzy, but had questions that wouldn't wait. "Will, you'd have been in your twenties when you bought it in Europe fighting the Germans. That'd make you 175 years old to me. Have you been here all that time?"

He rolled back over. "It doesn't work like that, Rag. I got here, same as you, waking up to old Gabe swinging his flaming pig-sticker at me. Since then, I've been training.

Everyday. Couldn't say how long. Months maybe. I know, it takes some getting used to. There're soldiers here from my past, and soldiers like you from my future. Near as I can tell, you're the only one here yet from as far in the future as you came."

"Why me? Why was I chosen?" I was no super soldier. I wasn't some legendary hero fit to fight the unknown who-or-what in some kind of final battle for existence. I know who I am. I'm just a guy who always wanted to be a soldier. I rose above the ranks of mediocrity of the army of my time by not being a quitter. More than that, I was someone who wouldn't bend the knee to be a slave. I wasn't fearless. Just a guy who would do what it took to protect my homeland. America. Well, the NorthAm. I wondered. Did my team's sacrifice make any difference?

"Rag, today was the last easy day. The ticket is to play it cool and be patient. They'll let you know what they want you to know when they want you to know it. That's all I can say." He pointed at his head. "Get your tiara on, princess. Tomorrow, you're gonna feel better about it all. Trust me. G'night." He rolled over for a last time and soon was snoring.

I lay onto my back. It made no sense. But here I was. Flesh and blood. Alive. I ate, felt pain, and needed sleep. Just like an alive person. Not like some kind of angel. I took the thin oblong ring and placed it on my head as Will had done and closed my eyes. I thought of Stokes, and Jess, and our final push to blow the dam. I wondered what happened after I released the detonator? Maybe I'd get to find out.

The diadem wasn't stiff or uncomfortable as I'd assumed. It warmed to my skin, and soon I was snoring.

06

"Ragnar Beck makes an impression. Doesn't he, Alator?"

Mars had taken a pause in the middle of the weekly meeting to watch the arrival of the latest candidate. It'd been a while since he had reason to laugh. Seeing Gabriel eat dirt was a good one. Gabe was little too stoic most of the time, even for Mars's liking. He had taken it easy on the new candidate, but he should've seen that coming.

Humans are predictable, but every once in a while one of them will surprise you. Which is why Mars preferred them. And as much as he trusted Gabriel, he also felt the warrior needed a little something to keep him on his toes. Eternity could get a little routine. Even when waging war.

Alator was getting ready to send his company off for a skirmish. "Yes, Mars. Michael was right to intervene when he did, lest Gabriel have to fight without restraint. The terms were set, and I expected a good showing. But will his pride now prevent him from allowing a fair trial of this new candidate?"

Mars agreed with Alator about his fellow Stalwart. Gabriel was prideful, but not to the point of downfall. "I don't think so. We need to get that company built, and even if Gabe's pride's a little worse for the wear, he won't let it hurt the unit. Michael will keep him in check, just as he does you and Ocelus."

Three companies of Ultimates, always in flux, kept Mars busy. Michael, the commander of his Stalwarts, in turn kept his three best warriors—Gabriel, Ocelus, and Alator—on track with always having at least two of the companies at full strength. Attrition was a constant in war.

"Besides, with a few more like Beck, Gabriel might have a company to give yours a good shellacking next time we have a field exercise. That is, if your boys make it back. You sure they're not going to screw the pooch against Hadúr's bunch?"

Alator frowned. "You jest with me, Mars Gradivus! There's no match for your Ultimates in all the realms. And against Hadúr's army? Even if the negotiated accommodations sent to my company were to meet his constructs with only bare hands, you would not be displeased with the outcome."

It was easy to get Alator's goat. "Just messin' with you, son."

Mars's face went dark from a need to convey that despite the jokes, we remained serious. A general could be flippant, but behind any perceived ease of formality on Mars's part, his Stalwarts always had to know their master would not tolerate losing. "I know you'd fall on your sword if that happened." Mars let the implication hang for a moment. "Perrault's done a good job leading the company. Is he still up to the task?"

The human had proven a good company commander, but it was just a matter of time before he'd buy his farm.

"He is, Mars," answered Alator. "So long as I am not permitted to fight, he is adequate in the role."

It burned the Stalwarts that they couldn't fight, but rules were rules.

Mars nodded. "I'm glad Perrault has your confidence. You have my blessing to depart." He raised his spear and let Alator give his obeisance before being dismissed.

"To the glory of Mighty Mars."

The thunder of Mars's spear banging the stone floor signaled the end of their audience. Traditions helped maintain *discipline, even if Mars found them a little tiring. His scribe stepped out from behind a column. "Quintus. Move my meeting with Ocelus to tomorrow. I have more negotiating to do with Di Qing before I'm ready to give him a mission order."*

Mars hadn't negotiated with the pompous ass in an eon. Time hadn't made him any easier to deal with, and since the Ultimates had given his clay soldiers a solid pasting at the last encounter, Di Qing was being even more fickle in the negotiations. The sticking point was whether Mars's warriors could bring their Annihilators. If Di Qing was going to use magical wards to shield his troops, the Ultimates sure as hell were going to bring along their best weapons.

"Yes, my lord," said the scribe, bowing as he spoke. "And—"

Mars held up a hand. "Now, give me a few minutes alone, Quintus. I want to check up on this new man."

Ragnar Beck had gotten Mars's attention.

Unlucky for him.

✳   ✳   ✳

"Will, I had the most vivid dream about—a trebuchet." I vaguely knew what one was, but after the dream I knew the ancient artillery piece inside and out. How to calculate counterweight, how to load it, heck, I bet I could even build one from scratch.

Will stretched his arms and removed his own diadem. "That's the diadem's work. Onagers, mangonels, catapults, they're all pretty similar. You may get the chance to use them."

The diadem taught us while we slept. Incredible! I felt sharp, at ease, and very hungry. I also had that drive, the one that makes you feel like there was something very important you had to do. "Last night's lesson was the trebuchet?"

"Not for everyone. Mine was a refresher on the 81 millimeter mortar. I could run a whiz wheel in my head. No such thing as too much repetition. You never know what you're gonna find yourself needing to know. Come on, time to get the blood moving."

PT is PT. Whether you're a grunt freezing your butt off on a parade field at zero-dark thirty in the a.m., or a resurrected soldier in some otherworldly existence doing god-knows-what for god-knows-why, the burn of oxygen-starved muscles stings the same. Just yesterday I'd been struggling through a swamp with my skin rotting off me, hordes of enemies trying to shoot me dead, and today I was running all out, my heart pounding and my muscles tingling. It felt good.

Gabriel led us in calisthenics. Some of the exercises were new to me. Gabriel was on an elevated platform, just like a drill sergeant from my basic training days, doing the exercises with us as we counted off repetitions. The other one, Michael, paced around the formation. Watching. We were on our hundredth burpee before I started feeling even a little winded or tired. This body was better than ever. If this was the result of dying, maybe I should get killed more often.

Two hours later I paired off with Will, not the slightest bit tired or achy. I'd been in prime condition before I got here, but realizing that I was not the least bit strained after what should've been a grueling PT session was as supernatural as the Cradle itself.

We'd just started to trade some light jabs when Will snuck an overhand right past my guard and clocked me between the eyes with full force. I kept my hands up and blew bloody snot out of my nose as he pummeled me, tears clouding my vision as he tried to break my guard again. I held him off, threw a few open-palm hooks to the side of his head, and landed a knee in his ribs, hard enough to hurt him. He grunted and faded back, then broke into a grin.

"I told you, yesterday was the last easy day."

I paired up again for a few more short bouts with others in our training circle. Jakob, a big guy with a buzz cut and crooked nose, presented palms outstretched to show me his hands were empty. Then he tried to murder me. I learned later Jakob was a Polish national who'd been a Legionnaire, fighting for France in Algeria. I thought Will meant the Algerian War of Independence. The one in the twentieth century. He meant the *first* war in Algeria, in the eighteenth century. Anyway, Jakob survived that to get killed fighting Spain against the Carlists. He was tough as nails and hard as granite. What he might have lacked in technique he made up for with brute strength and resilience. I don't think any of my blows even made him wince.

Karl was a Prussian with a dueling scar across his cheek. Maybe I was wrong, but it seemed like he thought he was better than the rest of us. Aristocracy. He wasn't anywhere near as skilled at hand to hand as Will or me, but I was warned that with a saber in hand, he was a terror. I'd have to wait for another day to find out. He got killed in one of Europe's never-ending wars of the eighteenth century, so I guess he was used to the concept of war being eternal.

Hikaru was Japanese. He made a chopped bow to me as we faced off, then attacked. His fists were iron. His grip was a vise, twisting my arm in a way it was not meant to be twisted. I headbutted him with everything I had and kicked him in the knee to break his grip. After our bout, he gave me a slight smile. It wasn't a friendly one. He was letting me know that next time, he would break something of mine. Will didn't know from where or when the stout Asian had made his last stand in combat. "Some folks just ain't chatty, I reckon. Hikaru's one of those. But he's a good soldier. I've learned from him."

I was still feeling aggressive from my last bout. It felt good to be alive, or whatever you'd call the state we now occupied. But madness or reality, as I took a turn out of the circle to watch others fight, my curiosity returned as the pain in my ribs from Hikaru's last kick subsided. "What is this place, Will? Why are we here?"

"I told you. We're training. To be Ultimates. We've been chosen by Mars to fight for our side. It's an honor. Everyone around you has made it here like you and me. We all died in glorious combat, I guess you'd say. No one here died in their bunk in an air raid. Near as I can tell, we're a lodge of heroes who all died on some kind of suicide mission."

Will confirmed my suspicion. The men I'd trained with today were hard warriors, not conscripts or slaves. "Seems like a pretty tough selection standard you ask me, Will. One that's only useful if you can resurrect the selectee."

"And that's just what they've done, cousin."

"What *who* has done, Will? I still don't know how it is I'm here. Or why. And what's the Cradle preparing us for?" The sense of curiosity I'd had a lack of upon rising this morning was returning. I attributed it to getting punched in the head so many times today.

Our overseers made the rounds as other bouts continued. Will was about to speak, but a quick glance to see that Michael was nearing held him up, and he cast his eyes down at the sand, as though he were ashamed.

"What gives, Will?" I said a little too loudly. "Why can't we speak about these things openly?"

His whisper was a warning in itself. "Careful, Rag. Oh, hell. Here he comes. I told you to be patient."

Michael made a beeline for me. "Ragnar Beck, stand where you are." Bodies shifted and a new ring formed, leaving Michael and I in its center. "Attack," the giant ordered. "Do not hold back."

I stole a glance at the faces of my fellow soldiers to see even the stoic Hikaru grimace in pity. Karl rolled his eyes. Jakob made the sign of the cross.

"Attack me, I say, lest you be fearful and unworthy. If that is so, say so now and I will return you to oblivion. We have no need of—" I didn't let him finish as I launched a cross step side kick. I was in the air, anticipating the contact my fully outstretched and in-line form was about to have with his midsection when his fist hammered me to a halt in midair, driving me into the sand like a stake. Except stakes were meant to be driven point first. He'd stepped aside, entered, and sledgehammered me faster than I could see him move, dropping me like a dead log. The air left my lungs. I felt every bone in my body bend.

"Look at me, Ragnar Beck." Michael's voice held some miniscule amount of benevolence, but my ears were ringing so I could've been mistaken. "First you must earn the right to be called a soldier. Then you will be treated like one. Demonstrate you can follow orders like a soldier, and later, the reasons for your mission will be explained."

I made the dying croak of a tractor-trailer flattened frog. "Yes, sir."

"See him to the healer."

It wasn't my imagination. He'd driven me inches deep into the ground. If it had been concrete and not a sand pit, I'd be mush. Hands scooped me up and brushed me off as I was painfully lifted from my half-grave and onto my feet.

Will just shook his head. "Told you to play it cool, didn't I?"

※　※　※

The healing field radiated over me and in minutes I was fixed, but the lesson stuck. My existential curiosity needed to be suppressed if I was going to make it here. So, for now, I would commit myself to becoming a good soldier. And that's what I did. Weeks went by. Too many to keep track of. I woke each morning with some new bit of knowledge inserted in my brain like a memory of something I'd actually done. There were weapons I'd never seen or heard of, and in my mind, I'd held them, sharpened, stripped, oiled, and practiced with them vividly. From pike to Napoleonic cannon up to my own best friend the M-7. I'd had little opportunity yet to have anything much more sophisticated than sharp things to practice with, but Will assured me the day was coming when I would.

And each day I awoke caring less and less about how I'd come to be here, or what my purpose was. I only felt the urge to train harder. Something deep inside told me there was a task awaiting me, and that somehow the very universe itself depended on me becoming an Ultimate. Whatever that was. It was a tantalizing whisper of a dream that stuck with me, something that beckoned to me like the sirens that called to Ulysses.

When I arrived there'd been a few dozen of us in the Cradle. In the next weeks more soldiers made their sudden appearance in our ranks—Gabriel's flaming sword always their greeting. And each time I saw the ritual repeat was no less surreal than the first.

Gabriel and Michael would call us together. We formed a circle to watch the whirlpool form, a vortex of swirling gray mist that materialized into the image of a battlefield, somewhere in time. Clearer than any Hollywood production, we first watched the candidate's actions leading to their dying in glorious combat, a sort of guide recording the vital stats of the player's last game.

The mists evaporated, leaving the empty sand in our circle ready for the next part of the ceremony. "This soldier has been found worthy," Michael said in his booming voice. "Prepare for the challenge." A grand sweep of Michael's spear, and the candidate would appear out of thin air, facing the giant Gabriel, sword aflame, challenge issued in those same words I'd heard as my welcome to the afterlife.

"Before man was, war waited for him. And unto eternity, those who would call themselves warriors must always prove themselves worthy."

The first time I was a witness rather than the star attraction, it was to welcome Antonius into our ranks. He'd had been a real-deal Roman soldier. We watched his battle against dozens of bearded and fur-clad barbarians in a thick pine forest that made me think of old Europe. He went down swinging after killing more of them than heart disease ever would. If Gabriel put him off with his avenging angel act, I couldn't tell. Antonius went from death, to resurrection, to vicious soldier again without missing a beat.

He gave Gabe a run for his money, as I had, but was fought to a standstill by the much larger Stalwart before being told by Michael to stand down. A kindly older brother took him away as Will had done for me, and he was assigned to one of the other platoons.

Part movie, part gladiator duel, it took me back to my appearance here just a short time ago. "Is this what it was like for me? You all watched my battle against the Lotus mob up until I blew up the dam?"

"And a good showing it was," confirmed Will. "It's a helluva thing, seeing a man's life and death in full color. Just as us older guys have seen yours, pretty soon you'll have seen your share."

"But Will, that man must have died thousands of years before me. And he just shows up today? What gives?"

Will eyed Gabriel and Michael. "Remember to keep that curiosity in check. When it's time to know those things, we'll know them. For now, something tells me this unit isn't at full strength."

He was right. And after a while, it became the closest thing to entertainment we had in our brutal training prison. Or so I thought.

I couldn't place the next candidate's race or language, but the battle was another ancient affair. Spear and sword wielding troops in light leather armor fought against invaders coming over the top of a stone wall on siege machines and ladders. Like the other candidates, this one fought bravely and with skill before falling to greater numbers, having given his all. It had become an almost commonplace event.

On sight of Gabriel, the stout, scarred, and bearded man fell to his knees, sobbing. At Michael's direction, two of us stood the man on his feet, put sword and shield in his hands, and pushed him into the confrontation with the waiting Gabriel, still brandishing his weapon of flame and steel. The poor overwhelmed soul was nothing like the savage fighter we'd just witnessed in his final moments. He again collapsed in sobs and prayers, discarding his sword and shield to prostrate himself.

"To the well of souls with you," Michael said—and the man was gone.

"Been awhile since I saw one from that far back," Will said to me out of the side of his mouth. I stared at the empty spot. "Those Old Testament kinda characters never prove out. They just don't seem to be up to the task. You watch. I reckon the selection committee's gonna get back to the twentieth century. Modern guys just seem a little more capable when confronted with all this hocus-pocus."

"Where'd he go?"

"You heard Mike. The well of souls."

All I knew was, as bizarre as "here" might be, I didn't want to go to whatever place the well of souls was.

"Return to training," was all Gabriel said to get us moving again and out of our shock.

Gabriel was our head trainer/judge/master. In other words, a drill sergeant. Will was right when he'd told me that I wouldn't get used to a thing. The day's activities constantly changed. Michael made infrequent appearances, observing and noting how we progressed. I caught him watching me trade throws with Hikaru one time. Another, I seemed to garner his attention while I coached Will on the finer points of running an M-100.

That's right. I learned, *and* I taught. Gabriel was the master of every weapon and tactic, but I have to say, he was not what I'd call a great instructor. Being some kind of demigod or angel-like being, he couldn't relate to how a human learned things. He expected perfection with little instruction. "A barbarian should be pleased to kill with thunder," he berated Magnus on the rifle range as he missed the target for the second magazine's worth. "You're a disgrace to your fathers."

We all took turns teaching and coaching in the finer points of the weapons and tactics from our times. Tactics reflected technology. While troops marching in ranks worked well with Napoleonic weapons, when we used M-7s the squad quickly saw how the patrolling formations from my era were superior.

Days of training were separated by nights filled with more lucid dreams of the how-to-of-all-things-deadly. I'd gotten to know some of my fellow eternal soldiers a little better. I learned that all had a perception of their time here similar to Will's; they felt as though they'd been in Valhalla for no more than a year. I'd have thought about it harder if I hadn't been so damn busy.

We sat around the table, a few minutes of freedom before lights out.

"Tis the will of the Allfather," Magnus said. "But Valhalla it is not." Magnus was a red haired giant, fierce but friendly. Introducing myself the first time, his face lit up. The name my parents had stuck me with had never brought me any goodwill before, but he seemed keen to speak with someone named Ragnar. I'd helped him get acquainted with the M-1 Garand. By my standards, it was ancient hardware. By his, it was unimaginable technology. Gabriel approved my coaching him for an afternoon, and

I had him hitting a 12 inch circle at 600 yards before we were done. I'd made a friend.

"Truly, Thor himself wields such as this." He'd been here longer than me but was still having trouble adapting to weapons and tactics of the time period post-middle ages. There were more from his tribe and time period in other squads, but some had been found wanting. Not for lack of courage or aggression, Will told me. Everyone but me seemed to disappear for short periods. A day. Maybe two. Karl vanished for a day. When he came back, he seemed even cockier than usual, if that was possible. Most returned. Some didn't. The well of souls got filled, I supposed.

And though the diadems we wore each night took us all through the tutorials of a curriculum to make us PhDs in the tools of the two-way shooting range, we all hadn't learned at the same rate. Magnus confided to me that it worried him greatly. "I do not wish to be sent away, even though I think the ones who fail are given peace. A strange reward for failure, while the rest of us toil on."

"Don't you know, that's how it always is?" Will said, sitting on the back of his chair so he looked down on us at the table like a gargoyle. "Even in the afterlife, being competent just means you get saddled with more work. That's the definition in a nutshell of what it means to be a soldier."

"I wouldn't be so sure those who've departed are yet reaping their eternal reward," Jakob said. "Purgatory is full of souls waiting to earn their eternal reward. Those departed from our ranks were found wanting. It is by our good works and prayers that we will help them enter the joy of heaven." Jakob crossed himself.

Karl made a grunt of disagreement.

"Something you'd like to add, Baron?" Will teased.

"There is no eternal reward. There is no heaven. No hell."

"Here we go again." Will rolled his eyes. "Please, Professor Schopenhauer, enlighten us."

"What do you think this place is?" I prompted Karl, who sipped his coffee as though it held more interest for him than our conversation.

"I will tell you. We are here by our own will. We are soldiers. This is the essence of our existence. This place is our perception of how the ideal soldier's life should be. It is our attachment to the pleasure of soldiering that causes us to continue to suffer this existence. So here we are."

"Knew *that* was coming," Will mumbled.

But whereas Will discounted Karl's take on things, it had an effect on those around the table who'd not offered opinions. Many of them newer to Valhalla than me and still adjusting, as I was. Eating stopped. Eyes fell to laps. Hikaru remained stoic as he continued to shovel his dinner. His finesse with a sword wasn't matched by his comportment at the table. He spoke English as well as any of the squad when he chose to. If he had thoughts on the matter, they were drowned in the steaming soup he slurped so loudly.

"What do you think this place is, Will?" I asked for the hundredth time since I'd known him.

He shrugged. "Jakob's a Catholic. Pretty clear he thinks we're in God's army, but I ain't seen Him yet. Karl's a pessimist. Hikaru, well, he won't say. Magnus believes in the old Norse gods, but I'm thinking he's like me and doubts this all fits what we each grew up believing. It would sure give my Bible totin' granny fits. As for the rest of us"—he jutted his chin around the table—"no one's had anything new to say since I've been here. We all have our theories."

Gabriel and Michael circled around the mess tables like sharks, silently judging as the squads interacting after another long day of training. Michael hadn't made an appearance in several days, but he reappeared tonight, intimidating and mythic-like as ever in his iridescent armor. I tracked him for a moment when he seemed to sense my gaze out of the hundred men in the room, his head snapping to meet mine. I did not look away.

"What about you, Rag?" Will asked. "You've been here long enough to have your own theory. Spill it."

I smiled at Michael, hoping he could hear me.

"I think it's about time they let me get my hands on some of those ray guns at the far end of the armory."

※　※　※

As we broke up after dinner, Magnus pulled me aside. "Ragnar, there is more that no one has told you. There is a god here." His whisper caused my hairs to stand on end. "It will be your time to meet him soon."

By the time I placed the diadem on my brow, I didn't care. I dreamed of tables for plunging fire with a .50 cal machine gun.

The next morning we fell in for PT. I knew something was up when Gabriel made a beeline for our squad. When I heard my name, my stomach flip-flopped as though I was at the top of a roller coaster, headed down. "Is Ragnar Beck ready for testing?"

Will came to attention. "Yes, Gabriel. He is."

"You may accompany him." Gabriel moved to the head of the formation as Will waved me to follow him out of ranks. Michael stood by the gates, his armor glowing faint-

ly in the pre-dawn light. I marched ahead, and for the first
time since I'd arrived, my knees felt weak. We followed
Michael beyond the walls, the golden spires of the towering
city just visible in the pre-dawn.

I'd been out of the compound many times since arriving. To the many ranges and live fire lanes. To the nearby
mountains to carry a ruck that weighed as much as I did,
up a rocky trail to where the air thinned and my lungs
burned like fire. But never to the surreal painting that was
the cityscape of Capitoline.

I guess I should've been more curious about Aricia, but
I wasn't. The Cradle sat some distance from the glowing
city. In strained glimpses of the ethereal Capitoline in the
distance, I saw movement and activity that told me there
was life there. I knew there were others like Gabriel and
Michael. Demis. And others not so grandiose or statu-
esque in stature, who we saw occasionally performing tasks
around the grounds and many buildings that made up the
Cradle. But the longer I remained here, the less curious I
was. The only thing I cared about was the pursuit of perfection as a warrior.

Until now.

"What's going to happen?" I whispered to Will.

It was Michael who answered. "There's nothing to fear,
Ragnar Beck."

Michael halted on a large white disc, and Will pushed
me onto it with him. We levitated and sped away. Unless
you were close enough to be pummeled by one—as had
happened to me—it was easy to forget the true size of a
demi. Michael had to be seven feet tall. He was dispas-
sionate and unemotional, yet his words did console me.
There was little sense of motion as we flew, only a light

wind against my face as we hurtled toward the shining towers and pointed steeples. On gold streets vehicles moved
with precision. More of the demis and others not as grand
moved unhurriedly. We changed course and in a gentle
bank aimed to a lone, tiered castle atop a forested hill. We
came to rest just as effortlessly as we'd launched into flight,
landing at the foot of a wide staircase rising to the massive
building at the top.

I knew the palace of a god when I saw one.

Braziers lit the way, the flickering fires an anachronistic
touch to my sensibility, out of place after the ride on the
flying saucer. As was everything here, the stairs and columns were flawless, in their grandeur no hint that they
could've been formed by ordinary human hands. I suddenly felt self-conscious in my sandals and tunic. At the top
of the stairs, the vaulted chamber held a throne. That's the
only way I could describe it. And atop it I knew immediately was the god Magnus warned me awaited. Breastplate
and great helmet. Spear, sword, and shield. A wolf cape
clasped around his massive shoulders. His scowl made my
soul shrivel.

Michael raised his own spear high. "Great Mars, I bring
before you a soldier."

I followed Will's cue and took a knee, bowing my head.
I heard a heavy sigh.

"Let's make this quick, Mike. I've got a lot on my plate
today, and I haven't had my coffee yet."

07

Long ago, Mars introduced himself to the candidates as they arrived, usually with good results. There was a middle ground. If you pulled them from too far downtime, their little brains couldn't handle the shock. The same happened as Mars pulled men from farther uptime. Between the two extremes, mankind was more capable of getting in line and accepting authority.

Just as the nature and capability of man was better understood, so was the timing of their first meeting with Mars.

Mars presided over his weekly report from Gabriel, Michael at his side. "Ragnar Beck is acclimating well enough, it seems. The time for him to meet me is at hand."

Gabriel couldn't keep the chagrined look off his face.

"What is it, Gabriel?" Mars asked. "Will you never overcome your disdain for working with humans?"

There was a gleam in Mars's eyes. He was speaking in a high manner, just as Gabriel did. Coming from Mars, it contained an edge of mockery over the Stalwart's sense of superiority.

Gabriel bowed. "It is as Mars wills."

"Pfft. Don't give me that. It's their free will and curiosity that make them better than the alternative. If I were to wipe those aspects from their nature, they'd be no better than the animated muck they fight."

Gabriel dipped his chin. "As you say, Mars. Yet they would be less trouble."

It was an old argument between the two. Mars let his subordinates know they could air their concerns. He was that kind of general. Up to a point.

Mars gave little Quintus the scribe, the high sign. "I have an opening tomorrow morning, Michael. Does that suit?"

Quintus flashed a confirm the date to Michael and Gabriel, knowing that Mars wasn't waiting for them to agree. He was merely being polite.

Michael, commander of the Stalwarts, bowed. "It will be so, Mars. Gabriel and I will escort Beck to you at first light. I think—" He stopped. Michael was holding something back.

"What is it, Michael? Speak your mind."

"Mars, Ragnar Beck is more curious than most. His performance has been superior, but his persistence in questioning the nature of his being is unusual. Otherwise, he is proving an excellent soldier. Perhaps, a stronger conditioning is necessary before we proceed?"

Mars thought it interesting that Michael and Gabriel both had some reservations about Beck. "Minerva's gift suppresses as much of those impulses as lets them still be the kind of soldiers I want. Their curiosity can't be eliminated without also ruining their initiative and ingenuity on the battlefield. You take the good with the bad, son. If he stays in line after meeting me, then he goes to the Plains of Eternity. It's time to find out if his sense of order is more important than his love of the craft."

※　※　※

If Mars was a god, he didn't speak like I imagined one would. His voice didn't boom with thunder, or echo through the halls, or have that formal diction that avoided contractions like the burning bush giving the Ten Commandments.

Instead, he sounded like an annoyed first sergeant, or maybe like that old movie where the general gives a pep talk to his troops in front of a giant American flag. Great movie. Great flag. The stars and stripes hung in my grandpa's home, and one draped his coffin. I still loved that flag the best, more than the NorthAm flag I'd worn on my shoulder.

"On your feet, men," ordered the god. "Jensen, how are your troops coming along?"

Will stood at attention, and I copied him.

"Fine, sir. Better every day."

"And this one," Mars said, meaning me.

"Ready to take the challenges, sir."

"Very well." From his seat above, Mars looked me over. I locked my eyes on the base of his throat, looking neither up nor down, fixed on the spot I'd always been taught a soldier should look at when being inspected by a superior. It was the best I knew how to do for a god.

"Ragnar Beck," he began. I flinched. He knew my name. "We expect everything from you. You're here because you've already proven you know how to deliver. You're a good soldier. Not yet an Ultimate. We don't have eternity to teach you all there is to know. But with what time we do have, we're going to make sure you've had the best training possible to face what lies ahead for this army. Don't fail. Dismissed."

I snapped a salute, not knowing if that was protocol, did an about face, and marched. It was heady stuff, being addressed by a god. I kept my best military bearing as I took the stairs down, and waited on the flying disc at parade rest, feeling Mars's eyes were somehow still on me.

We lifted. Carried on the glowing disc and travelling without engines or noise. The presentation before Mars had been one of those moments come and gone too fast. Should I have asked questions? It didn't seem like I was there to have them answered. I was still a soldier. Mars had given me an order. *Don't fail.* That was good enough for me.

On the short ride back I took the opportunity to rubberneck from altitude while I could. "Will, is that a compound like ours?" I pointed to an isolated spot on the horizon that reminded me of our own Cradle.

"Yup. So I'm told."

"Are they full of resurrected soldiers, like us?"

Michael was neither annoyed in his tone nor sympathetic to satisfying my curiosity. "Fix your mind on what is yet to come, Ragnar Beck, not the things ancillary to the next moments of your existence."

As he said it, my curiosity withered and was forgotten.

We descended just outside of camp, the only place I knew on this incredible world other than the Hall of Mars. Once through the gates of the perfect stone wall, instead of returning through the arches of the training ground, Michael headed for the domed building I'd seen many times, expecting us to follow like the obedient soldiers we were. I was ready to see somewhere new, though my apprehension about a "challenge" made me feel shy as a kitten about to tackle stairs for the first time. I readied myself to expect another surprise attack like the reception I'd received from Gabriel on arrival. I stuttered at the entrance for a quick scan. Inside, a lone attendant in armor much like Michael's stood behind a rostrum. Otherwise, the only thing I spied sat beneath the peak of the dome. Two columns the width of a door waited ominously in the center of the rotunda.

"Hestus, is the way prepared?"

"It is." He swept a hand across the glowing panel, and a shimmering wall filled the space between the columns.

With the tip of his spear, Michael pointed to the wall of electric blue. "Pass through and be tested, Ragnar Beck."

I hated surprises. I hesitated.

"You'll be fine, Rag," Will assured me. "You're ready."

I gulped and stepped through.

※　※　※

"*Les manteaux rouges arrivent.*"

I don't speak any languages but NorthAm English and a little Spanglish. But I knew that was French. Whispered. And I understood him perfectly. "The redcoats are coming." This was something new. As was my body.

I was dressed in buckskins, behind a tree, my long rifle close to my chest. The drum beat of a marching cadence was very out of place in the woods. Left and right of me, bearded men dressed likewise were doing the same as me. Waiting in ambush. An honest to goodness Indian was beside me. Black war paint on his face, chest, and arms. He was Abenaki. I knew that somehow. I felt my face. A thick beard covered it.

Just as suddenly as I'd left Panama and woke only to have Gabriel's flaming sword trying to split my skull, I was in a new fight. Mars's command to me was unambiguous. *Don't fail.*

I knew things. My name was Phillipe Ricard. My family had been in the New World a long time. My father was a Voyageur. Before him, a lineage of coureur de bois—runners of the woods—trapping, trading, and living with the Indians. The English claimed territory belonging to New France as the war in Europe exploded. I was only too glad to join Captain Beaujeu and the Abenaki volunteers. Beaujeu had high regard for the natives, especially my Abenaki brothers. Wearing warpaint just like the Abenaki, he led us to Fort Duquesne. We weren't there in time to ambush the British on their way to lay siege to the fort, and he was killed when we attempted to cut them off. For once, the British marksmanship had been superior. I clutched my long rifle.

I'd shot one of Braddock's horses out from under him. I came close, but it'd been just a little too far for me to hit their general. But now I wasn't just Phillipe Ricard. Now I was Ragnar Beck. And I could do things Phillipe couldn't dream of. It was going to be a pleasure to nail British scalps to the trees to avenge our captain.

I snuck a glance around the white bark of the birch I hid behind. The leaves were thick. Just enough breeze blew to make them rustle, concealing our sound and scent and cooling the summer air. The British are in retreat, trying to make it back over the Monongahela. Native guides led the way on the trail. The Mingo were not as fierce a band of warriors as the Abenaki, and the foolish British had few natives to guide them. I'm only part Abenaki, mainly French, but I feel a part of both worlds. The guides hurried past, their fear betrayed by their speed, oblivious to our presence. The sound of drums became louder.

They retreated along the road they'd suffered to build wide on their way to lay siege to the fort, but this time the cannons they worked so hard to bring with them had been abandoned. They hadn't been of much use in the thick forest. I knew all these things, yet I'd only just found myself here.

Pierre leaned out in slow motion from behind his hiding place, and I did the same. The frizzen was still closed over the pan. I eased the hammer back with my thumb, finger on the trigger to keep the last click of full cock from making the dreadful metallic sound. I released the trigger slowly—testing with thumb on the hammer—and eased off, feeling the sear was engaged. My muzzle rose as slowly as the drip of maple resin down a tree. Sights settled on a red jacket, I tracked him through the trees and led slightly. I continued my swing until his next step brought him into a patch of fading sunlight, and I pulled the trigger.

The push in my shoulder, the cloud of white smoke, and I was blind for a moment. I kept my face on the gun and continued my swing for another microsecond, then took a knee. Around me, more thunder rained out. Below me, the sounds of panic and chaos, as panicked English voices shouted commands. A charge from my powder horn, the extra millisecond to hold a patch over the muzzle, and I pushed a ball down. I needed another accurate shot ready before I assaulted.

A high-born English voice from a PBS period piece sounded off. "Second rank. Ready volley. Fire."

I stayed behind my tree as lead balls whipped the air to either side. Next to me, a grinning Swift of Foot had just reloaded as well. This was our moment. I leaned out, bracing my forearm against the tree, and took a quick look over my barrel. Saber held aloft, the redcoat officer yelled more orders. Before he lowered the blade in time with the command for the next rank's volley, I fired. I hesitated on the sights just long enough for the cloud to clear, and I saw him clutch his chest and fall. I was already reloaded as our whoops began. We charged.

A few sporadic shots came our way, but the remaining redcoats were breaking, running, fleeing for their lives. Down the hillside, weaving between trees, I brought my rifle up. While still at a run, I shot another man in the back before he made it into the woods opposite the road. Onto the road we rushed. I butted a kneeling soldier in the face. His surprise look was erased as his face exploded, blood and teeth flying.

Rifle in hand, I drew my hatchet from my back and crushed the skull of another, catching him with his hands cocked back to use his rifle on me like a club. I followed him to the ground with more circling chops until I saw the contents of his skull. A quick assessment. We owned the road. Blades and clubs and hatchets were at work. Down the road, gunshots. Organized volley. Someone was still in command, making a counterattack.

I shouted, "With me!" I ran, vaulting over corpses and the dying, weaving through pairs of combatants engaged in the bloodiest of games. I left the road, through the forest, up a spur, and down again. I reloaded on the run. No patch this time in front of my ball. No time. On the road, an officer on horseback directed two ranks of infantry. Angled away from me, they fired a volley into the woods. The second rank stepped forward as several of the first rank fell to shots from my friends beyond the woodline.

The officer on the horse was imposing. Calm. A giant for this time period. He pulled pistol from his saddle and stood in his stirrups to fire at a lone Abenaki warrior as he gave a war cry and ran full tilt out of the woods toward the skirmishers. I paused to watch the officer in his deliberate fire, track and follow through, and fell the overly aggressive youngster. He should've stayed in the woods and waited.

I fired. I wasn't alone. I hit a skirmisher broadside, and he dropped, opening up another target for those with me. One uniformed soldier fell after another. The British ranks were breaking. The mounted officer fell with his horse, multiple balls finding meat, the shrill neighs of pain and death louder than the gunfire. This was my chance. First onto the road, I dropped my rifle, ducked beneath a butt-stroke, and with blade and hatchet in each hand, set to work on the sergeant. My knife sliced hamstring. A rotation, a twist, a tight circle, and my hatchet found the back of his head. I spun away and kept running. My goal stood in front of me.

I wasn't the first to reach the tall soldier. Saber in one hand, pistol held by the barrel in the other, he skewered one of my bearded brothers, then clubbed with the pistol butt, using the motion to pull his blade free. He was skilled.

But not as skilled as me. Hundreds of hours spent trading blows and cuts with the best warriors from all times had made me the deadliest on this or any battlefield.

I was on him. I deflected his slash with my hatchet, catching the blade with the arc of my swing, finishing the motion to leave arms wide, center exposed. I spun and kicked, my foot landing on his chest as I extended fully. He flew backward but did not fall. He was stout. I closed, knife reversed, countering his saber again with my hatchet. He parried, I attacked. I drew blood with my knife, then tiring of the exchange, sent a flurry of attacks. Feet, knees, blade, hatchet.

He fought well. But as my blade sunk into his heart and the air escaped his lips, I grinned and eased him down before removing my blade. A rapid turn in all directions to look for my next opponent. There were none. Victorious cries and raised fists told me we'd avenged Captain Beaujeu. Lieutenant Alain picked up the saber of the giant I'd slayed and offered it to me.

"Phillipe! My god! That was something to see. You fought like a whirlwind."

The Abenaki whooped, then one grabbed my hand holding the bloody hatchet and raised it overhead. Even my French brothers joined the chorus.

Swift of Foot was by my side now. "I know it is not your way, but the honor is yours, Phillipe." In his hands he held a bloody dark scalp, pointing to the gray mane of the giant at my own feet. I dropped to both knees and grasped a handful of hair, then passed my knife beneath it with a sawing motion. I raised the bloody mess overhead and gave an Abenaki shout. From my victim's waist, I pulled his blade from a leather scabbard, using his own knife to nail the hair and skin to a tree, a warning for the English fools.

"Drive the English into the sea from which they came!"

I raised my head to the sky and let loose with howls and whoops until my voice was raw, my ears deaf.

Mid-yell, I was back in the rotunda.

Will, Michael, and Hestus stared.

"Jumping Jehoshaphat!" Will's mouth hung open. "You scalped George Washington!"

08

The words from Will sounded to my ears almost like an accusation and I was worried I'd done something wrong. I was Northam, after all. Was I supposed to help Washington? The thought hadn't occurred to me. I was entirely devoted to the cause of Phillipe from the moment I arrived on the battlefield.

"Was I not supposed to, Will?" I'd dimly recognized the face and it was obvious now. George'd never have to worry about his false teeth again.

Will only shrugged.

"But you saw?" I pressed. "You saw the whole thing?"

Will's eyes-wide nod told me he had. I suddenly felt even prouder of my performance. Though we were about the same age, I felt as though I'd just reeled in a bigger fish than the older brother who'd taught me how to cast.

Michael gave me a subtle tight-lipped pucker of a smile, his first hint of any approval toward me. "Return to train until your next challenge, Ragnar Beck. And speak not of today's events to any who have not yet participated in the same. The penalty will be severe if you do."

In my post-combat buzz, I didn't want to think about what that penalty could be. I was feeling too good. Anyway, I was a rule follower. "I understand, Michael. Mum's the word with the newbies."

He frowned at my informality. Like I said. I was feeling good. It wasn't every day you get to best a legend. "William Jensen, you may share with him the possibilities that come with success."

"Come on," Will whispered out of the side of his mouth. I was a kid who'd killed his first deer. Or maybe, it was more like that perfect Christmas morning after the presents had all been opened, and Santa had brought me everything I'd asked for. This was so much better than the bitter victory at the dam. Even if I still secretly suspected none of this was real.

"I've figured this out, Will," I said as we walked back through the arches. The air was clean and crisp, and I was anxious to get back to training. "It's a virtual reality game. But better. We get to flex our muscles out in the wild, trying out our improved combat skills. Is this where you and the others have been disappearing to?"

He stopped short. "I know what you're thinking, Rag. You're not the first fella from your time to float that idea. This isn't a game. What you just did *was* real. Where you were *exists* in time. The people you were with, the ones you killed. They were real."

I felt the nausea again, like when I'd suddenly materialized here. I'd killed George Washington. My face must've betrayed the enormity of what I'd done. "You're telling me that actually happened? That I was there? In the French and Indian war. America doesn't get to have its most important founding father because I drove a knife into his heart?" It was the most fantastic and terrible Twilight Zone episode ever.

Will shrugged. "Some America. Somewhere. Not ours."

I was dizzy. Was he talking about a multiverse? When I asked, Will frowned.

"Beats me. I don't know what a multiverse is. They don't ever tell us much. You know how they speak. Michael calls it 'the Plains of Eternity.' Come on. I've got some friends I want you to meet."

It was the noon meal break. Our squad was nowhere to be seen—out of the compound somewhere training. I didn't see Gabriel, so I thought it was a good bet he was supervising our squad while Will was babysitting me. I hoped that was the case. If Karl were leading training, he'd have everyone lined up in two ranks, marching as he criticized their intervals if they weren't perfectly dress right dress. Old habits die hard, I guess. Since Karl was still around, he must've performed satisfactorily—like me—but he hadn't shown me that he was ready to leave his outdated concepts of military tactics behind.

Will on the other hand had been hurtled from antiquity but unlike Karl had achieved a competency in the tactics of my era. That put him at the head of the squad. There was no question Gabriel led, but like an officer with a dependable NCO, he let Will run things in the way best suited to achieve Gabriel's intent.

Will led me through the mess to a table where a squad I recognized was just finishing. "Smitty. Wilson. Got a second?" The two he'd addressed reminded me of Will. They looked like pure midwest American stock. The one who answered confirmed it.

"Sure, cousin. Meet you outside."

I'd seen Will socialize with some of the other squads. I just figured he knew more of the candidates in the same way he knew more of the ropes around here by being on the scene longer than me. Outside, his two friends joined us for some prison yard talk.

"Meet Ragnar Beck."

I shook hands with the two.

"So, just had your first little adventure?" Wilson asked. "I take it everything went well. You're still here to tell the tale."

I looked to Will for approval to admit it. I didn't think he'd set me up to violate Michael's order, but I was suddenly feeling very much unsure about things, like I was back to square one in my new world. The feeling of elation at my combat victory was long gone.

"It was me that brought Smith and Wilson here," Will explained. "When Michael said I could tell you about the possibilities that could come from your successes, this is what he meant." He thumbed at his friends. "But it took me a few trips before Michael told me about recruitment." Will used the same hand to poke me in the chest. "He spilled the beans to you after your first action."

"Recruitment?" I asked stupidly.

"Remember that primitive Hoosier that got disappeared the other day?" Smitty was talking about the newcomer who collapsed in front of Gabriel without so much as raising a fuss to defend himself. "Near as we can figure it, the head shed's always looking for talent. Sometimes they find a guy who looks like a winner, only they get him here, and he doesn't have the right stuff."

Will picked up the explanation from his friend. "After my third challenge, Michael asked me who I would recommend to join us. Someone I knew who was the kind of soldier they were looking for."

Smitty grunted. "Thanks for thinking of us," he said sarcastically.

Wilson shrugged. "Beats being dead, I suppose."

Smitty tried to make it clearer for me in his early 20th century American lingo. "You shine like a star, and you can recommend a candidate for them to bring back. That way it's not so much like they're choosing someone from a look-see of his one little moment in the spotlight. More like, the guy's got references."

"I'm not sure what impresses them more," Wilson said. "Surviving, or buying the farm in the same kinda way got us here. My last jaunt was right out of Henry the Fifth. Only I wasn't on the winning team, and I didn't get to hear any Saint Crispin's day speech. I was on the side getting shot to hell by clouds of arrows."

The Battle of Agincourt? I wondered. "How'd you come out?"

Wilson scoffed. "I went down skewered on a pike."

"But they brought you back," Will reminded. "That's what matters. You didn't go yellow."

I thought I understood. "So, Michael thought well enough of my performance that if I keep doing well, he'll let me recommend one of my teammates for resurrection?"

"If you want to call it that," Smitty said. "Seems a little blasphemous if you ask me, but ain't nothing seems too out of bounds anymore."

Will took on a pall of seriousness. "Mars said that what awaits us is the war to end all wars. Gabriel and Michael have let slip the same thing. Nothing less than the battle for all existence. And we've been chosen to defend it. Defend everything. I chose Smitty and Wilson because I knew they were just like me. I don't know if you impressed Mike because you're so darn good, or that time is short, and that's why you got the early nod. But this is what Michael wanted me to clue you in to. If you think there's someone from your time who can help us in this fight, figure out who they are and be ready when he asks."

A weight as heavy as a ton of bricks landed on me just then. Would I be saving the souls of Stokes and Jess and the rest of the team by bringing their names forward, or would I be sentencing them to an eternity of war?

That night I prodded Will for more information. "Did Smitty and Wilson buy it the same time as you?" I was used to reading or working a 3-D puzzle at bedtime in my previous life. Instead, I craved whatever the diadem was going to show me as I slept.

Will lay with his arm across his face, voice muffled. He was trying to ignore me. "Not exactly, but we all had our last stand in the Meuse. If you're lucky, you won't replay that one yourself."

I'd gone back to trying to figure out how we were all here at the same time—whenever this time was, wherever here was—from so many different periods across history. Maybe that's what the well of souls was? A Purgatory, or a limbo, a timeless place where our souls stayed in darkness until we were pulled here. I'd asked Jakob could explain it to me. He seemed convinced his Roman Catholic worldview explained it. My folks were dyed in the wool Baptists. All I knew is that when I died, I was supposed to pass through the pearly gates to that kingdom in the sky, to walk on streets of gold. But that obviously didn't happen. Had I faltered in my faith? I had to admit, I'd always been one of those who questioned if there was a heaven, and if so, was it truly like that stuff I'd been told as a kid? But here

I was, being slapped in the face with the stinky dead fish of an afterlife.

My first notion might have been correct. I was suffering a nerve agent-induced psychosis courtesy of the Lotus Hegemony.

"Stop trying to understand it." It was as if Will were reading my thoughts. "You're a soldier. A good one. Get your diadem on. Tomorrow, you'll be even deadlier. All I know is, if this is the afterlife, at least it ain't boring. G'night, Rag."

09

I woke up with a new understanding of horseback cavalry. "Will? What's the worst thing you've seen on the Plains of Eternity?" I used Michael's terminology for the gateway to the world of our challenges. His groan told me he wasn't yet awake, and I'd pelted him with the cold, hard hail of another question before he'd even had the chance to get his feet on the floor.

"It's all war. You had your flesh eaten away by a Chinese weapon. That sounds like one of the worst things to me. What could happen in war worse than that?"

I was still struggling with the "reality" of what I'd done to George Washington. If my actions were real, then they had real repercussions. I'd changed history for a developing America. What other frightening possibility of a crime could I be responsible for next?

"Will, have they ever put in you in a position to do something really horrible? Have you been with Genghis Khan? Razing villages of women and children? How about Nazis, doing Nazi stuff?"

He was on his feet and not looking too happily with me. "You know I don't have all the answers. You've been here long enough that you know as much as I do. You're going to start going to the plains regularly now. If you don't want to end up in limbo, I'd concentrate on something more useful."

That's why he was squad leader.

I didn't have to wait long. A few days later, we were on one of the live fire ranges. I was kitted up in WW2 era garb, a flamethrower on my back, looking forward to a movement to contact exercise with the entire company, when I got pulled out of formation. I didn't have Will to hold my hand this time.

I was feeling pretty cocky after how I'd breezed through a fight as primitive, bloody and cruel, as I'd had for my first test in the French and Indian War. Lately we'd been practicing bunker assaults against automaton defenders, using weapons and gear almost contemporary for my own period. I felt prepared for ancient and modern warfare, and everything in between. What could be next?

"Hestus, is the way prepared?" Michael called. In the rotunda it was just him, me, and Hestus, the airline gate attendant.

"It is." The shimmering wall appeared, and Michael did the same grand routine, pointing the way with his spear.

"Pass through and be tested, Ragnar Beck."

I sort of knew what to expect when being slingshotted by surprise into a new reality now, and made a quick assessment. I was in a jungle that made Panama's seem like a manicured arboretum. I didn't have as concrete a body of knowledge about who I was in this scenario, but a quick peek at my light brown uniform and the AK-47 in my hands told me plenty about who and where I likely was. I'd read about the Vietnam War like some kids read Manga. As a young troop Grandpa had served under veterans of what had been America's longest war. Longest, that is, until his and my dad's multi-career spanning war came along. The history of the war in Southeast Asia was a popular topic in my household.

I was crouched behind a tank. It was crawling, crushing foliage beneath its treads to make a path as we followed. All tanks are big when you're right next to them. Even so, this wasn't anywhere near the size of one of the M-11 Cashes I was used to. This wasn't a main battle tank. It was some kind of light reconnaissance or amphibious model. The wheels in my brain started turning. A PT-76? I could be wrong, but I guess it didn't matter. There weren't too many engagements where the People's Army of Vietnam used them, at least until the end of the war when it was the South standing in its own and the North rolled into Saigon.

If I listened, that inner voice was telling me who I was and how I hated the imperialist invaders. I'd suffered through high-altitude bombings and had seen my unit all but wiped out before we reinforced, resupplied, and made our way anew east from Laos.

"Du, are you scared?" There was a raging fight happening somewhere the other side of this jungle. It seemed we were about to break through into it.

Phuc was talking to me. He was my oldest friend. At nineteen, we'd both been in the army for two years. We'd survived everything together, but this was our first chance to fight, to bring the war to the traitorous South and to the Americans.

The part of me that was Rag felt revulsion but I was going to play along. If I was supposed to be a hard-core commie, then I'd be a hard-core commie.

"No, Phuc. I'm not afraid. And you shouldn't be either. Remember what Uncle Ho has sacrificed for us. We do this for the people." I kept pace, the belch of diesel exhaust making me cough as the tank ratcheted ahead until it broke through, the crack of trees splintering under treads heralding its arrival. The "pings" of ricochets off the glacis told me it was wisest to stay put, but curiosity got the better of me. I took a cautious, low lean around to see what awaited. A wide kill-zone around a camp, layers of razor wire, and block houses in the center. I knew where my cruel judges had sent me.

This was Lang Vei. It was 1968. This was the Night of the Silver Stars. And Michael had sent me here to kill the Green Berets inside.

I knew what I had to do. A tracer round skipped off another tank breaking through the jungle, the orange trail from the camp burned in my retina as I threw myself prone. I knew what should follow. It was the .50 caliber marker round for a 106mm recoilless. *Get some, brothers*, I thought as I kept my head down. A thunderous boom nearly deafened me, but my heart soared to see the tank on fire, rounds cooking off inside it. Some smooth Green Beret had gotten a tank kill.

Behind me, my squad mates were dead, or soon would be. We'd been close enough to the other tank that the frag and the white phosphorous it ejected burned through their clothes and skin as they screamed. Phuc had dropped with me, following my lead. I was his squad leader, after all. His eyes were wide in disbelief as I shot him.

I have a side, and it's not yours. The RPG he carried was now in my hands. The PT-76 I'd been hiding behind was now a good fifty yards from where I'd hesitated in the woodline. Its main gun fired, missing the center block house. I loaded a B-40 rocket and took aim at the lead wheels, for a spot right where the driver compartment should be. I cocked the hammer and fired. Contact! The tread came off, and smoke poured out of the hole in the skin.

I grabbed another rocket and loaded. Another tank broke though the wall of green and paused to fire. I aimed at the same spot and sent another. A delay. A lackluster explosion on impact. Then the fire. Small at first, then a growing inferno as it found more fuel to feed it. The tank commander leaped out. I fired at him for all I was worth as he stumbled, but couldn't hit him. It was dark and a futile effort without being able to see my sights. Someone in the camp cut him down for me. If I wasn't careful, I'd get the same treatment.

Two for me. But no more rockets left.

Rounds whizzed overhead, and I threw myself down again. *How to help the guys in the camp without getting prematurely killed?* I wondered. Jumping up and yelling, "I'm on your side," probably wouldn't have a positive effect. Unlike my first challenge, there wasn't a way to victory here. There was no plan. I just didn't want to die. Not yet.

Sometimes in the midst of battle an opportunity presents itself, and without conscious thought, a course of action plays in your mind like a movie preview. It was the buzz of an aircraft overhead that did it for me just then, and the burp of a two-cycle chainsaw engine revving up over and over again. Flares drifted through the heavens, and what I needed to do right then was as clear to me as if I'd been sent a message from Mars himself.

If the Spectre gunship raining rounds from its Vulcan could see better, maybe I could help turn the attack on the camp and save the lives of the A-Team inside. I crawled back into the woodline, then ran. I plowed through the jungle, heading for where I hoped another tank and a column of infantry was waiting to plow into the open. The firefight was in full hurricane force from both directions. I had to hit the deck and crawl many times as I pushed ahead to find what I was looking for. Behind another tank a squad knelt, waiting for the breakout to happen. I tossed a frag and opened up with my rifle on automatic. I caught them with their pants down. Being a traitor was fun. I made it to the back of the tank where my prize awaited. I grabbed the can of diesel and poured it over the tank, sloshing and spilling every drop I could.

"What are you doing?" An officer with pistol in hand, a puny Makarov, shocked and confused by my perplexing action, fired. He hit me. I dropped the can, found my rifle, and stitched him. He'd missed me with the rest, but at least one of his shots had buried in my thigh. It was a dull slap of an impact, not at all what I thought getting shot might feel like. The diesel poured out of the can. I pulled my lighter and tossed it. Diesel doesn't ignite well. I cursed when nothing happened. I pulled a grenade as I limped away, tore at the pin, and tossed. With a crump and whiz of shrapnel, the fire started. The tank rolled ahead, the flames igniting the paint, the other cans on the rear deck blazing to life in a sudden burst as the tin can lurched out into the kill zone, unaware of what had transpired outside. Like a moth, I fluttered after it, oblivious to the bullets and explosions around me.

A white flare erupted high above, drifting under its parachute like a lazy tuft of cotton. In the camp, I caught glimpses of tall Americans and the tiny soldiers at their sides as they fired from sandbagged bunkers and pits. My leg gave way and I fell. This time, I'd been hit by something much bigger than a little pop-gun. The buzzing of the aircraft engines was louder. I opened my eyes to see the mouth of the dragon spew fire from the sky as the tank exploded, and I vanished with it in a trillion ragged pieces.

And then I was back in the rotunda. I knew what awaited. The abyss would be a welcome shelter from the rage of Michael's scowl and curse.

"Impudent cur! Back to the well of souls with you!"

Michael levelled his spear at my chest. I was ready for oblivion, so I no longer needed to act fearfully obedient. If this was all a dream, then what did it matter if I stopped being a whipped dog and bit back?

"I may be a cur, but at least I'm not a commie who'd kill his own people. You don't want to explain how any of this works or what I'm doing here? Fine. But you'll never get me to kill another American." George Washington technically wasn't an American yet when I killed him. So he didn't count. I closed my eyes. How bad could the well of souls be? If that's where I'd been cooling my jets between death and appearing here, it would just be a return to nothing. I wouldn't even know it. That's what Jakob thought.

A very annoyed voice made me open my eyes. "As you were, Michael." It was Mars. Michael's spear tip was still pointed at my chest, and the face of an irritated Mars floated overhead. "Stand down, Mike."

Michael brought his spear to port arms.

"YOU!" Here was the thunderous boom I expected from a god. I popped to attention, like Michael. "Time to stand tall before the man, Beck. You know the way. Get your butt moving, soldier. NOW!"

The image vanished. Michael ignored me, brashly turned, and stormed out of the rotunda like a child sent to his room.

"Move with haste, Ragnar Beck," advised Hestus. "A conveyance awaits."

Was I crazy, or was Hestus amused at my predicament?

I didn't find anything funny about the situation but took his advice and double-timed out to where a glowing disc sat. It took off as though sensing Mars's directive to make it snappy, and in minutes deposited me at the base of the grand stairs. Two at a time, I vaulted to the top where in the great hall Mars was not alone.

Giant demigods as large as Michael and Gabriel in shining armor and great red and gold cloaks stood around a table, Mars at its head. I was on my own to figure out how one's supposed to report to a pissed-off god. I marched ahead to a respectful three yards away and snapped to attention, rendered a hand salute, and held it, waiting to be recognized. I stayed frozen that way, ignored for several minutes. I tried to listen to the conversation, anything to be distracted from the ass-chewing or epically painful death that awaited from the god I'd disappointed. The pounding of my heart in my ears drowned out the discussion occurring around the table. I was sure what would follow wouldn't be a one-way trip to oblivion; more like, I was going to be burned to a cinder on the spot by a massive lightning bolt once Mars took notice of me. I stood so long that my saluting arm ached and my attention wavered. Just as it did, the moment came.

"YOU. Beck. What d'you have to say for yourself?"

10

Mars could say this much for Beck: the human was proving to be a pain in the ass. But the god had known a few pains in the ass who were nevertheless worth having around. Otherwise, he would not have stayed Michael's hand.

Beck dropped his salute. "Sir. My actions reflected my assessment of the test conditions, sir."

Mars let a sly smile curl the corner of his mouth. "This oughtta be good. Explain."

Beck didn't fall apart before the god; he stayed in a statue-perfect attention. "Sir, it was a test of my ethics as a combat leader. I'm an American, sir. I have ancestors who fought in that conflict. That particular battle put me in a position to fight against Americans and against a unit that my ancestors served in for generations, sir. I would have served in that unit too, had it still existed during my life, sir. That battle was one where a Special Forces A-team survived outrageous odds against a tank attack, unsupported by other American forces. In fact, sir, other American forces refused to help them.

"I made an assessment of the situation, sir. To be sent to the Battle of Lang Vei as a combatant on the enemy side could only be a test of my ethics. To do anything other than what I chose to do would have been an act of moral cowardice on my part, sir. If anything, sir, I should have been with the defenders, not the attackers."

"*Who told you to think, soldier?*" Mars paused to consider the countenance of the soldier standing before him. Beck looked as though his guts had been turned to ice. "*And who said you get a choice? I told you not to fail. All you had to do was prove you could lead a small team and assault a bunker just as you'd been practicing, and you'd have succeeded. It should have been an easy test of your ability as a combat leader. Instead, you failed.*"

What Mars had seen, he'd liked. What he saw now, that Beck wasn't ready to back down, he liked further.

"*Sir, I made the choice to do what I saw as right. Knowing what I know now, I would do the same again, sir.*"

"*Beck, you said you recognized the battle. How? It was a small incident that occurred many generations before your soul landed on the earth. You some kind of scholar? Explain it to me, professor.*"

This pain in the ass was ready for that one and launched into an explanation.

"*Sir, I'm no scholar. I'm just a,*" Beck stammered. "*I'm just a soldier, like my father and his before him. It's all I've ever wanted to be. I grew up reading everything I could about the greatest units and soldiers throughout history. I'm not an educated man, sir. I'm just a soldier.*"

He was humble. And honest. He was a pain, but he was also a good soldier. One Mars felt was too good to dump for being a free-thinker. The god accepted his explanation. But what to do with him? An idea presented itself to Mars. "*I've heard enough, Beck. I'm busy. I don't have time for this bullshit.*"

Beck looked as though he was ready to have a powerful finger leveled in his direction before being whisked away to hell.

"*I'm going to give you another chance. That's a rare thing around here, you understand me, mister?*"

A glimmer of hope formed in Beck's eyes. "Sir! Yes, sir!"

"Get back to the plains and show me what you've got. Now. You screw this one up, and you'll never soldier again. Got me?"

"Sir! Yes, sir!"

"Dismissed."

Beck delivered a salute, held it just long enough, hit a sharp order arms, and double-timed a retreat.

Mars had surprised his staff.

Neton smirked. "You've grown tolerant, Mars."

And perhaps the god had.

Olloudius frowned. "I've heard about this one. Does he suspect the Plains of Eternity are but a testing ground, and that his soul is not in danger of being released back to the cosmos while there? Is that why he acts so reckless in battle there?"

Mars shook off the suggestion. He had heard Beck's musings with his confidants over meals. The human very much thought what he did on the plains was real. "No. He doesn't know. I believe he's a rare one who loves the craft as much as his rectitude. If that boy proves out, we may have another company commander in the making."

✖ ✖ ✖

"The way is prepared, Ragnar Beck." Michael was nowhere to be seen as Hestus went through his ritual for my benefit alone.

The rippling electric blue curtain awaited. I stepped through, not a clue where I would end up or what violence awaited me. Would I be raiding the English coast, leading a Viking mob? Would I awake in the body of a saber-wielding winged Hussar, charging the Turkish army sieging Vienna? A German U-boat commander, trying to save my flooding boat amidst a hull ringing from exploding depth charges? Would they actually send me back and have me perform the same role as before, forcing me to prove that I'd do it all over again? In a millisecond I imagined everything I'd ever seen in every war movie in my life, wondering what Mars had in mind for my redemption test.

"Officer's call."

The creek water at our bivouac was so alkaline the horses wouldn't drink it. I spit out the coffee we made from it. We'd been on the move since midnight. I blew my nose, grateful at least for the respite from the grit-filled air kicked up by the horses that I was still ejecting from my lungs.

"The general's back, Lieutenant, and he looks impatient."

I tossed the rest of the cup into the dirt. "On my way, Sergeant. Thanks."

The terrain was so rough, we'd spent as much time leading our horses as we had riding. We were almost common infantry. The river snaked back and forth on itself in the deep gorge just the other side of the bluffs we traveled behind. We'd been led northwest, finding small campsites along the way, until the lodge-pole trails broke west across the river. We stayed on the main trail—by now almost a mile wide. It was so dusty because most of the grass had been grazed off. We'd call these clues important battlefield intelligence in mine or most any soldier's time.

But none of that seemed to register with *him*.

Lieutenant Varnum was the chief of scouts. He'd sent a message to the general before dawn that they'd found the camp. The general rode up to see for himself. The Crow swore that about 15 miles ahead was a large pony herd and a village. They'd also seen parties of Lakota cresting a ridge in the distance. Varnum's cheap spyglass couldn't confirm what they said they knew, so he dismissed them. Lieutenant Varnum had brought up that even if the camp wasn't as large as the Crow said it was, we should still consider that the Lakota had seen the 7th's campfires.

But none of that seemed to register with *him*.

Last night, a load of hardtack had fallen off a mule in the pack train. Two soldiers went to retrieve the boxes. A few miles back, they found several Indians going through the cases of foodstuffs. The fools shot at them, missed, and the Indians got away. Where else could they be headed except back to the village? No question our column had been discovered by the Lakota.

But none of that seemed to register with *him*.

When Custer returned from his scouting trip, his briefing at the officer's call was nothing if not succinct.

"The largest Indian camp on the North American continent is ahead, and I am going to attack it."

Mars had sent me here as my test. As my punishment. Had I not known this battle inside and out, the clues were there for even the worst detective to find. This was my moment.

"Colonel."

"What is it, *Lieutenant*?" I'd started off badly. Most of the regiment referred to Custer by his Civil War brevet rank of "general" even though he was a lieutenant colonel.

I rehashed the intelligence. He waved me off. "The Lakota most certainly know of our presence, Lieutenant. And what does it matter?"

"Sir, there may be thousands of them. If we could do a more detailed reconnaissance—" I didn't get to finish.

"They're scattering now, as we speak. If we don't hit them, we'll be chasing hostiles through the winter. We have no choice but to attack instantly. Are you a coward, Lieutenant?" Before I could deny it, he gave his order. "Battle plans will have to be made on the move. We'll advance in order of readiness."

※　※　※

Mitch Boyer was our interpreter. He was mixed breed, French and Indian, not that you could tell. He looked as Indian as any of our scouts but spoke English as well as I did. He'd been trained by Jim Bridger himself, the greatest scout who'd ever lived. He was such a valuable man that Sitting Bull had a bounty on his head of 100 horses.

As the meeting broke up, Boyer came over to the officer's gathering and spoke up. "General, I've been with these Indians for thirty years, and this is the largest village I've ever heard of."

Custer waved him off.

I caught Boyer's attention as the group scattered. "It was a good effort, Mitch."

"And you. Not an easy thing to do to tell a god that he's wrong."

I winced. "Not the first time for me today."

Mitch shook his head as he followed Custer with his eyes. "Watch yourself, Lieutenant. That man will stop at nothing."

So far, my pre-ordained knowledge of the Battle of the Little Bighorn was not helping.

I raced to saddle up. Here was another opportunity to try and change what I knew was coming. I'd formed a friendship with Captain Benteen. His H company was ready first and taking the vanguard to lead the regiment after Custer and the scouts. I weaved Zeus at a gallop to find him. Benteen was a good cavalry officer and tactician. Plus, he was not a member of the cult of personality that followed the general.

"Captain, I've been talking to Boyer and the scouts. They think there may be thousands of Lakota ahead. We're too small a force. If the general tries to divide us for some kind of pincer envelopment, we'll be too small to fight them off. Don't let him divide the regiment, sir."

Benteen looked at me oddly. "Why do you think he'll try an anvil and hammer maneuver?"

There wasn't much I could say. "I'm just thinking it would be a bad idea, that's all."

"If he does, you'll have better luck telling the moon differently, Jim." He spurred and rode off.

Major Reno was second in command. I was torn between what *I* knew and what Lieutenant James Sturgis knew. Sturgis didn't have a bad opinion of Reno. My recollection of the history told me there were some real negatives about him that were brought out afterward. Before I rejoined E company, I sought him out and made the same suggestion.

"You're not in the cavalry to be cautious, Lieutenant." He slurred the word cavalry. It was true. He was a drunk. And it was too late. The column was moving out.

I joined my company, my fellow lieutenant Algernon Smith in the lead. "Trying to get yourself sent to the stockade, Jim?" he teased as I rode next to him. "First, questioning the general, then late to repair?"

"No Alge," I sighed. So far, I wasn't having any impact on the events that would transpire.

"Not to worry, Jim. We'll have Sitting Bull with us in a cage to show off in Philadelphia for the Centennial. We're going to be famous."

"Yes, Alge. We will." I drew my pistol, thumbed to half cock, and found the empty chamber. I thumbed in the last cartridge, cocked, then lowered the hammer and reholstered. "I think it's a day to carry all six."

※　※　※

The sun was sweltering by the time we halted. My mind worked overtime as we rode, trying to think of a way to change what was about to happen. The officer's call confirmed what I'd remembered. Custer had stripped out of his buckskin jacket and wiped at his brow with a kerchief as he told us his plan.

"We're dividing into four battalions to take advantage of the terrain."

It was just as I'd remembered.

Benteen's eyebrows shot up. "Hadn't we better keep the regiment together, General? If this is as big a camp as they say, we'll need every man we have."

Perhaps the seed of my idea had taken hold and sprouted in Benteen's head.

Custer frowned. "Captain." The general paused to let his words take effect. "I want to be assured there are no Lakota on upper Little Bighorn who can endanger us from the rear. You'll take your battalion and split southwest to scout. You have your orders."

Benteen caught my eye as he departed. His hackles were raised. He was essentially being sent to the rear and out of the fight, and he knew it. Benteen's opinion was as poorly received as mine had been.

Reno looked as proud as a pickled beet, heading one of the battalions opposite Custer's. We followed the dry creek bed northwest toward the Little Bighorn and destiny. I wasn't scared. I'd been killed before. Twice now. I wasn't sure what Mars expected of me. What I knew was, I had to try something to impress him, or it was the well of souls for me. No brilliant plan came my way. Instead, my thoughts were filled with Stokes, and Jess, and the rest of the team. My real team. If I couldn't do something to win Mars's favor, they would stay in the void that was the well of souls.

Nothing came to me.

I rode with Custer's battalion, and as I knew would happen, we finally came to the moment where the last thread of the garment that was Custer's command came unraveled. On Custer's order, troopers set fire to the lone tepee of an abandoned camp overlooking the valley. Our scouts spotted a band of warriors in the distance, fleeing. We'd as much as sent a signal fire to the heaven's that we were coming. Ignoring the 12,000 ponies grazing on the plain and the two-mile spread of the massive camp, our general assumed the Lakota were fleeing at the sight of us, and that the camp was breaking up. Custer called Reno to him, beckoning him with his own hand, to attack from the south end to try and "bring the Indians to battle."

I watched firsthand as Reno's battalion rode down the creek after the fleeing Indians. It wasn't long before the Battle of the Little Bighorn, the battle I dreaded, finally started.

I moved to where Custer and Captain Keogh watched Reno's skirmish with the Lakota from our new viewpoint on the bluff. The Indians, rather than flee, had gathered in strength. Reno's battalion was in a fight for their lives.

"Damn Benteen!" Custer swore. "Where is he? He's been gone for hours. He should've returned by now." Reno's battalion was beating a retreat back to the bluffs, and wisely so. Riders and warriors on foot were in pursuit of Reno's strung out group as they fought. "We have to support them. A flanking maneuver! We have to get ahead and flank them." It was another chance for me to turn away defeat.

"Sir, the bluffs are too steep ahead. We won't find a place to ford any further north. Better we return to support Major Reno and cover his retreat from his jumping off point, don't you think?"

Custer scowled at me. "Damn your impudence, Lieutenant! You're a poor excuse for an officer. Have I taught you nothing? When attacked from two sides, the Indian will always turn and run. We have to flank them! Divide them! Then we'll have them in our pincer." He ignored me and turned to talk to his brother Tom and Captain Keogh. He ordered us to mount, and I left to find where Zeus was grazing on a tiny patch of green.

We'd rode just a little further when I witnessed him do the only decent thing I'd seen him do since the campaign started. He broke ahead to where the scouts led us and halted the party. He translated through Boyer. "You've been hired to scout. Not to fight."

He released the scouts. Some part of the general knew we were in for a deadly fight. I wondered if my protests had helped him see the futility of our situation as more and more Lakota spread across the valley. Three of the Crow departed. Boyer and one of the Crow, Curley, chose to remain. Boyer led us north again.

I accompanied Captain Yates with two companies as we descended the bluff to make a feint at the south end of the village, to draw warriors away to protect their women and children to allow Reno to retreat, and ultimately rejoin our force. Custer would move farther north, confident that Benteen, having heard the battle, would also return and bolster our numbers for an attack into the camp.

An hour later, I was dead.

Our feint worked, in a way. It did draw warriors away from Reno's retreat—and brought them and the whole village straight to us, by the hundreds. We fought our own retreat back up the bluff to rejoin Custer's and Keogh's battalions, losing several men in the maneuver. I killed more than a few with carbine and pistol before I let Zeus take us up the steep wash back to the bluff. By this time, the Lakota were raining bullets and arrows on us in a way that made the very air our enemy. Our dwindling battalion fought ahead to join Custer. Horses unaccustomed to battle threw their riders. The Indians climbed up both sides of the ravine. We shot them by the score, but rather than flee as Custer had expected, they kept coming. For once, I agreed with the man who'd been considered the Civil War's most brilliant cavalry officer—it was time to move north again; the only direction left to us.

With only two hundred of us left, we were surrounded. Two thousand Lakota on horseback and on foot swarmed. It was here our firepower faded. Yes, some of the Indians outgunned us with their repeating Henrys, Winchesters, and Spencers. Our trapdoor Springfields were excellent at distance, but our slow rate of fire hurt us in close combat with our better armed adversaries. Yes, my own carbine jammed at least once, just like the books had said. The folded copper case stuck in the chamber of my trapdoor, the extractor too weak to pull out the 45-55 copper case, and I had to pry the rim out with my knife. My experience was proof that the historians had it right. And I was sorry they had.

The Indians gave accurate fire from distance too, as they picked us off from several hundred yards away. I always appreciated good combat marksmanship, and theirs was admirable. Pistol in hand, I dropped a warrior on horseback, just as an arrow penetrated my back, the point sticking out beneath my chin. I dropped to my knees. I looked for Custer. In his buckskin pants and blue wool shirt, he stood out. My friend Algernon rode to his position to join in his last stand, just before everything went dark. I'd failed. My only regret at the time was I hadn't seen Custer die.

Looking back on it, I suppose it was a good thing that I was going to be given another chance.

11

I was back in the Rotunda.

"The way is prepared," Hestus said, pointing to the gate. I ran a hand over my shirt. The arrow was no longer protruding from my chest. I took a deep breath. It's a hell of a thing, seeing your inside bits hanging off an arrow tip, right where the knot of your tie should be, your own blood forming the tail.

"The way is prepared," Hestus repeated.

He hadn't moved. Neither had I.

"I heard you the first time, Hess. Give a guy a break. I'm still not entirely used to this whole die, lather, rinse, resurrect thing." Hestus was more emotive than Michael or Gabriel, and in a very human way rolled his eyes as he made a non-stop stabbing motion with his finger toward the shimmering surface. "Okay, okay. I get it. No rest for the wicked."

I passed through, hoping that this next challenge wouldn't be so pointless.

I was in the same dusty and grimy uniform. I was atop Zeus. Algernon was again bragging to me that we'd have Sitting Bull as a prisoner to show off at the Centennial exposition. Hestus had sent me back to the Little Bighorn.

Groundhog Day all over again.

"I know a girl from a nice family in Philadelphia, Jim. She has a lot of fine friends we could introduce you to. A strapping cavalry officer like yourself just back from capturing Sitting Bull could make a big splash with the debutantes of Philadelphia. That is, if you make a good showing of yourself today and stop speaking out of turn to criticize the general. What were you thinking? He's going to strip you if you're not careful. Don't you want to be famous? Just think about showing off your saber to a group of high society fillies at our heroes' welcome."

I swayed along in the saddle while Algernon kept up his pep talk. I was back again because I hadn't lived up to Mars's expectations for this test. That had to be it. "Sounds great, Alge. I'll do that. Let's go kill some Indians so I can meet a nice girl. Awesome idea." I kicked Zeus in the side and galloped off, leaving Algernon agog. Reno's battalion was in the valley, the whoops of the Lakota punctuating the gunfire a mile away. Captain Yates would be my sounding board for a better plan to bring to the general. I was too late.

"Lieutenant Sturgis, excellent timing. I was just going to send for Smith. Good news. We're to lead a feint to draw out the Lakota and give Reno's battalion some breathing room. Bring up E troop to join us. Now. Time is of the essence."

"Yes, sir." I galloped off, following orders as I'd always been taught. Yates had already received his instructions from Custer. It was true, our feint would take the pressure off Reno's retreat. But dividing our forces while Custer forged ahead trying to find a ford across the Little Bighorn wasn't going to work this time either. It would only be getting us strung out further as more of the Lakota poured up the ravines and gorges on foot to surround us. What did Mars expect me to do?

Our diversion was successful again, maybe more so this time. I killed a few more Lakota, raising my tally to ten. Not as impressive as it sounds, because I knew where they'd be coming from. I easily spotted the teepees where a band of them had appeared from; the ones that had almost killed me previously. This time I knew it would be men exiting the lodges, and not women or children, and I cut them down one at a time until my carbine failed to extract a round and my Colt clicked on an empty chamber.

Time to go.

We made the same retreat back up the bluff, a hornet's nest of Indians after us. We fought as we moved, the Indians crawling up the gorges and firing at us the whole way, more arrows, more bullets, more whooping. I remembered making the same whoop myself as another person in another war. It didn't seem such a glorious sound to me now.

After another mile of tough fighting along the bluff, we rejoined Custer and Keogh's battalion. The general was in conference with his brother Tom and Keogh in the center of a defensive formation. I kneed Zeus as I leaned forward, using his neck as a shield, charting my course to where the general stood. I reigned in and hopped out of the saddle when I saw Mitch Boyer stumble away from Custer's position and fall to the ground, bleeding. Curley, the Crow scout who'd opted to stay with us, was trying to get him on his feet. I rushed to help.

I pulled the kerchief off my neck and held it against Mitch's chest to stem the flow. "It's too late for me," Mitch said as he pushed me away. "You'd better leave now, for we will all be cleaned out."

Curley, who I didn't know spoke English, insisted that Mitch come with him, pulling at him to mount his horse with him.

"No, Curley. I'm too badly wounded. You're very young and don't know much about fighting. Leave us. Keep out of the way of the Sioux and go tell General Terry that all here are killed. Custer will stop at nothing. We have no chance at all. Go."

Curley hesitated. "Go, Curley," I said. "Do as Mitch says. Go find General Terry's men." Terry's regiment was somewhere north, waiting to cut off any retreating Indians. Only days ago, the general had offered Custer four companies from the 2nd Cavalry and a battery of Gatling guns for the expedition. I helped Mitch into a tiny depression and watched Curley lead his mount off the bluff and away, arrows narrowly missing him as he dropped out of sight.

"I hope he makes it," I said to Mitch, knowing Curley did. At least, I'd seen his picture in the books—a survivor of the Little Bighorn. "Think those Gatling guns could've made the trip with us?"

Boyer relaxed into the pit like a bed. "No." He drew his pistol. "Remember, Lieutenant. Always save the last one for yourself." He raised the pistol over my shoulder. I turned to see a warrior a few yards behind me, club raised overhead in full run when he fell to Mitch's shot.

I'd had enough.

I drew my own pistol, not caring about the battle around me. The blood pounded in my ears as I strode ahead. Custer had his Webley Bulldog pistols in hand. He didn't see me as I raised my own. I continued to march ahead. It was one of those perfect moments when the rest of the world faded into unimportance. Only instead of it being a young man stricken by love at first sight across a crowded ballroom, I was a raging instrument of revenge, bent on killing...not a madman. An incompetent. His eyes turned in time to see me fire. My bullet found Custer's head just before my world went black.

I was back in the rotunda.

I don't know who killed me, Indians or cavalrymen. Some movies you leave before the credits and you don't get to know who the actors were. But I knew the ending. Hestus's frown didn't diminish the evil grin I wore.

"Got that out of my system, Hess."

I didn't know it was possible to irritate an angel. Hestus rubbed his temples and sighed. "The way is prepared."

Time to try again. I thought I knew what I would see when I stepped through. I hate being right so much of the time.

※ ※ ※

Everything played out the same. Our feint worked, and once again I managed a few more kills than the last run. Practice makes perfect. Back on the bluff, the Indians were attacking fiercely from all sides. Again. I'd made no more of a difference this time than I had before. I made it as far as seeing Mitch and Curley when I changed course. It seemed I was powerless to change what was going to happen. So why did Mars want me here? Was this punishment? It couldn't be worse than the well of souls. That was an eternity of nothingness. This? This was hell. An eternity of fighting a losing battle. But why?

I didn't know if I was right, but suddenly, as I ducked and threw a warrior with a club charging at me, I had an idea. Men around me fought individually. Some of them well—all of them bravely—but individually, as had I. I'd been fighting the whole time like all these men. Fighting, and not leading.

Algernon was kneeling behind his fallen horse and loading his carbine. Zeus was still by my side. I hopped on and rode through the maelstrom. "Alge. Get that horse up. Any of you who can ride, we're going to assault over this bluff and drive the Indians back. We have to break their assault. Our only chance is to drive them off this bluff. Get your horses up. Let's go!"

I hopped off. Zeus had stayed near me this long, he'd stay with me a little longer. A dead trooper lay with a Lakota across him. I rolled the body off and grabbed the rifle out of his dead hands, and checked him for ammunition. His 45-70 would have better range than my carbine with its reduced loads. I grabbed his Colt and the few extra rounds he had. Another search for more ammo among the dead, and I was ready.

Algernon had his wounded mount up. With him, E troop had a dozen cavalrymen left, ready to fight. I remounted. "Follow me!"

We charged over the bluff into the ravine. Pistol in one hand, I fired at the first warrior I saw. I caught him by surprise, Zeus's gray chest plowing into him at the top of his run up the slope, sending him flying back down into a clump of his friends. I shot them too as their own whizzed wide past me. They snapped shots off at me. I took my time. Zeus's surefootedness was something I could take for granted as I worked, like a tank commander from his turret, his driver doing the rest.

At my sides were Alge and the cavalrymen of E Troop. Our skirmish line advanced, and we pushed the Indian assault off the bluff.

For a little while.

Zeus fell. I felt the bullet hit him, the sound of his flesh being penetrated with the dull slap and thud of the ball. To his credit, and there was much credit to give him, he toppled slowly, giving me a critical second to get free and land on my feet and not under him. He was dead.

I dropped behind him and went back to work. I laid the rifle across him and started choosing targets. I made a quick guess and raised the leaf of the tangent sight to 400 yards, cocked, opened the breach, loaded, and chose. Across the river, I spotted him. My counterpart was a fine looking warrior. Older than the ones I'd shot so far. A wide bead necklace around his neck, he didn't hide or hunch but pointed in my direction to send his next wave at me. This was a chief, standing tall and proud. He should've ducked instead.

My range estimation was right on. Smoke on the ground drifted to my right, and I held slightly left into the wind as I pulled the trigger and froze. The shove of the rifle was stronger than that of my carbine, the white smoke cloud from the muzzle larger too. The fine looking man fell. I was loaded again. I had the range. I chose the men around him and worked them one at a time.

I was on my feet. Around me, the troopers were still mounted, firing from horseback. Algernon was off his mount. I found him. On the ground, horse next to him, obediently waiting. I rushed up, bullets impacting the dirt to either side of me. I reached his mount, grabbed a handful of reigns, and coaxed him to let me mount. We had to push them back farther. The only way was to take the fight down the ravine and push them back across the river.

"Let's go! Stay on line. With me! Charge!"

I spurred my mount and dug in as he took off at my command like a lit rocket. For about ten yards. Then the same sick, dull splat hit and I was somersaulting over his massive head, down, down, down. I came to in time to see a woman smash my brains in with a stone.

This time Hestus seemed less perturbed. He was almost contemplative in his countenance as he pointed. I knew he would.

"The way is prepared."

※　※　※

My plan to counter assault off the bluff wasn't going to work. I held us at the edge of the ridgeline. We owned the high ground, but that's not much of an advantage if you don't have the numbers. Or solid defenses. Or when you don't own all sides of what you're trying to defend. What I wouldn't give for hand grenades or some 40 mm.

Custer had used the time we gave him to organize. There were fewer than a hundred men clustered together with and around the general. I'd started calling him that in my mind. Whatever else I may have thought about him—brash, reckless, bigoted—he was no coward. He gave better than he got as he took his share of Lakota from distances around the bluff top and of those who'd made suicide charges into the midst of what remained of the 7th.

"Fight your way to the general," I yelled. It was time to consolidate for our last defense. More of us fell making our way to where Custer fought on both feet. He'd dropped his

Remington Creedmoor rifle, an excellent choice for a distance arm—a poor choice for what we were in—and had his English pistols out, one in each hand.

I pushed my men ahead of me, leading a horse by the reins behind us as cover. When I got to the outer perimeter, I shot it in the head. The poor animal could only serve as a breastwork for our defense. It dropped, and I used it for cover. Others had done the same.

The Indians were massing. I'd run out of ammunition.

"Steady. Aimed fire. Choose your targets." I walked up and down behind our line as the men calmly worked. I recovered a hatchet off a dead Indian and drew my knife. It was that time. The time for bad breath fighting.

It doesn't matter how skilled or mean you might be. You can't fight your way out of a swarm. I fought as I backed up until I was standing next to the general. Though he had a hole in his shirt that seeped blood, he remained on both feet. Another warrior made a lunge and poked at me with a spear. I parried with my hatchet and slashed with my knife hand. He dropped the spear, and I finished him.

"Well fought to the end, Lieutenant," Custer said behind me.

"I wish Reno and Benteen had made it to us, sir." Here at the end it seemed wrong to criticize him. Hindsight is truly 20/20. And I had the best hindsight of them all.

"As do I, Lieu…" Custer's head snapped back, a bullet in his temple. One found my chest a moment later. I picked up Custer's pistols. Both were empty. Pretty soon it didn't matter. I fell and blacked out. I woke for a moment to see an Indian open my guts with his knife and hold my liver over his head. I screamed.

I was back in the rotunda again.

I reflexively checked myself. I was whole and clean. No matter that being in the rotunda meant I was "back," it was impossible to immediately accept that being snatched from history and my grisly end was behind me and that everything was again normal. Whatever that was. My stomach growled, and I felt nauseated again. That at least was normal. How long since I'd last eaten?

Hestus had company. Michael and Gabriel waited with him. Something different was afoot. Before I could get my bearings, Mars's face appeared, shocking me to attention. "How does it feel to lose, Beck?"

I was dumbfounded. Tongue-tied. Gobsmacked. Losing sucked. But I couldn't find the words to express my disgust at having lost the Battle of the Little Bighorn so many times.

"Do you want to try again?" Mars's floating head asked wryly. If this was a trick question, I didn't know how to avoid the trap.

"Sir, I'll take the challenge as many times as I need to demonstrate my commitment."

I think I surprised him. One eyebrow shot up.

"Hmm. I don't think that'll be necessary. Return to your unit, Lieutenant. You're now a platoon leader."

Lieutenant. Platoon leader. I hadn't left my rigid position of attention. I saluted.

"And Beck. Don't fail." He was gone.

The edge of Michael's mouth made a mirthless twist. "Time now to return to your unit. New duties await you."

I marched out beside Gabriel. As we walked, Gabriel used a new tone with me, one I had not experienced before. He was taking me into his confidence. I was no longer a recruit. "There have been changes while you were absent. The minimum number of soldiers have attained certification by testing. The company is advancing from one of acclimatization to one ready for advanced training. Ranks have been assigned accordingly. Mars has selected you platoon leader. I continue to lead this company until such time as one of you is capable."

We passed through the gates, and he continued without soliciting my input.

"More will be brought to replace those who have been released."

"Who's been returned to the well of souls?" I asked. "Any from my platoon?" If I was a platoon leader now, I had the right to know if there were spots to be filled with new recruits.

Gabriel's grunt seemed to me like approval. "Two have been sent away. The Scythian, Anacharsis, failed to adapt. Likewise, the Hessian, Lengerke, has been found wanting."

Two empty spots. "Where did they drop the ball? On the Plains of Eternity?"

Gabriel sighed. "Correct. Both could not tolerate the challenges of battle technology more advanced than their own times. The nomad's fear of heights made him incapable of a simple airborne operation. The German was claustrophobic. His refusal to fight in the discomfort of gear to protect from a chemical environment means he could not advance. For both, their fears halted them from entering combat."

I pictured Anacharsis as a jump refusal, retreating from the aircraft door against the momentum of a stick of paratroopers behind him. It was a mark of cowardice. In his own 7th century, just the idea of flight was the stuff of myth. It was difficult to accelerate many of the primitives to modern warfare, but not all. Some of the ancient recruits had adapted, like Magnus. There was nothing the Viking hadn't tackled, if not with gusto, at least never showing fear.

The loss of the nomad wouldn't hurt us. He was difficult to train and not a team player. Lengerke, on the other hand, was disciplined and intelligent. His loss would be felt. I already had their replacements in mind, and Gabriel sensed it.

"You have earned the right to recommend a worthy soldier to join your ranks. Tomorrow you will choose. For now, return to your unit. Platoon leaders' meeting on the field at 05:00."

My mind was racing. The Little Bighorn was all but erased in my emotional memory. I felt a primal drive ignite. It's a fire most akin to the one that drives humans to couple. The previous blind date disasters all but erased by the prospect of possibly meeting the right girl in the next encounter. The anticipation of being a combat leader refilled the wellspring of my hope.

My first instinct: if I was now in a position of leadership, there were going to be some changes in how this unit was run. Before I could interrogate Gabriel further, he departed, leaving me at the entrance to the mess. My stomach gave a sharp twinge to let me know it recognized our destination and it demanded attention.

A cautious step just far enough inside for me to scan the room and find my squad's usual table among the four platoons. Heads turned. Loud banter dimmed. Even the murmur that might be expected died off. The proverbial pin could be heard dropping. In a place where time didn't exist, where soldiers from history were brought back from the dead and tested in combat at all points across that history, my appearance generated shock.

Then, cheers. Everyone was out of their seats. A wave of men rose like a tsunami and carried me into the sea of their midst. I might have had a lump in my throat. I was back among the brotherhood.

"You've been gone a week," Will all but shouted over the din of congratulations as he slapped my back. "Where've you been?"

There was only one answer.

"OCS."

12

Will looked at the single gold sunburst on my collar whereas he wore four crimson chevrons. "No one's come back after so long. We just knew you'd been cashiered, cousin."

Around me, the rest of the platoon laughed and made their own exclamations. Even Karl, who rarely smiled, grinned as he reached through the crowd to take my hand. "Back from the dead seems to fit poorly, ja? It is a surprise to see you after so long, even in a place where the impossible is commonplace."

Hikaru held a bow for an extended second before fading back to let Magnus through, who lifted me off my feet in his bear hug.

Jakob was next to him. "I prayed the rosary for you every day, Ragnar. Prayed for your safety and for your soul. It is good you are among us again."

"*Lieutenant* Beck, we should say." Will was first to notice my new rank and the first to call the others to show respect for it.

"Where were you?" Magnus asked. "It must have been a trial of fire."

I laughed. "It was." I took a quick look around to make sure there were no unfamiliar faces; no one who had not been onto the Plains of Eternity yet. "Would you believe Mars made me fight the Battle of the Little Bighorn about a half a dozen times?"

Will was the only one to react. His jaw dropped open wide like the ramp of an APC.

"What is this, big little horn of which you speak?" Karl asked irritably, whatever moderately good mood he'd once had now gone.

"Can we talk about it later, men? Right now, I have a hunger in my stomach the size of a black hole. Will, are we still bunkmates? We can have a squad leader meeting after chow. I have some ideas I need to discuss with you all. If we're to get this unit ready for the final battle for existence, there are some things that have to change around here."

Three steaks later, my friends were crowded into our small room where I took the only standing space as they shared spots sitting on our bunks, ready to listen. "I've been promoted to platoon leader. Neither Mars nor his demis have spoken to me in any kind of candor about how we're to conduct business, but I've connected a few dots. I want to talk this out amongst ourselves."

Their quiet told me they understood my purpose. "Gabriel said the unit is considered ready to start advanced training. The promotion of some of us to formal leadership positions with actual ranks seems to be proof. Will, what happened while I was gone that got you your stripes?"

My friend shrugged, his ropy neck muscles standing out as he did. "Nothing like what you went through. Seems I'd already done enough on my little vacations to prove I wasn't a dirtbag. Day after you left for the gate, ole Gabe and Mike pulled me out of ranks, pinned me on the spot, and kicked me up a notch to platoon sergeant."

"It was more than that, William," Jakob said. "You were complimented on your superior tactical skills. It was said that your challenges on the plain were completed in a superior manner. We did not need convincing, though. It is natural that you should move from our informal leader to the position."

Karl, Jakob, Magnus, and Hikaru each had three crimson stripes on their collars. "I see Will and I haven't been the only ones to get promoted."

"Yup." Will smiled. "We needed four squad leaders. And for the first time I can remember, Gabriel actually *asked* for my opinion on something. I recommended these four gorillas, and he agreed."

Only Hikaru seemed put off at being called a simian. He growled and then a tiny smile followed to tell me that the enigmatic samurai indeed understood Will's friendly aspersion. Of all of them, Hikaru was still the one I knew the least about. It would help if the man would only communicate beyond yes, no, both communicated by the grunts.

I made a humming noise before I dove in to my next thought. "Gabe said we lost a couple in the platoon while I was gone. A couple of the—" I didn't want to say *primitive.* "A couple of the brothers from far earlier eras than some of us."

Karl took my meaning. "It is true. Many have failed to adapt to the demands of warfare beyond those from their own time. Yet many of us have done so." He gestured to Hikaru, Magnus, and Jakob. "Even Will had some level of unfamiliarity with the tactics and weapons between his era and yours to which he had to adapt, Lieutenant." Karl was the first to address me solely by my new rank. It confirmed something I'd secretly suspected about him. He may have been an aristocrat in his own era, but his sense of superiority was subdued by his commitment to a military bearing.

"Very well. Tomorrow, Gabriel is letting me select a candidate to join our ranks. I have someone in mind who I think will adapt quickly." Stokes was who I was thinking of. He was a proven commodity from my era. "Which brings up one of my next points. Will, you know more about the compositions of the other platoons. Have you encountered anyone here from a time period farther in the future than myself?"

Will looked as if he'd tasted something sour. "Nope. It's got me thinking too, LT," he said, using the more informal form of lieutenant. "There are things in the armory even an uptimer like you haven't seen before. What's your guess about all that?"

I'd been considering these things for a while, and it was time to air my thoughts. "I don't know. It tells me humanity has a future past mine, but why all those future soldiers aren't represented here, I can't say. Maybe it's this. We're all here because we died fairly heroic deaths, against the odds, carrying out what were surely suicide missions."

My NCOs nodded.

"I saw the direction warfare was headed even in my time. It's one of kill counts and technology. Maybe in the future, opportunities for valor just don't happen. Or not as frequently. Because surely, there are warriors more capable than us who died in their beds instead of buying the farm in combat. Guys who survived their battles and are probably better tacticians than any of us. I keep expecting to see Audie Murphy or Napoleon appear, but they haven't. Alexander the Great. So why aren't they here?"

Karl winced when I mentioned the Frenchman.

It was Jakob who was ready with the answer. "Because there are rules that we are not aware of that even Mars must abide by. The confines of a higher power. The Holy Trinity. There can be no other reason."

Hikaru's entrance into the conversation startled me. I'd almost forgotten he wasn't a mute. He spoke with sure conviction and a precision that matched my perception of him. "It tells us much about the battle we face. The way of the warrior is found in death. To choose death when given the option is the ultimate test of the warrior. The ultimate proof he is samurai. Mars wants only the most committed warrior for this fight. And yours is the last generation of man to produce such."

It was the most words Hikaru had ever spoken in my presence. I didn't want to discourage his future input, so I kept my reservations unspoken about his judgement as to what made a warrior. I always thought it was best to make the other guy die for his cause—not to die for yours—but it was hard to argue given our circumstances. Plus, I was in no position to prove my own thoughts on the matter. I'd chosen death myself.

"I also see it as meaning our battle is such," Magnus agreed. "Ragnarok comes, and the gods want only the most committed."

"*Götterdämmerung* indeed," Karl seemed to say to himself in a whisper.

"The end times," Jakob said. "When at the last trump the dead will be raised and judged."

Will frowned, one of the few times I'd seen him wear the expression. "Beats me. All I know is, we've been playing a lot of games up till now, and I don't see how doing more of the same is going to get this unit ready for any kind of war."

"Bingo, Sergeant." I used one of my favorite panto-mimes and pointed at him with my index finger before placing it on the tip of my nose. I did it on purpose. It was time to break this somber mood and move forward.

Jakob interpreted aloud. "Right on the nose."

I continued. "Regardless of why we were chosen, we're here. For the longest time I was convinced I was in some psychotic delusion. Now, my doubts have been erased."

"What did it for you, sir?" Will's frown had transitioned to a single raised eyebrow.

"Because I realized not even my subconscious could conjure a reality as concrete and detailed as this. About my third go at trying to save the 7th Cavalry, I surrendered to the inevitability that this is all real. And that means the reason we're here I have to accept as real as well—we have the most important war in all existence coming for us.

"Which means Will is spot on. This unit isn't ready for war. And if the powers that be aren't making it so, then it's incumbent on us to get this unit fit for battle. Gabriel called me to a platoon leaders' meeting tomorrow morning to start the day. I'm going to force a discussion about how we move forward in our training."

We'd done mainly squad- and platoon-level battle simulations. Nothing I would call full-scale combat. We'd also still been playing as light infantry no matter what time period of weapons and tactics we'd been saddled with. Where was the armor and artillery? Where was the air and naval support? Where were all the tools available to a modern combined arms force going into all-out war?

I examined the other men. "Who else is anxious about when we're going to get our hands on the toys sitting at the far end of the armory?"

Even the stoic Hikaru responded with enthusiasm when I brought up the only section of the armament stores that we had not yet played with. It didn't take a science fiction fan like myself to understand that the things I saw sitting in those racks represented technologies from far in the future.

"If we're going into battle, it seems to me it's time we stop messing about with swords, muskets, and single shot rifles. Heck, even an M-7 is an antique compared to what looks to be sitting in there. Seems to me that's where we need to invest our training time—with our best weaponry, in company strength—and soon. If there aren't any future soldiers here to teach us how to use those plasma rifles and death rays, it's time we taught ourselves. Any thoughts to the contrary?"

If there'd been a flaw in my thinking, I was certain at least Will or Karl would leap to point it out. Silence told me they saw the situation as I did.

I nodded. "I'm meeting the other platoon leaders and Gabriel at 05:00. Any idea who the other looeys are?"

"I'll get you up to speed, boss," Will assured me.

"Good. If there's nothing else, gentlemen, I suggest we adjourn." My sergeants each made their departure. Only Hikaru made a gesture of obeisance with a curt bow before exiting.

"You think Gabriel is ready for some constructive criticism about the training schedule, Rag?" Will reverted to my name now that we were alone. I was glad I didn't have to tell him to do so.

"We'll find out."

We went over the makeup of the other platoons as best Will knew it and then settled into our bunks. Lying in bed thinking about the tack I'd take with Gabriel in just a few hours, Will's drawn-out yawn told me he was about to go under as he set the crown on his head.

"Hey, Rag, what was Custer like?"

The question caught me by surprise. I hadn't once thought about the famed leader of the doomed 7th Cavalry since returning. He was the second personage of historical fame I'd had a brush with so far. "Partly arrogant prick. Partly hero. He was no coward."

"Did you scalp him too?" Will laughed a sleepy chuckle at his own joke as he faded.

"No, wise-ass. *Him* I shot in the head."

✳ ✳ ✳

At 04:45 I stood on the empty field waiting for the three other platoon leaders to join me. For the pain of missing those last few minutes of precious sleep, I was rewarded with the secret satisfaction of being first to repair.

Will had given me the scoop, and I knew who to expect. Almost as one, my three fellow platoon leaders walked onto the empty training field. I tried to pick them out per Will's description as they made their way to where I waited. Will hadn't been the first chosen to join the Ultimates, but he seemed to be one of the last remaining from those earliest times—however long ago that was. He still thinks it's only been about a year by his reckoning. In that time, he'd personally seen all the members of our unit appear and take the first challenge at the hands of Gabriel.

Coghill was a Brit. Thin and a bit stuffy, he met my preconception of what a Victorian officer was probably like. He'd been in the Queen's Infantry in colonial Africa.

I wondered if it was the Zulu Wars where he'd earned the distinction that brought him here. Like all of us, whatever his origin, if he was still here it meant he was tough and intelligent.

Jeong I recognized. He was blocky, short, and dark. I'd noticed him before in training with his platoon. He was tough as granite and took a punch like few I'd ever seen. More importantly, he delivered blows that broke bones. He'd sent many an opponent to the infirmary and into the magical healing field before they could be returned to practice. He was from closer to Will's time than my own—the Korean War—and died defending his own country against the forefathers of the Han I'd died fighting against. The opportunity hadn't come up for me to get to know him, but I wanted to compare notes with my fellow veteran of the war against the Han.

Once I'd sorted out those two, it meant the third in the party marching my way was the Russian. Denisov was about my size, meaning larger than the average soldier in our company. He had icy blue eyes like Magnus. That and the red hair told me it was true that the Russians were the heritors of the Viking bloodline. Will said Denisov was a murdering Bolshevik who'd risen to command during the Great Patriotic war—we called it WW2—and bought it against the Nazis. Of everyone here, Denisov was the only one Will held animosity toward.

"I wasn't alive to see those times, but from what I saw of that Red's last battle, he fed his men into the meat grinder without a second thought. That he did the same to himself tells me he's a fanatic. I don't trust him. If that's the kind of on-the-ground tactician Mars wants, God help us all."

"Gentlemen," I greeted my fellow platoon leaders as they converged on me. Handshakes all around gave me a quick measure of each man up close. They were all hardened professionals. I wondered if I gave them the same impression.

"Beck." The Brit spoke first. "You're an American, is that so? Twenty-first century? Saw you go down against the bloody Chinese. Well done."

"Thank you, Coghill. I don't have the benefit of seeing all of your last battles, but I know you all by reputation. It's an honor." I wasn't sure if I really meant it in Denisov's case, but it was time to be polite.

Jeong's face betrayed purpose. Maybe anxiety. Perhaps, it was the same concern I was feeling about what would come next. "While we are still alone, I ask you all—do you share the same concern I have that we are not yet prepared for war?"

I immediately felt an alliance forming.

"I certainly do," I said. "How we're training this unit needs to be addressed. I'm hoping Gabriel's going to have a new direction for us. Otherwise, we need to spur the change that will make us combat effective. Playing with swords and sticks and wrestling each other needs to end. It's time to bring out the big guns."

Denisov nodded. "I am accustomed to a system where orders are blindly followed and collaboration is minimal. We have a core of well-tested individuals, but we are not a fighting force yet. Just as disturbing to me is that we know nothing of who our enemy is. It is difficult to prepare if we don't know who we fight against, or even when."

Jeong frowned. "We are not here of our own free will. But it is necessary to be treated as more than slaves if we are to lead an army to victory."

"Pipe down, chaps," Coghill whispered. "Gabriel's on an intercept course for us."

We wordlessly faced on line and braced to attention as Gabriel arrived. Likewise, we popped off salutes, held until Gabriel acknowledged us with a nod.

"You have been selected to lead. You will remain in these roles until such time as you prove unfit. We approach the time when Mars expects you to advance into a unit worthy to be called Ultimates. You are not yet worthy of the name." He paused. When he did not resume speaking, it seemed appropriate to entreat him for information.

"Gabriel, we have concerns about just that. Do you have a commander's intent for us to follow? A training plan? We're ready to proceed, but are the next steps left for us to recommend, or do you have a directive for us to follow?"

"Information," Denisov blurted. "We need intelligence about our enemy—his strength, weapons, and capabilities. It is hard to prepare without such basic knowledge."

"Why are we not yet training in the most advanced weaponry available?" Jeong followed. "If we have proven ourselves capable in all forms of personal combat as part of our selection to be Ultimates, then it seems logical for us to move to the next phase, and quickly."

Coghill braced to attention. "Sir, I also formally request we…"

Gabriel boomed. "Enough."

I joined Coghill and the others at a rigid attention. Gabriel had powers beyond our understanding. Angel or demigod, whatever his title, I for one didn't want to be the subject of his wrath. When he commanded, there was no choice but to fall in line.

"You are soldiers. You obey. Mars rules here." I remained frozen. Gabriel's voice softened. "But I am pleased by your enthusiasm for the task ahead. Information will be forthcoming when it is time." We all relaxed slightly, and I allowed my eyes to settle on the angelic giant. "For now, our task is to fill the last of our ranks before you proceed to the next level. To that end, assemble your platoons. Ragnar Beck, choose your candidate."

Michael called me to him, his voice the first indicator that he was present, followed by the rest. "Remain out of the candidate's sight, at the rear of the formation. As you know, the challenge is difficult enough. It would not do to further confuse the new arrival."

"Yes, Michael." I made my way to the outer edge of the circle as the cyclone of mists formed. It spun faster and faster until I was looking at the dark jungle night and the last hours of my own life. I watched snippets from my team's last days with a focus on Stokes. I hadn't been with him when he led one of the ambushes against the Han in the Darien. It was well done, as I later knew. He hadn't told me that he picked up a live grenade, tossed by a Chinese soldier, and returned it into the kill zone. He hadn't told anyone. The picture sprang forward to the firefight on the golf course, the attack on the defenders at the dock, and the slog across Gatun Lake and into the mangroves to our final objective. It wasn't so hard, watching us die again, the revolting death creeping up our faces as we finished our mission together.

"A soldier has been found worthy," Michael began. I knew the rest of the liturgy and prepared to see my friend appear, hoping that he wouldn't let us down. In a flash, Stokes was here. Gabriel gave his same speech, the sword ignited, and it began.

Stokes didn't let me down.

The sword was in his hand, and he wielded it against the same telegraphed, long-arcing blow that Gabriel always used to give the new arrival a chance to get with the program before he really tried to take them apart piece by piece. Stokes deftly stepped to Gabriel's sword-hand side and pushed him as he brought his own blade over head to strike at Gabriel's head, only to miss as the giant whirled away to bring his shield up, tip pointed at the resurrected aggressor.

Stokes caught the shield Will tossed to him, and the battle continued. What Stokes may have lacked in technique, he more than made up for in violent aggression and mature combat decision-making. He never overextended himself. He never retreated but instead closed, delivered blows, and took an angle of departure that let him control the engagement. I remember my own fight with Gabriel, the elation that my body was no longer the sickly, failing thing it had been by the time I'd reached the dam. Stokes was feeling the same thrill of having his strength returned to him.

But against Gabriel, even that wouldn't be enough. I'd gotten lucky and taken advantage of Gabriel's underestimation of my mortal combat abilities. Gabriel was capable of learning too. As Stokes rose to the occasion with each exchange, Gabriel increased the force of his blows and the speed with which he could deliver them until several fine crimson streaks on arms, legs, and chest had appeared. Stokes dropped his shield with the last flurry of blows. Gabriel's sword swung—and halted—poised at my friend's throat. For a moment, I wasn't sure I wasn't going to see his head fly across the yard.

"Stay your hand, Daniel Stokes," Michael yelled. I exhaled in relief, unaware until that moment that I'd been holding my breath. It was different watching my friend go through the experience, even though I knew the point was to test him, not kill him. "Stand easy. You have passed the first challenge."

Will, stepped forward. "Easy there, cousin, let me help you." Will patted my friend's back as Stokes hurled his guts onto the sand.

"What's happening? Where am I?" Stokes asked, no differently than me or any of us had asked at the same moment. Like a well-rehearsed play, the scene was underway without a change in the script. I was tired of it. Time for a change. I pushed through the crowd to where a dizzy Stokes tried to focus.

Will's brotherly tones continued. "Deep breaths, my friend, deep breaths. It'll get easier. You're okay."

"You're with friends again, Danny. It's good to see you, brother."

Stokes snapped to meet my eyes, and recognition made his face light up. "Rag! What the hell's going on? Aren't we dead? Is this heaven?"

This part I'd worked out in my head already.

"No, brother. It ain't heaven," I chuckled. "Unless your idea of heaven is fighting for your life every day. Nope, we call this place Valhalla."

13

I was taking fire. The shooter got a few rounds off before ducking behind cover, waited, then did it again. I'm counting "one-one-thousand, two-one-thousand" in my head from behind this little rise of tree roots and shrubs. I didn't quite see where he'd shot at me from—I was too busy scooting to better cover—but I'd see him the next time he popped out. It's common for humans to *think* they're doing something random when what they're *actually* doing is obeying their internal stopwatch down to the whole second. He had a five second pause between his first two salvos. My bet was he'd do it again.

He wasn't smart, slick, or subtle. I thought these guys were supposed to be the masters of jungle warfare. He popped out from behind the same tree, aiming at where I'd been the last time he saw me. Before he could fire, I dropped him. His face exploded in red and he vanished. I might've done just that—shot him in the face and not the brain—which meant he might get back up and in the fight. I had other things to worry about right now, believe it or not. I was supposed to be running a platoon, not playing gunfighter.

"Talk about going to the well once too often," Will said, announcing himself from behind me as he hustled through the slippery elephant grass, dragging my RTO behind him. "He almost had you dead to rights. Would've too if he hadn't been married to that same spot. That'd be a grand start as platoon leader, Rag."

Will didn't look like Will. To my eyes, he had a faint glow, like all of us transported through the gate to this battle. We might be in different bodies, but however the magic worked, we all recognized each other for our true selves.

"Yeah, yeah, you're a regular Sergeant Alvin York. I'm sure you'd have handled it much better, wise guy. Did you get Second Squad moving?" The coarse threads that had held my top NCO's E-7 stripes on his uniform sleeves left a ghostly after image. Kind of like the ghost we all were, haunting these new bodies. My own drab shirt was blank on the collar. My last uniform had rotted off me, and I'd left the new one sterile. It was unnecessary to put my single silver bar on. I was the "old man" and everyone knew it.

"Yes, sir. Magnus had to motivate some of the downtimers, but they should be up on line at our left flank by now."

The unit I found myself in charge of was a mix. My full Valhalla platoon was here. Interspersed with us were nearly an equal number of soldiers from this time. I was still miffed that Gabriel and Michael didn't seem obliged to give us advanced warning of what was to come, but it was actually a relief when my entire platoon was directed to the gate, appearing together on the other side on the Plains of Eternity. It meant that finally we were going to get some real combat experience as a unit. And what an experience this was turning out to be.

Bougainville.

"Will, I want those gun teams from Second and Third squads working the murder hole we know is at the top of this draw. First and Second squads behind them in reserve to bound ahead if we get bogged down or take too many casualties. Make it happen."

"Roger. You know, if we all had M-7s and a couple of M-100s, we'd have this wrapped up in a day. I'm tired of getting hobbled by all this ancient hardware. We could drop 40 millimeters on them from here and fire a couple of Lancers that'd home right in on their position. Then we wouldn't have to play this primitive game they want us to play."

Will calling our weapons primitive made me chuckle. The M-1 carbine in my hands was lighter than any rifle I'd ever carried. "This coming from a guy who used to think the '03 Springfield was the most devastating weapon of war ever invented." I passed Will my canteen. He'd been doing the grueling job of a platoon sergeant, implementing my orders to coordinate our assault up the hill. That meant a lot of miles trudging back and forth and a lot of potential exposure on the two-way shooting range.

"True. But I've been here before. Well, not Bougainville, but on the Solomons with the Marines. You know what would impress me even more?" He took a swig. "Radios. If we at least had one per squad, we could speed this little exercise along."

Will took the words right out of my mouth. "Someday they'll let us play without one hand tied behind our backs."

Jablonski, my RTO, had gotten used to our exchanges. Ski and the other non-Valhalla crew had been assigned to the American Division just before we landed on the island. Most had been in the army only a few months. If he thought anything strange about us referring to his fellow replacements as "downtimers" or our frequent talk about better weapons and tech, he'd long ago chalked it up to some kind of salty veteran lingo unique to those of us who'd been fighting so long.

The rest of us had been with the Americal since they stood the division up on New Caledonia, training it in place in anticipation of a Japanese invasion of the island. Like all the trips to the Plains of Eternity, I experienced the same merging into my current persona, knowing much of my character's life. Not unlike my own career in the afterlife, Lieutenant Smith had risen to the rank of sergeant before getting bumped up to take a platoon after his performance on Guadalcanal. I should say, *our* performance on Guadalcanal. While I was him, I had his memories of the campaign and knew the lessons he knew. As with all my previous training trips into this time-tripping reality, melding my own knowledge and skills with my host's made me even deadlier.

But just because I was a compendium of death didn't make me invulnerable. There was always bad luck that you couldn't account for. And luck was as much of a factor in combat success as skill.

"Private, let the company know we're starting our next push. I'll be in touch." My request for mortar support had already been turned down; our weapons section was the other side of this ridge supporting the rest of the company. If we had to do this alone, then I didn't feel the need to keep the captain very much in my thoughts. He was overwhelmed running a company. My old 7th ID special ops platoon leader, Lieutenant Hokkanen, could've run circles around the guy. I knew I could. No time for daydreams. I focused my attention on the task at hand. Mars's "don't fail" command was never far from my mind.

To my right I heard the choppy bursts of a .30 cal machine gun. Karl had gotten First Squad's gun team grazing the hill. About time. To my left, Magnus had moved his Second Squad ahead, and his gunners were busy laying down short bursts. I decided to work over to where they were and let Will stick with First Squad on the other side of the draw. Time to light a fire under these guys.

"Come on, Ski. Stick close."

The kid's eyes had the same yellow tinge as mine. Until nearly my gramps's time, disease always killed or crippled more soldiers than combat. Atabrine was all we had to prevent malaria since the Japanese cut off our source for making quinine. For some of the troops, the drug made them psychotic, or so ill it might as well have been the violent fevers of malaria they were suffering from. I had to order those troops to coat themselves in DDT to avoid being bitten by disease-carrying mosquitoes. Cancer they could worry about later—if they lived through this. But they didn't know that, and it was nothing to worry about even if they did. Surviving today was all that mattered.

"I'm with you, sir." Ski was a good troop. I'd stopped trying to comprehend the nature of the Plains of Eternity. Whether this was real—some other timeline in the multiverse—or whether it was the most perfect VR tank that could give a gamer the ultimate experience, it no longer mattered. Every one of these lives was real to me, and I wanted all my men to grow to be old men. But the pessimist in me knew that war didn't care about what I wanted.

I led us to where the 1919 was busy chewing holes in the jungle. The damn things were magnificent but heavy. Just the gun alone weighed thirty pounds. Humping the gun, the tripod, and enough ammo to last more than a few minutes of bursts was a task better suited to pack animals than three men. Magnus had just finished giving the gun team their last instructions when I found him.

"We've got the motherless dogs now, sir. I was just about to take the rest of the squad forward."

"Let's go." I tapped him on the shoulder as we trotted ahead, the alternating call and answer of choppy bursts from both our thirties working from both sides of the steep draw. The Japanese gunners had stopped their return fire. Had we lucked out and silenced their gun? Were they changing barrels? It was time to press this advantage. We made it up the ridge to where the rest of Second Squad was on their bellies. The trees had thinned out, black volcanic rock peeking through the grass to let us know this island was formed by the same kind of hot fury we battled through. The chug-chug-chug of the Japanese Type 92 machine gun was back, and rounds whizzed over our heads.

"Stokes," Magnus yelled. "You're up." In his short time with us, my friend had already become a fire team leader. He'd had a few trips through the gate and each time returned with more confidence.

"Just waiting on the go-ahead, Big Red. Let's hit it, men." Five men followed Stokes on their bellies through the grass, over the top of the rise, and were gone. I waited for Magnus to take the rest of the squad over before I followed, bringing Ski with me.

I have a good arm. I pulled a pineapple out of my buttpack, ventured a look over the grass to where the enemy hidey-hole was tucked behind more of the black boulders, drew back, and heaved. I ducked just as a brown uniformed Japanese rifleman popped out from an outcropping. My grenade exploded, spoiling his chance to get a decent shot at me. Figuring that I'd made a few of them duck, I popped up again. Stokes was out front. He rushed for a few seconds before diving for cover, launched a few rounds at a time with his Tommy chopper on semi, then rushed again. His team did the same, Stokes the only body with the telltale glow to my eyes, and covered the distance up the draw in seconds. Grenades arced ahead, and small arms fire kept the defenders' heads down. Stokes was leading the way.

What would happen next was inevitable. I almost felt sorry for the Japanese. Who am I kidding? I wasn't going to feel any more pity for them than I would anyone else trying to kill me.

Magnus and the rest of his squad had moved up our right flank. They had a better view into the tunnel that was the pillbox's kill zone and were raining fire uphill into the funnel. From way on the other side of the draw, I could hear Karl and Jakob's squads doing the same. The gun teams below had ceased fire. It was Valhalla gunners running our thirties. A gunner sucked into staying on the trigger and losing awareness could chew up his own men when they moved onto the objective. There was nowhere to shift fire to, so knowing they'd done all they could, they would already be picking up shop and moving up to support us. I helped train those men. Pavel had been a Cossack. Gaston, Napoleonic cavalry. They'd been enemies at one time, experts at sabers and bayonets. Now, they were two squared-away machine gunners. Wildflowers transplanted to new soil and blossoming brighter than ever. That's who all my soldiers from across time were. Death flowers. If they hadn't blossomed, Michael would've pulled them out by the roots.

Stokes was again proving he was as hardy a variety as any of us. He was still in the lead. He was about as far forward as he could go, just at the edge of what had to be the last hard cover before the pillbox. He tucked his Tommy gun away and pulled a grenade pin with his teeth, just like the movies. Show off. He made a curving toss around the rocks, tucked back, and was stepping back around the cover to fire into the enemy position, timing it perfectly. Across the gulley, Will and Karl directed our guys into the fight as the Japanese fired down on them from above. There were troops dug into foxholes guarding the machine gun nest over there, more than we had on our side of the draw. Once we cleared this machine gun out, I'd take Hikaru and the third squad up and over and come up behind them to wipe out any remaining resistance to First Squad.

I was making a beeline for a small depression on my way to where Magnus was leading the rest of the squad forward when Stokes yelled out, "Fry 'em." Stokes pushed the downtimer private ahead, manhandling him into place by the flamethrower tanks on his back. "Let 'em have it." Without further prompting, the dragon let loose its fury. A gush of sooty flames arced out, the momentary wet splash of the jellied fuel on the rocks replaced by the hot whoosh and crackle. Screams told us all we'd found gold.

Now was the mad time. The time when the thrill of murder overpowered any caution or desire for safety. It was every man on his own to rush forward, to blaze his own trail. To claim his territory, where he was the king, where he owned everything at the end of his muzzle. I was no different. Because it was only after bringing death that we could hope to rest, take a sweet drink of hot canteen water, savor the breeze that waited at the top, and fill our lungs with breaths of the clean air that might be found there. To pause and thank God—before doing it all again.

I claimed my own spot, running to where a narrow path snaked through the rocks, cutting off a downtimer running to the same channel leading into the rocky cove. I was playing gunfighter again instead of directing the mission. I could do both. There was a time and a place. I was leading by example.

I held up short of the opening to grab another grenade, only for the kid at my back to run in to me at full force, pushing me out into a pretty big angle of exposure. A sandbagged position and the gaunt, terrified faces behind the guns told me I'd guessed right about wanting to toss a grenade first. I forced my way back as shots filled the space I'd just been in. The grenade was out of my hand and away. I brought my M-1 up and let a quick work of the trigger act as the piercing light ahead of my locomotive of hate as I charged ahead. Up and over the rim of sandbags, I gave three bodies in the pit my full magazine of tiny .30 carbine bullets before I dropped down and changed mags.

My caboose followed and was in the pit behind me, shooting the same bodies I'd just filled in. There was no such thing as too much lead in someone who wanted to kill you. "Good job, Private. Try not to run into me next time. You almost got me dusted."

"Sorry, sir." The kid's chest heaved, winded from the adrenaline dump and the nonstop bulldozing we'd done to get here. The tinny ping of his M-1 rifle ejecting a clip hadn't yet been answered.

"Reload, take a breath, and let's go." The kid thumbed a full clip in, slapped the bolt, and nodded. The tide of flames and gunfire around me had picked up again. To my right, Stokes was still leading. He was ahead of me now and dead in front of the pillbox. The Japanese fortification was all but invisible from below. Rough aggregate cemented volcanic boulders into a wall with firing ports. Stokes ran at one as he let the spoon of a grenade fly, paused for the fuse to burn short, then stuffed it into the nearest slit and ducked. Fine clouds of dirt blasted out of all the openings.

This time he didn't have to encourage the flamethrower-wielding private. With men on either side of him advancing as they fired weapons into dark crevices, the trooper stumbled to Stokes's side, pushed the nozzle of his wand into the gap, and let loose.

Flames poured out of the firing ports. Splashback landed on the kid's sleeve. He froze, dropped the wand, and patted with his bare hand as the flames spread. My stomach clenched as his terrified screams grew. Stokes grabbed the torcher and pulled him down, rolling the flaming private in the dirt. In a moment, it was done. The tiny splash of fuel had been extinguished. The amazed trooper gawked open-mouthed at his singed uniform sleeve.

"Watch it, son. That stuff burns."

"Stokes," I yelled at him. "Finish that bunker. I'm going over top." A thumbs-up from Stokes, and I turned my attention to the next problem. Magnus and his squad disappeared down a tiny goat trail off to the right. I had another route in mind. "Third Squad, where're you at? Come on, Private." My caboose was still with me. I backtracked to the pit to find Hikaru bayoneting a body. The gasp of releasing air told me that though we'd filled that man in several times over, it still hadn't been enough. Heidekker was his downtime persona, but it was close enough to Hikaru that it was simply taken as a nickname we old-timers used whenever we slipped. His weapon briefly rose before he recognized me. "Up and over." I pointed the way I wanted him to take his squad.

"Third Squad, you heard the LT. Move." His English was harshly accented. I wondered if anyone noticed or cared? Did what they hear from us match how they saw us here on the Plains of Eternity? It didn't matter so much on Third Squad, as they all had the angelic glow. Hikaru said little as his squad moved in buddy teams, spreading out to climb up the craggy rise. Our men had done worse a dozen times over, across battlefields harsher than this. Without having downtimers to direct or encourage, they went to work like a team of mathematicians attacking a huge equation scrawled across a blackboard, deliberately and intuitively. Where one paused, his partner seamlessly blended action to solve the next term.

My RTO had found me. "Sir, captain wants a report."

I took the telephone handset. "Smith here." I heard the distant crump of mortars. I suppose we'd done fine without them, but did everything we did have to be the hardest, bloodiest way possible?

"What's the holdup, Lieutenant? Why aren't you through with that objective? I gave you the easiest mission. Get moving. We need you back with the rest of the company. We've got heavy resistance, and I need every man."

I groaned. "Just mopping up here, sir." I tried to not make my "sir" sound as insolent as I heard it in my head. Maybe I succeeded. "We knocked out a fortified position. We'll have the west face of hill 488 cleared presently, over." There would be more hidden positions and maybe another bunker or two on the east side. We'd hit them from above and work our way to the main body soon enough.

"Oh." I'd caught him by surprise. "Well, good job. Battalion wants results. Let me know how soon you can make your way to the CP. Finish your push to the top and report back. Out." I handed the handset back to Ski.

"You're welcome, Captain," I said into the empty air.

"The old man doesn't sound like they've done as well, sir." Ski was putting it mildly.

"Second Platoon will come to their aid, Ski. C'mon." I was proud of our assault. We hadn't lost a man. Attacking a dug-in machine gun nest was a grisly task. It was never routine, but for us it was unremarkable. We'd done it before. Too many times, maybe. At least we hadn't had to do it with pointy things as our only weaponry. Until you've been there, the thing you don't appreciate about that kind of fight is the noise. No explosions. No bullets whizzing by. Just the prolonged moans and wails of men hacked to pieces, dying slowly where they fell. At least here the death was quick.

Another half hour of letting Hikaru's squad take the lead with Magnus's working next to them, and we owned hill 488.

※ ※ ※

"Here. Pay you back," Will said, holding his canteen out to me. The platoon was together again. Karl, Hikaru, Magnus, and Jakob were with us. I took a swig and passed it back.

"Thanks. Casualties?" One burned arm—the kid who stuck around too long to see the results of his flamethrower work—a twisted ankle, and not a single wounded or killed. "I consider that a miracle. Good job."

"How may enemy KIA?" Will asked me.

I did a quick tally of my reports. "About forty."

Jakob read everyone's mind. "It is impressive. I wonder our endpoint. How long will Michael leave us in this place before we've been sufficiently proven?"

"Who knows?" Karl said. "We may be here for a while. It would seem there are many opportunities left for our new commander to be challenged, ja?" The woodpecker-like tapping sounds of machine guns echoed from the next valley.

Magnus laughed, the kind of hearty laugh I would expect from a Viking. "And a fine battle it is for such. But I think it is not only Ragnar who is tested. We are also being judged as leaders."

"It's our first time together on the plains as a unit," Will said. "And throwing us against these odds is a helluva first test. I oughta know. I played in this theater before. Not far from here with the First Marine Division. Michael made me run that three times before I finally made it off the beach, and another three times after that before I survived long enough to get the hang of it."

"You never mentioned that," I said with pity. It made my Little Bighorn adventure seem petty in comparison to what I imagined it had been like for Will.

Will shrugged. "We've all had just as bad."

Three days and three hills later, we'd apparently achieved a passing grade and found ourselves in the rotunda. Gabriel and Hestus were there to welcome us. It almost felt like coming home. I did a quick head count. We'd lost several in the platoon, and I was gratified to see them in our ranks, their end on Bougainville just another temporary death for an eternal soldier.

Gabriel greeted us flatly. "Return to your garrison. Today is a day of rest. You are the first platoon to clear their challenge on the plains. Form your unit in the morning for training, Ragnar Beck. You may depart."

I was too tired to question him, too tired to let my curiosity about the other platoons interfere with my desire to breathe the clean air that waited outside the rotunda. I was sick of the jungle. We hadn't slept the whole time we'd been gone. The last day we'd had no water resupply. We'd fought another uphill battle against dug-in fanatics and slaughtered them mercilessly. Even though my body here had undergone none of the actual strain and miles of combat, mentally, I was cooked. I knew everyone else was roasted too.

Thinking only of my bed, Will walked beside me. "Rag, I know about Pearl Harbor. The US had no choice but to fight. I think I know how it all ended, but can you tell me how your history recorded it?"

"The quick version?" I yawned. I was exhausted, but the hole in my stomach made me rethink my priorities. Food first, then bed. "We took every island away from them one bloody leap at a time while we firebombed their home island. Then, to avoid killing a million men to fight them on their home turf, Truman dropped two nuclear bombs on them. They rebuilt and became one of the great democracies that fought the Lotus Hegemony to the last man. They were a terrible enemy who became a great friend."

"Nuclear bombs? Heard about them. I bet that took the starch out of their collars." Will gave a tired chuckle. "Sounds like a good choice to me. Those yellow bastards were tough. Much worse than the Boche. I haven't yet fought anyone as committed. Wonder if that's why Mars likes to send us to that playground so often?"

"If there was a bloodier conflict, I pray we don't go there."

Hikaru was next to me, listening. He'd shown no compunction about killing his fellow Japanese. Not like I'd shown when I had to fight on the opposite side of other Americans. It'd almost gotten me sent to the well of souls.

"It is good to know the warrior spirit of my people did not die after my time. Perhaps that resolve fuels them yet."

Stokes trudged behind. "I hope so, Hikaru. Maybe next time we'll get to fight the Han together and you can help us get revenge for what they've done to the whole world."

I couldn't even begin to think about what waited for us next.

14

"His curiosity continues, Mars. And it infects the others."

Mars gave a curt nod. Michael was right, but the god wasn't concerned. "Yes. But he's just spinning his wheels. And if anything, it seems to be having the effect of motivating his men to work harder. No harm done."

"Do we allow him to select another candidate?"

"Yes." Mars spoke the words quickly, his mind drifting to all that remained on his plate. There had been a great deal of negotiating with the other generals as of late. His other two companies had been busy, and it was nearing time when he needed Gabriel's unit fully loaded and ready to deploy. "Make it happen, then close the books. It's high time we get them ready for a real battle."

※　※　※

"All present and accounted for, sir."

"Thank you, Sergeant." I returned Will's salute and did an about face. Gabriel in turn took my report while Michael looked on.

We'd been left to our own devices as far as military customs and courtesies, but Will and I were Americans. We'd more or less forced our way of doing things on the platoon. We came from different armies, and while the basics were all the same, old habits die hard for a soldier. Some saluted palm up. Antonius, our oldest soldier, still did the cross chest fist of a salute from the Roman Legions. I was good with that. A mixed military unit like ours had to allow for such things. Identity and pride were a good thing. I doubt the Vikings of Magnus's time had any kind of strict C&C, but by the way he'd taken to it, I'd say he enjoyed our traditions. Whatever our task masters expected of us in that department, we must've lived up to their expectations as they never commanded us to perform differently.

It was impossible to disregard the eerie feeling of being the only ones on the training field. It meant that the three other platoons were each still in another time, deep in the midst of combat. Torn between pride at our accomplishment and dread at what our fellow eternal soldiers were going through, I swallowed the butterflies in my chest, assumed a rigid parade rest, and waited to be addressed. It was Michael who spoke.

"Ragnar Beck, there is yet time to fill the ranks. Your selection of Daniel Stokes proved well chosen. Do you have another candidate to recommend to be called from the well of souls?"

I'd already given this thought. I'd prepared Stokes for this, my intuition telling me that just such an opportunity would come. How my recommendation would be received, I had no clue.

"Yes, Michael. Jessica Chow is the candidate for the challenge." A murmur started behind me. I hadn't let anyone else know who I wanted with us, not even Will.

"Quiet in the ranks," Will grunted over his shoulder.

Gabriel's statue-perfect face animated, a single eyebrow raised quizzically in a very human-like display. I'd produced anger in the giant before, but never this. Michael pulled a scroll from his waist pouch. He unrolled it, the glow causing shadows to dance over his face as he read. He held still as more information rolled past, the dark lines and flickering lights making me wonder what it was he saw. The light dimmed, then he rolled the anachronism closed and returned it to his waist.

"I will call this soldier into our midst. Ready yourselves."

I did an about face. "Get them ready, Will."

Will returned my salute. I'd succeeded in shocking him too. He whispered, "Hell's bell's, Rag. A woman?" He did his own turn. "Platoon. Fall out and form up."

"Stokes, with me," I ordered. I already knew what Michael expected. "We have to stay out of the way," I said as low and calming as I knew how. "It wouldn't be fair to confuse a candidate with a familiar face right off the bat. It'd be a distraction. You haven't seen one of these yet, but you remember what it was like."

Stokes shook his head. "It isn't even gonna be a problem, Rag. No one could distract Jess when it's fight time."

The swirling mists showed the highlights of Jess's actions in combat as they had every other candidate about to be materialized out of limbo, ending with her death. By now, the battle in Panama was a familiar scene to the platoon, almost as familiar as to those of us who'd lived it. I checked the reactions of the men. Even Karl, the staunch Prussian martinet, involuntarily nodded as he watched my former teammate do battle in the past. The mists faded and the ceremony continued, Gabriel assuming his position in the center of our circle. Was it my imagination, or did he look even more fierce than I'd ever seen him?

There was neither flash, nor noise, nor mystical fanfare preceding a candidate's appearance. One second Gabriel faced empty air, the next, she appeared.

"Watch this," Stokes whispered. "She's gonna eat his lunch."

I tuned out Gabriel's usual chant, my heart pounding in my ears as if I were the one preparing for personal combat with the giant. What would Jess do? My reputation was riding on her performance as surely as if it were me out there fighting. Our friend gasped. She looked at the sword in her hand, then at the crowd around her, and finally at Gabriel and his fiery gladius.

"Defend yourself, cur," Gabriel shouted.

"Oh no," I whispered with dread as I watched Gabriel close. He swung, blindingly fast, the arc of his strike shorter, less telegraphed than I could recall his first attack against another candidate before. The tip of his sword sliced through her coarse white tunic, leaving no doubt he was out for blood. Jess brought her sword up as she leaped back, weight forward, eyes wide. She sucked in a deep breath, and I felt my own blood turn to ice.

"Son of a bitch!" I shouted.

With a scream, she launched at him. "Aiyahh!"

Jess had studied martial arts since she was a child. I'd only heard the names of the styles she was proficient in, trained by her family almost from birth. She'd always downplayed her background to us. I think she was secretly ashamed of being Asian—because of the war with the Han—even though she had no reason for being so. The Han were as different from us as little green aliens landing in silver disc-shaped spaceships. If our roles were reversed, I'd have been a braggart, given the uniquely amazing background she'd been born into. I didn't know anyone who thought of her as being anything other than a loyal American. Or at least, not after they got to know her. Certainly not those of us who'd gone through selection and training with her. Now, she was proving herself all over again to a whole new group of warriors, given a chance to be in an army she'd never chosen to join.

Her first flurry of attacks, Gabriel deflected. The giant had supernatural strength and speed and could best any of us at will. But after his first cheap shot, he held back, allowing Jess to demonstrate her skill and aggression. He was going to take her full measure. I relaxed a little. What I feared would be a one-sided affair was developing into what the challenge had been for the rest of us; a test instead of a beatdown.

Catching the shield without missing a beat, she kept her focus and launched again without waiting to let Gabriel set the pace. She was as fast as any person I'd ever seen, probably faster. She slipped under his guard, stabbed, sliced, kicked, elbowed, and passed, almost before Gabriel could react. She slid behind him, working his unshielded side before breaking contact and pausing before taking a new angle of attack. Her fierce scowl told me she was disappointed her melee had done no discernable damage to her opponent.

Gabriel launched his own flurry of attacks, his delivery faster as he turned up his velocity to match Jess's speed. Her shield met his next slash with a loud crash, his blow lifting her off her feet. She let the force of it carry her back several feet. She landed with weight forward, in perfect balance, and again she attacked.

She was in the fight to win.

"Enough. Jessica Chow. Stay your hand. Enough." Michael's voice had the same effect on her as it had on all of us at this same point in our fight. It was the voice of command. She froze, shield up, sword ready.

"What the hell's going on here!" Jess's eyes burned with fire as bright as Gabriel's sword. I was proud.

"I told you!" Stokes yelled. Before I could stop him, he was pushing through the crowd. "Jess! Jess, it's okay. You're safe. I'm here, baby!" He rushed to her. Her face melted in recognition, and she dropped her tools of combat on the sand.

"Daniel!" She threw her arms around him.

"Oh, boy," Will said beside me. "This puts a new twist on things. What have you gotten us into, Rag?"

※　※　※

"Pipe down," Will yelled over the noise. I'd been trying to address the issue as best I knew how. We were in the empty mess. I stood on a chair with the platoon seated around me. Stokes had taken Jess away to start the nearly impossible process of orienting our newest warrior to the incredible circumstances of our existence. Michael dismissed us from the training ground to let me handle the situation.

The response to Jess had been unexpected. I'd seen less discord when candidates appeared who'd been mortal enemies of some of those in our midst. Even I'd accepted my own enemies who'd been transported here. The few Chinese soldiers we had in the company had gone to other platoons. None of them were from my own time. Even if they had been and were under my command, as long as they pulled their weight, they were like the rest of us. They hadn't chosen to be here. There was no reason for me to hold a grudge against them. As long as they proved worthy, they were one of us. I explained the same to my disgruntled platoon.

"You all know as much as I do. The bosses tell me we can fill the platoon with more bodies, but that time is short. No one's had any complaints about Stokes. He's pulled his weight and then some, and he's only been with us a few weeks. Chow isn't going to be any different. Does anyone doubt she's already as competent at personal combat as all of you? You've seen her in action."

"You brought a woman among us. Why?" It was Mazhar the Turk who shouted at me. "Surely there were others more worthy?"

"I said pipe down, soldier," Will yelled. "The lieutenant's in charge here. He doesn't owe you or anyone an explanation."

"It's okay, Sergeant ," I said. I wanted there to be a free exchange between us. Allowing the men with reservations to air their grievances was going to be important to morale. "But we're not a mob. We're soldiers. Let's keep a military bearing, got me?"

Magnus stood, waiting to be recognized. I gave him a nod. "I fail to understand why some of you have concern. The woman is a warrior. Proven. No different than any of us. I went into battle with many at my side. Women from my clan suited to war and so tested were treated no differently than men. If she does not continue to inspire confidence, they will cull her as surely as they have done to many others who were once given chance to prove worthy."

A few approving nods went around. Mazhar's scowl convinced me he would continue to be a problem.

Jakob rose. "Sir, in your army, were women warriors common? Were there many like Chow?"

I scoffed at the suggestion. "No, Sergeant. Not by a long shot. She's unique among her peers, men and women alike."

"I see, sir," Jakob said. He was going somewhere with this. "Why was it that in your time, a time so unlike that of the rest of us—except perhaps Magnus—that women were placed in harm's way to protect your people. Were the men of your time so lacking that women had to be relied upon to fill your levies for soldiers?"

"Kind of curious about that myself, Lieutenant," Will said. "If you wouldn't mind explaining it to us. The future of my army sure took an interesting turn after I was gone."

Among us all, I had the firmest conviction about Jess's suitability to be with us, so it was fair for me to explain why that was. "I'll try."

I explained about my family history, and how we were a living witness to the societal changes that shaped the army I served in. Women had served with men for all of America's modern history. There had been obstacles to them serving in all fields—especially combat—but that faded by my grandpa's time. In the Long War, there were women fighter pilots and women serving in all kinds of combat conditions, even if they were not in jobs thought of as frontline types of specialties.

The last bastion of maleness was the infantry and special operations. During my grandpa's time, that was challenged. And by my dad's time, it was common to have women who'd met the standard and served alongside men in those combat units. There weren't many, but my dad said the women he served with were treated no differently than the men. They'd proved themselves worthy. What had changed by my time I've described already. The culture of the later 21st century made for a military hampered by rights and feelings. Of a guaranteed equality of outcome rather than achievement by effort.

Karl looked like he'd swallowed the canary when he asked, "Did women perform as well as men? Had women in your society physically evolved into the equal of men? Had humans changed so much in the few hundred years since I walked the Earth?" I was ready for that.

"It wasn't that. I'd say it was more like the commitment and discipline necessary to meet those challenges had evolved along with the opportunity."

Karl wasn't satisfied with my answer, and the way he smirked told me he wasn't convinced. "So, in your time, sir, women were the equals of men in strength?"

"As a whole, no. But as individuals, sure. Many were. But allow me to explain something very important about these select women. Once it was accepted that there were women who could pass the same challenges given to men in order to serve in those combat capacities, women started to integrate into those roles. It was never many, but there were some. My gramps told me there was resistance at first. It became less of an issue as time went on, but then, a very harsh reality was realized, and ignored.

"While many women tried out, and a select number of them succeeded, the statistics couldn't hide the biological reality. Their longevity in those positions was much, much shorter than that of their male peers. The number of injuries and the damage they accumulated to their bodies in a shorter period of time left many of them crippled and no longer able to remain in those units.

"Sure, the same thing happens to men, but it happened at alarmingly higher rates to the women. About the middle of the Long War, one female warrior spoke out about her experiences, and her honesty had a big effect on what happened next. A Marine officer wrote an article about her time in combat next to men. She took a stand against a lot of the proponents of blind equality in the military. Most of the loudest of the cheerleaders for women in combat weren't soldiers themselves, but politicians and social engineers.

"Her name was Petronio. She was a Marine officer. It wasn't until many years later that her contribution to the controversy was appreciated. She was one of the first women to speak out about the physical toll that being a combat Marine had on her. As a result of her many injuries serving alongside men in combat, she wrote about how the reformers were ignoring the reality that men and women were in fact very different, and that she was proof of that."

I couldn't yet tell what effect I was having on the men, but I knew I hadn't won them over. It was time for me to start my final assault on their conceptions. "What if in order to serve, you knew that what you were doing would forever change your body? What if as a man, you were told that to serve, your body would be stressed and injured in such a way that you would bear the burden of that service forever?"

Karl scoffed. "That is a known fact for us all, Lieutenant. I understand that compared to my time, you lived in an age of miraculous medical science, but a lifetime of soldiering scars us all. It's the price of service. In my day, a soldier drank to ease his pain. Even if you do not die in combat, your body is fed to the machine and used up. It is the way."

To this, all the men around me grunted hearty approval.

"And I agree." Before I was resurrected, I was like everyone else in my unit. In my twenties, I already practically lived on anti-inflammatories. I wore collagen stimulators on my joints and back each night to try and stave off the pain from the huge loads we carried daily. Between them, my gramps and my dad had three artificial hips and knees, and both had discs regenerated in their necks and backs from their service related injuries. "And they proved that as a whole, those injuries piled up faster for the women and most of them had a pretty short career in combat arms. But the women had an even greater potential injury to worry about. It was well known that along with the potentially long-term damage to their musculoskeletal systems that their hormones predisposed them to, their endocrine systems were also being damaged. As a result, many were so injured they were never able to have children. Ever."

Karl snorted. "So, at last you are honest with us, sir. Not even in your time were men and women truly physically equal. Yet, such ignorance of the facts persisted and your generation stuck their heads in the sand and still permitted such an afront to logic. Madness."

"I won't disagree that it was madness for the institutions to ignore those facts in favor of political considerations," I allowed. "But hear me out about this. Petronio blew the lid off of what everyone knew was true, that men and women weren't equal, and still it was ignored. And even if the leaders of the time chose to ignore those issues, the women themselves knew those things. So, here's my question to you all." I said it to the room but looked directly into Karl's eyes. "What does that say about the commitment of those women who knew all those things, yet *still*, they chose to pursue a life on the cutting edge of war? What if you *knew* there was a very, very real risk that you would never father a child, yet, because of your love of your country, still chose to sacrifice that part of a normal life in order to serve? Would you still do it?"

Karl's eyebrows raised. I was making headway. I'd come to a conclusion about those things long ago. My dad railed daily against the social indoctrination I received in public school. My gramps and him spent much time trying to counter what I was being fed daily by the social engineers that controlled most aspects of education during my time. It was a crime to even *think*, much less say, that anyone was differently abled based on a characteristic like the genes you were born with. You could be sent to remedial education for such behavior. It's why standards disappeared in the military. They had to eliminate them. Otherwise, the fraud that was their worldview would be exposed.

I was raised to treat people as individuals, and to judge them on their actions, not on their inherited characteristics. So, when it came to women in the military, I never had an issue. It was when the NorthAm was in a full-out war for survival that our military woke up and discarded the interference of such bankrupt philosophies and policies. When women like Jess stood up and performed just like the men—so they could be counted among the best of us—it only cemented my view on women in combat.

"It wasn't just risking life and limb like any warrior, the women risked more. Unlike your age, Karl, in my time women could control whether they would be mothers. But that choice to bear children could be irrevocably decided for them based on their desire to serve. I've always thought of that as an incredibly special distinction. A mark of a warrior's commitment that we as men would never have to reasonably consider. To me, anyone who would risk such a thing is a special kind of warrior. So, what does that tell you about a soldier like Jessica Chow?"

Will stuck a finger up. "What about the treatments you told me about? The ones to make the women less susceptible to those injuries?"

I nodded. "Yup. What happened was, without totally acknowledging the reality of the issue, the military started offering women an option. The Petronio program. It offered women who wanted to serve in such high-demand occupations a hormonal treatment that was proven to offset the effects of such severe and prolonged physical stress. Many women who decided to serve in those roles volunteered for the treatments. It worked. The medicines allowed them the ability to serve alongside the men in combat for much longer, with about an equal risk of injury as the men were subject to. When their service ended, they were taken off the treatments, with a chance at returning to a normal level of female hormones and the chance to bear children if they so choose. Not a given, but a chance."

"And Chow was one of those? Were they made into men?" Jakob blurted out in shock.

"No, Jakob, nothing like that." I couldn't begin to imagine what he and the other men were thinking. The science of my time was way past anything they could imagine. "It rendered them sterile while getting the treatments but did enhance their recovery and reduce the severity of their physical injuries."

Hikaru's frozen features remained unreadable to me. He met my glance and took that as a cue. "Women are fierce warriors. They too are samurai. It does not shock me that there are women warriors of your time, Lieutenant. I do not understand the manner of their service in your time, but it cannot be denied that our new soldier is capable. She is perhaps already more capable than many we have seen join our ranks. Not all appeared among us so well trained. But through hard training they adapted and improved to be the soldiers they now are. It seems evident our new soldier will not be lacking in skill or fierceness."

Will stood. "Gentlemen, this is not a democracy. It's not vital you all agree. If your pride can't withstand serving with a woman, I'm sure Michael will gladly hear your complaint and offer you a trip to the well of souls. What's necessary is that you follow orders. The lieutenant's choice is an order, and you're all going to follow it. End of discussion. Sir?"

Will had brought the matter to an abrupt conclusion, maybe more so than I'd wanted.

"Chow has to prove out every day just like all of us," I said. "She gets no special treatment here. What I want to leave you all with is simply this—she's a soldier, same as any of us. If you treat her that way, I'm certain you'll know that to be true soon enough."

"If it was not permitted, it would not be so." Michael had entered the room without any of us noticing. At the sound of his booming voice, we were all on our feet and at attention. How long had he been listening? The giant made his way to where I stood.

"While you focus on superficial things, your preparation goes neglected. You are not yet judged worthy to be called Ultimates." Then with what I thought was almost encouragement, he said softly, "But you are nearly so.

Ragnar Beck." Michael looked down at me. "The roles are filled. There will be no more additions to your platoon. Training continues. Proceed."

Will waited for Michael to leave. "Squad leaders, get your troops in formation. You heard the man. Teatime is over. Back to soldiering."

There were a few grumbles, and Mazhar still looked like he'd eaten sour persimmons.

"We're going to have to watch him," Will said when it was just the two of us left. "Maybe some PT will sweat the prejudice out of him."

I was ready to get this body moving. Not having someone shooting at me would be a bonus to the day as well. "It'll at least get everyone's minds off this never-ending selection they keep putting us through. You ever get the feeling they're maybe moving the goalposts on us?"

"Are there goalposts? Or is this it? An eternity of training for the amusement of the gods?"

Despite Michael's hint that there was a light at the end of our tunnel, what Will said struck a chord with me. "You might be on to something there. C'mon. Let's get at it. Stokes will get Jess calmed down, and they'll join us later. Might be a good day to hit the range and get back to standards on our best weapons."

"Roger, sir. Wonder when we'll see the rest of the unit back? Hard to imagine anyone having a worse time than we did on Bougainville."

"I know that's not true. You were on Guadalcanal."

"Pfft. Getting killed on the beach wasn't so bad. You can keep your Little Bighorn experience, Rag. At least no one gutted me alive."

15

"I have our new soldier bunking with Stokes," Will said when he joined me in our own quarters. "I didn't ask first, but do you think that's a good choice?"

I'd been going over squad assignments and was already considering where to put her so it would cause the least disruption. "You mean, do I think that's going to keep her from being assaulted by someone like Mazhar? If he tries it, they'll be raising him from the dead again. Jess'll take care of it before anyone else will get the chance."

"That, sure, but I also mean what about her and Stokes? Their little reunion made me think they were more than just comrades. Am I wrong?"

"No. They're a couple." It was going to be difficult to explain to an early-twentieth century prude like Will. The social customs of his time were very restrictive in regard to how men and women interacted. I'd read the Great Gatsby after we watched the movie in school. I thought the book would make more sense to me. It didn't. Sex was a taboo topic in their culture. The stuff on the tank when I was growing up was a hundred times more explicit.

"You may not believe me, but they're professionals. They have a code of behavior when they're together that's never caused an issue. I trust them to act in a way that won't hurt the unit." They'd joined us on the range for the rest of the day's training once Stokes had Jess a little more acclimated. Jess was the happy warrior, delighting in her new body as she worked through all of the light and heavy weapons, stuff she was already so familiar with from our time. If we had to backtrack and get her up to speed on muzzle loaders or crossbows, it wouldn't be difficult.

"Hmm. Good to hear. I was sure you'd already worked it all out beforehand, but you could've clued me in to your plan, cousin. It was a bit of a surprise."

"Sorry, Will."

"S'okay. But, Rag, can I tell you something?" He looked like he was trying to walk on eggs. I was pretty sure where he was leading.

"You think I made a mistake bringing her here?"

Will paused long enough to give a quick shake of his head. "Hmm? No. It's not that. It's—well, she's normally what I would call an attractive woman. And while it's been a good long while since I've been around one, what I'm curious about is, I don't feel like my old self. The kind of thoughts I would normally have about someone like her— even though she's a soldier in my unit—I'm just not having. And now that I'm thinking about it, since I've been here, I can't recall having those kinds of thoughts at all. Maybe it's because I've been fighting for my life most days, or maybe I'm just a guy who's nearly a hundred and fifty years old, but—"

For a soldier, he was the least profane or crass of any among us. A real reflection of his time. Some things he wouldn't discuss plainly. I didn't make him spell it out. "No. It's not just you."

The kind of aggression and harsh physical training we were going through should have our testosterone meters pegging out. The side effects of that should be present as well—but weren't. "My guess is, we're not the same in that regard. We've been changed in ways other than just being resurrected into better bodies."

Will shrugged. "Well, it's good to know it ain't just me then. Reckon it does free up some of my thinking time. Speaking of which, what's next for us?"

Coghill and Jeong's platoons were back. Denisov remained missing.

"Only Mars knows."

※   ※   ※

By the morning, Denisov's platoon was formed with us. Quick handshakes all around and a few brief words were all that was needed to understand the hell each platoon had gone through.

"Solomon Islands, W-W-2," I said.

"Gallipoli," Coghill said. He didn't need to qualify it with a war. There was only one.

"Fallujah. The first," Jeong said. That raised my eyebrows. I'd heard stories from my gramps and read several accounts. Why they hadn't simply surrounded the town in a siege until all the inhabitants starved was always Gramps's question.

"Rag, never forget that politicians don't want war to be cruel. A siege would've saved a lot of American lives. We should've surrounded that whole city and waited until they were eating rats to stay alive." We watched one of the movies about the first battle of Fallujah together. I thought it was pretty good, but Gramps kept commenting about all the technical inaccuracies.

"But the lawyers will always find a reason to say no, even if the law of land warfare permits it. See, it's perfectly acceptable to hobble the guys on the ground and spill their blood, just so long as everyone else can feel like their hands are clean. They don't care about your blood, but they'll lose sleep over some savage." Gramps knew I was going to join. He wasn't trying to discourage me, but he always told it like it was, just like I was already a soldier.

"And it only got worse, Rag. By the end of your dad's time in the Long"—everyone in my household knew the decades-long war in west Asia by that name—"you couldn't kill anyone without ten levels of permission, no matter if they were trying to kill you. Your dad was smart, but he came close to going to Leavenworth for bringing the hate to those bastards—for doing his job to bring him and his men home. As much as I think your generation is going to be in a war with the Han soon, I don't mind telling you, it did my heart some good to see the Lotus Hegemony clean up our mess over there. They aren't having any compunctions about killing the booger-eaters, are they? Their leaders aren't trying to win points with long-hair simps at home by persecuting their own soldiers for doing their jobs."

He didn't live to see how right he was. I'd have to pump Jeong for a rundown on Fallujah later. I was very curious to know how he'd fought it out.

Denisov was the last. He looked fatigued. Whereas a few words would suffice for the rest of us, for Denisov, it wouldn't be so simple.

"The battle of the Eurasian Steppes, I suppose. Names come after battles are decided."

Coghill frowned. "Which war? "

"It was your war, Beck," he said, pointing at me.

This was a surprise. None of us had been to my own time. I both dreaded and relished the potential to do so on the plains. Dreaded because I'd suffered their brand of inhumanity before. Relished because I still wanted payback.

"The Han?" It was the first any of us had been sent so far into the future. I felt for Denisov. Going back in time was a mind trip. Going into the future I died in? It had to have been a real Alice in Wonderland experience. I wondered if witnessing my last battle had helped prepare Denisov and his troops.

"Everything they did to you, Beck, they did to us. And more. Three times I used tactical nuclear devices to halt their advance. They could not defeat us except by their weapons of genetic warfare. They are an enemy more evil than the Nazis I fought in the Great Patriotic War. If Mars would send me back, I swear—" Gabriel took the field. Denisov finished quickly. "You and I will speak. We have much in common now."

I trotted to the front of my platoon and took report from Will, who whispered, "What do you make of the guy with Gabe?" When I did an about face, I stole a sideways glance to see who he meant. He wore full body armor, helmet hanging at his waist. The armor had a similar radiant iridescence like the angels'. But where theirs was graceful like a two-seater Jaguar coupe, his was bulkier and sturdy like a Ford truck. Meaner. He looked like a human tank, and I was immediately envious. His nationality was hard for me to determine, but he was human, of that I had no doubt. He was brown, with almond shaped eyes, his hair so blonde it was almost white.

"Today you begin the final steps in your training," Gabriel announced. "Captain Goshang Perrault will be acting company commander. He is an Ultimate. You will take direction from him as you would from me."

Gabriel departed. The smaller man, though not small, stepped forward.

"I'm here to guide you in the next level of your training. I'll meet with officers and NCOs immediately to discuss how we'll proceed, but the short of it is this—the fantastic stuff locked up in your armories that you've seen but haven't yet been allowed to touch?" A sly grin crept over the man. "That time is at an end. Welcome to the future."

✕ ✕ ✕

Now I knew what Magnus felt like the first time he'd seen a cartridge-firing rifle. An M-1 Garand or even an M-7 from my time—the finest implement of battle ever made—was now as obsolete as an atlatl was to a 155 mm howitzer.

The Annihilator Mark Three was my idea of the future.

"Annie will be your best friend," Captain Perrault said as he hefted one overhead. "Plasma bolts are the most powerful projectile in the small arms inventory. We have lasers, but they're big. For those of you who understand the technology, it's straightforward. For those of you who don't, tonight the diadems are going to start instruction on theory and application."

My pulse quickened. I didn't care what made it work. I just wanted to feel the weight of the sexy new rifle in my hands. I was the kid looking in the window of the department store with the greatest Christmas toy display ever assembled, and I wanted one. More than I've ever wanted anything in my life.

"The bolts Annie generates don't move at the speed of light like a laser. And they don't need to be focused. Plasma projectiles are superheated gas, magnetic coil-contained, and propelled. Against lightly protected flesh, their range is effective to thousands of meters. Gravity effects the bolt, just like a bullet, but much less so. You also won't need as much lead for a moving target as you would a bullet, and you'll learn how the auto-ranging and firing solution software makes the job almost effortless."

He pulled something off his side and tossed it in the air. A glowing orb shot over our heads, causing some to duck.

"Watch." The captain shouldered the weapon and tracked the bright flashing ball as it flew an erratic course higher and higher above us. When it was so far above we could barely see the small blip, he fired. A tiny bolt of lightning fired with a sound I can only describe as pure science fiction—how every super futuristic ray gun was supposed to sound—and a bright orange flash told us all the target had been vaporized.

I'd known lust many times. For the first time in my life, I was in love.

"Like every weapon," the captain continued, "it's only as effective as the soldier who knows best how to use it. In the rare chance that the electro-optics are knocked out, you need to understand how to hit with the weapon with the human eyeball. So, we'll start out with what you're used to now—using plain old iron sights.

"Once you've all mastered Annie, you can look forward to learning the other weapons in the inventory, until finally"—he thumped his fist against his chest—"you'll be outfitted like a real steel gorilla. Powered armor is the greatest thing since the invention of sexual reproduction."

Not a lifetime of military discipline could contain me. I joined the mad howl with the rest of my wolf pack. If I'd had any misgivings about the afterlife, any frustrations about our lack of understanding as to our existence, I couldn't recall them now.

"Good." The captain surveyed us, pleased at our wild enthusiasm. "But it's business as usual. You can all look forward to more time on the plains, solving problems in combat as a unit, and returning for more training until I think you're all fit. Then and only then will you be ready as a company. Ready for the final test to become Ultimates. Are you ready to begin?"

"SIR, YES, SIR!" was the deafening reply.

"I believe you. Platoon leaders, fall your men out while we have our conference. It's time to leave the Stone Age behind."

16

Will headed me off at the pass. For two men born a century apart, we thought like brothers. "I've got about a million questions, but right now, I'm anxious to get my hands on one of those new irons."

"I'm with you. Let's see what our new CO has to say." Perrault was as tan as his hair was pale, the incongruity making him look like the cover character from some fantasy novel. In his glowing armor, the combination left me without doubt he was of some future human race. Swedish and Malaysian with dominant traits of both? That was my best guess. I wanted to ask him about that and suddenly had a curiosity to find out something about the future history of the world I'd died defending.

The men were dismissed to do what soldiers spend a lot of time doing: waiting. The other officers and NCOs converged with Will and me to where Captain Perrault waited.

"Gentlemen, stand easy. I know who you all are," he began. "You'll get to know me soon enough. I am not a tyrant, and I try and keep things informal when possible, but I will not tolerate any break in discipline. Are we understood?"

"Sir?" It was Coghill. "Are we to assume that you arrived here from our distant future? Are these the weapons and technology from your own time? Is that why you're here?"

Jeong, usually reserved, was also forward. "Captain, where are you from? You represent no race of man I can place."

The captain frowned, then sighed. "I should've known. Let's get this cleared up right now. Do all of you remember what you were told after your first trip to the plains? To keep your voders closed?"

I'd suspected as much. The veil of ignorance we lived under wasn't going to be lifted any time soon.

"You all know there are rules here. What you don't know yet is that many of these rules are in place for your protection. Yes. I'm from a future more distant than any of you. Until you've all advanced in training, what I could tell you might jeopardize your performance. Just as all of you've been able to learn more about your future history from up-time warriors like Lieutenant Beck, I could tell you also. But at the appropriate time. For now, I want you all to concentrate on your next critical tasks: getting your company certified to Mars's satisfaction. Shiny?"

That was new lingo to me.

"Shiny, sir," some of us replied.

"The correct reply would be, 'bright and shiny, sir'."

"Bright and shiny, sir," we said in unison.

"Excellent. Let's get weapons issued and familiarization underway. We've got some casts to watch and some work to do before we can get any range time in. Return to your platoons and make it happen. For the time being, you're all ignorant Neanderthals until I tell you you're not. Dismissed."

Will stutter stepped us all with a question. "Captain? Will you be taking over daily combatives and physical training?"

Perrault's face scrunched. I wasn't sure if it was irritation that Will had spoken after his dismissal, or the suggestion that our new command cadre would be PT-ing us every morning.

"No. Continue to conduct your calisthenics and your *wrestling* as you see fit. No more questions. *Dismissed.*"

We waited until we were well out of earshot before Will and I started our prison-yard mumbles. "Guess I'm getting off to a bad start with the new boss," Will said.

"An appropriate question from a platoon sergeant, cousin." I too was curious how daily routines would be affected by Perrault's assumption of command. "He mighta' been pissed because you asked a question after he dismissed us, but it also struck me that he didn't think much of our PT program. See the look of disgust on his face when he called our combatives wrestling?"

"If I had powered armor, I might think hand-to-hand was a waste of time too."

"Speaking of, be sure to remind Hikaru he leads training in the morning. And tell him tap-outs will be obeyed. We've got no time for troops to go to the healer."

"Roger. And who cares what Perrault thinks of our caveman tussling? Let's get our new shooting sticks."

We were just getting comfortable with Annie when a few days later Jess was pulled out to take her first turn on the Plains of Eternity. It was my role to escort her for the obligatory perusal by Mars himself and mentor her transition into the way of life of an eternal soldier.

"Beck, I've been following your progress," Mars addressed me. I hadn't been before him in some time. "Not bad. Don't let it go to your head. One screw-up wipes the slate clean." His gruff, clipped manner of speech had to be affected, and for our benefit. As an immortal, perhaps he had too much time on his hands and he'd watched Gramps's favorite, Full Metal Jacket, too often. "This one?" He pointed at Jess. "You think she's ready?"

"Yes, sir. More than, sir."

"Chow. You have the confidence of your platoon leader. Don't let him or me down. Whatever you do, don't fail."

I remembered how I felt my first time, standing before our omnipotent leader. My guts were frozen like an iceberg. Jess looked how I remember feeling.

"Yes, sir!"

"Michael, make it happen. Dismissed."

As we floated back to the base, Jess tried the same subtle interrogation I'd tried with Will. "Is that *the* Mars. Like, the god of war?"

I already knew Michael would intercede. "Think not of matters ancillary to the challenge that awaits, Jessica Chow. Ready yourself."

I was allowed to witness her trip to do battle in the Korean war. She did as I would've expected, leading a defense against a wave of North Koreans, beating mess kits and marching like a herd of zombies at her platoon's dug in position. After mowing down bodies until she was knee deep in hand grenade pins and spent brass, she fought hand to hand with an entrenching tool until she fell.

Before she was back among us, Michael broke from his usual stoic silence. "Well chosen, Ragnar Beck."

Jessica looked pleased with herself as she appeared back in the rotunda. "Whoa. What a rush."

"Return to training, soldiers. Lieutenant Beck, you may now educate your comrade. Take your leave."

"C'mon, Jess," I said as I led her away. "I'll get you up to speed. And pretty soon, you're going to be as salty as the rest of us. Valhalla has a way of doing that."

✳ ✳ ✳

Mastering Annie wasn't too difficult, and even guys like Magnus who'd struggled with twentieth century weapons found the Annihilator Mark Three an easy tool to learn. But we had our problem children. It was still cringe-worthy to see how a few of the troops from way downtime were easily flummoxed whenever something new was introduced.

"Take a break, Shapur," Stokes told the Pathan from the middle ages. "Walk it off and we'll try again. You'll get it this next run."

"Its will is against me." Shapur shook his clenched fists. "A horse that refuses the halter." He stomped off the line, following Dan's advice.

The captain gave his feedback. "The other Neanderthals are capable. Is it a lack of motivation? Your diadems have taught you, as have I. Perhaps a trip to the plains is what's required?"

Perrault's disparagement wasn't helping.

We were running everyone through the next qualification course of fire—pop-up targets across multiple ranges. Those of us who'd already passed were coaching the rest. The standard was 100 percent hits using single shots on the dismounted humans, and a short burst to disable vehicles. Shapur was among the last yet to qualify, failing three times already. He continued to confuse the single-shot and pulse fire setting. With a short bow, the man was a marvel. He could fire a dozen arrows in a matter of seconds, knocking the shafts on the same side as his draw hand, launching and drawing on the run, as effortlessly as I would shooting the same small targets on the move with an M-7, but with equally deadly effect. Maybe more. Arrows made for tremendous wound channels, much larger than bullet holes. I'd seen the results myself. A man with an arrow in his chest bled out faster than a man shot.

"I can relate," Stokes said after Shapur stormed off to walk tiny circles as he cursed his new nemesis, the Annihilator Mark Three. "It's like every time I had an operating system for a device down pat, they'd go and release a mandatory upgrade, move all the icons around, change their color, and it'd take me a month to learn it again. Many's the time I wanted to murder some guy in a cubicle who's only job was to make my life miserable by screwing up my tech. Shapur runs an M-7 well. He'll get Annie too. It'll just take a little extra work."

Stokes said it for Perrault's benefit, who was within earshot, but ignored us as he stood behind another pair of shooters, showing a similar level of disapproval.

"Keep at it, Dan," I said and stepped off to speak to the captain. As much as I sometimes questioned how our time was spent here, seeing how easily our company of culturally and technologically disparate warriors had advanced nearer to the pinnacle of what Mars expected of his Ultimates, I understood. While it would've been a simple step from where Stokes, Jess, and I had come from to learning this level of tech, for the others, it would've been impossible without the lengthy and arduous process of education.

"I have to supervise the other platoons, Lieutenant. If you can't get your last few men functional, we have to move on."

"What happens to them then, sir?"

"If they're unfit to be Ultimates, it's the well."

I gulped. "They'll make it, sir." No one was getting sent to oblivion if I could do anything to help it. If I had to shoot it for Shapur, he'd make it.

Luckily, Stokes was right. Shapur got it on the next try, looking like the kid who recovered his spot in the spelling bee by getting onomatopoeia correct after flubbing c-a-t. We got him and the last of our downtimers qualified and were on to the next goodies, anxiously awaiting the prize that teased us behind the last glass wall of the armory: powered armor.

Captain Perrault got us up to speed on hand flamers, crew-served lasers, energy mortars, and all sorts of fantastic instruments of mayhem, making them all our new best friends. Jess was the only one to break away to take additional trips to the fields—which was no burden as she took to each new implement of death like a duck to water—until one morning as we formed up for morning combatives, Michael and Gabriel marched onto the field. We'd seen very little of them since Perrault came on board. Them being together and aiming their attention at my platoon like one of the guided hyper-velocity rockets we'd just learned to use told me immediately something big was in the works. Michael halted to tower over me, the glow of his armor tainting my vision like purple sunglasses.

"Ragnar Beck. Report with your platoon to the fields of eternity. It is time for your next challenge."

17

Mars had made it known that if Beck succeeded in his next challenge, it would be proof that he had what it took to run the company. Denisov was the god's next choice. Mars had taken Beck at his word that he'd studied military history well. The lieutenant was more of an intellectual than he wanted to admit and he had that balance of in-the-mud courage and smarts that made Mars believe he could succeed.

Even at this.

"Michael, here's the scenario for the plains." Mars stood by as Quintus handled the details. The god watched Michael's face for a reaction as he scanned the order, enjoying the surprises. Beck had Mars enjoying himself lately. Bringing a woman to Aricia to try out for his Ultimates? That was a bold move. "What do you think, Mike?"

The angel looked grim. "It has been some time since you have tested any against this challenge, Mars."

"I didn't know you to have any pity. What, you think it's too tough?"

"No, Mars. But I sense that even you think it impossible."

"Mike, if I didn't know better, I'd swear you were developing a sense of humor."

※　※　※

The MACO was yelling in my ear. "B Squadron. That's your shitter. Let's see if these guys can finally do this at night without killing us all. Good luck."

We were in the desert. A giant Sea Stallion helicopter belched black smoke as the crew chief stood at the ramp, waving us to him.

I gave the marshalling area control officer a thumbs up. I nudged Will next to me. We were all dressed in blue jeans and wore black fatigue jackets and black watch caps, and we carried suppressed .45 caliber grease guns and CAR-15s. I squinted as frozen dust sandblasted my face, kicked up by the rotor wash like a cyclone.

I knew who I was, where we were, and what we were doing. I found Jess and Stokes. The whole platoon had the faint halos identifying us as the other-timers in this reality. Even with the inherent melding of ourselves and the person we were transmuted with, it would only be the three of us who understood that magnitude of the where and when we were thrust into.

Stokes yelled as we jogged, bent over and shielding our faces with our hands. "Are we still stateside?"

"Yes," I yelled back. "It's 29 Palms. We're not there yet."

"So there's still time to change this?" Jess yelled. "How?"

"What is it?" Will asked. "We're just training, not going into combat right now, right? That's what I'm feeling."

He didn't know yet, but Mars had really dropped us into the mouth of the volcano this time.

I paused at the bottom of the ramp to let the rest of the platoon mount. The down beat from the rotors was strong, and the sand no longer blasted my skin, but the JP-4 fumes were stronger here and brought on that nauseated feeling that comes with being slowly poisoned. I pulled the three of them in close. "This is bad, Will. Real bad. We know what's going to happen. It's 1980. We're training to go rescue 53 American hostages held in Iran. It's a mission that never got the chance to succeed. Mars keeps telling us not to fail. Right now, I don't think that's possible."

Stokes said it for me. "We're screwed. Well of souls, here we come. No getting space-marine armor. No Ultimates. No final battle for the existence of the universe or whatever it is we're training for. Shit."

Stokes mumbled his curses just loud enough for everyone to hear. The others didn't know what we knew. Yet. I was going to have to tell them. We were billeted by squadrons, so we didn't need to pretend we weren't who we were.

The ride was brief, but what of it there'd been had been rough. Our pilots were not experienced flying in no-light conditions, and the last few months hadn't made them significantly better at it. We'd just done our first full mission-profile practice. We'd practiced our actions on the ground so many times I could do the assault on the embassy and the hostage rescue in my sleep. But this was the first time we'd practiced as a full force, taking a flight in total darkness on the RH-53s along a simulated route, the same as it would be to our jumping off point. Our hotwash afterward was unanimous—it was a miracle we hadn't crashed. It was yet another vote of no confidence in the pilots.

What only me, Jess, Stokes—and now Will—knew was that no matter how much we trained, the crews would never be able to perform their part of the mission. Ergo, it was doomed to failure from the beginning. At least, if what happened on the plains was what happened in history.

I tried the gentle touch. "Danny, take it easy, okay?"

Stokes could run his mouth at the wrong time. This was one of those times. Next to him, Jess was withdrawn. I could tell she was thinking the same things Stokes was saying, arms folded across her chest, chin tucked as though trying to ward off the cold winds of the bad news we were burdened with.

"What is the issue?" Karl asked. "This rescue mission is from your history, yes? You up-timers know the outcome of this event. You know what pitfalls to avoid. How can that not result in a victory for us?"

The normally fearless Jakob—assured that all was according to his creator's plan—looked more concerned than I'd seen him when bayoneting frenzied Japanese at Bougainville. "Why does Stokes despair so? The captors are no match for us. We are the most highly-trained warriors of the time, plus, we bring to the plains our own superior skills. We are unstoppable in a fight. What is it that worries you all so?"

We'd all become a little immune to the stress of stepping through the gate with no prior knowledge of where, when, or what we would face. What I'd figured out was this: as if our training wasn't enough of a selection process, the plains chewed up a soldier who didn't believe that everything they needed to overcome was already within them. Everyone here was as hard as the rock of Gibraltar. So, if Mars had sent us here, it wasn't to rehash what we'd already proven by our other jaunts across time. It was to rise to a new challenge. But sending us to replay the Iran Hostage Rescue? It was the ultimate puzzle.

"Everyone know the gist of where we are and what we're doing here?" I'd learned to read these guys. Hikaru's millimeter-sunken frown was a brightly lit marquee to me that joined the other more obvious signs of doubt in the crowd.

"We're in the United States. It's March, 1980. We're in a desert location in the US practicing for a hostage rescue mission inside a foreign country. That country is Iran. More than fifty Americans are being held hostage by Islamic fundamentalists at the US embassy compound in the capital, Tehran. The country has been in revolution for almost two years and blames the US for their ills."

Without asking permission, my contrarian, Mazhar, interrupted. "Persia is a civilized land, and they are a civilized people."

I let it go. He'd gotten over his prejudice against Jess and hadn't given me a bit of trouble since the day of her arrival. I credited the prospect of finishing our final selection and training as motivating his sense of inclusion toward our newest member.

"Maybe so, or at least in your time, Mazhar. Sociopolitical background and religion notwithstanding, our unit is tasked with bringing the hostages home safely."

Everyone was tapped into the consciousness and memory of the person they ghosted and knew what their hosts knew. But I'd been taught in the army that the things that go without saying are the things that actually bear repeating over and over. "Let's make sure everyone is tracking." I went over the mission plan. Our portion was straightforward: do what assaulters are born to do. We'd hit the hostage takers so hard and fast they'd never get a shot off, rescue the hostages, and leave the country of their captivity with a lesson they and the world would never forget. You don't mess with Americans. It was the getting there and out that was the difficulty.

Magnus's face beamed. "It will be one of the greatest moments in all of history. We will accomplish something so daring, so fierce, the story will be told for a thousand years. We've done difficult things together, my friends. Many battles we have fought and won. But this fight will shake the pillars of Valhalla! Mars chooses us to do this great thing because Odin whispers in his ear that we are the chosen warriors!" The red giant leaped to his feet, raising fists over head at his own declaration. I had to admit, he was always enthusiastic when a fight loomed and a helluva good team motivator.

Will covered his face with both hands. I wanted to let Magnus down easy and not pull the rug out from under him all at once. I couldn't hide my own disappointment as I sighed the words. "If only."

Karl the pessimist understood. "Man plans, the gods laugh."

The Viking's perplexity would've been comical if the stakes hadn't been so high. His hands dropped like a deflated Macy's Thanksgiving Day balloon. The tiny squeak that came out of him belonged to a mousy child, not a berserker.

"No?"

I broke the news. "We're never going to get past Desert One. The mission fails there. The helicopters turn out to be the weak link in the chain. Enough of them don't arrive to even start the mission, and during our departure, some aircraft collide and kill good men. The hostages stay put for another year."

One of the men, Ruben, raised a finger to be recognized. Ruben wasn't what I'd call a rocket scientist, but he was solid. For what the young paratrooper did in the invasion of Normandy, he should've gotten the medal of honor. We'd all seen him, and we knew—and so did Mars—which was why he was here. "So what you're telling me is that what we got tonight was a little taste of what's to come? The pilots can't cut the mustard?"

Jess had recovered from her funk. "It's not clear. The Iran hostage rescue mission is something I've read about my whole life. It's hard to blame the pilots. They were trying to do something they'd never trained for. Night vision tech was barely a thing. The aircraft weren't the best they had."

It didn't surprise me she knew so much about this mission, but even I was taken aback at what she remembered on the spot. It spoke both of how significant the mission was in our history and how serious a student of warfare Jess was. Stokes shed his vexation and sat up more attentively as she spoke. She hid a lot of her intelligence by being quiet. I didn't have to encourage her to continue.

"Some say Air Force Special Ops should've been used, and that the Navy and Marine assets were put there for political considerations so that all the services were represented. See, the US had just lost a war. The country was demoralized. This was going to be a message to the world that the US was still the most powerful nation in the world, and it was important to someone at the top that everyone had their piece of the pie. The ground mission commander blamed the pilots, but it's more complex than that."

Karl shook his head in disgust. "So, for the sake of glory, the best were not chosen?"

"Something like that," I admitted.

"How do you know these things?" Jakob asked.

Jess hadn't been with us long, and though she'd impressed everyone with her physical prowess, they hadn't yet seen her flex her brain the way I knew she could. "They wrote books, made movies—heck, there was a TankMax game that let you play the whole mission out as if everything worked according to plan."

I'd forgotten that! It was an older game, and supposedly it had the input of historians and even some of the surviving members of the actual operation. As a kid I'd read a review of the game that talked about its realistic attention to detail, but I never downloaded it. The VR experience was only rated as two stars. Maybe it wasn't as immersive as newer games, but now wished I'd never read the reviews. Hindsight's a bitch.

Jakob cheered. "Excellent! It is providence that we have a scholar to guide us. You have the solution then?"

Jess's face fell. "I don't have one."

Karl stroked his chin. "Logic tells us that with a complex problem, one first isolates that which is understandable. The helicopters or the pilots are the weakness, yes? So we eliminate one or both of those problems."

"No, Karl, we're not going to kill the pilots," Will said for me.

Karl groaned. "Don't be absurd. That is not my meaning. But, if the helicopters were, say, unusable, then the planners would have to look at one of the alternatives, yes?"

Destroy the helicopters? I didn't think that was the answer, and it was Jess who confirmed it. "The helicopters parked outside in the hangers aren't the same ones used in the mission. Those are already on the carrier. That was one of the problems they identified later. The mission is so secret, it's considered a security risk to let the maintenance crews on the USS Nimitz know the birds are going to be used for something very important, so some of the mission helicopters get cannibalized for parts, and none of them get much airtime to work out any bugs in them."

It was Will's turn to groan. "The most critical, most fragile part of the plan to move the assault force into place and to bring the hostages out, and they don't use birds in tip-top shape? I don't know much about newfangled machines, but you don't show up to the races with a horse that's never run before. One Model -T isn't necessarily the same as another Model-T. Did they really want this thing to come off?"

The room broke down into full blown despair and frustration. Stokes was the one to shout everyone down. "Just a minute, just a minute. Do we absolutely *know* that the same thing is going to happen this time? I mean, it doesn't make sense to send us here to just crash and burn in the desert."

I was the one to shoot him down. "Danny boy, you haven't been on the block as long as the rest of us. Anyone here have an experience where something played out differently than what you knew had happened, or where something went the way you thought it would?"

The grim looks on their faces told me they hadn't.

"Sure, we've had successes, but I keep thinking about my back-to-back-to-back trips to the Little Bighorn. That never turned out differently than the history I know, and I sure never got a win out of it, no matter what I tried. Mars even made a point afterward to rub it in my face that I couldn't change the outcome."

I remembered Mars's smug face asking me how I liked losing.

"I never got an easy go of it at Guadalcanal," Will said. "It wasn't history to me, but the future. I played through and got slaughtered more times than I can count. I can't say knowing how it went down would've helped me though. It was a miracle I made it as far as I did my last run at it. All I learned was sometimes it's just luck that gets you through."

Karl scoffed. "Waterloo. I did not escape a beating at the hands of my fellow Prussians, no matter that I knew the outcome. Mars did not permit me to outfox my fate."

Jakob stiffened. "You did not tell me that you ghosted Napoleon?"

Karl laughed. "I did not play that role. I commanded a unit of cavalry close to the Nightmare of Europe. Little meddler, his family called him. They knew, even when he was a child. Had I ghosted the emperor, I might have slit my own throat."

And yet it *was* possible to change an outcome. I'd proven it my very first time on the plains, inadvertently denying the 13 colonies their first future general and president.

"So, what do we do?" Magnus said, loudly enough to silence the rest. "Do we play through and see what happens? It is March now. When does the mission actually occur?"

I struggled. "Hmmm, as I recall, it's soon. That right, Jess?"

"Mid-April, 1980, we move out to Egypt to stage."

Will caught my eye. "We're here pretty early if all we're supposed to do is take the ride we bought the ticket for. Don't make much sense to me."

"We have a little time," I said. "We'll keep working the problem. In the meantime, let's get packed up. We're heading back to Bragg in a few hours. I'm going to see the colonel. I seem to remember after Eagle Claw failed there was another plan. Snow-something."

"Snowbird," Jess corrected me. "It was a much bigger operation. More of an invasion than a covert surgical strike."

"Tell me what you remember of it. Maybe if I can plant that seed, it'll grow into something that'll let us win." Jess grimaced.

"What?"

"From what I remember, the colonel's brought up his lack of confidence in the aircrews to the higher-ups several times, and's been ignored. Bringing this up might not get you the receptive ear you're thinking. As I recall, he was known for being hard to work for."

"Pfft. I gotta try. Besides, I had Custer as commanding officer. How bad could this be?"

※　※　※

There are ass-chewings, and then there are ass-chewings. I've had ass-chewings. I've heard of ass-chewings so bad that the recipient didn't have enough posterior remaining on which to ever sit again.

This made all those other ass-chewings seem as gentle as a bedtime story read to a dying child.

As my parentage and intelligence were evaluated, I said a prayer that if I fell, I'd stay dead rather than replay this beatdown. I'd never heard a colonel use language like that—and all directed at me, his West Virginia accent getting thicker and thicker as he discussed my lack of sapience. I was a major in this unit. What would he say and do to a sergeant? If I was lucky, I wouldn't be tossed out, leaving the rest of the platoon to figure this one out without me. The colonel's last words to me were his kindest.

"You moron. Don't ya think I know all that? Get out of here!"

I should've listened to Jess. She was the expert here. This had been the king of all bad ideas of all times, and I'd lived through a lot of time from which to make the comparison. I made a dash for the billets before he came after me with his Browning Hi-Power. He was very good with it. If he acted on his murderous thoughts towards me, a hundred yards wasn't far enough away to guarantee my safety.

"And?" Jess greeted me.

"What they all say is true. That's the meanest SOB ever lived. He survived being shot in the gut with a Russian fifty-cal. If he hadn't, Mars would've picked him up already. He's been given a nearly impossible mission, made completely impossible by a bunch of generals in Washington. We're stuck. He knows it. Still, he'd rather skin me alive than hear about it."

"So what, then?" Will asked me.

Karl looked very smug and professorial. I wasn't in the mood for his aristocratic condescension at the moment, but I was out of options. "We attack the part of the problem we understand. We have enough information to act on. It is the pilots and the helicopters that are the solvable term of the equation we have."

"I don't know about you, Karl," Stokes said., "But I don't know anything about making helicopters airworthy. None of us do."

"Ja. This is so." Karl dropped into his own accent, reminiscent of a movie character. All he needed was a monocle and a cigarette holder. "So then, who does?"

"Well, the Navy maintenance crews on the Nimitz, for one," Jess said.

Karl rewarded her with a nod. "Yes. Exactly."

Stokes had been absorbing Jess's briefing. "The Nimitz is already in the Indian Ocean carrying the birds we'll be flying for the mission. How do we get the squid rotor heads read-in so that they know how important those birds are?"

Karl frowned, disappointed the golden beads of wisdom dripping from his superior brow had not enlightened the peasants surrounding him.

"How is this not obvious? We must do it ourselves."

18

We were crammed like sardines into the back of our Combat Talon C-130. The flight from Oman across the gulf to Desert One wouldn't take long. Our airfield waiting in the Iranian desert had already been marked with remote control IR landing beacons, buried by the Air Force combat controllers.

I was getting to witness many historic firsts. Tactics and techniques pioneered for this mission were things we took for granted in my day—like flying in total darkness. Some were things we'd had to actually relearn because the lessons had been left to evaporate like an unsealed gas can by my generation of head-in-the-sand leaders. I'd met the "Brand X" group of special tactics airmen who'd infiltrated Iran to get the mission started. I was amazed human men with testicles that large could still walk like normal folks. They had a part of the operation that I'm glad we didn't have to fix. What I'd learned ghosting this mission was an adage I'd wished I'd known in my day. Special operations was a three-step dance: Get there, get it done, and get back.

I'd gone on my last mortal mission not knowing the "how to" of any of those things. And now I was here.

"Won't be long before we find out if this worked," Will whispered in my ear.

"Thanks, Captain Obvious." I was nervous, even if I shouldn't have been. Fight, die, fight again was my new norm. It was just that if this didn't work, I truly had no idea what to do to make it different on the next run. Or the one after that.

Before we loaded up to head back to Bragg from the rehearsal at 29 Palms, Karl had focused us on the problem—how to get the helicopters to not conk out prematurely.

"We start with what's available to us. The flight crews. If we can convince them of what we know, it would be the first step in a chain to right the listing ship, ja?"

Stokes rolled his eyes. "What? Tell them that we're angels sent from heaven and that we know the future? If someone told me that, I'd call the counter-intel guys myself."

We were constantly under the watchful eyes of the secret-keepers, making sure the mission wasn't compromised by loose lips. We had people monitoring our phone calls and letters and following us around whenever we were off the compound at Bragg.

"No." I had a glimmer of an idea. "Karl's right. But we do it like this. We haven't had a lot of back and forth with them. If we tell them we've got some inside info and why we have to share it with them in an unofficial kind of way, we just may be able to use our reputation as super-secret commandoes to our advantage. These flyboys don't know what we do or don't know."

The unit we were in already had a very special aura about it. That came with secrecy.

"We'll leave it to you to be our Shakespeare then," Will said. "I can't wait to see how you're going to write this one. Ready to be our Prospero and talk our way out of death?"

I took the core of our platoon, and we found the crew of our bird, working in a poorly-lit hangar as the winds pelted the tin walls with more of the same frozen bits that had sandblasted us earlier. The crew chief was the first to notice us as we slid through the pedestrian door. Before we got to the helicopter, the whole crew was assembled, looking as though they expected trouble.

By the time I was through, if I hadn't made new friends, I at least hadn't made enemies.

"If the birds let us down, the whole thing's going to get put on you. This thing's so secret, that it's setting you up for failure." I explained how we suspected the RH-53 minesweeper helicopters on the Nimitz weren't going to be ready.

The lead pilot looked suspicious. He squinted at us. "What you're saying isn't off base. We know we aren't up to the task. But it isn't our fault. We've brought these things up too. The Air Force has brand new 53s outfitted for just this kind of mission. The pentagon is insistent the birds are going to be Navy and flown by Marines and Navy. That's it. When it was suggested that we let the Air commandos do this and just paint 'US Marines' on the tail, I hear someone almost got murdered."

"That's why we have to do something about it, or no one else will," Karl said.

"What can we do?" the other young pilot said. "Jeff's right. We've spouted off as much as we dare without risking getting shitcanned off this mission. We've talked about refusing to fly. They'll just put us in jail and get someone else. It wouldn't be fair to saddle some other crew with our job this late in the game."

"Let me ask," Jess stepped in. "Have you done anything to these aircraft to increase their performance? Like, remove anything or add anything?"

A grizzled looking man stepped forward. No one wore name badges or ranks, and there was only bare Velcro where aviators wore them on their flight suits. Everything about the man told me he was a Chief, the ultimate enlisted rank in the Navy. "I won't ask how you know, but yes. We've removed one of the engine air particle separator filters to give us more lift. Why?"

Jess took the cue. "We know the weathermen are blowing it for us. They're failing to take into consideration in all their weather predictions some important things. We know. We've spent a lot of time in the desert. What would happen if those filters were off and you ran into one of the haboobs that are famous for blowing up out of nowhere in that part of the world?"

"What's a haboob?" the lead pilot asked.

"It's a wall of dust as thick as concrete and so big you can't climb above it or fly around it. And they come out of nowhere. What would happen if you got hit by one on the flight in?" Jess persisted.

The older man considered. "It'd deadline one of these helos faster than you could imagine."

I tried again. "We have to figure out something to make sure you arrive at Desert One with enough birds to fly us. And if we don't, we're going to end up leaving those Americans where they are as well as embarrassing our country. Whatever it takes, we have to solve this."

The younger pilot threw up his hands. "We've tried."

A few more go arounds and there was nothing to do but leave the dejected crew and head back to finish packing up.

"Think we accomplished anything?" Will asked me. "Because it doesn't feel like we accomplished anything."

There was a knock at the door. It opened up and in stepped the grizzled crew chief. "Hope I'm not disturbing anything, gentlemen. May I come in?"

I called over my brain trust, and we put the aviator in a chair and circled around him. I sensed something was about to break for us. "What's on your mind—Chief, is it?"

"Yes, sir." He sighed. Loudly. What he felt was as clear as an iron girder bending from an incredible weight, the sound of breaking strain in his voice. "I believe all the things you're telling me. What I'm about to suggest, it could be construed as treason, I suppose." He hesitated.

"You're among friends, Chief," I said.

"Our pilots—these guys are broken. You have no idea the size of the gun being held at their heads. I'm not sure what you told us makes that any better for them."

"It had to be said," Stokes told him.

"I'll just come out with it then. I have an idea. We're folding up our helos and they'll be carted back to base today. I'll be back home with them. As far as I can tell, we don't have the spooks following us around the way they're glued to you all. I can make some things happen that may help, I think."

The hair on the back of my neck stood up. Jess looked at me and mouthed, "Jackpot."

"I know the toughest, smartest warrant officer that ever whipped a flight line into shape. Someone I can confide in. I have a friend—well, more than a friend. My sister is the GS-5 who does the orders for all personnel assignments at the Department of the Navy."

Jess beamed. "You mean, you think you can get the right person with the right knowledge onto the Nimitz to take charge of the prep for the helos?"

He shrugged. "All I can do is try. My man is portside. I'm going to spell this out for him, and if I can get him to agree, I'm pretty sure I can get the strings pulled and make this happen without anyone being the wiser. Or end up in the brig and headed to the gallows for sedition."

"Espionage would be the charge," Stokes added unhelpfully.

The chief turned a little paler. "Well, I suppose I'll have you all to join me for the necktie party if that happens. This whole thing's a mess. But it's going to come to a head soon. The whole country knows it. I don't know how much time we've got. Carter's up for reelection. I didn't vote for Grits, and I don't have much faith in him. But he's got to be feeling the pressure. The whole country wants this. And with that movie star cowboy breathing down his neck, he can't hold off much longer. You're right. If we don't do something to make this right, no one else is going to. I'm in."

I offered my hand, and he took it. For the first time since our arrival, I felt like there was hope.

Jakob crossed himself. "God told Abraham that if he could find ten righteous men, he would spare the sinful. In our case, I think we have found the one virtuous soul who may save us all."

※　※　※

"Touchdown in ten," came the word.

"Good," Hikaru said from across the aisle, gear and explosives stacked like cordwood between us. "Flying is unnatural for men."

The low-level, harsh, and sudden nap-of-the-earth flight had worn us all. I loved roller coasters. I could've been a fighter pilot, but Gramps let me know I wasn't cut out for it. "Boy, you were born to pound the ground, like all Becks. If it wasn't so, the good lord would've given you a head for math." My cast-iron stomach had never failed me, but even I was feeling queasy from the bumpy ride.

"You've spoken to the Rangers?" I double checked with Magnus.

"Yes." My friend grinned back at me. "As much fun as it would be to see them launch a LAW at a fuel truck, it would be better if we did this quietly." In the books, it was a big deal that not long after landing at Desert One, we would be compromised by vehicles, passing innocently and unsuspectingly through our not-so-private landing zone. I'd hammered this possibility with our people over and over; an advantage of being a major on this operation. I had a little clout. Not much, but enough. Two were fuel trucks carrying black-market gasoline. The other was a bus full of passengers in the wrong place at the wrong time. The Rangers helping with the ground force protection were given the mission to secure the airfield perimeter. With Magnus's coaching, we hoped to make things a little less lively than what had occurred.

After an approach, a tight turn, and a final attempt, we bounced hard and were down. The ramp lowered as we taxied and stopped. A dirt bike and a Ranger-laden gun jeep sprang off into the darkness with one of our assaulters in charge. We were already on our feet, loaded and ready to get onto the soil of our next combat.

It was hot, unlike the deserts we'd trained in. "Take charge of them, Will, and get ready to help fuel the helos while I check in." The other C-130s were coming in, sending up clouds of thick dust as they taxied into positions around the unimproved runway. Soon the rest of our force spewed from aluminum bellies in mass birth.

I found the marshalling area and checked in. The boss was there, larger than life, talking to our combat controllers. "It's a goddam superhighway," the boss yelled. "We've got a bus load of women and children to deal with, and two trucks in custody." We had a plan for that. Our new guests would be getting an all-expenses-paid trip to Egypt on the C-130s when they departed. Not seeing the flaming fuel truck, I knew we'd already changed history.

"Helos inbound," one of the radio men reported. The boss's grin was like a small moon. In the distance, the beat of rotors stood out behind the idle of the C-130s. I sensed his relief, and it told me he had major doubts the mission would get this far. He'd been right.

"We're a go. Get ready to refuel the birds. We're on our way."

History was about to be made. And I was here to live it.

19

We'd set into motion as best we could the influence we hoped might change the outcome at Desert One. From the US we stopped off in Germany to pick up the Special Forces team who would rescue the three hostages held separately in the Ministry of Foreign Affairs. The hostage takers were radical students, not trained military tacticians, but not made entirely stupid by their bizarre fundamentalism. Spreading the hostages out was a deft move. To rescue them all at the same time meant we needed more help at a time when few qualified bodies were available. In 1980 USA there were only two units certified for counterterrorism. Our unit was still small and new. The Berlin boys were the older, more established group who'd been training the mission from right in the heart of terrorism that was Europe in the 1970s.

I'd read about that unit and even Gramps—who was unimpressed with most depictions of Special Forces in books and movies—told me if he could go back in time, that was the unit he wished he could've served in. Being a kind of time traveler myself, I wondered if there was a way I could swing such a trip. I'd be bound to learn something more useful than I had at the Little Bighorn, where all I'd learned was sometimes there was nothing you could do but die with your boots on. I hoped this was not a repeat of that lesson.

The dozen long-hairs from Germany met us at the staging spot in Egypt. They had a kind of cool factor that made me curious, but we were too busy for me to do much more than give a friendly nod to them in passing. I wasn't alone in feeling differently about the other new faces that joined us. If the SF team were brothers from another mother, these new additions were more like sheep among wolves, not operators.

"Who are these characters?" Will asked me as we watched the loadmaster put the out-of-place passengers into seats with us on the already crowded C-130. The security vehicles, the fuel bladder, us, and all our gear made a sardine can seem roomy.

"Our drivers."

A military unit is a tribe, and a member of a tribe can spot an outsider from a mile away. They wore our jeans, black-dyed field jackets, watch caps restraining unmilitary-like haircuts and unshaven faces, but that's where the similarity ended. They were a mix of a dozen Iranian-born civilians and Persian-American soldiers—Farsi speakers pulled from their mundane life in some support unit and given a "special opportunity" to serve their country. The civilians were Persian immigrants who by day were actually truck drivers. These were the chauffeurs who would drive the tractor trailers to take us from our hide site just outside Tehran into the city to finally start our assault. The intel people had found folks who fit the bill and were willing to take the risks with us.

"They look wound tighter than a pocket watch," Will said. They clutched at the nylon straps of their jump seats, wide-eyed as though they'd never been on an aircraft. At least, not a military plane. Certainly not one flying into combat. The smell of burning aviation fuel could make anyone not used to it nauseated and uncomfortable, and until we got in the air, the smell wouldn't leave. Some of them looked like they were going to puke, and we hadn't yet even started to taxi. Most of us slept or feigned the same.

Will chuckled at their discomfort. "Not the first-class luxury flight the agency boys lured them with, I bet. Plus, all the stewardesses have facial hair and carry pistols."

"Yet, here they are" I said. "Will, you know the saying about being scared yet doing the job anyway? Getting tortured in an Iranian prison for being a spy would be enough to keep anyone home on the couch. Good on 'em for stepping up."

"Agreed. Who are those two rounding out our rodeo troop?" Will indicated who he was singling out with a subtle sideways glance. He had the knowledge of the person he ghosted but still didn't know any more than his host. As an element leader, I'd only gotten the brief just before we loaded up the 130s for our flight into Iran and our first stop, Desert One.

"Expat Iranian generals. The agency wants them along."

"What for, and why are they armed?" The two were sweaty and fidgety, wearing plain green fatigues with pistol belts pinching their muffin top waists. "They're more scared than the truck drivers."

"Someone thinks they might be of help. I'm going to ignore them unless they give me a reason not to."

Will frowned. "Meaning?"

"Meaning the boss has told us that we should deal with them accordingly. If they go off the reservation and present a block to mission accomplishment, they get put down. End of story."

My friend shook his head. "This really is a thrown-together mess, isn't it? Marine pilots flying Navy minesweeper helos. Air Force. Army. Civilians. Surprised someone didn't fight to get the Coast Guard in on this too. You know what they say about too many cooks? Think our backdoor conspiracy did the trick? If ever there were a time for an unsung hero to save the day, this is it."

"Let's hope our Navy warrant officer is that man." I imagined our savior dressed in khakis, giant coffee mug in hand, round gut and Navy regulation beard, cursing and cajoling swabbies in grease-stained uniforms as they slaved over the RH-53s, deep in the bowels of an aircraft carrier. "Because if we have to start back at day one again, I won't have a better plan."

"Here's hoping we only have to do this one once then."

※　※　※

From out of the 130s, we watched the ground controllers direct all eight helos into position. Eight. All here, all running. Blades still spinning, we rolled the fuel bladders out of the 130s and helped the aircrews hot-fuel our "shitters"—black smoke pouring out of the engines just like their nickname suggested. Helicopters were unnatural to my way of thinking. Was there anything in nature that flew by whipping its appendages above it? The tilt-rotor craft from my time were decades old, but wings at least meant that if there was an engine failure, we could glide like a bird instead of drop like a bag of wet cement. Helos had been good enough for Gramps. I guess they were good enough for me.

I felt hope for the first time in a long time. Loaded on the helos and flying a lurching course just above the ground to our hide site, even the downtimers in the element sensed something significant had happened. I sent a silent prayer into the universe, thanking whatever power was out there for the blessing of Navy chiefs and warrant officers. Maybe this was all the proof I needed that there was a god after all.

Siyanda, a Zulu warrior who had adapted well to training, nudged Karl next to him. "This means history has been changed?"

Karl frowned. "Perhaps. There is still much that can go wrong. But it seems our destiny is in our hands."

Magnus beamed. "Mars has a cruel sense of humor, but there's no denying we've blazed a new trail. The pillars of Valhalla tremble in anticipation of what we do next!"

"Good old Magnus," Will said to just me through the side of his mouth. "Ever the optimist."

"Cousin"—I'd taken to Will's vernacular—"I've been nuked, gassed, infected with a bioweapon, skewered, gutted like a fish, blown up, shot enough times to qualify for a government subsidy as a lead mine, and even I feel there's a chance this may work out."

Across from us, Jess gave a thumbs-up. Over the song of the rotor whine, she'd heard me.

Stokes just grinned. "It's time to settle an old score. I want payback. If I got brought here just for this, then getting killed is the best thing to ever happen to me." Jess beside him made a quizzical frown. Stokes quickly retracted. "Sorry. Second best thing."

Jess smiled. I saw her real self. Had anyone but us been able to judge the exchange, one grizzled operator just made a kissy face at another. "Just kidding." She winked. "I'm with you. This could be the righting of the greatest wrong in history. It's time to balance the books."

I'll try and explain what I was feeling while I was flying through the darkness and into the undiscovered country that was this unexplored future. This mission was the most debated "what if" of the last part of twentieth century history. So much so that it still hung over everything we did through my gramps's, my dad's, and even my time. Had this mission succeeded, there were arguments that the Middle East would've looked different for decades. That maybe even the Long wouldn't have happened. Some of the arguments were compelling. Some held that it would've only escalated things. It was a common topic of conversation at our dinner table growing up. Who knew?

If you could've stopped the assassination of JFK, would it have meant a different outcome for the Vietnam conflict? What if you could've assassinated Hitler? Stalin? How about Mao? Would that have set the stage to keep us from eventually having the Divine Leader of the Lotus Hegemony? It was too much to take in. Time travel was the stuff of fantasy. Trite, hackneyed, pointless. Yet here we were. And it mattered to me because this was the fulfillment of a fantasy that every American fighting man had entertained for generations. What if the Iran hostage rescue had succeeded?

The odds had shifted that I was going to find out.

The following evening as the sun lowered behind the tops of the wadi we sheltered in, all elements crammed into the backs of the semis—hidden behind false walls and cargo boxes in case our caravan were stopped and searched. If an overly-zealous cop or revolutionary guard got past our obsequious driver and the bribes he'd offer, then they had better have a close relationship with their maker because they'd meet him on the spot. Nothing was going to stop the assault. Certainly not some keystone cop looking for a little baksheesh or to make off with a new TV or whatever he thought was in one of the trucks.

The boss had taken a live reconnaissance of the embassy and briefed us as we loaded up at the warehouse to rescue our suffering fellow Americans. After this much time ghosting their hosts, there wasn't a one of the platoon who didn't feel every bit as American as I did.

"You boys don't screw up now, you hear?" I'd never wanted the approval of anyone more in my life.

"No, sir. America's depending on us." The boss's nod sent us rolling ahead. We slowed until the headlights of the semis showed they'd all made it out of the canyon and onto the road, and we sped off. The sun was down and the dim lights on the horizon called us. Somewhere in their midst, Americans were under the gun of fanatics. It was time for the reckoning.

Relatively speaking, me and my close core were riding in style, interspersed in a pair of beat-up Volvo sedans. Stokes drove with our civilian guide next to him to direct us into the city, Magnus and me in the back seats. Behind us in the other sedan, Will, Jakob, Karl, and Jess kept pace. We had a special task to accomplish before scaling the compound walls, and I considered it yet further proof that my previous agnosticism was in error. It had to be divine intervention that gave me such a place of honor. I knew the cruel Mars didn't favor us, so it could only mean there was a benevolent supernatural force in the universe.

The city had light traffic. On the dark streets, pedestrians averted their eyes as we passed, trying to avoid the attention of roving patrols of morality police looking for religious infractions or "western spies." Brutish thugs hoping to find an unescorted woman who had not yet learned her place. With luck, perhaps one with her head uncovered, who could be beaten on the spot for her immodesty. The oppressiveness of the capital and the pall of fanaticism blanketed everything.

"Looks even bigger in person," Stokes mumbled at the first sight of the huge compound and its massive walls. "The state department spares no expense. We need more men."

The US Embassy in Tehran was as big as an amusement park. We could've found it without our guide. I checked the route as we went, not entirely trusting of our navigator, but finding no fault in his course. Massive brick walls enclosed twenty-seven acres of sovereign US territory now located in the heart of the Islamic revolution. Within its perimeter—woods, motor pool, consular buildings and offices, the residences of the ambassador and other high-level diplomats—it was a virtual city within a city.

Just like the boss said, the militants had become complacent after possessing the symbol of the evil West, unchallenged by the most powerful nation on the planet now for nearly six months. Where was the great Satan now?

They were about to find out.

We slowed to make the turn, and I leaned around Stokes for a better view down to the main entrance. It was barricaded of course, and roving militants stood in the street. I eyed the parapets. No one was on the walls. Turning onto Roosevelt Avenue, we were waved past by a lazy checkpoint of slovenly, bearded youths, rifles strapped to their backs like afterthoughts.

"Watch it, Stokes," I said, forcing myself to lean back in my seat, cool and collected. "Speed up a little. We want Jess to hit that checkpoint just as we reach ours." She was a little behind us, leaving a gap so as to time our simultaneous arrivals at the two guard stations. I felt the sedan accelerate slightly in perfect response and rolled my window down. The night air was crisp. Magnus next to me did the same. For the hundredth time I checked the tightness of the suppressor on the end of the .22 pistol held between my knees. Stokes slowed as we came to the end of the block. Just as he nosed toward the next checkpoint at the corner of the long wall, I leaned out.

"Hello, brother," I said in my best Farsi. The three guards looked in our direction. As the headlights illuminated their faces, I shot the closest between the eyes. I shot the next from inside the car. Magnus was already out of the vehicle, firing a single, well-aimed round at a time. *Click. Click. Click.* I was out the door and joined him on the street. Stokes pulled ahead on the sidewalk, popped the trunk, and grabbed our rifles. He put them in our hands just as we finished dragging the bodies out of the street.

"They got theirs too," Magnus said, pointing down the long wall to where the other sedan sat, Jess and our partners silently cleaning up the mess they'd made, mere shadows slithering through the murk of darkness. The first of the semis turned down the street, lights extinguished. Jess waved them through.

"Keep eyes out," I said unnecessarily as we waited for our blocking force to relieve us. In a flash, two pairs of assaulters trotted up, each carrying HK-21s. The sound of bipods snapping into place was followed by the rustle of bodies falling prone next to our parked sedan.

The Blue element leader took a quick look at the stack of bodies. "Secure?" he asked in a word.

"Never knew what hit 'em," Magnus answered. He was taking on a very midwestern drawl after his time around Will and me.

"Take off, Red. We got it."

Our guide stood frozen, back to the wall, trying to press himself into it. I slapped him on the shoulder. "You know where to go. Thank you."

In easy view was the stadium where the helicopters would land to retrieve us. The Air Force ground controllers were already trotting off to secure the field within for our landing zone. The truck drivers and other enablers were going with them to wait in the stadium until the helos landed and shuttled us to our departure airfield.

Soon, Rangers would be seizing the Manzariyeh airfield, the destination for our helos once we abandoned the embassy. C-141s would land, waiting to accept the 53 hostages, all our enablers on the ground, and finally, ourselves. We would fly to Germany while combat air patrols from the Nimitz provided cover. Our hostages would be free, and the world would know that America would never back down to terrorism. Never.

But that would be a long time from right now. There was work to be done.

"God protect you," our guide said, and was off, pushing the elastic orange band up around his sleeve to identify him as a friendly. He'd gotten us here without a hitch. If he wasn't a US citizen yet, I hope he got pushed to the head of the line for his spot. He'd earned it

Ladders were going up against the wall, silently contacting the stone, the duct-taped padding absorbing their noise. Other than our team's suppressed shots, there'd been no shooting yet, and no noise above the sounds of our vehicles to give us away. On the other side of the wall, the hostage takers still had no idea we were here. Our luck couldn't hold out too much longer. It was time to move.

"We're up, Red leader," Will told me. He'd been getting a head count while I'd made a quick report to the boss and gotten the go ahead. Blue element owned the streets, and Red and White were here, ready to move.

Jakob was already scaling one ladder. The rest were full of dark, climbing bodies, laden with weapons and explosives. I nudged in and sprinted to the top, then slipped over to another ladder and made my way down faster than a squirrel on a greased pole.

We had the farthest to travel in the compound, to its very edge where the staff cottages and many office buildings and consulate waited. White element was dividing to take the large residences of the ambassador and deputy chief of mission. Wordlessly, we trotted ahead, ready to start the precise violence we'd waited so long to deliver.

Spread across the line of our last concealment, a line of decorative trees edging the road from the motor pool, my teams divided, ready to assault. The signal would be the explosion that would punch a grand exit in the wall we'd just scaled. In the stadium across Roosevelt Avenue, the combat air controllers would call the waiting helicopters to start their approach. Overhead, the AC-130 gunships would be circling, ready to vaporize anyone or anything moving to our location to interfere. Karl nudged next to me, ripping the tape off his shoulder to reveal the American flag beneath.

"Any second n—" Karl's "now" drowned in the explosion.

I yelled the sweetest word in the human language.

"Assault."

20

Will led half the element, and I the other half as we each raced to our respective groups of buildings. Harried shouts in foreign tongue were extinguished by another more perfect language, the *whump whump* of suppressed shots from an MP-5. Karl peeled off with his team as Hikaru led his to the next building, and mine with me to the last. On the steps lay a body with a neat hole in the forehead, the door at the top of the short rise ajar. I followed my men through.

Was I nervous? Did I feel excited, or anxious? I've gotten those questions from younger warriors. My answer's always the same. The waiting's the hardest. Once the action starts, I'm just a worker; a guy doing a job. Can you imagine someone who repaired computers getting all sweaty and nervous every time he popped the cover off a hard drive? Or the guy who makes shakes at the fast-food restaurant—do you think his hands tremble like a surgical intern holding the knife for the first time?

Running into a building where someone's waiting to kill me is always just another day at the office. That's what I tell them, confident that they'll soon be like me. Either that, or they'll be gone.

Like water from a fractured dam, our rush and flow were an unstoppable force. Doors were breached. Flashbangs deployed. Shots fired in succinct cadences. "We're Americans, here to rescue you."

Shouts and shots echoed from in front of me. It was only fair that someone else got to do some killing, but I held out hope. So often when you start near the end of the stack, you end up taking the brass ring by the time you get to the end of the ride. Those in front of you peel off along the way to take every door and the space behind them. Hostage takers instinctively keep their prizes deep in their lairs, like dragons on treasure hordes. The last room was a large series of adjoining office spaces, and where we had good information that the largest group of hostages were held.

Sometimes, intel is correct.

I found myself on one side of a door. A shotgun blasted the wood above the striker, and the assaulter faded back as someone else's hand tossed a flashbang. I was first through, the leading edge of the avalanche. Thinking is the enemy of acting. Conscious thought slows performance. If I'd ever suffered from such a malady, it had long been cured. I moved and my light settled on a bearded form with gun in hand. The front sight on his chest magically stayed in place as I worked the trigger and followed the collapsing mass to the ground, locked on to him by an invisible tractor beam.

"We're Americans, here to rescue you. Stay down. Stay down."

I pushed down the wall, ignoring the screams of someone on the ground—striking me as neither feminine nor masculine—simply the human sound of terror that couldn't be contained. Movement! Shape! Outline! Color! My mind recognized what was happening, and I acted. The thin woman held by her throat, the wild-eyed man using her as a shield, the pistol in his hand. It was not just my weapon that barked. My first shot snapped his head back, and the woman was free from his grasp. She sank in an instant as more shots joined from around me faster than thought, faster than my brain could capture the images in my mind.

"We're Americans, here to rescue you. You're going home."

"Bolt cutter," one of the men called. Some of the hostages were shackled, deep gouges in their ankles attesting to the duration of their bondage.

"Get them together, and let's get moving," I said to Yuri, the gruff Russian who'd died at Stalingrad. He'd killed more Germans than lung cancer. "Get me a count. I'm heading out to check on the others."

I passed out of the building, reversing how we'd come in. Outside, the rest of the element was assembled in protective formations, dazed-looking men and women surrounded by my troops inside the stockade of a human fortress. One of the men reached out to touch the shoulder of an assaulter, the American flag the object of his reach.

"Thank God. Thank God," he said over and over.

The buzz of a chainsaw came from overhead, and the orange light of tracers ripped in a line that danced somewhere the other side of the wall. The gunships were raining hell on something just outside the compound. We had genuine angels on our shoulders looking out for us, and I had no worry.

"Twelve hostages, uninjured," I said. Hikaru and Karl gave me an additional five, all uninjured as well. Will had sent a man to find me. Between the consulate and the staff cottages, another five hostages were recovered. One was too weak and injured to walk and was being carried on a litter. For the first time, I got on my radio and called in.

"Red leader reporting twenty-two Hotels safely recovered. Fourteen Tangos down. No injuries to shooters or Hotels."

"Copy Red leader," came the reply. "Tax day. Festival, festival, festival, how copy?"

Tax day meant we had all the hostages accounted for. Festival was the signal we could move to the exfiltration sight. White element must have done just as well, and the Berlin boys had recovered the three Americans at the other site.

"Copy. Moving. Out." I was buzzed, but we weren't out of the heat yet. I spoke loud enough for the hostages to hear me, saying words I'd practiced in my mind a million times, never daring to hope I'd be saying them for real. "We have all of your fellow Americans. No one is left behind. Help anyone who needs help to walk, tell the person next to you. My men have to keep you safe as we move. Ready?"

A voice answered. "Are you kidding? Let's go home!"

"Karl, lead off. Move us out."

Up the wooded boulevard and back to the ambassador's residence, I knew this was a long way from over. We'd heard the explosions within the compound earlier and soothed the hostages—I mean, the rescued—as we waited to move out, explaining it wasn't sounds of combat ahead.

"Not to worry," Magnus said in more of his mixed Viking-American. "The sounds of Thor's hammer are just good men using explosives to fell trees—in case we have to land the helicopters in the compound. Either way, y'all will be flying out of here on the wings of the Valkyries."

Hikaru's cringe at Magnus's verbal tragedy caught my eye. To the samurai who spoke always with clipped efficiency, Magnus's attempt to ease the hostages was painful to the ear. What would our rescued tell the world? That they'd been saved by hillbilly Norsemen? It was one of those sweet moments that I lived for. The stuff that would fuel laughter and comradeship when someday we sat around a fire, reliving the events of this night of nights.

Outside, the machine gun teams played the call and answer of a church choir, a burst from one HK-21 north of the compound answered by a short burst from outside the southern wall. The lack of other shooting had already answered my internal query; they were discouraging the curious or foolhardy from investigating with measured doses of .308. There hadn't been another rain of steel from the gunships, though I knew they were overhead watching us all with lightning held behind their back more deadly than that of Magnus's gods.

The hole in the wall was as beautiful as the pictures I'd seen of the Parisian Arc de Triomphe. What it perhaps lacked in artistic detail, it made up for in its precise, miraculous, and instantaneous creation. The breachers who created the parting of the Red Sea were there, beckoning and guiding the rescued through.

"You're almost there. We've got you." While passing through the gaping hole, brick and stone cleared from the path with care by the breach team in anticipation of just this moment, one of the rescued burst into tears as she stepped into the street, the prison of her captivity behind. I heard the man next to her.

"We get back, I think we'll stay in Virginia for a while. What do you think, honey?" It was the stuff of American lore. Kindness. Strength. Dignity. Wrapped in humor. It was another moment to store in my memory and share later. The same man again spoke words of comfort. "Listen, it's our taxi, come to take us home." He was right. The beat of the helicopter rotors was just ahead.

We stayed a moving wall, our bodies their shields, the stadium just ahead. I was prepared to peel off men to assist or even carry our rescued. We knew many had been treated harshly. Some were bound or chained for weeks at a time, not allowed to stand or walk. I knew the marks of brutality well, and the rescued had them. Gaunt, withered, bruised, and bent, yet as they marched with us their spirits glowed from within, and I swear to you I saw pearlescent halos of an aura radiate from them. I've survived death. I've seen incredible things. This was one of them. They moved with a heavenly light, and it spread around us all.

Through the gates the noise of the turning blades was deafening. I had to shout to the control officers to be heard as I reported. We pushed the rescued one at a time through the corridor of bodies of the waiting medics and aircrew for the headcount. Names were given and compared to a list, then the rescued were escorted with haste up the ramps and onto the birds. It was at this point my heart pounded the hardest and I suppressed a shiver. We were close to the end. It was the way of the universe that this was when the masts broke and sails ripped and sagged, that hopes were dashed on rocky shores.

But not today.

Two helicopters rose, the hum of them dying the other side of the tall stadium shell to be replaced by the roar of fighters somewhere high above. The jets of the combat air patrols of F-4 and A-6 aircraft pierced the heavens, and I felt some of the warmth return to my body.

It all happened quickly from there. More sorties of helos landed two at a time, the next for our brave enablers, relieved but visibly proud, and load by load the last of us. I was on the final bird. We'd intermixed the elements, filling the birds hastily. I found myself sitting next to one of the older members of the unit, a man I knew had served in three wars. I'd read about him as a kid.

Will was on the other side of me, and I nudged him and whispered, "See who's next to me. It's Pappy."

I'd told Will about him. There were a lot of legends in this crew of operators, and he was one of the most legendary. When it was just our element we'd spoken very freely. Among the other members of the unit, we of course concealed our true selves and our knowledge. We had to be careful. I was about to say something to the man when he spoke to me.

"Look out the port, sir. It's happening."

I turned in my seat and strained to see through the tiny plexiglass window behind me. The contingency plan to follow our successful rescue was underway. I'd completely forgotten. It seemed so unlikely and surreal a possibility that what I saw hit me harder than a right cross from Gabriel or Michael.

We banked and for a brief moment, I was shown the image that even now if I close my eyes, I can see in perfect detail. The embassy was in flames. The tongues of the circling dragons rained fire from above. The gunship's Vulcans and 105s razed the grounds and the buildings within the walled compound, hell unleashed on earth. There would be no trophy or monument for our crazed adversaries, or the twisted demagogues, or the gangs of ignorant thugs to celebrate over. My mouth fell open and my eyes felt wet. We. Had. Won.

We banked violently in the other direction, and I turned around again in my seat. There was nothing more to see. Will wiped his eyes. He felt it too. It was a feeling unlike any I'd ever had after combat. Sure, there was always the relief, the letdown of the adrenaline, and the joy of being alive. This was different. We'd rescued innocent people. Innocent Americans. Righted a wrong that Mars himself surely felt couldn't be accomplished.

The world really was black and white sometimes, and every effort to make it into shades of gray was just a grubby attempt to ruin clean water by adding dirty water. I'm not naïve. Of course, some things were too complex to break down into two camps. But sometimes, it was good versus evil. Right versus wrong. This time, I knew with every fiber of my being, we were the good.

Gratitude filled my heart and I said a silent prayer of thanks for being here. For all I'd suffered, for all I'd been through, I was truly grateful.

I felt more than heard the clipped grunt of laughter next to me. I snapped out of my reverie to see Pappy, the legend, laughing to himself. Everyone processed things differently, even hardened warriors. Was it my misjudgment, or was the laugh…irreverent?

He saw me looking at him, sensed my curiosity, and leaned closer. "Mars on his throne is pleased today, I'm sure."

I felt myself go pale. "Say what?"

"Nothing." He retreated.

"Go on, Pappy," Will coaxed. "What was that about Mars?"

The sinewy older man shrugged and muttered. "War. I've seen plenty of it. I jumped into Normandy. I was still in my twenties when Korea happened, and I jumped into the battle of Won-Ju. Three tours in RVN. This is my last. I'm proud of them all. Most proud of this. We did good. But I'm done."

He paused and got that far off look. "It makes even less sense to me now than when I signed up, thirty-seven years ago. It's all a game. We're just dancers twirling for the amusement of the gods."

The stunned look on Will's face told me he sensed the truth of it too. With astonishment in his eyes, he leaned close. "Is he right, Rag? Are we just performers? Bit players, killing ourselves for bigger parts in a Broadway show. All for an audience of one?"

I sighed. "Mars."

That by itself wasn't what pushed me, what made me want to force a confrontation with our tormentor. Our general. Our god. Small g.

21

We found ourselves back through the gate. Will and I were both subdued after our sudden epiphany, spurred to consciousness by the wisdom of an old warrior. But it was hard to stay that way, the bubbling excitement spilling out of the platoon like champagne, reinvigorating our sense of righteous victory. Even Hikaru, the most stoic of us, beamed. If right now we were sent back to 1776, every one of these soldiers would pick up a long rifle and march to the Battle Hymn of the Republic. They knew what it was to be an American. So, it was hard to give too much more thought to our circumstances. For the time being, there was only a well-deserved break. Tomorrow would wait for tomorrow.

I'd told everyone to take the day off until I heard differently. Gabriel had no objection and confirmed that we were alone. The other platoons were on their own trips to the plain. I didn't know if there was cause for concern—or even pity—on behalf of my fellow eternal soldiers in the other platoons, but I gave it no more thought. I'd become callous after so much time in combat. We won our battle. Let them win theirs. If getting back to Valhalla first meant we got some downtime, it just proved once again—it pays to be a winner.

It was then that the next seed sprouted from the soil of my simmering discontent.

"Rag, can I talk to you?" Stokes stood in our doorway. I hadn't slept late but was lying in my bunk, planning our next evolutions of training and yearning for the chance to finally put on the hardshell hanging in the armory. The armor that meant that I was finally an Ultimate.

Stokes looked frazzled. Shaken, even.

"What's up, Danny boy?" I said, sitting up.

Will was already awake. "Want me to walk, Stokes?"

"No, Will. I think I need both of you to hear me out."

I offered him a spot on my bunk, and the three of us huddled. I didn't want to rush my friend. Whatever was troubling him, he'd tell us soon enough. But when nothing came out, I started to pull off the bandage for him.

"You did a terrific job on the rescue, Dan. Better than the downtimers themselves could've done." I wasn't sure what he was conflicted about but thought maybe it had been the mission. Or the challenge of becoming an Ultimate. I thought it was time for a pep talk. "You've become awesome. Can't you feel it? We're stronger, faster, smarter, better trained than any warriors we've ever imagined. And what we just did—I'm still floating when I think about it. I'm glad we're in Valhalla." I hoped that would be the push to get him to talk.

Stokes nodded while he stared at the ground. "How did we celebrate?" he asked meekly.

"What do you mean?" Will said, confused by Stokes's direction. I was as well.

Stokes scowled at us both. "You know. Celebrate. Did we hoist beers around a fire? Grill steaks? Get loud and fight? How did we celebrate the biggest night of our lives?"

I frowned. "Not sure what you mean, Dan. We—"

"We went to bed," Will answered for me. He said it with a kind of realized puzzlement. "We turned in."

Stokes nodded. "Does that seem right to you—for a bunch of soldiers?"

I frowned. "It's what I felt like doing, I guess. I'm always ready to get the diadem on and get some more training. Aren't you?"

Stokes scrunched his face. "Yes. Yes, I am. Doesn't that strike you as odd?"

I thought about it. Now that he said it, it did seem odd. Something stirred in me as I tried to remember the last time I did something like what Dan described. A lyric or poem half-remembered came to my lips. "Saturn dreams of Mercury," I said dreamily, not sure what I meant.

Stokes gave a singular nod. "Yes, Rag, that's it."

"What's it?" Will said, still confused. "I don't get it."

"Just that. Rag used to be the most curious person I'd ever known. He was always in his specs, reading, or even had a real book with pages in his hand. He played games and worked puzzles all the time. He was always sharpening his knife. Don't you remember that about yourself, Rag? And always talking about what your gramps taught you. We used to make fun of you, but we all respected that about you. Admired you for it. Where's that gone, Rag? The thing that made you, *you*?"

Now I knew what he meant. It was like a part of myself, remembered, not lived. I shivered. "I'm different."

Dan's face held something I'd never seen in him before. I swear it was fear. "Yes, Rag. You're different. And so am I."

What wasn't he saying to us?

"What happened, Dan?"

"Jess. She and I." He let the words hang. "You know we love each other. That we were going to get married and leave the army together someday. You know we were always professionals. That our romantic life was…disciplined."

Stokes and Jess never took their romance lightly. Except for the occasional verbal playfulness that only two lovers could show in public, they let it be known early that they would never act on their feelings while in uniform. And they lived it. They took leave together—on the few occasions when we could—and we always assumed that's when they had a "real" romance with each other. They were the picture of discipline and always soldiers first, lovers a distant second.

"You said it, Will," I reminded him. "About Jess being attractive but feeling nothing about her in those terms, like a man."

Will scrunched his face, replaying the incident, and turned to Dan. "You mean…"

Dan nodded. "Last night. We thought we would be close. Only—it's like it couldn't happen. Like that part of ourselves was—dead. Corpses, acting like a man and a woman."

Now I knew what Dan said was true. I'd felt myself change. I was harsh. Calculating. Detached. More like a robot. I was no longer a man, let alone more than one. Not a super being. Instead, Dan made me realize that I was less than I had been. We all were.

"Rag, I still don't know what this place is or why we're here. But this isn't some kind of resurrection. It's more like hell. We're being punished. We may look like our old selves, remember our old selves, but we're not. And the longer we're here, the less of our selves remain in us. We're like the ghosts inside the people we are when we're on the Plains of Eternity. But not just there. We're ghosts here too. Just fuzzy memories stuffed in a body."

※　※　※

"Ragnar Beck, you have an audience with Mars. At once." Gabriel didn't depart after issuing his edict. Always the authoritarian, he ignited the rage I'd been holding. He waited for my reply, the most pregnant of pauses in the history of such; I made him wait.

We'd been back for a couple of days—alone the entire time—returned from the plains to find the other platoons were still deployed. How long had we been gone, really? Subjectively, our platoon spent weeks together in 1980. How long was that in Valhalla time? Some trips to the plain I'd returned to find time had passed symmetrically, day for day. Some challenges, weeks on the plains translated into a single day in Valhalla. There were no answers from our overlords. Only our disregarded questions and Gabriel's disdain to make it always clear we were inferiors here.

I'd been told more than once that "Understanding isn't necessary to your purpose as a soldier. Rise to the challenge or fall. That is all."

The training, the challenges, the satisfaction of knowing I was on my way to becoming an Ultimate, that I'd been chosen to lead—all of it fueled my ego. And I knew it. I was becoming a soldier greater than any who'd ever walked the earth. On my way to being a kind of demigod myself, if I'm honest. Hard to not to think in those terms given where we were and what we were doing. But I'd let the human, curious, skeptical part of me wither. I'd become what they wanted me to be: a soldier blindly following orders.

Until after our return from Iran and Stokes snapped me out of it.

I was meeting with Will and the squad leaders when Gabriel interrupted. Our platoon had trained for weeks in the intense rush that was urban close quarters combat as members of one of the finest units that ever existed and achieved the pinnacle of success. As far as I was concerned, Magnus's prediction was right. We'd rocked the pillars of Valhalla. I was convinced that we were now the deadliest force in the universe.

My plan was to jump right back into hard, realistic training. But now, we would leave behind the ancient slug throwers and incorporate our newest arsenal of death-dealing weapons. The Annihilator Mark Three was going to feel very good in my hands again. What foe could be out there waiting that we couldn't overwhelm and crush at will?

Gabriel's sudden heavy-handed intrusion irritated me. I'd become a little less cowed at the presence of our supernatural overseers. Stokes gave me ample reason for my contempt. Plus, I was tired of being treated like a trained pony—trotted out to prance on order, to perform on command without so much as a sweet sack of grain my reward. But Gabriel's interruption ended up being as timely as the dinner bell ringing at the first growl of your stomach.

I'd waited just long enough to let Gabriel know I wasn't his slave. "Thank you, Gabriel," I finally said over my shoulder to him. "Mars beat me to it. A parlay with our master is exactly what I had in mind. I'll leave just as soon as I've finished briefing my NCOs on today's training plan. I know the way, thank you."

I made a dismissive nod and tarried just long enough to gauge Gabriel's reaction. I knew I was being disrespectful. I didn't care. He raised an eyebrow but said nothing before departing.

Will drew air between his teeth. "Watch it, Rag. I know you're steamed, but don't forget—Gabe and Michael can crush us at will. Plus, Mars is a god. Let's not test them. Don't go in there with a gut full of burning coals thinking you're going to pin his ears back."

Karl's usual detached aloofness changed to uncharacteristic concern. "We all prefer you remain with us on this plane of existence and not become...dead. Be the neutral tactician, not the rage-filled berserker." He cast a sideways look at Magnus. "Perhaps it is best to say nothing at all to the god."

"I thought you didn't believe in gods, Karl?" I said.

"You know I do not worship Mars!" he spat back. "But by any other name, he is a god. If he is not omnipotent here, it is not apparent to me. And a god demands subservience. At least continue to fake it, Ragnar. Swallow your resentment. For the good of all. We need you to lead us."

Karl's unusual outpouring struck me. "Thank you, Karl." I felt some of the heat go out of me.

Magnus was grim. "Karl speaks wisdom. Let this slight against us go unanswered, Ragnar. It is our lot to follow their will. Isn't that clear?"

I was cooler, but I disagreed. "If we're fighting for something, it's high time we know what it is. There are some questions that need to be answered. And now."

Jakob seemed to be the only one on my side. "If there are answers, I would like them. We have been patient enough. There is but one God, and I feel the Holy Spirit within me, even now. My faith is unshaken. Whatever trickery this is, it is time we know what it means for our eternal souls."

Hikaru stepped forward. "We have debated all this before. It is unhelpful. Instead, I will stand at your side. You should not go alone."

I smiled. "Thanks, Hikaru, but no. If I do get zapped to a cinder for some kind of blasphemy, best it happens to me alone. But I'll play it smart." I winked at Will. "Not to worry."

Will shook his head. "Promise us if you find yourself in a deep hole with Mars that you'll stop digging, okay? Karl's right, we need you."

Most, but not all, of the boiling lava warming my forehead had settled, and I no longer saw in red. "Thanks. I'll play it cool. See you all soon."

I made my way out the gate and found a glowing conveyance parked outside. The sky was its usual pale purple, the distant towers and their golden spikes no longer a subject of my curiosity. They could be the facades of a Hollywood set for all I knew or cared.

As I flew, I thought about our latest adventure on the plains. If it was to be my last fight before a god cast me into oblivion, I couldn't have asked for a better one. Maybe this was how Michelangelo felt after he polished the last chisel mark off the surface of the David. If there were such a thing as perfection, we'd just achieved it. I need to tell you about it because as you know, in my mind, it happened. As real as anything I'd ever known to be true.

My magic carpet made its descent to Mars's palace. Reliving our triumph on the way filled me once again with the feeling of invulnerability. If I wasn't bulletproof, I was at least bullet resistant. Winning had a way of making you forget the dangers, the risks, and the painful defeats. Maybe if I had servant to hold laurels over my head while whispering in my ear that all glory was fleeting, it would've helped. I'd promised the men I'd play it cool. Now, I felt the bile rise again and I doubted it would be a promise kept.

22

"He suspects the truth, Mars."

The god of war knew that Michael was right. He kicked himself for not seeing how this could have happened. Having a woman in their midst was the lynchpin to unlocking the realization that they were not the resurrections of themselves they'd been led to believe. Mars's entertainment at the variety of new developments Beck had brought to Aricia had clouded his vision.

"He does at that, Michael. He's closer to the truth than anyone's been at his stage before."

"What shall be done about it, Mars?"

"That's going to be up to him. If he falls in line, we proceed. If he doesn't, I have to release him before he poisons the others."

"If he does, the company will be wasted. Others may choose to take refuge beyond."

It was within Mars's power to return Beck to the void now and avoid the confrontation all together. "That's a strong possibility, Michael. Let him come. If I can salvage this, we'll be better off."

What if Beck knew Mars couldn't keep him and the others here for eternity?

※　※　※

I marched up the stairs. The fire was back in my chest, as hot and bright as the braziers that burned in columns leading to where Mars sat alone on his throne. Posed like a painting with spear planted next to him, pelt draped across his shoulders, his eyes were fixed on me as I marched forward. *Be cool, be cool*, I chanted in my head. At the appropriate distance, I took a knee and bowed my head in my best act of obeisance.

"Lieutenant Beck reports to mighty Mars as ordered." I kept my eyes on the deck.

"Rise."

I did so and remained at attention. Mars eyed me for an uncomfortable few seconds before he spoke. "That was a pleasure to witness. Job well done, *Captain*."

Captain! Did I just receive a promotion?

"Others have attempted the same and failed," Mars continued. "That sad little bit of history deserved a proper resolution. No one has done that mission the justice it deserved. I was greatly pleased."

I remained frozen, unsure what to say. In such moments, I knew it was best to say nothing until prompted.

"Stand easy, Beck."

I snapped to parade rest.

"The rest of your company are having a more challenging time. What I saw out there on the plains leads me to give you the nod to step up and take the company. What do you say, Captain?"

Where was the indignation I'd felt on my march up the stairs? Where was the searing desire to confront Mars with our list of grievances? The revulsion at our realization that we were no longer fully human? He'd drowned the coals of my fire with flattery and reward. And it worked. My chest swelled with pride from his praise. I really was a robot. I'd been programmed to respond to his approval in just this manner. Not just by Mars, but by a lifetime of soldiering. If anything, my betrayal of my principles made me feel a little more human again.

"Thank you, O great Mars. I will lead in your name." I felt a little queasy as I said it, but part of me meant every word.

"You are nearly at the end of your training, Beck. Perrault will get you up to speed on the last of the qualifications, then it's all on you, company commander. Questions?"

As busy as my mind was right then, my mouth refused to move. There were too many things whirling inside my skull to find one to put into words.

"Come now, Beck. I've watched you in action. I know you're a thinker. Knock off this stolid stuff and get the stick out of your ass. Your general is ordering you to speak. Now act like a man about to take command and ask me questions. Relax. That's an order."

A switch inside me flipped. "Yes, sir." My tongue loosened like a rusted lock that had been sprayed with oil. "Our hostage rescue mission. You said others had tried the scenario on the plain. Some of us are up-timers, so it was history to us. Did—"

"So were those who'd tried before you, son. This isn't my first rodeo wrangling young cowboys into shape, and I know what you're wondering about. The scenarios I choose for you on the plains are tailored to test and reinforce different things for different soldiers. For this last, only a real war scholar could've affected the outcome. Your team's solution was adequate. It depended on some assumptions, but it paid off. Once you got on mission, the actual combat was very one-sided. Not the worst fighting you've been in by far. Still, it was very entertaining."

Entertaining. Was that it? Were we really here just to entertain the god of war, like Pappy mused about after the mission? Something kicked off inside me, and finally the flame I'd felt earlier return.

"Is that our purpose here? To amuse you?" I'd said it as an accusation, a dog growling at the call of his master.

Mars's storm hit me like a gale force wind.

"You forget yourself, Captain!"

What ease I'd felt before making the accusation, what fury there'd been, was gone. I snapped back to attention.

"Americans," Mars mumbled in a fuming way. "I give an invitation to speak, and you use the opportunity to mock me. Of all races and creeds, it's always Americans. Sparta produced less arrogant fools. Still, there's a reason I keep doing it." He snapped his fingers, and I once again felt the constraint relax.

"Sir, with all due respect, we've been told very little about our purpose. We all get the sense we're to partake in some great battle. It would help—"

Mars held up a hand. "Isn't it enough that you're warriors tasked with perfecting yourselves? Stand at attention."

I braced again. The fleeting sense of freedom and inquisitiveness that I'd had was snatched away once again.

Mars frowned. "If only I had more soldiers to draw upon so I could ignore Americans. So short a span of time your tribe occupies humanity's plane. If your time weren't such a fertile harvest for warriors, my task would be easier." I heard his lament yet couldn't say a thing in our defense.

"Steel yourself to the task." Then he recited.

"To every man upon this earth
Death cometh soon or late.
And how can man die better,
Than facing fearful odds,
For the ashes of his fathers,
And the temples of his gods."

I knew the quote but couldn't place the poet.

He continued his lecture. "Humans at times come close to understanding their place in the universe. You're being given the chance by my divine power to become the ultimate warrior. For now, that must be enough. Are you up to the task of leading, or is there another I should select?"

The words left my mouth without thought. "I serve at your pleasure, O great Mars." Deep inside, I knew I was not the automaton that mouthed those words, but there was nothing I could do about it. I was helpless to say anything else.

"Fine." The heat went out of him. I sensed a fatigue. He was worn. Disappointed perhaps. From behind a column, Michael appeared, and Mars recognized him. "Return him to his company." Then to me, he said, "Perrault will remain with you for your final training. Before you lies a last test of your fitness to command the company. Remember your purpose. And do not fail. Dismissed."

I bowed, stepped back, turned, and followed a step behind Michael. I waited to speak until we were on the disc and flying away. The constraint I'd felt before Mars, locking my tongue against my will, was gone. Michael was an intimidating figure. I'd experienced his power and had every reason to fear him, but he no longer had the choke collar around my neck I'd felt with Mars. Anger would not serve me. I swallowed it. "Michael, I need your help. Will you answer some questions?"

The implacable Michael surprised me with a clipped laugh. "Did not Mars impress upon you your duty? Given an order by his general, a true warrior can have no questions."

Now my anger returned. "Not good enough, Michael. I'm waking up from this nightmare. I know we aren't human anymore. Our free will's been taken from us. We're conditioned to want to please Mars. When I'm in his presence, I feel his control. We may be conditioned to serve, but we're not slaves. We're still men. This lack of information is eroding at our unit."

He seemed to consider this. "What is not clear?"

"Mars said our last mission entertained him. I asked whether that was our only purpose here, to entertain him. Then he came down on me like a ton of bricks."

An eyebrow raised. "What makes you think you are here for such pettiness? You insulted Mars. Such a slight to a god is not usually rewarded by a promotion, Captain. Consider yourself extremely fortunate to be forgiven."

Michael must've witnessed the whole thing.

"Michael, we don't know what we don't know. What's our purpose then?"

"It is as you've been told. A battle awaits. To your tiny human perspective, this is a place of miracles. But even here, there are rules. Rules all must follow. Even I. We will speak no more of it."

My wish was going to remain unfulfilled. We landed.

Michael's dismissal to me was less severe. "See to your warriors and encourage them. If you are truly warriors, what comes next will be rewarding." With no more explanation, he left me.

I had a long walk alone to the compound, thoughts still jumbled. I found the men in the mess. Will looked relieved, and my inner circle were on their feet to meet me.

"That was quick," Karl said. "I for one am surprised to see you."

Magnus smiled. "I had doubts we would see you back, Ragnar. Did you rediscover restraint on the trip to the great hall of Mars?"

Jakob crossed himself. "I prayed for your safe return, and the Lord has answered my prayers."

The look on my face must've said it all. Hikaru, Stokes, and Jess remained quiet.

"Oh boy," Will exclaimed. "You look like you got taken behind the woodshed. What happened?"

"Mission failure. I got nothing."

"No answers from our master?" Stokes asked.

"Nothing black and white, but—" I paused to think. "Maybe something. Stokes is right. We're under some strong mental conditioning." I told them how when Mars gave me permission to speak, I used my free will to ask him about our situation—I left out that I'd been less than diplomatic about it—and how he jerked me back into obedience.

"Well, at least you tried," Stokes said. "It is what it is." He gave Jess a forlorn look, and she returned it with a kindly smile that said she understood.

I continued, "I think I got something useful out of Michael though. He can't or doesn't want to exercise the same control over us that Mars does. I talked turkey with him and though my questions irritated him, he didn't shut me down like Mars did when I sassed him. I bet if Michael could've silenced me the same way, he would've." For the first time, I'd tested the limits with both classes of our overlords and learned something we hadn't known before.

"Maybe that helps us, but I don't know how," Will said. "Good to know that there's just the one who can bend our wills in addition to whipping our asses, I guess."

"But there was more," I said. "Michael said something I've heard before, that this is a place of rules. Mars said something too, about being worn out with us Americans, that we were tiresome, but that he didn't have a lot of choice about recruiting from our ranks. It makes me think they're constrained in a way they don't like, either."

"What do you think it means?" Jess asked.

"I'm still not sure, but it makes me think that Mars isn't the all-powerful being a god should be."

"Heads up," Will whispered. Gabriel and Captain Perrault entered the hall.

"Attention," Captain Perrault said. "Congratulations on your latest accomplishment. With your platoon's return, this signals the final phase of training. Today, you'll don your armor and begin the task of learning how to use it as an Ultimate would. Fall out to the armory in ten minutes." The silver-haired human from the future strode toward our circle. "Congratulations to you on your victory and your promotion, Beck. See you at the armory." He disappeared with Gabriel out the nearest entrance.

"Superior little prick, isn't he?" Will said. "He knows you've been promoted by Mars and still didn't even ask your permission to order the company around."

"Let it go, Will," I said. "That uptimer is going to get us up to speed on the armor, and after that, I think we're rid of him. Though—" I had a thought.

Jakob was first to hear the gears in my head turn. "What is it, Captain?"

If I tried, I could be curious. Away from Mars's gaze and encouraged by my desire to protect my fellow warriors, I was still able to touch that part of me. That tiny glimmer of inquisitiveness sparked into something I'd pestered Will about my first day in Valhalla, before succumbing to my singular drive to become an Ultimate. "Will? Who told you that we were going to be in a battle for all existence?"

Will frowned. "Huh?"

"When you mentored me into Valhalla, you were the one who first told me that we were training to fight in a battle for all existence. Where did you hear that? Was it Gabriel or Michael who told you that? Was it Mars himself?" I'd stopped pestering Will about the "why" of it all soon after arrival. Was it conditioned incuriousness that took hold? Or infatuation with becoming a great warrior? I now suspected it was the former.

"I guess it's what I was told when I arrived. I don't even really remember."

Hikaru squinted and became verbal for the first time in recent memory. "What are you thinking?"

"We're going to keep playing along for right now, understand?" I said to my NCOs. "There's another source of information we haven't tapped. And he doesn't have any more supernatural abilities than we do. Perrault's been here the longest of anyone we've had contact with. And when the time's right, he and I are going to have a very intimate conversation."

23

"On my order, by squads, bound."

Mark 5 combat armor has made me a living weapon of war. I could flip a small car with one hand tied behind my back. I can fly. Well, it's more of a powered jump. At the top of my parabolic arc, I can linger for several seconds before descending. Pretty close to flying. I carry as much in deadly armaments as a tank. I'm connected to everyone so closely through my helmet system that it's like drinking from a firehose. It's almost too much information, especially with my command package.

It's tech right out of every military sci-fi fantasy story that ever tried to imagine what future infantry in powered armor would be like. But better. It's been envisioned as the future of warfare for so long that it had to happen once the tech existed to make it reality. I just never thought to see it.

I've read more than my share of those mil-sf books. Plenty of times I've imagined fighting in powered armor. Of being a one-man tank that could fly and deal destruction over a square mile. The first imagining of it was the best, but I could no longer recall it. Reading for me was like hunger once. But I remembered it now as an abstraction, no longer craving the satisfaction of the feast.

What curiosity I still have tells me that if we developed powered armor this good, then one of two things has happened in Earth's future. One, we became so deadly at war that it became unthinkable to the point that we established an everlasting peace. But what's more likely is that the human race has wiped itself out. Those are the best reasons I can think of why Perrault is the most up-time of up-timers among us, and that the Mark 5 armor is the pinnacle of weapons for an Ultimate. Otherwise, why would Mars have run out of dead-ender heroes from the future from which to staff more of his army? We've kicked around those possibilities, and more, and we've all come to the same conclusion.

If this is the E ticket, we might as well enjoy the ride.

"Karl, push out another ten klicks and block our left flank. I'm still concerned about that valley mouth being a likely avenue of approach for any counterattack." The valley to our west was wide and flat, like a river delta below a mountain range, but dry as a bone. If there were an armored division waiting to respond, that's where I'd bet they'd come from. "I'll bring your squad up in reserve once we're sure we won't have a horde of whatever coming up our six."

"Understood, sir," Karl replied. He'd become less and less communicative once I'd placed Will in charge of the platoon, bumped Magnus to platoon sergeant, and made Jess squad leader. Karl's ego had been bruised, and he wasn't hiding it.

I was running the platoon for this exercise, still the only ones to make it back from the plains in time to use our new toys. The rest filtered back to Valhalla to jealously see that we'd already finished Perrault's tutelage, now fully familiarized with the war-gear of our dreams. I mean that figuratively and literally thanks to the diadems. Our uptime tutor was finishing the rest of the company's training while we were sent to flex our new muscles on the plains. When Perrault was done, we would be a company of fully-trained mechanized marauders. The last box to check before being named Ultimates.

I hadn't yet found my chance to have that talk with him. I was waiting for the right circumstances to carry out the plan I had in mind and I was running out of time. Soon he'd return to his own unit, where I assumed he ran his own company of Ultimates, fighting or training to fight on Mars's battlefields. If the opportunity didn't present itself, I'd have to force the discussion. Emphasis on the force part.

I landed and stayed down a second to pull up the blue force tracker, watching just long enough to make sure Karl was moving his squad as instructed. He was following orders but taking his sweet time about it. Looks like I need to have a conversation with Karl too.

I opened the platoon channel. "Lieutenant, hold at phase line Ceres. Same intervals."

Will answered immediately. "Roger, Captain. I have scouts ahead. I'll advise if there's any significant activity across the FEBA." He had Jess and Hikaru's squads at the forward edge while I kept Jakob's squad with me in trail a few kilometers behind.

"Good job, Will. Keep it up."

This was a first for us on the plains. We weren't ghosting. We were ourselves. We received the briefest of brief op orders from Michael before passing through the gate. "Mars wishes you to send a message to his enemy. The city in the northern hemisphere of this region is to be punished. Make the reach of Mars's wrath known. Do not burn the nest to ash, but pull the twigs and straw asunder."

I had about a million questions. "What's the disposition of the—"

Gabriel answered for Michael with the same flame in his eyes his sword held, though we had not seen the fiery blade in a while. "Michael has given you Mars's orders. Carry them out. Leave Mars's enemies quaking. There is nothing more needed, or are you refusing an order from Mars?"

Magnus whispered from behind me. "They're not just testing the platoon, Mars tests *you* again. For loyalty. For obedience."

I'd already received the message loud and clear—without my Viking brother's translation: Mars was still pissed at me. Not enough to bust me back to private, but enough to want to see me flounder or rise to the occasion by making things as difficult as possible. Talk about your jealous and vindictive gods.

"Platoon," I said aloud, ignoring them both as though I'd received no rebuke. "Button up and form by squads. Lieutenant Jensen. Lead the first squad through the gate and set up security for the rest of the platoon and await my arrival. You're authorized to use tac nukes if there's no other way to open the beach head." Each squad had a low-yield nuclear missile. It made a nice mushroom cloud and could make a grid square a wasteland. I was warned they were to be used sparingly.

All I knew was I didn't know enough for this mission. With no other contingencies I could think of to cover, it was time to fish or cut bait. "Hestus, is the way prepared?" The gatekeeper's solemn nod and the appearance of the shimmering door told me it was.

"Order of march—one, two, three, and four. Command element travels with three. Move out."

We were all used to blind drops through the gate, but even after so many, there was something a little unnerving about this one. We weren't being sent to fight rock-wielding Neanderthals as the first challenge while installed in our spanking new souped-up murder machines. Of that I was certain. Something told me we were headed to a killing floor full of butchers every bit as kitted out as us.

I wanted to be first through the gate and into the unknown. But I'd learned that as the CO, I couldn't lead from the front every time. It was my job to command, which meant letting my subordinates do their jobs. It was hard at first, and I'd had to change how I thought about things. Instead of acting or reacting as an individual, I had to always consider how to influence the mission through my direction of critical tasks around the battlefield. My job wasn't to be the "doer," it was to be the "director." It was much harder than I'd anticipated.

But here was a compromise. After letting Will take the first two squads through, I led the third squad with Jakob just a step behind me. It put me right where I needed to be in order to make an early decision once I saw what we were dealing with on the other side of the gate but acknowledged the needs of my ego to be up front without frivolously exposing myself.

Trust me, it's more fun to be the killer man than to supervise all the killer men. Such is the burden of command.

Surprise number one. We weren't on Earth.

A sky as pink and red as a winter sunset bathed us in light from double suns directly above. Our dark gray armor was a little lighter in color than the terrain, which reminded me of volcanic cinders. Exotic jagged peaks and sharp ridges broke up a huge basin divided into several flat terraces of varying low elevations, each topped by the sprawl of a civilization. It was a megalopolis that must be home to millions. This wasn't some village of horse thieves to be punished for raiding Mars's stables. This was a nation.

"Lieutenant, report." Will waited for near the gate with two of his soldiers. The rest of his men were already pushed out many kilometers to our front in a wide spread. My display showed where all had found cover on high ground overlooking the city, holding and awaiting further orders. Ready to rain hell on anything that appeared. Perfect.

"Negative contact."

I took a quick assessment of the terrain, the city, and our force. A few commands in my helmet and I pushed the operation concept to everyone, pausing only a second before I narrated the plan over the platoon channel. "The mission is harassment and destruction of all vital infrastructure. Weapons free. Engage any hostiles or perceived hostile activity." As near as I could figure given the paucity of intel we were provided—which was next to nothing—this was as clear as I could translate my directive into a military mission for us.

"Lieutenant, take the first two squads ahead in a bounding overwatch to the marked phase line. I'll travel behind with third squad." Karl would block the valley to our left.

"On my order, by squads, bound."

Will had already zipped ahead in a series of lightning-fast bounces to get back to the first two squads waiting at the phase line. I'd kept up with Jakob, taking a few short bounces, as he directed his Third Squad to pause in trail a kilometer behind them. "Maximum Z one-hundred," he reminded the squad. Keeping leaps shorter and covering less horizontal distance than we were capable of was wise. There's always a temptation to use our abilities to their fullest extent, but we needed to maintain better security for our initial movement into the unknown. When it was game on we could rain destruction down from the peak of our tallest jumps.

I could've relied more on the feed from Will's scouts, or had Jakob send one of his men high for an extended recon at altitude, but sometimes you just want to get the lay of the land with your own eyes. No one was shooting at us yet, so I used my discretion as the commander and took the risk.

"Going high," I said on the platoon channel to let everyone know it would be me up above. I bounced.

I lingered for a few seconds at about three hundred meters, coaxing another burn from my jump jets to do so. My command suit was a little lighter than the assault suits. What I gave up in the variety of armaments everyone else carried, I made up for in speed and range. It let me get to different spots on the battlefield faster and do so for much longer between needing packs swapped out. Even so, we'd learned that an assault suit carrying every weapon in the inventory could run full-tilt for 28 hours. I didn't think we'd be here near that long.

I scanned across the landscape and zoomed in on the first movement I saw. Surprise number two. Our opposition weren't human.

I picked a landing spot just a few hundred meters ahead of where I'd bounced from, landing near Third Squad's line of halt. On the way down I sent a high-mag image to the platoon. "Opposition ID. Non-human bipeds." We hadn't prepared for this, but I think my communication captured the essence of what I saw. And I doubt it surprised anyone given the setting we found ourselves in. I know I felt a little Alice-in-Wonderland-ish, and I'm sure the others did as well. But whereas little Alice in her adventure had only a blue gingham dress to protect her, we had impervious armor and big, big guns. Lots of them. We could've flattened the Queen of Hearts and all her knaves as a light warm-up.

Squat, irregular, and unclothed, the aliens' skin looked like the lumpy flesh rolls of a hippo. Their heads were triangular and neckless, sitting atop triangular shaped bodies. The way they were built made me think this was a high-gravity world, but in our armor, I had little to no natural feedback that this was the case. Whatever natural selection had taken place to make the walking dog-plop people look the way they did, who knew the cause? The band I'd seen were moving hastily from one structure to another. They moved purposefully, and I perceived they were reacting to our arrival. Taking cover? Going for their guns? Loading up into flying saucers to fight us? It was time to go to work.

"Assault, assault, assault," I said. I dropped to Jakob and Karl's channels, not wanting to distract Jess and Hikaru as Will directed their alternating bounds through the city. "Jakob, keep the same distance in trail and be ready to take Three to support any sustained fight. If there's any counter assault by the natives, we'll be first to respond. Karl, any activity to report?"

I could've done without the "harumph" he used as preamble before responding.

"Negative. Sir," he added as an afterthought.

"Keep on it, Karl. It's a big area. Be ready to break off if I call." I shot him a grid. "I'm sending your squad here next. Those look like storage." A farm of a dozen large globes several stories high, windowless and plain, sat at the far edge of the city. "Appear to be critical infrastructure. Gaseous or liquid containers. No way to tell. You're going to destroy it all on your way out, so start assessing the target."

That ought to satisfy his ego.

"Understood, Captain." He'd perked up a little. I suppose I'd feel the same way had I been away from the middle of the action, but it was the kind of thing you kept to yourself. Karl had been raised to be an officer. To lead, you must know how to follow. And every assigned task was important to the mission, whether it led to glory or not. Surely, he knew those things.

I broke comms and checked the tracker again. We were already spread out across a box twenty by fifteen kilometers. The lead squads hit the edge of the built up area and let loose on whatever was in front of them as they made a quick advance deeper into the city. They were moving slower now, street by street, pausing on rooftops to use flamers, grenades, and the small shoulder-launched missiles against select targets.

Will's directions to the lead squads as they went to work were perfect. "Make it count! This place is a few hundred square klicks. We can't lay waste to everything we land next to." I found no reason to provide additional guidance and let him keep running the show. I hated a micromanager and didn't want to be one myself.

I let my suit take over on auto, keeping pace with Third Squad as we bounced, and diverted attention to watch as troops chose their targets, crashing through walls or roofs to assess whether the building rated ordnance or not. A harass and disrupt mission was all about destroying the enemy's home turf. Where they felt safe and where they fueled the sustainment of their own war machine. Being able to identify vital targets was important. As we had absolutely zero intel beforehand, Will's direction to the troops to breach where they could and evaluate before expending ordnance was needed. I'd had no doubts that Will was going to make an excellent platoon leader, and he was proving me right.

"Sir, think we can fill in?" Jakob said as he landed next to me.

I highlighted a few grids that'd had been cleared. Groups of the natives were leaving shelter, likely assuming the assault was now past them. What I saw made me think they were assembling in an organized way. What looked like weapons confirmed it for me. Many of them now had what looked like a musical instrument, a tuba maybe, draped around their tapering form. I doubted we'd interrupted a brass band convention.

"Scatter those locals before they can make trouble behind our forward elements. Do it."

"Yes, sir," Jakob said with enthusiasm. We needed a first sergeant, and I was thinking Jakob might be the obvious choice. I didn't care if the other three platoons felt left out of the company's leadership slots. There'd be time to reward them with higher levels of authority and responsibility later.

I let Jakob move out with his squad. "Going high," I warned and took another tall bounce. I hit the top of my arc and reassessed our battle area. A flashing light and its accompanying warning buzzer vibrated in my bones. My Annie, mounted on my shoulder, fired several bursts automatically, and a ball of fire erupted only a hundred meters off to my right. Someone had launched a missile at me. I plotted a regression and let my backpack lob several HE grenades in that direction as I dropped.

"Stop playing peekaboo," Stokes said to me on a private channel.

"You saw that?" I asked. Danny was many klicks ahead with First Squad. I pulled Annie off my shoulder as I landed on a rooftop. A rectangular vehicle raced from around a corner in my direction. I sent two short bursts at it. Both hit. It caught fire and careened into a building. No one came out of it. I found it very satisfying.

"Just happened to be looking back in your direction. Stay safe, Rag. Keep your feet on the ground. We're getting into some action up here. Out."

Action? "Jensen. Sitrep."

Will got right back to me. "Resistance is organizing. We've finally attracted some kind of militia attention. They have energy beam weapons and explosive launchers. Two small groups have hit us, but we've—" He broke off. I kept quiet as I listened to him redirect troops on his lower channel and waited. "Sorry. Got some armored vehicles and dismounted troops moving on us."

"Will, consolidate your squads. I'm bring help up." I broke the comm. "Karl, bring your squad in." I checked the map, swiped a highlight marking where I wanted him and sent it. "Take the left flank of the city on a ten-klick skirmish line with this as your right boundary." I added another overlay. "Once you're past this phase line, carry out your destruction of that tank farm."

"Moving," was all he said. Not enough words to judge if he was still feeling insubordinate. Finally, he added.

"Without your express permission, I've mined main leys across the western valley and set them to high proximity. I judge that will do the same as holding my squad in place to watch empty space, sir."

There it was. I was too busy to brace him just now. It would wait.

"Jakob, close up intervals and sweep up the right side. We're going to reinforce first and second. Make best speed."

He answered by immediately issuing orders to the squad. "Half-klick intervals on the bounce to support forward element. Cover to cover. Odd numbers ready. Jump."

I took my own path, straight up the middle. I was heading for Will's position, six klicks ahead. Staying low, I bounded onto the shortest buildings. It must not rain much here because the roofs were all flat, some with large atrium like openings. I paused on the next roof when I noticed that on the grounds beside it was parked a fleet of the rectangular vehicles, much like the one I'd destroyed. I grabbed one of my two bombs and tossed it into the center of the parking lot before bouncing again.

The bombs had some heft, almost all of it from the containment apparatus that prevented the miniscule amount of dense matter that was the bomb from going high order. In armor you could be as close as an arm's breadth from the edge of the very circumscribed ring of destruction and be none the worse for wear. But if you misjudged, you'd be vaporized. I'd rather use them on something more exotic than their taxi service, but this would have to do. I didn't want to return to Valhalla with any unexpended ordnance, and in another few minutes we'd be out of the city. I checked the clock. Twelve minutes we'd been on the ground.

"Moving up from your six, Jensen," I said as I took another shallow leap over a short rectangular building. It was narrow, and a half-effort hop would let me bound over it to the other side. Beyond was a wide street before the next tall building. I was still trying to stay low, and I planned a course to jog around that tall one to find the next best avenue for some more low altitude hops. From the ground, I might spot something worthy of the last of my bombs.

No sooner had I crested the roof than I realized my error. Another one of those marching bands of shambling dog turds filled the street. I landed right in the middle of their woodwind section. Ever see rats scurry from a burning trash pile? My sudden splash in the sea of hippos caused a panic. Good. What had been an error in my choice of routes was just another opportunity to bring chaos. Before the nearest could bring a weapon to bear, the flamer in my left gauntlet came to life. I turned myself into a lawn sprinkler and sprayed a wide arc. It had the effect I'd been going for. I was the growing eye of the hurricane.

In Viking fervor I heard "On the roof, Ragnar." Bolts from a pair of Annihilators rained wide around me into the crowd, further scattering and deterring the hippos from bringing their instruments to bear. Whatever color they were on the outside, they must've pumped red blood. One evaporated into a pink mist as a burst from an Annihilator hit it square on. Above me, Magnus and another armored trooper kept up the fire. I didn't hesitate to extract myself from my predicament. I took a leap and landed between them.

"Lieutenant sent us to bring you forward, sir." It was Mazhar. "Said you were too stubborn to ask for security."

"The captain didn't need help, Trooper." Magnus laughed. "He's hogging the glory to himself's what it is."

I checked the tracker while they scattered the rest of the hippos. Will had First and Second Squads on the move again. They were almost through the northern expanse of the city. Fires raged in all directions, plumes of black smoke rising to collect into a cloudy blanket, blotting out the suns. Without knowing why these beings were enemies, my assessment was I'd carried out my mission. We'd punished them. The place looked like pictures I'd seen of Dresden burning. A golden star flashed on my tracker. I zoomed to it. In the hills beyond the expanse of the alien city, a beacon signaled our exfil.

"All units." I pushed the grid location to the platoon. "We have an exfil rally point. First and Second Squad hold at the edge of the city and continue to provide suppression. Third Squad, finish up and make for the departure point. Fourth Squad, pass north from your zone to the RP."

I still hadn't heard the explosions I'd half-expected any time now from the storage tanks I'd assigned Third Squad to destroy. "Karl. Time hack to the tank farm det—"

"Whoa!" Magnus shouted as the storm hit us. The three of us were on the bounce, nearing the edge of the city, when the explosion happened. At the top of a high jump over a collection of burning ruins of huge rows of some kind of machinery, the leading edge of a shock wave found us. I hit the ground sideways and rolled, then collided with Mazhar at the end of my tumble. Even in armor, the ground hurts. The flames behind us died out for a moment before flaring again as oxygen returned. Had Karl used a nuke?

"Did he use nukes?" Magnus read my mind as he lifted me upright. He'd landed on his feet and moved to retrieve us without missing a step. He always had the kind of poise I thought would make for a movie action hero. "Let's get out of here." We were well shielded—so we'd been told—but just the concept of nukes had impressed Magnus greatly. "I don't want to grow a second head."

"Don't think so," I replied. "No time to find out. On the bounce." We were off again. I took a look as we made the last jump to put us past our defensive line. The west was one raging, blue wall of burning energy. I had no idea what would cause that. Whatever had been in those tanks was touchy stuff.

"Jakob, what's the status at the gate?" I asked as I landed.

"We hold the gate. It is open and awaits us."

Will reported for First and Second Squads. "Holding the rear. Small concentrations of troops. Don't seem to be in pursuit, sir." Maybe we'd spanked them hard enough to stay in their rooms, smarting from the lesson we'd given them. I hoped Mars would be pleased.

"Pick it up and move to the RP," I said as I made another of my continual assessments of the tracker. Fourth Squad was moving quickly to us from the left flank. There were only six icons. There should've been eight. "Karl, give me a head count on the move."

Pause. I pushed Magnus and Mazhar to bounce ahead. "You two start the count at the gate. I'll be last man. Move out." I changed to the platoon channel. "By squad, through the gate. Order, three, two, one, four. Karl, what's your count?"

He finally responded. "I am missing two. They were lost in the demolition. They did not follow my instructions."

Fourth Squad was bouncing high and fast from around the north end of the city, close enough I could see them in my naked vision.

"Wait at the gate, Squad Four leader." I was cool. But I felt the anger building. *Instructions? What instructions?* I didn't like what I was hearing. I needed more information. A voice snapped me out of my thoughts a split-second before explosions of impacts erupted from above the slopes where our gate beckoned. "Fast movers!"

I didn't bother to try and locate them before I gave the order, "Launch missiles."

Every squad had one trooper carrying an AA launcher. I had no idea what we'd be up against when we got the order to report to the rotunda and made some hasty decision at the armory as we loaded out. I assigned a subordinate task for each squad to assign a trooper to tote one of the two-meter-long packages. I'd felt guilty about it for a minute, especially when I sent the assault through the city. We were stretched thin across this huge playing field and having one man per squad carry a missile "just in case" had reduced the destructive payload each man could carry for use on ground targets. I thought I'd made a bad choice. Now, I felt a new confidence about my combat intuition.

Another rapid rain of blasts sprayed wide onto the slopes. I only caught a glimpse of the troublesome raptors, but if they were piloted aircraft, they were as bizarre as everything else here. A pair of un-aerodynamic dark triangles flying point rearward and without noise passed out of sight behind the peaks. The salvo of our missiles chased after them, leaving whisps of curving contrails behind them.

"Those were our only four missiles. Get through the gate!" I ordered as I ran. If the missiles didn't find their targets and we were still standing here when the birds came around again, we were toast.

I ran, pausing to push bodies ahead of me up the slope to where our shimmering gateway hovered in a shallow bowl beneath the next rise. The gate was a bright mirror at the end of a long hall, as out of place here as a reflecting pool in the desert. You couldn't miss it if you were blind. Magnus and Mazhar were doing as instructed, on either side of the portal marshalling my platoon through as rapidly as possible. I took a short hop ahead to where Will was directing his armored gorillas to get through the gate. "First and Second Squad are through. You next."

Karl stood at the head of a line of five, waiting to pass through. He was fixated on the gate, oblivious to the impending doom that the rest of his squad looked for in the air behind us as they queued. I felt my ears burn. He wasn't even at the rear of his squad, ensuring his men got out before him.

"Karl!" I said hotly as I marched toward him. "My orders were for you to wait at the gate." Before he could answer, I felt a shove. Will was behind me, yelling and pushing. "They're coming around. Get through, get through." Suddenly, I was carried along by the crush of the freight train I found myself in. Next thing I knew, I was falling onto the floor of the rotunda. I hit the smooth white tile, a shock after the black volcanic cinders we'd been on. I started crawling in the subconscious need to make room for those behind me. Hands lifted me, and I spun around.

"Come on! Come on!" I yelled uselessly into the shimmering door, urging any one on the other side to make their transition from there to here. A few more fell through into waiting arms until finally Magnus and Mazhar were flung through, just as a flash as bright as an exploding star drowned out all other light and vanished.

Stokes was closest to the now blank pillars, staring as I was at nothing. "Where's Will?"

My heart stopped. "Squad leaders, I want the count. Report." Three times I received it, and three times I counted on my fingers, disbelieving my math each time. With the two men missing from Karl's squad, the count should be 41.

Including me, we were 40.

Magnus removed his helmet. "Will was behind us. He was covering our backs when he pushed Mazhar and me through. I turned to pull him with us, but before I knew it, I was here."

"So, where're our missing?" Stokes asked with an urgency. "It's the plains. You die and return. That's how it is. Why aren't they back?"

Hestus manned his position at the console. His eyes remained fixed downward. Gabriel's face remained his judgmental frozen statue of classical perfection. It was Michael who I looked to for understanding. His frown was the herald of what I feared.

"It was not the plains as you have experienced them. You were elsewhere, in an equal reality. There is no return for the fallen from those worlds.

"They are beyond Mars's grasp."

24

"Karl, I want your report. What happened?"

I had him alone. I wanted to hear it from him before we reviewed the action with all my NCOs. I'd had Magnus take charge of the platoon to get everyone working in the armory while I figured this out. At the time, losing two men on the plains during a simple demo mission on the bounce had irritated me. Death was a temporary condition. I'd become immune to it. Here we knew of no final end for a soldier. Now I was experiencing feelings returned to me out of a half-remembered dream.

Sorrow, grief, and fear.

I still couldn't believe Will was gone. Michael's revelation that there were places where the immortal restoring force we'd taken for granted didn't exist was another jolt that made me feel like I'd stepped through the looking glass all over again. The words of Will's country wisdom my first day here came back to me.

One thing you'll get used to around here, you won't get used to a thing.

Karl was impassive. "I carried out your orders, sir."

"And got two men killed."

His tone was dismissive. "I could hardly have known that they would be killed, no more than you were aware that we were not on the Plains of Eternity."

I'd had enough of his aristocratic superiority. I braced him. "Don't play semantics, Karl! Dead forever or just dead on the plains is still a mission failure."

He responded appropriately by coming to a stiff attention, his heels clicked and his Prussian jaw locked.

"You got two men killed doing something so easy a trooper with one trip to the plains wouldn't have screwed it up."

His perfect military bearing, reinforced by a patrician upbringing and a lifetime of harsh discipline, melted. His eyes closed as though if he squeezed hard enough, whatever vision lay behind them would be crushed too. I'd pierced his shell with the truth. He'd screwed up.

"Stand easy, Karl," I said in quieter tones. It was time for me to be something other than the martinets he'd been schooled by. "Tell me what happened to Plei and Calvely."

Plei was from some southeast Asian empire. By his telling, a warrior prince. I had no reason to doubt him. Calvely had been an honest to goodness medieval knight. Neither were lacking in bravery—or they wouldn't have been here. But neither of the pair were among our most adaptable. Despite their willingness to work hard, they were among many of my platoon who, as we advanced in the technology of war, found themselves falling behind those from the 19th century and later.

"There was a small amount of resistance around the facility. Nothing challenging. We easily cleared the facility, and I directed the two to place the charges to provide for a thin overlapping spread so as to maximize the area of damage. I pushed the rest of the squad to continue our sweep north. As we converged on my last designated rally point to await the demo team's arrival, the detonation occurred."

Had the pair made an error in deploying or arming the bombs? They were fairly simple devices. There were many times I found myself unable to reconcile how things that were to me intuitive and simple, were seemingly out of some of the men's intellectual abilities. The more advanced the tech got—and the more most of it became easier to employ—there were still obstacles.

Will had frequently reminded me that for many of the men, doorknobs were an alien technology. How mind-bending was a Thompson sub-machine gun or a maser cannon? Was it that men of the later ages were more intelligent? I knew that couldn't be the case. History was built by examples of brilliance from over thousands of years. Heck, I doubted my generation produced a thinker or innovator who could've propelled the human race forward as much as the four guys those ninja turtles were named after—and they had nothing more sophisticated than hand tools, planes, levers, and pulleys to work with. Intelligence and imagination were more powerful than gizmos.

It was culture and superstition that held back most of the far-downtimers. Even the diadem lessons hadn't changed the core of their nature. Magnus was one of the exceptions. He'd shed preconceptions as fast as he was given knowledge to replace them, and without what I thought of as even a child's understanding of physics and chemistry, had adapted and mastered tech very rapidly. With help, of course. I remembered his awe at the M-1 Garand. I still cringed when I heard him mentor some of the troops with teleologic explanations as though instruments had a will, like "the desire of the weapon is to destroy, but you must guide the thing's want. The unaimed arrow does not hit the target." Painful. But for some, it was a bridge between magic and mechanics. It didn't matter if they understood the basis of the tech or not. I know most of this new stuff was beyond my understanding, even after plenty of diadem enhancement and hands on experience. Neutronium. Phased coil arrays. Proton packs. The things Perrault told us were fairly meaningless nouns to me.

"Did you check the yield and timer on the devices?" I asked him. On his squad leader display, it was information that could be accessed and checked with minimal effort. He looked at his feet.

"I did not, sir." Even time was a difficult concept for some to touch, the representation of measurements like seconds and minutes into numerals, beyond them. I hated to condemn the man in absentia, but I knew Calvely to have been illiterate. You didn't have to be well educated to be a soldier. It added up.

"Lesson learned. We have to keep in mind that not all of the men are so equally capable. Maybe I need to consider shuffling the squads around to even out some of the abilities." I had stacked the first two squads with up-timers. I needed to rethink that. When the rest of the platoons were back in Valhalla, I'd be having a similar discussion with the other platoon leaders and their NCOs. Maybe they'd already experienced similar misfortunes on their missions. I didn't want something so simple to hurt us again. Especially now that I knew the results were permanent.

"Yes, sir." Karl seemed to accept my counseling, and I sensed no insubordination or pridefulness in his manner. I was glad I chose to do this one-on-one. Whatever damage to his ego he'd felt by not being selected for promotion— further eroded by losing two men—I think he was over it. Or so I hoped. He was a hard one to read, perhaps harder even than Hikaru. My samurai at least didn't vacillate between extremes of petulance and obedience. He was a rock.

"Let's get our gear and weapons maintained, and after that I'll dismiss the platoon. We'll meet in the morning for our review."

"Captain, from now on will we be engaging in genuine warfare? Life and death? Not playing in a realm of fantasy?"

I still wasn't so sure about the nature of what I'd experienced on the plains. Every melee to date was no less real to me than what we'd just done. How would we know the difference? "I think it's about time we found out."

※　※　※

At the head of my company in full armor, helmets in the crooks of our arms, I felt proud. And rightfully so. There was no force in the realm of the living from any time that could match us. Michael was on the dais with Gabriel and Perrault. Stokes stood at the head of first platoon. I hopped him to platoon leader in place of our fallen brother. Karl hid any indignation he might've felt. I think maybe he realized that as a leader, he still had some growing to do.

The senior demi stepped forward.

"You have completed your training. An accomplishment worthy of the greatest reward the god of war can bestow. The honor to serve him." He raised his spear and passed its tip over our head in a wide arc. My armor turned from a dull grey to the same purple iridescence that emanated from the armor of those over us. I knew this didn't make us equals, but it's meaning was obvious.

"In the name of Mars, I judge you to be Ultimates."

I wish Will had been here.

Later, I invited Perrault to join us. "My officers and NCOs would like you to join us for a dining in, to honor your helping us achieve our new rank as Ultimates. Is that a tradition from your own time, Captain?"

He seemed a little perplexed at first, then as I suspected, some deep memory spoke to him, reminding him that such a thing was proper. Expected, even. "I'd be pleased to join you and your men, Captain. Thank you."

"It's informal dress, Captain." I tapped my armored chest. "We'll be in everyday uniform."

He seemed to think nothing of it. "I'll join you soon, then."

If he sensed some subterfuge on my part, then he was a good poker player. I gave no tell, and neither did he. I didn't feel the least bit bad about deceiving him. What happened next was going to be his choice.

My four platoon leaders and all the NCOs were with me in the mess. The other three platoons had been sent to fight on the Plains of Eternity, not on the same reality we occupied now. I was jealous. Not just because they suffered no permanent losses. They'd each participated in similar battles, on worlds populated by humans in a future so far-flung that the polities involved were as incomprehensible to me as my time was to one of the far downtimers. It did fill in some of the gaps in my curiosity about what was to come.

When I told the rest our revelations about my platoon's test—what had really been a test by Mars of my leadership—it had the sobering effect it'd had on us. There was a place where we were once again mortal.

Stokes was first to speak. "At least we know there's a way out of here."

"Death?" Denisov questioned.

"It's good to know we're not immune to it, I suppose," Coghill, the Brit, said analytically. "Keeps one a bit sharper, say what?"

"It's good to know it is not just me who feels we're no longer natural men. I'm relieved to see others sense it as well," Jeong, the Korean, admitted.

"I agree it's time to come out from the shadows of ignorance." Denisov had lost more men on this last proving mission than the rest of the platoons combined, though his fallen all appeared on the other side of the gate when it was over. If he strategized that way when Mars sent us to fight on this plain, we'd suffer more losses than just Karl's two. The Russian was the only one of us for whom Will had held distrust. I wished he was here to guide me with his uncommonly good advice.

"Then we're agreed."

"Ahem." Magnus cleared his throat as a warning, and the crowd parted to let Perrault enter. We'd pushed the tables out to create in a circle in the middle of the room. If the uptimer sensed anything, he didn't show any hesitation as he strode to where I waited. He was in tunic. Good.

"Glad you could join us, Captain." I moved into the center as the men spread apart to form a larger perimeter around the two of us. That finally brought a response.

"What is this, Beck?"

"I wanted to ask you some questions before you departed. I'm hoping you'll give us some consideration. I'd prefer to do it over dinner, Ultimate to Ultimate. If not—" I gestured to the mass of bodies forming the wall around us.

His eyebrows shot up. "If not *what?* You think you're going to turn this into a welcome challenge? Think you're warrior enough to beat me into submission? You must be thick as a Teak. *Orang bodoh.*"

Whatever he'd called me in his native tongue, I'm sure it wasn't to compliment my audacity. "That's up to you, Perrault."

He took a fighting posture, bladed to me slightly, hands ready. "You're an imbecile, Beck. That's what those words meant. What makes you think I know anything? Or that it's your right to know it if I do? Maybe you're not supposed to know more than you do? Maybe that's best for you, you ever think of that?"

"If that's the case, then it makes me want to know why even more."

"You're not going to know anything dead!" he spat, then took a few steps to close the distance—measured in their aggression, smooth and slow. It was going to be a fight!

"I've been dead. It's not so bad. Not as bad as being used like a slave."

I'd been inching closer and was about to shoot for his legs when he made a sudden hop directly at me. My forearms came up in reaction, and as I threw my first jab, he was gone. It had been a feint. He just needed to get a little distance from the cordon behind him. He sprang backward, somersaulted, bound over the heads of our human arena, and hit the ground running. He. Was. Fast.

"Stop him!" Magnus shouted.

Denisov was next to me in the stampede. "Was this your plan, Ragnar Beck?"

"Stuff it, Ivan Ivanovich."

Perrault hadn't gotten far. I burst out of the sunken mess, up the ramp, and out onto the central field to see Jeong waylay our fugitive. The Korean was a cyclone of spinning and flying kicks, all missing Perrault, as he always seemed to be just an inch out of reach—an imperceptible slide, a duck, a bob, a weave. I was almost on him. Jeong's next kick missed again, and Perrault stepped in and delivered a short strike. A knife hand jabbed out to Jeong's flank, and he dropped like the marionette whose strings had been cut.

Stokes flew past me. He leaped and while in the air landed a glancing overhand fist into Perrault's turned jaw, blindsiding him and sending him onto all fours. "Can't take us all down, pretty boy," Dan taunted. He was cocking to deliver Perrault a vicious kick. He'd done the same to me before, or tried to. Perrault wasn't done. His legs scissored out, then he twisted his upper body and swept Dan onto his back. I'd done the same to Danny many a time. I thought I'd taught him the error of his ways, but apparently not. Perrault was going for the mount when Hikaru sent a stiff kick to his chest, sending him tumbling head over heels backwards.

Both men advanced on Perrault, ready to give harm. I intervened, putting myself in between my men and the man. "Enough, Perrault. You're going to get beat senseless going up against all of us. Knock it off and talk."

He stood and wiped slowly at the trickle of blood in the corner of his mouth. He spit pink saliva at my feet and glowered at me. "Just do your job, Beck. All of you. You're going to be a lot happier if you do."

"Not good enough, Perrault. I'm through asking nicely. Answer my questions or I'm gonna split you from your skull to your ass."

"In your dreams, Beck."

I made a loop overhead with my arm, and the platoon responded by forming the ring again. "No fancy flying this time, Captain. Try it again and I won't bother trying stop everyone from pummeling you into a greasy spot on the sand."

"It's your trip to the well, Beck. Enough talk!" He took a cross step at me, intending to land a side kick. He was so fast he almost made it, but even with good one-step timing—which he had ample of—there was always enough of a telegraph that I avoided trying for such a committed type of attack myself. I easily slipped aside and punished him for his overconfidence with a fist into his thigh. He went with it and changed directions, whirling away like an eggbeater with several spinning back kicks.

I hated this kind of nonsense.

I didn't want to kill him. I wanted to change his mind by the most primal manner humans understood: total dominance. This wasn't going to be some kind of prolonged exhibition, trying to wear each other out. Real combat—real fights—were over in seconds. I was raised to understand what a fight was and what it wasn't. Dad taught me that if you found yourself in a prolonged fight, you were on your way to losing your life. Gramps taught me that if you find yourself in a fair fight, you didn't plan your mission properly.

I came at him hard.

See, I'm fast too. I backed him up, throwing hooks and round circular blows with open palms at his head to corral him. He tried to kick his way out, but I pressed close and kept him off balance. It kept him from using his most powerful and preferred tools, his legs. When his knees did contact me, they had little power. His reach was longer than mine, but he didn't like to use his hands as much. Or so I thought, until he like started at me like a sniper. He sent a pinpoint strike with the tips of closed fingers to the inside of my bicep. My arm went numb. He immediately sent another into my neck. My arm went weak.

But I didn't stop. Even with a temporarily lame arm, I rained blows on him still. Let him use his fancy nerve strikes. It wasn't going to save him. I'd backed him up to the edge of the ring, and when hands came from the crowd to push him at me, I was ready.

My hand slipped into my pocket, and I palmed the piece of lead slug I'd been carrying. Many weeks ago I'd found it in the armory. Some random, solid cylinder. No idea what it was for. It fit into my palm perfectly, so I took it with me. I just knew that someday it would come in handy. I probably didn't need it, but it seemed a shame to have carried it and not used it. He tried to shove me. If he could break me off him he could get back into the center of the ring, where he'd have room to use his length advantage and his long kicks again. As he started his reach for my shoulders, I planted my rear foot, sank, and corkscrewed up. I gave my head up to him to do so, but sometimes, the risk was worth it. Like now. I landed my uppercut just below his sternum. The air went out of him as he made that wonderful whooshing sound, and his fight went with it. For just a second. Which was all I needed.

In my experience, everyone is more cooperative when they can't breathe—when the world goes dim as darkness shades their vision like going into a deep tunnel. I don't care how well trained or resilient you are, when that happens, you know you're about to die. It was time to make that happen. A simple hip throw, I stayed glued to him, and as we hit the ground, I didn't stop.

If Dad and Gramps could see me now. Dad was the master of short circle power. Gramps, a master of much more. There was so much they tried to teach me that I'd never grasped, but Hikaru had opened my eyes, as had all my teachers in Valhalla. I was the master now. Training was all I'd cared about. I suppose if I hadn't been so consumed with learning how to be an Ultimate, I would have engaged my curiosity and maybe found a better solution than beating an answer out of someone, but now I knew to cut myself some slack. Mars had us conditioned, and I'd had to follow my programming. Fortunately, this was part of my programming too.

Don't fail.

I was using all my new abilities. Just not as Mars had intended. Perrault was struggling to breath. I'd put his diaphragm into spasm, and he couldn't fend me off as I snaked around him . Oxygen starvation tends to do that. I stretched out the arm I still held as I rolled. My other arm entwined around his neck, a leg wrapped behind his other arm. Hell strangle, Hikaru called it. *Jigoku-jime.* I extended my body and felt Perrault struggle like a fish flopping on hot concrete.

For a short while. He got weaker, then a little limp, with just enough tension left to tell me he wasn't completely out. It was that last moment when there was just a tiny dot of light in the center of your vision, that last connection to life close to being severed. I relaxed enough to let blood return to his brain. He made a wet suck of air. In a tiny croak, just loud enough for me to hear above the pounding of my heart in my ears, I heard it. "Yield. I yield. Enough."

My trust was as brittle as the thin layer of ice over a rushing river. I relaxed slightly more and waited. He didn't tense again and instead, went even more limp. Now I knew he meant his surrender. Because if he'd done otherwise, I'd have shut his carotids off again like closing a spigot. I let go and rolled him off.

He coughed into the sand and wheezed his words. "Beck, just you and me, okay. I'll tell you what little I know, but just you and me. You owe that to your men. They'll know. Trust me. The demis will know. So will Mars. They see everything. Don't bring the consequences of this down on your men."

Magnus and Denisov were nearest. "Get the men out of here," I ordered. "Perrault and I are going to have our chat. It's okay."

Despite my words, I was slightly reluctant. If the captain started up again, I wasn't entirely sure I could put him down a second time. At least, not quickly. My tiny cylinder of lead had dropped out of my hand and landed somewhere in the sand. Maybe it hadn't been the deciding factor, but it hadn't hurt. Fair fights are for suckers.

Magnus looked doubtful, but the Russian nudged him as he reiterated my directive. "You heard our captain." Magnus grunted disagreeably and was still looking back over his shoulder as he took his hesitating path behind the platoon as they went back down the ramp.

Perrault sat in the sand, catching his breath.

"Spill it, Goshang." I took a few more deep breaths to get my wind to speak again. "What are we doing here? My best friend was under the impression we're here fighting for the existence of all of humanity from the supernatural beyond. If that's so, then what's the big secret?"

Goshang Perrault gave a me a sad look. "If only. We're not engaged in a battle for humanity's survival. We're here fighting a war for the survival of Mars."

25

Fighting for the survival of Mars. What did that mean? The answer didn't come to me clearly, but another implication did. "You're saying we're slaves."

Perrault winced. "If you want to know, you must understand the risk. You could end up like me. Here for the duration. It was my choice. It may not be the choice you want to make. If you can't live with that, then let me stop now."

I tried to decipher his cryptic warning. "More bullshit about the rules." Whatever the constraints that defined how things were done here, I'd figured out that it bound not just the resurrected, but also Mars and his cohorts.

"Yes. The rules. And they're not bullshit as you so eloquently put it." He tried to stand, and I offered him a hand.

"Let's take a walk."

We strolled around the dark grounds. Slowly. What he told me didn't quite shock, but I learned I could still be surprised. None of it made me feel better. It was a lot like finding out the girl you'd wanted for so long had really bad breath.

"Mars isn't really a god, is he?"

I can tell he tried to laugh, but the effort started him coughing again. "I don't know the meaning of the word." I judged he was speaking with sincerity. When you've taken someone to the brink of death, they tend to respect you for it. "I was an educated man, Beck. I loved history. I know the myths and legends from the cultures that made those histories. But I'm a man of reason and science. Not a primitive like you. Mars is an immortal by our human reckoning. A being from another plane, close to but separated from ours. At one time he and those like him could touch our existence directly. Now, they're bound to this plane alone."

"This plane? You're talking about a multiverse?"

"Perhaps. That's an older term."

"You said 'those like him.' Rival gods? And their armies. Like us?"

"No, Beck. No. Not like us. Those creatures you fought? The ones you called hippos? They're nothing like us. They're artificial creations. Intelligent, animated meat. And the ones that made them, well, if you think Mars is a god, these make him a benevolent one by comparison."

"So the hippo-people weren't aliens?" I'd convinced myself that they were ETs and that we'd made a kind of first contact.

"That's the realm of Ah Puch."

"Who's that?"

"The Mayan death god. When he was isolated to this plane, he built his army from scratch using constructs. So have the other gods. We're the only humans fighting this war."

"Who are Mars's rivals?"

"Others who once held sway over humans. The old golds of myth."

How many ancient gods were there? I never studied mythology. Not at a serious level. "What are they? Some kind of powerful aliens? Supernatural spirits?"

"I don't know. Who can say? Mars and the others had influence over humanity."

"So... ancient Greece and Rome. Neptune. Mars. Achilles. All that was... real."

"Evidently. Though not as it was presented to humanity at the time. They're not gods. There are no gods. But they were all driven out of the plane where they could interfere with us a long time ago. My suspicion is this plane is not their home either. Wherever it is they came from, they couldn't go back. That's what I think."

"You don't know?"

He frowned. "The demis haven't given an 'orientation to the gods and their rules' course. I'm not part of the inner circle. I'm just a soldier. A useful tool. I made the choice to stay on and continue to fight as an Ultimate." He chuckled. "I like it. Same as you."

It was as close an interaction with him that I'd had to make him seem a comrade. And all it'd taken was nearly beating him to death.

Sometimes, violence is the answer.

"What changed that took them out of meddling in our human realm?"

Another shrug. "All I know is that it did, and now they can't."

"Let me take a stab at this." I've said it before, I was never a believer. I don't have a religion, or confidence about an afterlife—the whole heaven and hell thing. At best I'm a deist. More Thomas Jefferson than a true believer like Jakob. Still, my understanding of what was real changed when I showed up here back from the dead. "I don't know about souls or anything like that, but—"

He cut me off. "You came from a time of superstition, Beck. Primitive consciousness."

I was through taking offense whenever Perrault referred to me as being somehow stunted compared to him. I'd harbored similar uncharitable opinions of my own about the downtimers. I don't know how far in the future Perrault came from, but I was definitely a downtimer to him. His tone was conciliatory, and I let him continue.

"In my time we'd shed all notions of fantasy like a creator or an afterlife—all those fairy tales."

"Except you can't explain any of this either." I let it hang. His silence told me that having to admit as much to a downtimer was a blow to his enlightened ego.

"These beings have some kind of science we can't understand." Perrault chuckled. "It would send the philosophers of my time into a crisis. We're the proof that when we die, we go on. Primitives call it an eternal soul. My ancestors once believed in an essence, a life force that was our consciousness. Whatever it is that transcends our physical bodies, when we died it got captured and brought here."

I'd had a lead on this part. "So by your logic, it's a technology Mars has. But it seems they can't capture just any soul. There's something about *how* we died that makes it so their technology can interfere and divert us from wherever we were headed."

Perrault nodded in agreement. "Suicidal combat marked us in a way so that they can pull us here. Don't ask me the 'how' of it. But it's a loophole they're able to exploit in the system."

"System?" The implications were piling up like so many existential tailings left over from mining the meaning of life. I'd always tried to keep things simple—like eat, sleep, mate, kill. That sort of thing. It goes with being a primitive, much to my liking.

"There's clearly some kind of system, Beck."

"Do you mean god with a big G?"

He rolled his eyes. "There you go being a caveman again. Just when I thought you were making some headway in your development."

"You ask me you're halfway there yourself, talking about a soul. Semantics aside, you're telling me that our soul goes somewhere when we die, but ours were hijacked to come here for the use of Mars and his kind so that we do battle for their entertainment until the end of time itself."

Perrault got that look that told me I'd hit a nerve. "Right on the first count. Except Mars isn't just being entertained, he's fighting to survive. An army rolls in here and he's fair game, though it would be a hell of a bloodbath."

I tried to imagine just how horrific things could be if all of Ishtar or Odin or whoever's forces invaded and fought us back to the very throne of Mars.

"But between you and me," Perrault continued. "I don't think any of the gods want that. They just want to convince one another that it *could* happen if they felt like pressing."

I nodded.

"And then one more thing, and it's a big one. We don't stay here forever."

I gave a wan smile. "Yeah, we found that out. I thought I was through losing men in combat."

"There's more to it than that, Beck. I've been here to see it. When you've been here long enough, gone through enough battles and your unit is no longer combat effective from losses, you'll have earned your discharge. You get sent away. Through a different gate. And you don't come back here."

"And what happens then?"

Perrault shrugged. "I think you get to continue your journey."

I saw something in the man then. A fear that for all his uptimer superiority, his disdain at the superstitious primitives, he possessed a genuine fear about what would come after "discharge." And maybe that's why he volunteered to stay here forever. Every self-conceived hell has to be better than the real thing.

Another bolt hit me. "What about our friends who get killed on this plane? Like the men I lost fighting the hippos?"

"Early discharge, if you get me. Time served. Sent on their way."

A burden lifted from me. Will and the others weren't "dead." They were released from their involuntary service in Valhalla.

"On their way to...heaven? Is that what they're trying to keep from us? Mars is afraid it'll interfere with us fighting for him? That we'd choose to die so we could stop?"

"I guess. If you insist on being a neanderthal clinging to desperate fairy tales."

I pressed him. "Why haven't you gone, then?"

"I was offered a choice. To stay on. To build another company and fight again. I've done it three times now. I told you. I like being a soldier. An Ultimate."

"Have others taken the offer?"

"Yes. The senior who trained my company the way I've done for you. He stayed on. But he's gone now. He fell, I was told."

"So, this isn't Valhalla, then."

"Valhalla," he mused. "Lots of others have called it that. No. This isn't the eternal reward waiting for a soldier fallen in battle. But it's a place where a soldier can fight again and again. For a while. There are three companies, including yours and mine. Receiving new candidates. Testing them. Training them. Making them Ultimates. Then doing battle. Then when the unit is fought out, it's disbanded and everyone's sent on their way. And the process starts all over again."

I asked him more, but none of it made any more sense than what I'd heard so far. It was all just a snowglobe of plastic flurries whirlpooling inside my head. His conjectures weren't much better than mine and his disdain for "myths" and "fairytales" prevented him from exploring any explanation that wasn't rooted in materialism. A final question came to me as the hint of dawn that would regardless soon end our conversation as our next battle loomed. "Why are the gods at war with each other?"

Perrault spoke authoritatively. "Don't you remember what you were told when you first arrived? Before man was, war waited for him. War and death. Mars and the rest, their existence depends on it. That's why we're here. That's my best guess. And you know what? That's all right with me. I'm an Ultimate. "

"And you, Ragnar Beck, does it seem well with you?" Michael's voice didn't surprise me. Though the demi had once again appeared like a thief in the night, I'd prepared myself for just such an appearance.

I nodded at Perrault. "You said they'd know."

The captain's pursed-lip silence I took to be an expression of pity for me. For what surely was coming.

Gabriel didn't wear his stone-faced sneer. His face held an almost human concern. He stayed quiet as Michael spoke. "What Perrault tells you carries this much truth: Those who are released from Mars's service after honorable battle return to the path of ascension. But to fall in battle against Mars's enemies, what becomes of your soul is beyond his guidance."

26

Perrault hadn't yet been to the healer. Beck had given him a solid beating. Mars was not surprised. Perrault was a standout among his Ultimates, which is why he was chosen to stay on. Beck was better. A dirty bastard of a fighter.

Mars liked that. Still, he had yet to decide if the insatiably curious troublemaker could be reined in.

"Stand at ease, Captain." Perrault had served Mars well. No wrath was kindled against him. Mars knew when dealing with humans that they were fallible. And every so often, so was he.

"You did as I asked, Perrault. You gave him enough and did it in a convincing way. Do you believe Beck will continue without harming the morale of his company?"

"I believe so, Mars. He's pigheaded, but I don't believe he'll promote the idea of defections among the men."

"Then the useful deceit as to their true nature here continues. I'm satisfied at the outcome. The truth within the half-truths of what you let slip convinced him—that it's for the best he keeps what little he thinks he knows to himself. Return to your company. Well done. I have a mission for you and your men. Alator will have the details. Good hunting."

Among the gods there had been a great multitude of negotiations while Gabriel's company finished the task of getting its legs as Ultimates. It would have been easier to use constructs instead of mortal men as the Aztec and the others had done. But they did not know man like Mars did.

There was a reason he was king of the war gods—Mars Augustus. Choosing to use a handful of the right men, as much trouble as they sometimes were, would prove it to his rivals and adversaries.

Every general sought to pick a fight with Mars, and all at once. But it was Nergal, the Mesopotamian god, who was the biggest irritant.

"Quintus, send for them. Nergal's proposal is settled."

※   ※   ※

I was no better than Perrault. I realized that after he'd been dismissed back to his unit. I'd thought him an aloof jerk. Turns out I'd misread him. Badly. In his annoyingly superior way, he'd been trying to protect me. I had some answers, but the price for knowing even this little was that I'd crossed a line. Which meant I was set to become the same kind of sanctimonious stuffed-shirt I'd thought the uptimer was. I wondered if I'd see him again.

My men had backed my play, knowing they were likely risking punishment for our transgression. For that I was about to repay their loyalty with, "Sorry, guys. Whatever I know, I can't tell you."

The phrase about having your cake and eating it too made sense to me now in a way I'd not understood before. Unsatisfying didn't begin to describe it. I couldn't tell the others what I'd learned without causing the same consequences for them. They couldn't get their discharge and go on their way if they survived to the end. They'd have to stay like me and Perrault. Either surviving to fight another day or falling to goes who knew where—to the place where Will and the others were. Knowing this was worse than the next-to-nothing I'd known before.

Mars looked down at me with a smirk. "I've always had a soft spot for a soldier who can't seem to stay out of trouble, Beck."

I didn't feel the inhibition of control, but I also didn't have the petulant fire in me I had at my last audience with Mars. I only felt the regret that goes with grabbing the electric fence to test it for yourself.

"Don't look so beaten down, son," Mars said in an almost fatherly way. "If you're ready to get on the team and get back into the game, there's work to do. Battles to be fought. Glory to be had. What do you say?"

In for a penny, in for a pound.

"Yes, O great Mars."

The gruff chuckle of the god reminded me of Gramps. "Ha! That's the spirit." He waved a hand and a semi-translucent image came to life above us. "You did well against those simple shells Ah Puch fields. Not a great challenge. Just a taste of what you can bring to bear against my enemies. Your next mission isn't going to be such a one-sided affair. Not all my enemies are as infirm as those shambling meat sacks. This'll cheer you up."

A place appeared. A world—not the sphere of a planet—but a domain amidst the black with splotches of hostile red, orange, and yellow blending deserts and mountains. My eyes searched for any life-giving green or blue, until a grey island in a sea of orange magnified. Right angles and the depth of edifices resolved into a civilization.

Mars gave the place a name. "The home of Nergal."

Atop a square pyramid-like building stood a giant humanoid dressed in gold and silver, a horned cap on the angular head, surrounded by a red radiance. I was getting used to the idea of gods, so I found myself unimpressed. I didn't know from where or what culture this one once ruled over, but if the building was what I thought a ziggurat was, that meant the ancient Middle East. Like Mesopotamia, or Sumeria—or other places I only knew from watching quiz shows. What did impress me was the formation Nergal surveyed from his perch. In perfect groupings were columns of precisely spaced soldiers. Not human. Instead, some living caricature of man and beast-like figurines unearthed from an Egyptian pyramid.

"Nergal likes fire," Mars continued as I stared. "And fear. See the aura around Nergal and the leaders at the front of the formations? Melam. Nergal and his chosen wear the garments. Their properties won't affect an Ultimate in armor, but against anyone else, the fear it induces makes the flesh crawl right off an opponent."

In some of the groupings the warriors wore a backpack. Attached to it was a wand that they held across their chests at port arms. It screamed flamethrower, though there was an ancient quality to it, like some smith had created Bronze Age versions of the weapon. The creatures carrying the devices had wide, flat skulls with pointed horns, cloven hoofs, and stubby three-fingered hands. Dull black coats made them appear more like minotaur than demons to me.

I made a quick count by rank and file. I'd barely started when the image changed. There'd been maybe a thousand of the beasts. My company was not quite a hundred-fifty strong. And we'd never fought together as a unit with me in command. Still, matching our firepower against flamethrower-wielding bulls, they didn't seem much of a challenge. Unless there was something not yet apparent. There was always another shoe about to drop in Valhalla.

"This will be your first real challenge, Beck. Today you take your company into battle against Nergal's forces."

I had an important question. "It's for all the marbles now, isn't it, sir? No more Plains of Eternity practice? If we get killed on this plane, that's it."

Mars solemnly confirmed my understanding. "That's it."

"What's the objective, sir?"

Mars scoffed at my question with a tilted expression. "Kill them all, of course. Or die trying."

It wasn't a very grandiose commander's intent. "There's no territory to capture, sir? Strategic target? No decapitation strike against Nergal?"

"Explain it to him, Mike," Mars said.

Michael appeared from behind a column, with Gabriel at his side. The angel took another step, and with a wave of his hand a new image appeared. "Both forces will assemble here for battle." A domain of jagged peaks of black stone and ice. Snow blew across drifts on barren fields, separated by razor-tooth clefts of wide chasms that dropped deep below sight into blackness. "You will locate and destroy the enemy forces of Nergal, or perish. Nothing more. The beacon of the gate will then appear to return you to the dominion of Mars."

Mars rose, shrugging the wolf skin off his shoulders onto the throne behind. "Leave at once, Beck. This is your first time commanding the entire company. I've given you great responsibility. Make me proud."

Of course I had questions. If there were no objectives other than slaying a bunch of armed steers, the issue for me remained, why? Perrault said what we did was just some perpetual food for the gods—the fighting and the mayhem that now seemed little more than a flex between egos desperate to let their peers know who was top god. As a tactician, I needed more than that. If the intent was to dazzle, I would dazzle. If the intent was to devastate, I would devastate. It would help to know. But there was little to gain by incurring Mars's wrath again. It might even be the start of a new level in our relationship, playing the cog to his wheel. It was time to cut my losses and split while I was still on his good side.

With firm intent to carry out my orders as given, I saluted and turned to join Gabriel for the return trip, leaving Michael behind. Gabriel had never proven to be a font of knowledge, so I ignored him as we flew back to the compound. I was mentally organizing our loadout and order of deployment through the gate when he interrupted.

"You'll find the armory will not permit some weapons to be drawn for your deployment. In this battle you will be limited in armaments."

There it was. The monkey wrench thrown into the gears of my machine.

"Why is that?" I asked.

"Those are the parameters agreed upon," Gabriel said matter of factly.

"Were there rules for our raid on Ah Puch?"

Gabriel betrayed a tiny grin. "As such, no. It was retribution for a previous slight. Punishment for Ah Puch's arrogance and vanity, thinking himself more than he is. And convenient timing for your graduation training."

"Splendid. What will be allowed? Snowballs with rocks in them?"

Gabriel's visage of stone returned. "An Ultimate is not defined by his weapon. Do not let them become crutches. You have the wisdom and might of a hundred generations of warrior within each of you."

"An Annihilator Mark Three is a very comforting crutch, though, you have to admit." To that he provided no response. I think he was just too stubborn to admit I was right.

The morning sun was bright. Back in the compound I found the men on the field as they should be, in PT gear and carrying out the morning training ritual as if nothing had happened. Formed by platoons, they were engaged in beating the snot out of one another. If anyone had had enough hand-to-hand practice last night corralling Perreault, it wasn't evident. The spectacle of my Ultimates pitted against each other on the sand erased any lingering fatigue, and I felt the pull to be in the fray of the exertion myself.

"We've got a mission." The field froze to attention, those on the ground springing back up to their feet to join them. "Dismiss your troops to begin prep. Platoon leaders and platoon sergeants, on me."

Orders were barked, and the bustle of orderly movement was underway as I directed my attention to my assembled gathering. "Stand easy. I'll tell you what I know." I gave them as much as Mars and Michael had given me with as detailed a description as I could of our enemy and the terrain we were to fight on.

"It's more than we've had before, sir," Jeong said correctly.

Stokes shrugged. "It is a move in the right direction, treating us like real soldiers. Did your talk with Perrault bust loose some of this new openness, Captain? What did you learn?"

I played it cool. "Nothing that will help us right now, Lieutenant Stokes." I used a formal tone with Dan, hoping he would take the hint to let it go for now.

He took my cue. "Roger that, sir."

Coghill was enthusiastic. "Your assessment of their capabilities doesn't sound like it will make for much of a skirmish, sir. They're in for a jolly good pasting."

I'd waited to break the news. "Gabriel tells me there's a twist. Only the racks with green lights will release weapons to us for this mission."

Denisov shook his head. "Well, Beck. I'd hardly say your efforts have led to improving our lot. This seems punishment for your insolence." His lack of courtesy combined with his criticism raised my hackles. As it did it my first sergeant's.

Magnus growled like a bear. "That is *Captain* Beck, Lieutenant." Magnus had made it clear to me he shared Will's distrust of the Russian. The Viking balled his fists, ready to pounce if given cause. The Russian remained defiant with arms folded in judgement of me.

"We'll get this sorted later," I said. "I'll give a warning order outside the arms room, then we'll all find out together what we can bring. When we're armed and formed up at the rotunda, I'll give an op order and concept of operation, then it's through the gate. Questions? Get suited up. Lieutenant Denisov, remain behind a moment."

Alone with the malcontent, I took the high road. "Ivan Ivanovich, I'm frustrated too. But you know it isn't appropriate to speak to your commander this way, especially on the cusp of battle. Can I rely on you to lead? Or—" I let the last hang.

"I was wrong, sir. It will not happen again." He remained at attention.

I decided to let it go. "In the future, save it for when we're in private. Agreed?"

"Yes, sir."

I put my mind to other things and followed the men into the armory. Right away it was clear the battle was going to be fought in a more primitive manner than our last outing. Besides our armor, the most high-tech thing that released from the many rows of armaments were the bows. Made of some fantastic material, they were light, and the longbows delivered a wicked expanding broadhead over 300 yards. We could all hit a fist-size target at that distance. But we had half as many as we had hands to hold them.

As fast as we could, we outfitted each in the company with swords of their choice, long bows for two platoons, short bows for the rest, plus spears or halberds for all. We'd carried much more weight in uptime weapons on our last jaunt. This was simply making the best of a bad deal of the cards—as good a division between ranged, medium, and short-distance weapons as could be organized on the spur of the moment. I wasn't alone in eyeing our Annies and the maser cannons forlornly.

I pulled a two-handed sword off the rack for myself. Once strapped on, the belt and sheath took on the same iridescence as my armor.

"At least we have our armor, Rag," Stokes whispered. "Sounds cold where we're going."

I wanted to give my friend more of an explanation. "Sorry for having to shut you down there, Dan. We're short on time." I still hadn't worked out how to let everyone down easy. How to be less of an evasive prick than Perrault had been while still achieving the same level of protection for the others that he'd managed.

"Was it worth it? Did you get something out of him?"

"Not much, but let's talk later. Good luck with the van." I'd put Stokes and his—formerly my—platoon on the vanguard and first through the gate.

"Won't let you down, sir. Find 'em, fix 'em, finish 'em." He broke to his command voice, using his diaphragm to bark, "Squad leaders First Platoon, on me."

His platoon sergeant, the samurai Hikaru, yelled, "Karl, that means you."

Something about hearing Karl's name made my senses tingle, and I looked around to see where the Prussian was, wondering why Hikaru was having to call him. Jess, Jakob, and the newly-promoted squad leader, Ruben, looked about for him as well. His back to me, partially obscured behind a rack of hyper-velocity missiles, I could just see Karl's square head nodding in conversation. Denisov's crooked nose stood out in profile between the tubes of a locked rack of manpads. The two were having a private word. My intuition buzzed.

Denisov was a study in cool when he caught my eye. He didn't attempt to hide but stepped into the open and matched my gaze for a moment before turning, just long enough to make sure to let me know he wasn't hiding from me.

"What do you make of that, Ragnar?" Magnus mumbled to me alone. "Not very hidden, his contempt. What does Denisov hope to gain by his insolence against you? If he thinks he knows the old way, he is mistaken. We did not dethrone a chieftain by cowardly plots. We challenged him to open combat and let Odin declare the rightful leader."

"He's probably thinking more of a putsch than a challenge. He's a Soviet at heart. He learned from the best—his uncle Joe. I don't know what he thinks he has to gain. As if we don't have enough on our plate, I think we may have an enemy in our own ranks."

27

Magnus and I were through the gate, shoulder to shoulder behind First Platoon. It took only a millisecond to discover that our jump jets were disabled, another annoying surprise. I ran the function list in my HUD. Comms worked, as did the map.

"Negative contact, Captain," Stokes reported. We stood on an icy plateau. A steep escarpment to our left dropped to a wavy plain of icefields that stretched to a horizon of shimmering aurora to mark the edge of this domain. The expansive plateau we arrived on was divided by a fault line, the crevasse that split the plain close enough for me to see the sharp sawtooth edge of its far side, suggesting a deep chasm. At the extreme edge of visibility was a faint mountain range ringing all sides of the white-drenched expanse. It was what I imagined Antarctica looked like, if it were some island floating in space.

"First Platoon, push out." With no danger in sight, we could expand our perimeter. In a few minutes, with the rest of my purple-armored knights birthed two at a time through the gate, our last three platoons were through.

"Are we on the ground first, or are they dug in waiting for us?" Stokes asked.

"Let's find out." I broke to the command channel. "Second, Third, Fourth platoons. I want you each to send a scout squad out."

Our topo map was in its infancy of development, only what we could see from ground level had been reconstructed in our HUDs. We had to fill in the blanks, and quickly. Every set of eyes I could extend to investigate our new hunting grounds would instantly be translated into detail on the map. Very, very slick. I wish I'd had such fantastic tech back on Earth. If I could, I'd trade the map function for jump jets. Or my Annie. I assigned the three platoon leaders their tasks. "Dan, find a way across that crevasse in case we have to move the company in that direction."

"Gate activity," Jakob's voice intruded. "Ten kilometers, across the crevasse in the direction of the sun." It was as good a Three Ds as could be given. The tiny glow surged as it was rapidly filled, then blotted out by the dark shapes pouring out of it. I powered up magnification and hit the spot with a laser. Twelve-point-four klicks. Far enough that even magged up they were at the limit of what I could make out through the mirage of the misty layers of drifts between us. The dark patch growing on the horizon told me they were bringing the whole herd.

"We can scratch having to find them off the list," Dan said. "This isn't what I imagined it was going to be like as an Ultimate. Do the powers that be just want us to charge each other? I trained on the plains to lay siege with war machines, to use heavy cavalry. I figured if we were going to fight with these kinds of weapons, Mars would want that kind of show. This kinda fight's for casuals. It's just going to be a brawl."

Too right. It was turning a tarantula and a scorpion loose in a cardboard box to fight it out. I hit the company channel. "Company, we're not getting suckered into a toe-to-toe kind of fight. I don't know if these cows are as dumb as the blobs we last fought, or if they're all bovine Audie Murphy's, so listen up. There're three options I can see available. We can stay put and fight them across the crevasse until we run out of arrows. Then someone has to cross to finish the other off. It gives us no advantage. Too basic.

"Option two. We carry the attack to them. Problem is, the terrain denies us that immediate option. It's going to take time we don't have to find a narrow to allow us to take the fight to them first, so I vote for another option.

"Behind us." I pointed to the nearest of the slopes fifteen klicks away. "It'll take them the same delay it would us to find a crossing point, and my bet is they're wired to come after us. We use that time to get off this plain and to some high ground. We may find cover up there. It'll give us advantage with our farthest ranged weapons, and it'll make them fight us up hill. Opinions?"

Jeong was first. "Any advantage is better than none."

"Clichés exist for a reason," Coghill said. "The high ground it is."

Denisov's deep Russian voice spoke. "My platoon can do much damage to them while you take the company to high ground." His platoon was one of two that we'd armed with our best ranged weapons, the long bows. Before I assigned either him or Coghill to the task, he'd volunteered. I detected a bit of arrogance, as though he wanted to beat me to the punch. It was bold, brave, and taken to the extreme it fulfilled my criteria for a potentially-suicidal use of troops—a known risk of letting the Russian have the job. But if Denisov was involved in some kind of conspiracy against me, I couldn't think of how he could use this opportunity to slip the knife in my back.

I always liked an eager beaver.

"The job's yours, Lieutenant. I don't want a die-in-place action, Ivan Ivanovich. There's a lot we don't know about the capabilities of Nergal's troops. If Mars had to trade away every one of our decent weapons in order to let us keep our armor, it makes me wonder what Nergal got out of the negotiation. Let's find out. Your orders are to harass and delay, gather intel, report, and be ready to displace to our new position, understood?"

"Yes, Captain."

"Move out." It was time for the rest of us to get to the high ground and start a defense against the attack I assumed was coming. "Lieutenant Stokes, scratch sending a squad to recon the crevasse and take the lead. There's no one between us and the hills, so haul ass."

"Sergeant Hikaru," Stokes said in turn. "This is our azimuth of travel. Send them out." I gave the other platoons their jobs, and in a second, we were gone.

As we sprinted, Stokes commed me on the private channel. "It's a good plan, Rag. It's good to be doing something instead of waiting for a stampede of crazy cows to hit us."

Magnus and I were just behind First Platoon, with Coghill and Jeong's platoons to our flanks. I thought about what my old team sergeant or even Gramps would've said about my order to run like a gaggle of geese let out of the pen, headed for the pond. There was a time for tactical formations, and there was a time to un-ass the AO for a better one. This was the latter.

When I didn't answer, Stokes spoke again. "I thought running promoted cowardice, Rag?" Leave it to Danny to throw my own words back at me. I'd never been a fan of how our old army emphasized running as the most important exercise in our daily routine. Once we'd made it to the new special team at 7th ID, combatives and strength training took priority. While training for the Ultimates, the same had been true, but to the tenth power.

"And this proves what a waste of training time it is." I had ample wind to chuckle as we hit a familiar 4 minute-mile pace. No fighting force had ever existed that could cover a distance the way we were about to, loaded for combat as we were. Yes our armor was amazing, but it wasn't our steel suits that made what we were doing possible. Armor wasn't a panacea for weaklings. The armor could only do what we could drive it to do. Being Ultimates is what made the armor what it was, not the other way around. "If the terrain lets us keep this clip, we'll be at the foothills in forty minutes. Barely a warm-up for this crew."

"I could outrace a horse with this body and cross the finish ready to fight. Let's get some, Rag! I want to eat steak tonight!"

I was feeling the same exhilaration as Dan. The adrenaline and warmth of my exertion fueled my aggressiveness like red hot coals stoking a boiler to power the piston strokes of my legs, the steam built in my chest as I wanted to scream, "The dogs of war are coming for you!"

Our mental conditioning and superior bodies coupled with our natural warrior's aggression meant it was easy to let blood lust shut down our intellects. I'd become more and more aware of how we'd changed, and how it had to be me who kept us from the danger that this killer's overdrive could bring. I calmed my mind.

"Head in the game, Dan." I broke and opened the company channel for everyone to hear. "Fourth Platoon, update."

Denisov came right back. "We found a jumpable narrow five kilometers in, and I sent a two-man team across to gain intel." He'd found a crossing point. Even without our jets, I was confident that from a full run I could make a ten-meter leap. From what I thought I knew about our enemy from their bestial physiques, I bet they could do at least the same. A spot that narrow meant the enemy could pour across it too. A road in was a road out.

Ivan continued. "They returned quickly, with pursuit closely behind. My early assessment is that you're correct, sir. They're not dumb animals. They've divided their force. Half have moved off the plain off the escarpment, presumably to flank our main body from below. We have their lead element held up at this choke point. If they find another crossing point, our efforts to delay them will fail."

"I understand. Good work. Keep them pinned for now. Beck out. Jeong—" His platoon was closest to the drop-off of the embankment on our right. "Send a pair of scouts to get eyes on the enemy movement below us. I want stealth, not speed. Don't give us away."

"Sir" was all he said, and all he needed to say. We had another twenty minutes to reach the rising ground and what I hoped would be some kind of tactical advantage. It wasn't long before Denisov reported again.

"The main body of their force is here, sir." Our opponents had committed to a rapid advance, much faster than I'd hoped.

"Impressions, Lieutenant?"

"Their weapons are as you surmised, Captain. Crude flamethrowers. Their range seems to be limited, maybe a hundred meters. They cannot yet reach us, so long as we have shafts. I'm glad to report they respond as any creature should to a broadhead in the chest. We've felled many. Like us, they carry edged weapons, but no armor I can detect. They have the numbers, but we are armored."

He'd done as asked and gave us much-needed information about the enemy. Maybe I'd misjudged Denisov as a malcontent like Karl. If so, at least he was a competent malcontent. "Well done, Ivan Ivanovich." I meant it.

"We cannot hold them indefinitely though, sir. We continue to fell many, and though my men are using their resources to great effect, we will run out of shafts soon. Then we must fight at close interval. It is regrettable we do not have even bolt-action rifles. I could hold them at bay indefinitely. Orders?"

"Make your retreat to our position at your best opportunity."

"We would stay and fight them to the last, if that is your order, sir."

"Negative. You've done what you can. Conserve your manpower and pull out."

"Yes, Captain."

"Is Denisov looking for a medal?" Magnus asked. "Or does he prefer suicide missions?"

"I thought you Vikings loved that sort of thing?"

Magnus chuckled and left it at that, but in reality I was a little incredulous myself. Denisov was ready to sacrifice himself and all his men.

"Captain," Jeong interrupted. "The enemy force on the lower plain is moving nearer the escarpment. My scouts report there's a grade that would allow for possible approach onto our plateau a kilometer ahead."

Excellent! "Company, sitrep. The enemy is doing our work for us by moving to our position from below. Prepare to engage. I'll lead Coghill and Second Platoon's long bows into a defensive line overlooking the escarpment and concentrate on the flamethrowers and leadership. First and Third will fill in with short bows and take the close-range targets. I'll signal you to move up and rain shafts on them once they're committed to the ascent. Move."

Magnus and I crept forward on our bellies to join Jeong and his scouts near the edge of the drop-off. I couldn't yet see the herds I knew were somewhere below. "What've we got?"

"Other side of this drop-off it's a traversable slope," one of the scouts said. "This is the lane for their approach, sir. It's a front a few hundred meters wide, still steep, but I know we could make it on all fours. The enemy could as well."

"Were you spotted?"

The other man answered. "If they're as good as we are, then yes, sir."

I liked an honest assessment. I pushed some snow ahead of me into a wall and eased my head up for a look. The scouts had placed us well. Two hundred meters below, the bulls were massed in a long skirmish line matching the width of the inclined grade, and already climbers were ascending like a funicular railway. Behind them on the flats, hundreds of shiny black-hided monsters were formed in columns. A chill hit me as I remembered the Little Bighorn. Being on the high ground hadn't saved us from the Indians' superior numbers. But Custer's men hadn't been Ultimates, either.

I was spotted. Shrill honks and guttural coughs went up. I slid back and stood. "Coghill, form up and prepare to attack." It was time to check on Fourth Platoon's progress.

"Denisov, we're about to engage the enemy. Set up a rear defense when you arrive. How many enemy do you have in pursuit?"

The Russian was on the run, his voice bouncing with his footfalls. "We bring at least a hundred of the beasts to the gathering of the feast." I took that to mean they'd thinned their numbers by an equal amount. Back to the open channel.

"The waiting's over, men. On my command, Second Platoon advance and engage targets at will. Spread out and give First and Third room to get forward and work the steers coming uphill." The short bows were good to about fifty meters. Shooting downhill, maybe to seventy-five. I stepped forward for a last look as an arcing splash of fire shot up in front of me. More burning viscous fountains followed. The jellied inferno rained on our front line like a volcanic splash, sprayed from contrary firehoses. Their first volley landed short. Where the stream landed, it splashed into the snow and burned in small puddles, fiery rivulets trailed downhill unaffected by the snow. The ancient napalm made me cringe. A primitive part of me imagined my flesh boiling, and in my head heard the sizzle of fat on a grill. I caught a glimpse of black hides and horns scurrying up the embankment below us, behind them a line of the flamethrower-wielding tormentors slowly marching upright. If they could close the distance, they would rain their fire down on us before we could stop them.

When tactics were simple, they could be carried out swiftly. I'd lost time organizing the company. The bulls simply charged.

"Longbows, aim for the flamers first. Make every shot count! First and Third platoons, move in and take aim at

the climbers. Move." I stood, sword in hand, grandly pointing the tip at our enemy, trying to emulate every medieval
movie with knights I'd ever seen. The twang of bowstrings
and the rush of air on the shafts was drowned by the trill of
more spewing dragon-fire directed right at us. The torchers
had gotten closer. Archers dodged and hurled themselves
back to avoid the hellish lava. But as disciplined as my men
were, the only thing they missed was the satisfaction of seeing arrows find their mark in the slick black chests they'd
aimed at.

Coghill directed his platoon from the far left another
hundred meters up the escarpment, directing fire down at
our tormenters from the flank, as he also took steady, deliberate aim to land a shaft into one of the flamers, a squeal his
reward for a good follow through before breaking to avoid
another rain of lava.

An unlucky bowman between us caught a full deluge of
the liquid hell. He dropped and rolled in the snow as men
behind raced to pull him back from the edge, scraping the
burning paste off him as they went. I tuned the scene out.

"First and Third platoons, work the defilade." Bulls on
all fours were making a quick ascent, much faster than I'd
anticipated. Magnus had his own short bow up and joined
in the fight.

Fallen flamers were replaced by more from behind, aiming their wands at the highest elevation. Further back were
the leaders, the red aura of the melam garments leaving no
doubt who they were among the indistinct herd. They were
too far away to take out with anything but the luckiest of
shots. A waste of critical shafts. If not my respect, I at least
gave my acknowledgement that their tactical employment
of the fire weapons was disciplined. A single flamer tested

the wind with a short burst of liquid fire. If at its maximum ordinate the arc continued on to our plateau, an order was bellowed and adjacent flamers joined in. If the test fire resulted in the shifting wind sending the arc short, raining the fire on their own advancing troops, no one joined in. I prayed for fair winds.

Magnus chortled. "They're roasting their own for our benefit. See them burn! Friendly fire... *isn't*."

It was a truism. They did seem to be sacrificing a lot of their own troops to make this assault. Magnus sent a shaft from his short bow into a target, bypassing one closer—though on fire—who moved undaunted by the flames that covered its back. Magnus's shaft found the mark, and for a moment I wished I had a bow.

At the sudden appearance in its chest of the shaft, the beast paused, then fell to its knees as it tried to pull the arrow out. The expanding blades created deep, jagged wounds and in the chest made finding a reverse course through the rib cage all but impossible. The creature slumped as blood gushed onto the trampled snow.

Magnus yelled, "Let them burn, boys. Save your arrows for the uninjured."

The burning steer Magnus left to his fate now made it onto the plateau, dodged an arrow, and charged an unaware bowman locked on another target. The flaming juggernaut collided with him at full speed as he dropped the bow and fought to draw his sword. Ultimate squadmates launched themselves at the flaming mass.

I lost sight of the felled man as still more minotaurs crested the rise at us. I drove my blade below the ridge of an eye socket, the flames rising off its back a herald before its appearance. I paused to make sure I'd hit its off switch before I twisted and pulled my blade free. A breakthrough was happening. A formation of bulls made it onto the plateau and in the center of them, one who wore the glowing garment. The outer shell of black pushed through and parted the sea of my men, heading for where I'd seen the tackled trooper go down.

The screams were deafening. It was Karl. His helmet removed, pried off him while he was held helpless by a pile of them, exposing him to the element of primal fear that exuded from the horde. The leader stood and the bulls parted to let Karl depart from their midst. His howls and shrieks made my own skin tingle, the terror he must've felt at the hands of Nergal's weapon I now understood. They didn't need to kill Karl. They'd rendered him useless. And a liability. Karl crashed through a formation, breaking it, as bulls followed his path into the center to tackle and enchant another of my men.

Or they might have, against any other foe. Swords and fists made short work of the conflagration, and the melam-wearing leader disappeared into a puree of red mist as he was hacked into nothing.

I paused to look at the flaming body still at my feet. I noticed the thick liquid that made the creature's black coat so unnaturally slick and shiny, so different than the dull hide I'd seen in Mars's chamber. Viscous beads dripped from the tips of the horns but carried no flame.

"They're coated with something to retard the flames," I realized. "Their own fire isn't harming them." I had to reverse Magnus's recommendation to let the flaming ones burn to their own demises. "Platoon leaders, be advised. The bulls aren't affected by their own fire. They're not armored, but they're coated in something to protect them."

"Roger, Captain," I heard at least one response, Stokes's. I'd no sooner given my directive than a test stream splashed into our midst, landing on bare ground a meter from me. "Incoming. Scatter!" I yelled. Those nearby flung themselves away in anticipation of the volley to follow. The telltale of an incoming barrage was now well-known, as was the instinctive drive to flee the agony of the flame that infected any beast, no matter how poorly developed its brain. My warning was a hat on a hat.

The fire may have missed us, but it had the desired effect. We'd been driven back.

More of the fiery arcs poured onto our front, leaving burning pools where we had been only a moment before. The steel in Jess's voice matched her speed, and she darted past us through the burning patches as more horns crested the ridge. "Fill back in! To the edge. Follow me!" Her squad was already with her, arrows nocked and launching as they ran.

I took a step to join them when a gush of flames covered me, and suddenly I could see only smeary fire. I was tackled. Knocked to the ground. The impact caused me to drop my sword.

"Ragnar, you are on fire!" Magnus was astride me, wildly brushing at me with handfuls of snow as he scraped at my head to extinguish the flames. I felt nothing.

"I'm fine, Magnus. Get off me." I pushed him away and stood again. Flames danced on the purple sheen of my armor and soon faded, much to my relief. "I'm okay." It was a revelation. I'd assumed our armor would protect us. I'd hoped our armor would protect us. Now I knew.

A lot of military training is endurance. Much is to remove fear. I recalled how in basic training there were trainees afraid of the dark. Their first night patrol or land navigation test forced them to face a long-held terror. Gramps taught me to swim and when I was older, pushed me to the limit with crossovers and bobbing and other exercises until finally he took me through drownproofing. He tackled and mugged me as I swam. Held me under until my lungs burned.

It's not as bad as it sounds. Gramps wasn't trying to kill me. He used to say that drownproofing wasn't to teach you that you couldn't be drowned, it was to teach you that some water in your lungs wasn't a reason to quit. It was unpleasant—coughing and spewing water as lips parted the surface—but once experienced, you knew how to deal with it.

We'd just never been up against fire. Before I could be 100 percent sure, I had to check.

"Platoon leaders, report. Do we have casualties from the fire?"

Stokes sounded off. "Negative, sir. I have two men who've been doused good. The stuff burned off and they're fine." Jeong and Coghill reported similar. Mars was a helluva horse-trader. If he held firm to us keeping our armor and had left us with only sticks and stones, it would still have been a good bargain. It would've helped had we trained against fire before, but it was another case of better late than never.

I raged with newfound strength. So, Nergal liked fire, did he? And fear? If the bulls couldn't get us out of our armor, then neither the fire nor their fear weapon—the melam garments—could harm us. They were just dumb animals.

"Troops, ignore the flames. They can't hurt you in your armor. Stand your ground, choose your targets, and make it count. To the last shaft!"

"Closing on your position, Captain," Denisov reported.

"Are you current on events? Form up at our six and meet the enemy."

"With pleasure, sir."

"William Tell, Captain," Coghill said, meaning they had depleted all their arrows.

"We're Winchester too," Stokes joined a second later. I already knew that Jeong and Denisov were at bare quivers.

"Form up by platoon." Our basic formation would be the same as an ancient Roman testudo, but without shields. We'd drilled those formations well, with shield, spear, and sword—and been hammered into precision like the Legions of old by soldiers who had been there. I knew none of the men had forgotten their training, though it had been some time. Since we'd gotten ray guns and powered armor, I'd wrongly thought we were through with such primitive warfighting. My fault.

Sergeants barked orders, and in seconds the company was in square files. A task once learned well can be accessed like a file on demand. Both diadem and repetition on the training grounds had made it so. As had the many trips to the Plains of Eternity to live out just such. Like riding a bike after you've left it behind for water-skiing, the men fell into place with perfection. Pole weapons on the front ranks, spears and longswords the next rank, and flanks to cut through any who made it past.

A distinctive voice yelled out, "Leave us go amongst them." It was Jakob in the front rank, guiding his squad as a dozen bulls crested the plateau. "Ultimates care not what implements of war we wield. We are deadly with all. Squad, set!"

A deadly barricade of sharp metal lowered to meet the blind charge of dipped horns, cloven hooves pounding the snow where it still burned in islands around us. The collision was a freight train of bone and flesh breaking its momentum against a brick wall. Butts set into the snow, pinned by foot and pointed at a deadly angle, the attackers succeeded only in impaling themselves. Living shish kebabs, some of them self-broiling as the flames they wore as coats burned on.

"Push, men! Drive them back!" Jakob spurred his squad as a smoldering steer pulled himself hand over hand as though the shaft that impaled him was a rope, until a soldier beside him opened the bull's neck with a spear.

Hateful roars were proof the pole arms scored well as thick black bodies slid down hill. If we'd felled half, then hundreds remained. We'd kept them off our front, but we did not control the entire line, hundreds of meters long. Their strategy shifted and in seconds, pockets of two and three bulls had pushed onto our plateau, between our lines to attack from the flanks.

"Form the line. Close ranks. Close ranks." Men at the flanks slashed, stabbed, and hacked to drop the beasts as we closed the formation to again keep the bulls from getting between us.

The beasts were powerful. Armed with needle-sharp javelins of gleaming bronze, they prodded, slashed, and drove at us with short charges. Their spears deflected off our armor, but when one found a joint, it penetrated. The screams and blood of my comrades were the first indication we were not entirely immune to our enemy's assault.

But they paid a high price for each one of us they scored on. The pole arms and longswords of my men carved them into so much meat, it made me think of our enemy more and more as nothing but two-legged bovines.

We weren't just winning. We were slaughtering them. They were in chaos.

"Squad leaders. By squad, close and finish. Close and finish." I released the men for their reward—the bestial combat I assumed the gods desired. No longer time for the discipline of rank and file, no grand strategy or tactic needed. No influence I needed to exert to guide us to victory. It was at last blows and stabs. Hacks and slices. Blood sprayed from an orgy of blades and pointed weapons. I maneuvered into an open space and sprinted to where shining black hides broke past glowing armor. The first bull knew I was there when the tip of my blade split his chest from shoulder to shoulder as I continued past and drew the two-handed marvel around to split his partner's head like a ripe melon. I pivoted back to the first bull to find I was not alone.

Magnus appeared from the churn, a madman, the grin of evil driving the swing of axe, low and wide at a knee. With only a single leg to support the beast before me, I slipped the point of my opponent's thrust over my head and stepped aside to let it fall. I turned to find my next opponent and left Magnus to finish it on the ground.

The clarion call of a horn tore through my skull. I'd not heard it before and intuition told me not to ignore it. I sought its source. On a rise behind us shined an open gate, and beside it, giant Gabriel held trumpet to mouth.

"Return, Ultimates! Mars recalls you. Return! Return! Treachery and deceit by our enemies. His kingdom is under attack. Your general calls you to war!"

28

A single bull broke from the skirmish and charged to where Gabriel blew the piercing horn a second time.

"Get that cow," Stokes yelled as he took off after it, troopers joining him in close pursuit. Rather than feel sorry for the bull I took a quick survey. There were as many of them left as there were Ultimates, fighting in small patches. That meant we'd taken down many, many times our number already, and I had no reports of casualties of our own. With only pig-stickers, we'd torn through Nergal's best like a sharp knife through cheese cloth. Was this all Mars's enemies had to throw against us? The Plains of Eternity had more challenges, and I was proud we'd sweated hard on the training ground so we bled little on the battlefield.

So to speak. I'd personally lost a lot of blood on the plains.

I turned back in time to see Gabriel go into action. As he drew his sword, where the air touched the blade it ignited in clean yellow flames, pure and beautiful compared to the sooty fire we'd endured from the bull's crude flame-throwers. In a contemptuous swing, effortless and without concern, with a single hand his stroke met the beast at full charge, cleaving it in half.

Gabriel wasn't my favorite among the demigods, but he did have a style to him. He brought the horn again to his lips. "Mars recalls you. We must return to defend his kingdom."

I gave the order. "Denisov, cover our retreat. Company, in tight order, make for the gate." My Viking was hacking at another bull, his axe making the wet *thunk* as he joyfully sank it deep into the chest, oblivious to the sudden development. "Leave it. Let's go."

Magnus's focus retuned to me as he came out of another of the wild-eyed frenzies he fell into whenever given the opportunity to hack and slash. He placed a foot against the broad black thorax and levered the weapon free. "We're winning! Why does Gabriel sound a retreat?"

"He says there's a war in our backyard. Time to go. You be last man. Make sure no one's left behind."

"A war? Mars's grace is plentiful!"

We weaved through small formations fighting in the move against bulls in disorganized two and threes. All that was left were small numbers of the bulls, and I saw none of the enchanted-garment-wearing leaders left among them. They fought bitterly, their enraged lowing and snorts no less hateful here at the end of their melee than when we'd heard their first war cry. Their programming was to fight until there was no enemy left to kill.

I knew how they felt.

As I came to a dead stop, Gabriel was commanding me. Before I saw the anger chiseled into his face, I'd heard it in his voice. "Beck, take your company through the gate at once and prepare for glory." He sheathed his flaming sword.

"What's happened?"

"A ruse has been perpetrated, a violation most foul and deceitful. Aricia is invaded."

I thought about our assault on the domain of the hippo people. I'd never for a moment considered Mars's kingdom could be attacked. "We've been invaded?" I asked naively.

Stokes had his platoon forming in two files, ready to plow through the gate and slaughter whatever waited on the other side.

Uncharacteristically, Gabriel supplied me with details. "Mictlantecutli and other impudent curs from the under-world have conspired in cabal against Mars. This battle against Nergal's army was a deception to weaken Mars. But his mercy has made them forgetful. The god of war could never be defeated by honorless dogs such as they. You will remind them."

The name was meaningless to me. "Who are we fighting? Mick Atlanta?"

Gabriel ignored this query. "Prepare yourselves. Your own Cradle is in the invader's hands. Instead, we use another portal destination, to that of Perrault's company."

"We need our Annies," Stokes yelled. "Or is this another of these negotiated deals where we have to fight with one hand tied behind our backs?"

Gabriel drew his sword once again and moved to the shimmering portal. "In Mars's defense, there can only be total warfare, Daniel Stokes. Use all weapons in the arsenal against these blasphemers." He stopped Stokes by placing a hand on his chest. "But use the atomics with care. It is our home, after all."

I inserted myself into Danny's platoon, and with cold steel in hand joined the conga line, ready to run. I commed Magnus, knowing he was in the rear doing as I'd ordered. "Do we have the whole company? How many did we lose?"

"None. Even Karl has been recovered. He's shaken, but present."

"We're on the move. Keep it tight. Assault."

Passing through the gate I felt the tingle and stretch at the threads that connected my atoms to each other. The frozen plain and drifting snow were gone, but the gray stone floor and obsidian black columns lining the curving walls told me that just as Gabriel had warned, this was not our usual home port.

"Where's the arms room?" I yelled as I pushed past the spreading front of men to reach the arched entrance. It was night, and the sky above the stone walls was a sight I had not before beheld in Mars's domain. Trails from screaming yellow hyper-velocity missiles and white-hot burning balls of miniature suns buzzed and crackled as they flew upward to whatever danger they were aimed toward. Over the walls flared lights from distant explosions to tell me in an instant that it was true. This was not another test contrived by Mars to challenge to our abilities.

Aricia—our Valhalla—was indeed under attack.

"Make haste and follow," Gabriel said. I sprang to keep pace, feeling very under-gunned with only a sword in hand. Magnus broke onto comms.

"Captain, the company is all present on this side of the gate."

Until we could get properly armed, we wouldn't be much of a relief force. "Good. Platoon leaders, we're making for the arms room."

We moved out of the gate building to cross the esplanade that circled the compound. Stokes was on task. "Jess, Jakob, take our flanks." The squads bounced ahead to block for us as the rest of us swarmed out in tiny hops like frogs on amphetamines. No guards were present to hold the entrance, and I searched for movement as we went. For once, Gabriel didn't make me ask.

"Perrault and his company are engaged. They alone were here to respond. My fellow Stalwarts fight as well but must protect Mars. We are too few and cannot fight off an invasion alone."

"Who are we fighting?" I asked as I confirmed that all the wonderful capabilities of my armor seemed to be returned to their gloriously full function. Hikaru inadvertently answered my question.

"Hippos on the north side. Assault!" We'd no sooner broken through the entrance to the compound than to my right, Ultimates bounded out of sight over and around the compound wall to follow Hikaru. Bursts of plasma rays confirmed the attackers were well armed and a trooper in mid-bounce trajectory disappeared in a brilliant flare.

Gabriel growled. "It is defended! Beck, you must arm yourselves. Press on."

"Coghill, take your platoon to the north side and make contact with the enemy. Everyone else, seize the compound. On the bounce, Ultimates!"

In the lead, Gabriel launched himself and landed atop a floating sled covered with the squat blobs. His flaming sword swept in a dazzling figure of eight. Sparks flew and severed limbs and flesh sprayed like a woodchipper from his meat-grinder attack. A beam narrowly missed me and without thought I took a bounce, aiming myself at another of the sleds. I landed atop the barge alongside a cannon and drove my sword into the triangular peak of the head manning the controls. The blob spasmed and the weapon discharged, the unaimed blast impacting the nearest wall.

We were all fighting. And men were falling. The chatter of squad leaders reporting casualties branded me. Beside me a trooper stabbed and slashed with a sword in each hand. It was Jakob. In seconds we cleared the deck of the three remaining hippos manning the gun sled.

"With me," he yelled as he hopped onto the ground and with a single bounce launched again. Beams lanced down on us from the parapets into the bowl of the training ground. Ultimates leaped from the sand at full runs onto the walls to follow Jakob. I turned my attention to find Gabriel. His flaming sword held aloft, his rally point was clear.

"To arms, to arms."

I trusted my men to continue the slaughter and took a bounce to where Gabriel beckoned. "In here. Quickly." He disappeared down the ramp and I made sure those landing behind me flowed down after the demigod. With a swipe of his golden palm, the electric pulse of the armory's security field disappeared. The green glow around the racks and shelves said the demi had already disabled the locks, and everything was ready for the taking. The gloves were about to come off. I bypassed rows of plebian pikes, shields, swords, and ancient arms, whizzing past the museum pieces of ancient slug throwers galore, and on to the promised land where our energy weapons waited in the deepest cavern, the greatest treasure trove any dragon ever thought of sitting upon.

To find the cupboards bare.

"Empty!" Jeong cursed. Agitated Ultimates pushed in with us to bear witness to the nests of naked racks. Each cursed our fruitless hunt.

I tossed my sword down. If there wasn't an Annihilator to fill my hands with, the second-best-looking girl to fill my heart's desire would have to do. I'd blown past her on my way to the beauty queen's cubby, thinking I was done feeling her caress. Sometimes, second best is still pretty good.

"Dry hole, men. All issued out. Get strapped. Slug throwers it is." I pushed through my steel gorillas to retrace my steps. Spears and other pointed steel clanged on the hard floor in a chorus of tin percussion, and I found the men were already pulling M-7s off racks and passing them into eager hands.

"Get everything," Denisov yelled. Over his shoulder, he balanced an M2 Browning. "Leave nothing. Every man, take as many arms and all the ammunition you can secure."

Stokes swam upstream and deposited a stack of crates. "Take frags as you go. There are still some hyper-velocity missiles and anti-tank rockets around the corner. Grab them all."

Magnus was beside me, an ancient Johnson Carbine across his chest and bandoliers of the even-older 5-round stripper clips slung over his shoulders. "Forget that, Magnus. There are plenty of M-7s." I pushed one into his hands.

He accepted it with delight. "I'll take it as well. I love all my children equally." Across his back, the double-headed axe remained.

"Beck!" Gabriel got my attention. On his chest was strapped a gleaming gold branch as long as I was tall. I'd never seen it before. It looked like something carved, not forged. A walking staff, twisted and smooth, with runes and characters raised on its surface. He held it like a rifle.

"Mars commands us." The floating image of Mars looked down at me from the vaulted ceiling. The troops parted to let me pass. Mars was dressed as I'd never seen him, his armor glowing the color of white phosphorous. In the background were more of the demis—the Stalwarts—armed as Gabriel was.

"Orders, General?" I asked as I took a knee.

"On your feet, Beck! No time for all that!" Another image opened beside him. The kingdom displayed in relief. "Here's the situation. Perrault and my Stalwarts hold the palace. Another company is returning from the plains as we speak. Artillery continues to target their landers, but we don't have 100 percent coverage except directly over Capitoline. They've thrown the kitchen sink into this invasion. Some are going to make it down outside of the city to start an effective assault. Mick's got help from the other underworld chiefs, and threw them into the grinder first before his shock troops come in to do the really hard work of trying to take and hold the kingdom.

"Their invasion is still disorganized, but that's not going to last. We must protect my citizens. They're in the underground shelters, but they're not impenetrable. Michael's directing the ground fight from here." In the center of the metropolis an icon showed where the Stalwart commander had a command post established. "Perrault's is assisting, and when the palace sector has been swept, he's taking his company here." A red swatch blanketed a distant section of the city. "Here's where you're headed." A purple zone appeared adjacent to the one assigned Perrault, a section of the city where the peaked spires and tantalizing towers had teased me in wonderment many times before.

"Take the fight to them, Beck."

There was only one thing to say, and I said it with heart—the words bursting from my chest with glorious rage.

"Yes, Mars. Your Ultimates have returned to wage war."

29

My first encounter with the hippos taught me they were dull and slow. But when it came to slaughter, a brainless enemy with ray guns was as dangerous as a bunch of rocket scientists. Superior weapons were an equalizer all their own and the blobs' particle beams cut through our armor like a dull knife through butter. Of the men who'd bought us time to empty the armory, only a few had survived. It was men from Stokes's platoon who'd taken the brunt, leading the fight against the waiting defenders—with only armor, swords, fists, and courage to bring to bear.

Hikaru and at least two squads' worth of First Platoon's Ultimates were gone. We'd mourn them later. Daniel was reorganizing what was left of his platoon on the fly. Karl, all but forgotten by me, was between him and Jess. The scene didn't inspire confidence.

Stokes aimed his knife hand at Karl's re-helmeted brow, which meant his steel lid must've been recovered from the arctic plain. "If you can't do the job, I'm assigning someone who can. You're fired, Karl. Caruthers. You're squad leader. Take charge."

Another man saluted and began giving directions on the move out of the armory.

I was taken aback by what I heard Stokes just say. "What happened?"

"Sir, Jess found Karl off by himself, out of the fight."

Cowardice? From an Ultimate? I didn't think such a thing was possible

Jess explained. "He's melted down, sir. I'm not sure what to make of it. I found him muttering to himself, curled into a ball. He's not combat effective, and he sure as hell can't lead."

"He hasn't recovered from the fight with the bulls. That fear weapon screwed him up worse than I thought." There was no time to sort it out. Stokes had done the right thing. Karl swayed and hummed to himself as though he were on the deck of a ship riding a gently swelling ocean.

"Karl, what's your malfunction?" I asked.

The Prussian stammered in a dazed voice. "I'm able—and—I'm ready, Captain." He looked like the lights were on but the elevator didn't go to the top floor.

"Until you're recovered, you're not fit to lead, but we need everyone in the fight. Get it together and follow Lieutenant Stokes's orders."

Karl wordlessly ambled off, and one of his teammates shoved a rifle at him. He took it and wandered out with the same swaying gait.

"Leave him if he's a liability, Dan. Move 'em out."

He spoke to his platoon. "Outside, men. Prepare to bound by squad and await the order to deploy."

I hit the command channel. "Order of march." I pushed the movement plan to everyone and the broad arrows of our advance came to life on the map. "Movement to contact with the goal of establishing a front. Denisov and Coghill, take the lead. Travelling overwatch on the bounce. Jeong, trail. Stokes, you're with me in the center. Our goal is to push through the city and clear as we go. There are civilians bunkered there. On my command."

With electricity coursing through my veins, I gave the order. "At last, Ultimates! Our hour has arrived. We are unleashed! Advance."

At full tilt we could cover the thirty klicks to our assigned AO in minutes. Movement to contact in this environment was little more than a reconnaissance by fire. The problem was all that stuff a commander ideally likes to know: METT-TC—Mission, Enemy, Terrain, Troops available, Time, Civilian considerations. I had gaps in my knowledge as huge as the crevasses of the ice domain we'd just left. Out of what little Mars had given me to direct my group of marauders, what had stuck with me was that the underworld god "Mick" had gotten help.

What I didn't know about the "E" in that mnemonic had me worried.

"Gabriel," I pinged the demi. "Who do we have out there besides bulls and hippos?" I had Gabriel's icon identified in my HUD. He'd placed himself a few klicks ahead of me with Denisov's men. His deep, distinct voice held something different than his usual contempt, something I'd not heard before. Awe.

"Mictlantecutli, Nergal, and Ah Puch have joined forces. Michael reports the drone warriors of Ah Puch have landed in a first wave and are being engaged throughout the city. Nergal's forces engage with Perrault as we speak."

"Are we getting more help?"

"The third company is yet to arrive."

How many companies of Ultimates were there? "Is that all Mars has?"

"Yes."

That was a helluva way to learn our own order of battle.

"Where are the enemy gates?" I asked. The portals were a critical choke point. If I knew where they were, I'd bypass any enemy concentration, hightail it for their on-ramp to the kingdom, and hammer them cold.

Michael answered. "No gates. They cannot reach the kingdom of Aricia from their domains by such. It is only Mictlantecutli who can sail across the void to reach us. It has been an eternity since such has been attempted."

The ground-based artillery I'd never known was there continued to hammer the skies. I magged up and at the highest power, saw them. Saw something, anyway. Hazy blots in the skies, areas of distortion, very far away yet and detectable only because they blacked out the stars behind them. The rising streak from a cannon struck one and it exploded in a supernova high above us.

No gates. Scratch that idea. "Understood. Out."

As the first two platoons bounced out of the compound, I gave warning. "Going up for a look." It was another one of those times when as the commander, I couldn't delegate. I set the max limit for my jets and took a leap. My jets kicked in, and immediately it felt like I was once again tall in the saddle. Up, up, up. It was great to be free, even if at any second I expected my HUD to buzz the warning of a hyper-vel launch headed right for me.

Denisov and Coghill talked as the two platoons spread out in a long skirmish and began alternating bounds toward the city. I trusted them to do their thing and scanned around. I got a good pan of what lay ahead. At the top now I surveyed from the plains to the edge of the megacity, a kilometer above the ground with a line of sight to what lay beyond the towers and spires. I took the option and gave the command for a short pulse to hold this altitude for another few seconds, letting my HUD continue the intel capture before I inevitably had to come down.

"Captain! Too high, too high," Magnus's voice nagged. He'd taken the wiser choice of low, fast hops to get ahead of me, leaving a split-second after I'd taken my risky bounce for a firsthand eye-in-the-sky peek around. He was waiting in the stretch of open country on the way to the outskirts of Capitoline, exactly at the waypoint my HUD had marked as my predicted landing spot. "You're lucky it's the hippos. Don't do it again, sir."

"He's right, Rag," Stokes said. If there was a problem with the HUDs, it was that it let too many people keep tabs on me. I ignored them. I needed a moment to evaluate what I'd retrieved. With the jump parameters defaulted back to a tactical height, I let the suit plan the next series of hops.

"Noted. Same interval. On my mark." I touched down and with Magnus alongside, we bounced again. I let the automatic functions of my command suit take over, and I got to work. Around me, Stokes positioned what was left of First Platoon.

The program showed me a cursory breakdown. "We've got bulls and hippos across the city in small groups," I said over the full net, the moving enemy concentrations I'd spotted now marked on the map. "They're meeting resistance from small numbers of Mars's Stalwarts." If the demis of the Stalwarts were anything like Gabriel and Michael, they were hellacious fighters, but Gabriel had already told me they were too few for this fight.

Michael's voice came back to me. "Stalwarts are holding key avenues of approach to the palace. Mars is defended. Mictlantecutli has landed his first troops beyond the mountains and out of our defense ring. Stop them before they close on Capitoline or all will be lost."

A new icon came up on the map. A full fifty klicks from our present position, a marker indicated first one, then two, then three landing areas behind the mountain range that shielded the rays of the rising sun each day before it beat down on our Cradle.

And between the open ground that cushioned the city and where Mick's troops were landing, sat our Cradle. Flames rose from it, and there was a tug at my heart. Not so much a home, it was the repository of our rewards for achieving Ultimate status—our Annies! And so much more.

"We are in range of the enemy," Denisov reported. "Bulls and hippos are working together. Particle beams and gun sleds defend phase line Chapman at edge of the city."

Life is never easier than when the rubber meets the road. There was only one thing to do.

"Attack."

30

The boundary of the megacity was defined by the moat of a river, and just beyond it, a manicured greenspace worthy of a heavenly kingdom. I took a bounce. I'd only ever seen it from afar, but it had struck me as sterile and empty, unused by the citizens of Capitoline. But now, dark blotches of the enemy intruded. From our own side, a piercing golden ray shot from my left. Its origin could only be from one source: Gabriel. Impact. A gun sled had just pulled out from a wall of thick hedges as an eerily-silent ball of glowing energy expanded, as though consuming the matter it engulfed. So bright was its glow that even as my HUD dimmed, I had to squint as I watched. As quickly, the nuclear flare faded and evaporated. In its wake, only a slight mirage remained, and in a moment that too was gone. Where the sled and the artificial soldiers manning it had been, in its place, nothing.

It was the first shot fired along the front, and we'd sent it. Or rather, Gabriel had. The golden rifle had outclassed the memory of my sweet Annie, and I felt a new jealousy. There was a split-second of quiet, broken by Stokes.

"I want one."

Fire erupted from across the river like fireflies calling to us on a summer night. We answered. The familiar chatter of M-7s, M-100s, and every cartridge-firing arm we could grab rang out. They were all distinct, and I knew the signature of each one. "Jeong, bring your platoon up and support Denisov. Stokes, break right and join Coghill. Magnus, let's go." It was time to get up front and get eyes on the action.

I wove a course and landed behind a trooper as he launched a grenade then immediately bounced again, firing his carbine on full auto as he leaped. "Conserve ammo," I reminded. The HUDs worked with the optics on the M-7, but nothing to the extent they did with our Annihilators. "Semi only. Make it count. Forget pray and spray." It took a much steadier sight picture than with Annie, which meant that at these distances, firing on the bounce was a waste.

Magnus yelled, "Down." Bolts whizzed around me, and I dropped flat. An AT-12 fired from my right. It was as slow as a tossed rock compared to a hyper-vel, but none-theless the anti-tank missile crossed the six hundred meters in a flash to kill the gun sled that had almost gotten me.

As much as I wanted to go on the hunt myself, I had a job to do, and that meant using my brain instead of my guns. Which was a drag. Why did I have to be the com-mander? A bull and a hippo moved together on their bellies not far from where the AT had pasted the last gun sled, and I assuaged my need for action by launching a 40 mm at their position. The tube under my M-7 made the comfort-ing "bloop," and I counted down the seconds until impact. I stayed on a knee so I could watch. I know. Not smart. I hit the count of five when my HE landed right where I'd wanted it, a few thousand fragments tearing through both bodies.

It's important to stop and smell the roses once in a while.

I took a moment to enjoy the warm fuzzy feeling, then got back to business. I checked our advance. We had to drive them back or we'd never get across this open killing field. I sent directional icons to the platoons as I spoke. "Right, keep up a base of fire. Left, IMTs and rush. Go."

In armor, our individual movement techniques would give a lion an inferiority complex. From a crouch on all fours, we could leap like a cat pouncing on a mouse—if a cat could do it in 15 meter intervals—while never rising above the ground more than waist height. Squads of Ultimates doing IMTs, spread in line across hundreds of meters, pouncing, landing, rolling to a side to pop up and fire prone—while another squad did the same in alternating bounds—could cover the length of a football field in seconds.

And that's what we did. With such violence of action, we brought as much power to bear as a tank battalion rolling across the desert on line. If only we'd had our Annies. On the left, Denisov and his squad leaders did as I'd ordered while Coghill on the right kept up a furious base of fire across two klicks of the linear front. I sent a flare up and gave the order. "Shift fire." With Annie, the HUDS would disable the fire control of a weapon pointed at a friendly. Our slug throwers had no such governor. Finally, the storm of lead decreased to a light drizzle of sporadic shots, and Denisov pushed ahead.

As simple and dull as our enemy was, our superior tactics didn't level the playing field. Particle beam weapons, though poorly aimed, found their mark too often—even if only by lucky accident. The rank of Ultimate alone was not enough to bring us the one-sided victory we'd come to expect was our just due. As I'd later call it, the Battle of the Valhalla Arboretum lasted only minutes.

By the time we'd made it into the cover of the city, I'd lost half of my company.

"Hold. I want battlefield recovery of any serviceable enemy weapons." I had security push ahead to give us a little breathing room and let my platoon leaders make it all happen while I checked in. "Michael, we've crossed the phase line into the city and are continuing clearing operations. Any update on the landing forces' disposition?"

Silence from our ground commander. I'd also lost track of Gabriel and had seen no further magical golden rays during this assault to cross into the city proper. "Gabriel, are you in contact with Michael?"

Denisov raised me on a closed channel. "Captain, I'm with Gabriel. Make for my location. Quickly." He sounded grim.

"What's up, Ivan?"

"Gabriel's wounded. Badly." I was already on the move. He was 1500 meters to my left, stationary in the greenspace, and I lit out for him like I was on fire. In three bounds I was on his position. Denisov was in the center of a perimeter of three Ultimates, facing out. On the ground beside him lay the giant. A hole the size of a tree trunk was burned through his abdomen, and impossibly, he was propped on his elbows, speaking in labored breaths.

"I have not long. You must be… the Ultimates I know you to be. Ragnar Beck"—he gestured to me—"take this." Beside him was the golden rifle. "You have not… used it before. I have commanded my weapon to… to obey you and you alone. Use it wisely. It will… it will not—" He fell back and was gone.

"Can a demi truly die?" Denisov asked.

"It's a day of firsts, I think." I picked up the rifle. Even in the dark, its golden hue gleamed like a bright jewel. "Michael, we're on the move. Gabriel's down."

There was no response. I hated to think of what that meant.

Magnus was next to me. "Should we make for Michael's CP to give support?"

I'd already come to a decision on just that. "No. We've got to stay on mission. Platoon leaders, report."

Jeong's icon blipped red on the map as he spoke to me from where he formed our left flank a few klicks away. His platoon had policed the carnage quickly. "We have a dozen serviceable new weapons recovered and are ready to move."

"We've got four so far," Stokes said from my right. "Not much to them. Rudimentary sights. Point and press. Nothin' fancy."

"Any of the guns sleds useable?"

"Negative."

From where Coghill had moved his shrinking platoon to spearhead our advance into the city, he reported no enemy in sight. I punched up the map. "Denisov, peel a squad off to Stokes. Dan, you and Jeong are taking the lead. Our goal is to not get bogged down. We have to interdict the landing. Company, move out. Best speed."

I gazed at the rifle. It was as long as I was tall.

Magnus whistled. "Can you use it like he did?"

"Only one way to find out. Let's go."

Our path through the city was direct. My broad guidance to my Ultimates turned into a ballet of choreographed perfection—death dealers instead of dancers. A bound, a touchdown on a rooftop, another leap. Dropping frags, launching grenades; the burst—pause—burst of well-aimed fire creating a hail of mayhem as they sped over and past both bull and blob. The enemy was spread throughout the city, firing wildly as they ran, seemingly uncoordinated and undisciplined. But I saw the pattern—they all moved to converge in the direction of Mars's palace, with Michael's CP between.

"Michael, we are successfully interdicting enemy troops moving for your location. Do you need assistance? Please respond." Nothing. If his position was overrun and he was too busy to respond, things were bad. If he had gone to meet Gabriel in whatever afterlife a demi had waiting, then Mars had to take care of his own defense. I had my mission.

The men recovered more of the alien particle beam rifles along the way, and by the time Stokes reported that he was breaking out of the city, half of our number were firing particle beams.

I had yet to try the golden mystery I cradled in my arms. "Platoons, get scouts up and report." I took a leap a few hundred meters up to land on the ledge of one of the tall spires that shot up even higher. It was my King Kong moment on the Empire State Building. It was the last of the highest points overlooking another kilometer of shorter structures, where the buildings thinned in density near the outskirts. Squares and oblongs, spires and towers, all whose purpose I couldn't guess. Were they domiciles? Storehouses? Crypts? There was so much none of us knew, and now there wasn't time to wonder.

Another klick beyond, and the open plains awaited—a dangerously-exposed area which if we got caught in, there'd be no way we wouldn't be fried like ants under a magnifying glass. My dilemma: to race through and meet the yet-unseen landing forces of Mick-something, or to establish a defense here? I checked the map, got oriented, and magged up.

Twelve klicks out, there it was. Home. Our Cradle still burned. Whether it had been destroyed by ground assault or bombed from afar, I couldn't tell. If I took us there on a detour, would there be anything left for us to find?

I willed my view to max, and the HUD responded. At the far edge of sight, waves of tiny figures carpeted the cresting ridges, dark skyline behind. Shit. It was wishful thinking that the enemy would remain stationary once landing. Here they came. They'd covered near as much distance as we had. We were two trains on the same track hurtling toward a head-on collision.

We needed firepower.

Michael's voice broke my concentration. "Beck, I link you and Perrault together now."

I wanted to ask him where he'd been, but Perrault interrupted.

"Beck, I've got you on the map currently static. What are you waiting for, I'm—" It was my turn to cut someone short.

"Perrault, we're under-gunned. We brought knives to a gunfight, and what we've recovered off the battlefield is third-rate." The men had been reporting the particle beams were proving to be unreliable, and most were out of charge. It was only that we'd been so poorly armed that had let the enemy use to them to such effect against us. "Where's the third company of Ultimates I heard about earlier."

Perrault growled. "They're not coming."

It was my turn to make the same sound. I bounced him a slice of the view from my HUD. "Do you see the enemy advance?"

"Affirmative."

"Perrault, if you have atomics, use them! Give us some breathing room."

Michael reentered the discussion. "You will not use the atomics so near the city unless Mars himself orders. Hold them until that time. I am again in possession of full awareness of what transpires. Perrault, advance to engage and interdict the enemy. Beck, recover what weapons as may be found from your Cradle and rejoin the fight. I am sending what Stalwarts remain to join you at the front. Make haste!"

Whatever fight Michael had been in, he made it sound as though it was over. "Moving," is all I said. "We'll be along, Perrault. First, we're going to race for our Cradle. If there's nothing to recover and all we have are our fists, we'll be there. Guaranteed."

Perrault sent me a new overlay. "We're swinging wide and hitting them before they get off the high ground. Make it fast, Beck. Out."

Now that we were connected, my command functions let me tap into his order of battle. Perrault's company had 60 Ultimates left out of 100. We hadn't been the only ones slugging it out. Now I knew what had him questioning my tactics. He was looking to me for support as I was hoping for the same from him. If they'd taken such a pasting with their full complement of arms, it had to have been a much worse fight than we'd had.

As much as I'd been focused on feeling sorry for us without our Annies, it just proved that sometimes, the grass isn't always greener.

I plotted our destination and sent it to every HUD. "We're making a dash for the Cradle. I'll direct as we go.

Platoon leaders, from where you are now, make a break for it. Go!"

I jumped. From rooftops and from the concealment of the city leaped my Ultimates, like mortar shells from dozens of tubes. Stokes was already on the plains, taking the right flank to cover our drive to the Cradle.

"Incoming." An explosion some distance away confirmed the call.

Magnus called in the status update. "Rag, we've attracted attention! We're taking fire. They have some kind of artillery, and they're walking rounds onto us."

I gritted my teeth. "Denisov, keep the company on course. Take charge if I don't make the link up."

The Russian answered. "Where are you going, Captain?"

"I'm closest to the problem. Go." I was on the bounce, getting a fix on Stokes's team and the source of the enemy artillery. Three purple arcs trailed sparks behind glowing purple balls of energy, their origin from the distant mountains. The rounds struck, short and wide of where an icon showed me Jess zigzagged in an evasive pattern. The last of the tiny suns landed behind her, the explosion on her heels as she took the next leap. Another volley of three rounds rose from the horizon, the trajectory traversing ahead of the last rounds, the direction of our movement correctly anticipated.

"Get clear," I yelled. I'd had moments to examine Gabriel's gift. Right now, I was only absolutely sure of being absolutely sure there was nothing else I could do. I input a max ordinate jump and took the ride.

Magnus groaned. "Not again, Ragnar. We discussed this, sir."

"I'm busy, Magnus." My HUD displayed a new gold reticle that matched the rifle. A scale ran up one side of it, not dissimilar I thought to one of the pulse guns we had. I hit the top of my climb and fired the sustain jets. Even so, I had only a short time to pull this off. From the ridge of one of the nearest mountains, another volley launched. Good timing, that. I didn't have a clue what I was doing when I slid the scale to the top and locked the reticle. I pressed the button under my thumb, hoping it was the trigger, and wished for the best.

Gramps wasn't the first to ever say it, but it was in his voice that I heard it. "Better lucky than good."

The same silent pulse I'd witnessed the one time I saw Gabriel unleash the wonder I now held shot out. Silent. No recoil. Just the beautiful gold ray. It was in the same instant, twenty kilometers away, the flash of a small nuclear explosion answered the effort. Light speed was magic stuff. I glided back down as the show over the face of the mountainside faded away beneath a rising mushroom cloud.

Perrault yelled at me over the command channel. "Beck! No atomics! Where did you get one? I thought—"

Michael spoke. "Gabriel has trusted you with his Rod of Destruction. It will not be capable of another such use until it rebuilds the charge. However it is that you assumed its mastery, Beck, you did well. You cannot know all of its powers now, Ragnar Beck, and there is not time to teach you. Just know it will not serve in that way again."

I felt guilty. "Michael, I tried to contact you earlier to let you know that Gabriel fell. I'm sorry."

"Set your mind to task. We will speak of it later. Know that Mars approves."

31

Mars had watched Gabriel's last stand. A Stalwart had not fallen since the beginning of time. It had nearly been equally as long since one had been called to battle. Gabriel had died fighting. He was in his element. It was how he would have preferred it.

The rules were beyond violated. But with that came the freedom to battle without restrictions. Mars hadn't seen a Rod used in forever. He was glad they still worked. With one in hand, Gabriel was the equal of a hundred well-armed opponents. Nay, a thousand. But the Stalwart had overextended himself.

After an eternity of constraint, being unable to participate in battle himself, consigned only to guide and train the mortals of Mars's army, left to watch as they marched through the gate to do battle—that had made him hasty. Gabriel had forgotten that he wasn't an army unto himself. Not even against the mindless foes he slaughtered.

His back was turned when the particle beam tore through him. In the end he was more a warrior than the Ultimates, but less a tactician. He was as Mars had made him in their forced existence together.

Mars felt as though Gabriel deserved more, somehow. He had died like a common foot soldier. His final moments no different from the men who he oversaw—fighting a suicide mission.

"Mars, we must go to battle!"

Neton was a good Stalwart. Mars once tried him as company cadre, but it didn't work out. Even after this many millennia banished to tiny Aricia, the grudge he still held prevented him from working with the mortals.

Mars undertstood Neton's bitterness. They had, after all, abandoned him, too. Their worship slackened, and then ceased altogether. The way of principalities and powers shifted, changed as they knew they someday would. But even being less, the gods were still more than mortals and therefore deserving of their worship.

Banished, Mars built Aricia as the kingdom for his Stalwarts and for the children of the pantheon who chose to depart rather than succumb early to what would be a final oblivion at the end of time. That seemed all so long ago that Mars could almost forget what was before.

When men sought his favor. When the blood of sacrifices wet the earth and the smoke of fat drifted into the heavens.

But not Neton. He burned with hatred for those who had forsaken him nearly as much as he burned to prove he was still a warrior to be reckoned with.

"Let me defend our home, Mars!"

The god of war was inclined to let him go.

Michael restrained him from where he directed the battle. "No, Neton. You, Segomo, and Condatis will remain with Mars at all times. I have sent what brothers I can to battle in the streets and save as many of the heavenly citizens as they can. It is up to the Ultimates now."

Mars's Ultimates.

Gabriel's company was poorly armed and bereft of its leader. Ocelus had left to retrieve his company from the battle arranged with Mictlantecutli's forces. He had not returned or made contact since. With the invasion of Aricia, it could only mean that his company was lost. More treachery.

Alator's company had only just returned to be on hand for this epochal blitzkrieg. It became clear to Mars that a conspiracy by the underworld pretenders was underway to dethrone him!

He never suspected. He'd grown complacent.

Ah Puch and Nergal's automatons may have led this assault, but it was Miclantecutli who was surely the mastermind. The others were incompetent, content to rule in their bleak hells, too affixed to their dark domains to care about anything but the occasional joust to feed the churn as was their role. But Miclantecutli—Mars had nearly forgotten how ambitious he once was. Now he knew his quiescence hadn't been from a lesson well learned by defeat after defeat at the hands of the Ultimates. Rather, it was a deception while he schemed how best to bend the rules enough to build a better army.

The god of war donned his battle armor. He was no less eager than was poor Neton to fight, but a general must lead. He must plan. He cannot lose sight of the next battle. Mars had much to do to set things right again. "Michael. Turn the Ultimates loose. And when the battle is won, I want you to bring me a prisoner. I go to work now to plan what comes next."

Michael dipped his head. "Yes, Mars. It is Mictlantecutli who has contrived this insult, is it not?"

"You were always my best student, Mike. Yes. And I hope he's enjoying his moment because he's broken the covenant. And now the gloves are off. He's signed the order for his own destruction."

Michael smiled.

※   ※   ※

Whatever power I'd unleashed with Gabriel's Rod of Destruction, it worked. It bought us the time we needed to get to the Cradle. The boys were just mopping up the last of the trespassers when I arrived. I bounced right into what was left of the compound to find the boys working in daisy chains to pull the rubble away from the armory entrance. Perrault pinged me just as I touched down.

"Beck, hurry it up. We're deep into it." I checked the battle map, and Perrault's company was engaged across a narrow front. I dropped into a direct feed from his HUD and got my first glimpse of our enemy. Of all the evil I could imagine, of all the nightmarish constructs that existed in this reality I called my present, I could never have conjured this.

Giant spiders from hell.

Eight legged freaks. They were armored. And armed. On their backs were turrets with slug throwing machine guns. With their forelegs they held short blades they wielded in a flurry as they crawled. It was only the sheer number of them that prevented them from being more effective. Those closest to Perrault's front fought like demons as he and his crew mowed them down, only to be replaced by the fresh mob that swarmed behind them. Perrault had a kill zone a few hundred meters to his front. Alator was near because the golden ray of his Rod cut wide swathes in their ranks.

Their numbers covered the hills to the defender's front.

"We're on our way, Perrault. Hold fast."

"We're through!" Stokes yelled. "And the arms room's intact. But the shields are up. I can't draw weapons!"

"On my way!" I answered.

Two lines worked together to open the entrance to the ramp and the tunnel that led to the armory. It had completely caved in and a narrow channel had since been cleared and was widening by the second. I pushed through and found the way, then I dropped to my belly and crawled over jagged stone until I was delivered into the vault where the arms room began. The red glow from the locked racks lit the way. I had to leave Gabriel's Rod outside, so tight were the confines.

"Michael, I need help. We've gotten access to our arms room. It's intact, but everything's locked." This time Michael answered immediately.

"The armories can withstand an atomic strike. And the security fields are to protect the arms as well as to prevent their misuse. Do you still hold Gabriel's gift to you?"

"It's close by."

"It will serve as a key. The armory will recognize your authority. Make haste, Beck."

"Hold on, Stokes. I'm coming." I reversed course. In the short time I'd been spelunking after Stokes, the men had the entrance nearly cleared. The golden rifle was on the pile of rocks where I'd laid it. "Pass me that, now!"

Jess had been listening and was already retrieving the Rod as I spoke. "Here, Rag." She tossed it.

It was in my hands and I turned back to a find the arch at the bottom of the ramp was nearly open again. "I want a line formed behind me ready to pass weapons back. We're almost loaded for bear. Let's go."

Stokes was waiting at the last room, trying to push through the invisible field. "C'mon dammit, give. Give!" A meter past it lay salvation.

"Hold up, Danny. Let's see if this works." I didn't know what to do, exactly. I searched frantically. There was no control pad. No lock for the key I was supposed to hold. I'd only ever seen Gabriel wave his bear sized paw across the portal to disable the lock. An icon popped into my HUD, a red flashing star. I clicked it. Nothing happened. I waved the rifle around. Nothing happened.

"Michael, I have the Rod and I'm at the arms room entrance. How do I deactivate the field?"

Michael spoke. "Martius iussu, para bellum." The field disappeared. "The rod will now obey your command over the armory."

Perrault spoke again with even more urgency. "Michael, we're losing. We need the atomics. There are too many of them." Perrault wasn't panicking, but he was closer to it that I'd imagined possible.

I checked the HUD to see what was going on and my blood froze. A wall of bodies rose in front of him, with lead-spitting spiders raining fire down on him from a few meters away.

"Hold, Captain," Michael ordered. "Beck makes his way to your relief now."

"He'd better, or there won't be anyone left to save!"

"Here." Stokes held out an Annie to me.

I took it and slapped a belt of charge packs to my chest, felt them lock into place, and pushed through the gauntlet of Ultimates as they worked to empty the armory. Annie in one hand, the golden rifle the length of a timber in the other.

"Make way for the captain," Magnus roared.

Outside again, I had only a minute to devise a plan. "Anyone ready, come with me now." I pushed out my assault plan to all HUDs. "Platoon leaders, nothing fancy. Get your people fully loaded and on my tail. Perrault's company is going under. I'm heading straight for them. The rest of you"—I added the next element to the map—"hit them from this flank. If we're still alive by then, you should be pulling some of them to you. Good luck."

With me were Stokes and Magnus plus a half platoon's worth of Ultimates, growing by the second. Coghill burst out with them. "Captain, I have my platoon. What remains. Looks like a bit of a pickle but we're ready to follow you into the fray."

"That will do. The rest of you with Jeong and Denisov." I didn't wait for a reply. "Let's bounce."

I aimed myself along the azimuth to where Perrault was fighting and lifted off.

At full speed, we bounced a hundred klicks an hour, disregarding the missiles that came our way. They were slow, not hyper-vels. From high and low, our Annies knocked them down from the air as we advanced. I was feeling more confident about our odds. They had the numbers, but we had the firepower. Against slugs and chemical missiles, this would be not much more than a long, slow campaign of whack-a-mole extermination. Call me bug stomper. A white particle beam narrowly missed me as I descended into Perrault's perimeter. It didn't miss the man behind me. I landed.

"Perrault, fall back. We'll meet you and form up together." I chose a line for a new defense a few klicks behind his current position, where the plane was a little higher than the dry wash he and his men were holding now. Annie's targeting icon was in my face. A swarm of the creepy crawlies was coming through a pass a klick to my right and making for us. I raked a path through them ten deep, with a wall of fire joining me from either side as we bounced, all of us sending grenades from Annie into the mouth of the channel. More rushed in to take their place. A never-ending wave of them continued to pour from over the mountains.

"Fall back by squads," Perrault said in response to let me know he understood, and I returned my attention to the battle.

Maybe one in a hundred of the bugs had an energy weapon instead of a slug thrower. There was no way to pick them out of the crowd as the insects rushed us. It was cut them down as you see them, stand your ground, and hope any who got through weren't carrying particle beams on their turreted backs.

One of their beams from the rear of the pack cut through several spiders, slicing through allies only to continue and find one of my Ultimates. My reticle settled as I launched a grenade from Annie. The purple flash that followed the wake of my projectile told me I'd found the shooter. The secondary explosion fried a spot fifty meters around it, taking out any bug still standing after my grenade hit. Bonus points.

Michael's voice closed out all other traffic in my ears. "Mars directs me to choose locations for atomics."

"About time," hissed Perrault

"Beck, direct your grenadiers to these locations." I let the others keep up the fire and followed along as Michael guided me. "These locations are where their landers continue to arrive. You will find the atomics are no longer locked. Use them as you have been taught."

The nukes were hyper-vels but strictly line of sight. We'd used them in training only once, and even then, we'd been told the yields were fractional compared to their full potential. We had five of them.

"Who's got atomics?" I asked, the quickest way I knew to figure how to get them deployed. I received four affirms. Two were with me, two were with our element that peeled off to the far left flank and were just now starting to plow into the spiders from another angle. Where the other one was, I didn't know. Down with its Ultimate, I supposed, somewhere between here and what was left of our Cradle.

I drew out a plan and sent it to them all. "I want three-man teams. Two assaulters running cover for each atomic. You're going to have to go right over them. Get high, launch, and get out of there." The suit jets could be "flown" for a time using continued thrusts to avoid having to land. It was a long way, and like anything tech, the jets were not magic, nor could they run indefinitely.

Jess spoke up. "My missile's green. I know I'm in good company to ask for volunteers for a suicide run. Who's coming with me to get a front row seat?" Two voices sounded off. I hit dirt at the new phase line just in time to meet a party of Perrault's men bouncing in from ahead. They immediately went to work covering the next group bounding back, Annies pulsing in short bursts.

"I'm coming with you," Stokes said. "I'm not losing you for a second time."

Before I could say anything to the contrary, Jess shut him down. "You'll do no such thing, Lieutenant. You have a platoon to run. Wish me luck."

Three Ultimates on my right leaped straight ahead, over the sea of spiders, and were gone. Jess was a friend. More so, family. To Dan, she was everything. I wished her luck in that part of my mind I could devote to such a thing for a millisecond.

Perrault landed near me, turned, and let loose with an M-100. Spindly legs and segmented bodies exploded a hundred meters away. I flinched as a slug pinged off my armor. The sea of spiders was a rising tide again and was over the wall of bodies, advancing at us in a fearsome wave. "Beck, we've pulled back. Those of us left. Don't know how much good it'll do us. I've seen them do this before. They're not going to stop until all of them or all of us are dead."

What had he just said? "What do you mean you've seen them do this before?"

"Not now, Beck. We need those atomics, and now! Where are your teams?"

I checked. Denisov and Coghill were plowing them down from our flank many klicks away. It did look like they were successful in dividing the attention of the horde, but a tsunami is a tsunami. And what fed it was an ocean of spiders, streaming forward and filling every dip and crevice just like that rising tide. Deep in enemy space, small blips bounced.

"They're still on mission. It won't be long."

Perrault grunted. "All we can do is pile them up again."

The crew-served lasers were not proving out. They were meant to punch through heavy armor. They discharged in short, focused bursts. If the spiders had spider tanks, they would've have been worth their weight in platinum. Instead, they were the wrong tool for what we needed. M-110s would have been a better choice. The crews had taken to traversing the beam as it fired but they only cut into the enemy wave in narrow arcs, then had to cool. When it came to facing down what made Zulu Dawn look like a rugby scrum, a minute was an eternity. Now I knew. Not all the diadem lessons made up for real experience.

The energy mortars were faring better. Behind me, Jeong had sections running two tubes, sending salvos. What had started as a well-planned barrage deep into the spider lines had shifted to danger-close impacts just a few hundred meters away as the host picked up momentum. When they ran dry, we'd miss them. I was already planning our next peel back. We could keep doing this, making a tactical retreat a few kliks at a time, hoping we would attrite their numbers enough to make a difference, but quickly we'd be fighting from Capitoline's border.

Then the first atomic went off.

And the next. And two very far up the range to our left. A spread of destruction that covered the horizon from end to end. The mountains sheltered the heart of the fury—expanding masses of red and yellow that shamed the violence of the suns they mocked. It was beautiful. More beautiful was the evidence that spiders had morale. The bugs stopped.

"It's our chance to push them back!" I put out on all channels. "On line and advance."

I let Annie stick to my chest and pulled Gabriel's gift off my back. It had served me once. Why not again? Michael had told me in the vaguest of terms that it wouldn't work again for some time. At least, that was my impression. But how long was that? You never know unless you try.

Someone said in a panic. "Behind us!"

I spun, expecting to see bugs. Instead, descending behind us, the light of the distant nuclear fusion reflecting off their armor, were Stalwarts. One landed next to me, his golden rifle closer to scale for his massive figure than mine.

"A dunce such as you does not deserve Gabriel's trust." The Stalwart took a step forward, leveled his weapon from the hip, and fired. A green beam, wide and flat in the shape of a duckbill, shot out. Spiders dropped like a windshield had hit them at a thousand miles an hour. Just. Dropped. He swept it from side to side like a weed whacker. Spiders fell in droves.

He stopped. "If you are to wield the weapon of a son of Jupiter, then use it correctly, you weak slug!"

"Show me how."

"Like this." He pointed me to a small button I'd thumbed the only time I'd used it. Near it was a small indentation. A new icon came up in my HUD. "Choose the dispersion to match what you've seen of mine," the Stalwart explained. "Michael has determined these creatures are not constructs. The light of Pluto will silence them but be not the clod of a mortal I know you to be, for it will do the same to all that hold the spark of true life, even a Stalwart. Gabriel gave you much trust. Use it to serve Mars."

I tried it. The beam dropped the spiders like I'd turned off their switch, better than Gramps's bug zapper hanging in the backyard I once played in. "Thanks—what's your name?"

"I am Neton. And if we speak again, it will be only to herald the end of your miserable existence." He bounced off to my left before I could respond.

Perrault was yelling in my ear. "Beck, up and down the line the Stalwarts are mowing the bugs down! It's time for marching fire."

"Take charge. I have to join them." I bounced, seeing what needed to be done. I hit again, cut another swathe out of the horde, then bounced again for the farthest right edge of our formation and went to work. For a moment, I was no longer the guy trying to run things. I was just a janitor. I sprayed an Olympus-sized can of Raid into the bugs. Those that didn't drop took the hint and veered off for the center. More so, they weren't even firing back. They were in a blind panic. Ants running from the focused heat of the magnifying glass.

Powered armor and energy weapons made us the equivalent of a NorthAm heavy division. Maybe two or three. Ultimates filled the line between Stalwarts, hundreds of meters between each and together. We stretched across a twenty kilometer front. On the move, slaying as we marched, it was the bayonet charge of all eternity, Stalwart death rays and Annies creating a buzzsaw of sweeping, inescapable death.

My work on the flank was about wrapped up. The terrain rose rapidly in broken peaks where even the eight-legged soldiers couldn't get purchase. I took a bounce to see beyond the first string of foothills. From here I could see into the first of the string of valleys that ran parallel to the vast mountain range that was the back wall of the kill box the enemy had dropped into. Spiders retreated into the edge of the atomic devastation. Far out I saw the wreck of massive landers, the frames of the hulks reminding me of the skeleton of a mythical leviathan from a nightmare I'd once had.

"Captain Beck, your attention is needed here." It was Coghill.

"Beck here." Coghill's icon showed him still on our far left flank, where he and Denisov had raced to form the short arm of the "L" that blocked and diverted the spread of the bugs around us and down on Capitoline. "Sir, bit of trouble mopping up. The big fellows aren't coming to our aid. Thought you might be available to pop over, sir, and lend a hand with your street sweeper." It was a good time to play Johnny on the spot as the horde was shut down here.

"Good call, Coghill. On the bounce to you."

I took off on a course just behind our advancing line. The view was unmatchable. Small pockets of bugs were corralled in the draws and valleys leading up the retreating hills, and Stalwarts still fought hard battles against the cornered creatures who chose to fight rather than flee and be shot as they crested the ridges. Did they know they were dead-enders? That there was nowhere for them to escape to? I checked in with Perrault on the way. "I'm moving to help clean out the left flank. Sounds like they're getting held up."

"Do it, Beck. We've got maybe ten klicks of slow going to herd the bugs all the way back to their LZ, and from there we can pot-shot at them until the rads cook them for us."

"How far out do we have to stay to keep the same from happening to us?"

"Michael says about three klicks and we're safe, so long as we don't try and pitch tents and camp out. I have forward limit of advance planned and am pushing it to everyone now."

The map updated and I agreed, we'd be able to corral the last of the bugs and let them fry, or gun them down, whatever their choice.

Coghill was back over comms. "Captain, the bugs are making a counterattack. We've had them boxed in a canyon from three sides, but they've a bloody large number of particle beams in this lot. I'm losing men by the minute."

The unflappable Brit was harried. He'd commed me on a private channel—a mature choice for a leader, to keep the distress of the situation off the open net. That's one of the ways I knew he wasn't panicking. I plotted a three-bounce route that would put me at his position in a few minutes.

"Mortars?" I asked.

"I bloody well wouldn't be calling for help from you if we hadn't run dry on the high angle, sir."

I winced. Had our roles been reversed, I might've had the same annoyed response to anyone asking me something so obvious. "Copy. Almost there, Coghill. Hang tight."

The cut was deep and wide and would've rivaled the Grand Canyon had it not been only the one ravine. I took my last bounce and descended near the mouth and the shallow pitch of the wide mouth of what had once been a riverbed, or the facsimile of one. Bugs were in piles, and the partial remains of Ultimates interspersed with them. Coghill hadn't hit the panic button on me. This had been bad. Ahead were sporadic shots.

I broke into the long bounding trot the Mark 5 armor made possible. "Coming in from the canyon mouth," I said on open channel.

Golden rifle leveled, I sprang ahead, thinking to surprise a redoubt of bugs in some corner of the canyon still pinning down my men. Yes, I over-penetrated. In armor, you can get away with things you'd never do without it. A juggernaut attack is what I was prepared to give. I sprang and hit on both feet into a deep crouch to absorb the sudden stop as I froze. I was too late. The canyon was stacked with bugs piled dozens deep for as far back as I could see. Nothing moved. I was too late. I punched up the Order of

Battle, sending out a pulse that would hail and transmit from any UItimate their location to update the OoB.

"Coghill, where are you?"

Something hit me in the back like a freight train, and I crashed face first into the dirt.

"Glad you could join us, you low-born pretender." Karl's guttural accent stood out even in my haze. I crawled to my feet and turned. From a crevice in the canyon wall, concealed behind some loose boulders, two Ultimates stepped out—Annihilators trained on me. The tiny legends in my HUD identified them, but I already knew who they were. Coghill. Karl.

"Not a bad show for a commoner, old boy, but an eternity of suffering your crass leadership? I think not."

"Coghill," I croaked as I fought to bring Gabriel's rifle up.

The flash of two Annies was all I saw before the end.

32

"I will now call you Rasputin. You are no monk, but you are mad. Wake up, Beck." Denisov was pulling me to my feet. My head throbbed, and my body tingled.

"I'm gonna gut you like a fish, Boche." I couldn't focus yet, but I knew that cornhusker hillbilly drawl. It was the voice of Smitty, Will's fellow 20th century doughboy.

Denisov steadied me as I swayed. My vision was returning, so I knew I wasn't dead. "It was fortunate we had already beaten the monsters back so soundly in my sector. I thought to come to Coghill's aid as well, though he meant for only you to respond to his plea for support. I have been suspicious of him and the Prussian, but even I never thought they were so hungry for power that they would attempt this."

On the ground was Coghill. Or what was left of him. The parts of him exposed between the jagged holes blasted in his armor, especially what was left of the head, weren't recognizable. It was by process of elimination that I knew the dead man was the Victorian aristocrat. On his knees next to him was Karl, helmet off, armor scorched and dull from grazing hits by an Annie, the glowing sheen that belonged to an Ultimate extinguished. Smitty's muzzle rested in the nape of the bent neck.

"Say the word, cousin, and this kraut gets what he deserves." Smitty bent and yelled. "Is this how Will went out? You try and kill us all one by one? Traitor!"

"Hold up, Smitty," I coughed. "Ivan Ivanovich Denisov." I'd had the gnawing feeling since our first encounter that the Russian was a villain. Now he was my savior? "I saw Karl and you before we hit the arctic realm. I thought he and you were part of some conspiracy against me." I took a few deep breaths. The golden rifle was still on my chest, but my Annie was gone.

"Pah!" he spat. "He and Coghill made appeal to me that you were not noble enough to command. Such proletarian thinking. Yes, I am descended from royal blood myself, but such is not a mark of pride for the new man."

"You didn't come to me to tell me they were plotting to kill me?" On his shoulder mount was the M2 Browning. It immediately drew my fascination and attention. "Is that what tore up Coghill?"

Denisov smirked. "I apologize for not being here earlier. I bounced in just as the cowards attacked you. I raked them with my Annihilator as I landed. The last of my Raufoss rounds I gave to Coghill."

The explosive incendiaries from his .50 had torn up Coghill's Mark 5 armor like a chainsaw on a tin can. I'd have to talk to Michael about getting us more of the obsolete arms.

"The Prussian was stunned but alive from my Annihilator burst," Denisov continued. "I must have missed him in haste to avenge you. My mistake makes me glad. Now, we can fitly punish him for his crime, da? But how is it that you are unharmed? Your armor is not even scorched?"

"At this range, two Annies should've killed me. I don't know."

Just then Magnus bounced into our group. "Ragnar! You live! Is this the coward?" The axe came off the Viking's back.

"Wait, Magnus. I'm okay. We've got more important things to worry about." While I'd been lured into a frag party, a battle still raged. "Perrault, talk to me."

"Beck! Good to hear you're still with us." The cheer in his voice made me think it was for reasons more than just my being alive. He didn't like me that well. "While you've been resting, we've gotten this campaign rolled up. I'd like to play this out on the plains a few more times. Now I think I know how the Battle of RV-317 might have gone a little differently for me."

I had no idea what he was talking about, but it was good news. "Have we won?"

"That we have, Beck. We're holding the front, and in a half a segment, there won't be another bug left alive. They're pinned between our guns and a rad count that'd cook a stone down to ash."

I keyed the OoB, read it, and then hit it again. The same count came back. I was stunned. "Perrault, we've lost all but fifty of us. That's all that's left."

"It's true, Beck. And every one of them made it count before they went down."

I ran the short list of who remained. Both Dan and Jess were on it. Somehow, Jess delivered her hyper-vel nuke and made it to safety. Dan had held the line, as had the other Ultimates of Perrault's and my company. And now, there was less than a platoon's worth of us to brag about it. Michael's voice commanded my attention.

"Beck, Perrault. Return with the Stalwarts to the palace of Mars. He has much to discuss."

We both answered together. "Yes, Michael."

Perrault was up on the line still. "I'll make for your location, Beck. I've lost all my platoon leaders. I'm putting Jeong in charge of the mop up."

"You hear that, Lieutenant Jeong?" I echoed.

"Yes, Captain. I have the command."

"Good. Denisov will be with you shortly. Stokes, where you at?" I looked for my friend. His icon blipped next to Jess. On the line. Of course.

"Here, sir. The bugs are roasting before our eyes, Captain. Thanks to Jess and the rest."

"It was a job well done. To all." The ringing in my head couldn't diminish the warmth of pride I felt. "Jeong, report in when the last of them are dead. Captain Perrault and I are headed in to see the general."

"Beck." It was Mars's voice.

"Yes, O great Mars."

"Beck. Bring the traitor with you."

✳ ✳ ✳

It had indeed been an eternity since Mars went to war at the head of his army. He felt it high time to do so again. From his throne he lounged aloof and considered the chained prisoner Hestus and Albiorix escorted.

Michael, next to Mars, waved them forward. "Bring the invader to Mars for his inspection."

It was a pitiful thing. Vile and ugly. Who would make such a thing? After short study, Michael determined it was not a con-

struct. "Mars, this spider was not mocked by Mictlantecutli's hand. It is from the domain of the living."

The creature was more than a dumb animal. It was sapient in some degree, shrunken and withdrawn, and very much aware it was in danger.

"How is this possible?" Corotiacus asked from the double line of Stalwarts paneling the great hall. Mars felt the energy of his war councils of old.

"The Aztec pretender breaks the covenant in the most unlawful way," the god of war answered. "He's accessed the old domain through some tiny tear in the fabric of reality that separates our planes, and like a thief, he's pulled out what he could grab. This."

Mars leveled his grand spear at the thing. Stripped of its armor and weapons, it looked far less fearsome than on the field of battle. It was not without beauty, in its own way, filling its own unique purpose in the universe. But it was not made in the likeness of the gods. Mars was no creator of all, but he knew enough of such things to know an accident when he saw one. A failed attempt that survived the rubbish bin where such mistakes were meant to end up.

Perrault and Beck stood at the base of the gathering. Mars beckoned to the commanders of his Ultimates, bringing them into the council.

"Perrault. These are the creatures you once battled, yes?" Mars already knew the answer, but the Stalwarts were watching, and he desired for his Ultimates' commanders to have an easy first entry into his council of war.

"Yes, Mars. This is one of the aliens I fought against. And lost."

Next to Perrault, Beck couldn't contain his surprise. Mars identified the curiosity rise in the man, the desire in Beck to interrogate the silver-haired fellow captain once again. He would not provide them the opportunity. Things were afoot. Time was bleeding out and with it, opportunity.

"Dispose of this thing, Michael," ordered Mars.

Michael frowned. He wore many hats as chief of his Stalwarts. Among them was his responsibility for the mechanics—the nuts and bolts of things. He kept the kingdom running so Mars could concentrate on always feeding the churn. It was Michael's determination of the unusual nature of the bug-soldier that cemented the god of war's decision as to what was next.

Mars knew Michael's reticence was because after so long, here was something new. He wanted to play with the beast. There were more important things for him to do now.

Still, Michael persisted in the hope of research. "Allow your scientists to evaluate it for a short while more, great Mars. There may be advantages yet we can learn before the hour approaches."

Mars considered, rubbing his chin. He had a point. There were specialists among his citizens who could carry the burden for Michael.

"All right then, Michael. Let your egg heads have their fun. Boys, take it away. Get it out of my sight."

The chained thing shambled away under the prodding of spears. It was little wonder when Mictlantecutli found this race he was so strongly drawn to them. It looked like one of the foul creations that hung from his coat like a pet. But it disgusted Mars. Infuriated him. Having a horde of them unleashed on Aricia was beyond insult.

Mictlantecutli would pay… but not yet.

"Beck. Bring the traitor forward." Mars still had some difficulty believing what Michael told him had transpired. Surprises were now wearing thin on the god.

Beck's Viking—Magnus—brought the next prisoner forward. The Prussian had been stripped out of the armor bestowed on him in Mars's name while glowing links bound his hands behind him. The Viking correctly pushed the prisoner to his knees and lowered the edge of his axe onto Karl Von Stomberg's neck. The Viking pleased Mars. He wasn't bright, but he understood how things were done, unlike too many of the Ultimates. Magnus knew how to deal with such treachery without having to be instructed. So much had been lost over generations of warriors.

Mars pondered the dilemma before him. The mortal kneeling beneath his feet was no Ultimate. The Prussian had been proved out and done his duty in Mars's service to this point. Was this evidence that there lay a fault in the process of selection? If so, how had Gabriel failed to sniff out this wretched cur? Or the blue blood they'd already executed from their midst, Coghill? How had they made it through so many tests on the Plains of Eternity? They weren't cowards.

Rather than a failure of measure, it had to be an inherent failure in their nature. A coating on them that could not be scrubbed off. A sin that couldn't be cleansed by the fire of combat. What Mars suspected was they were prideful. It was pride like that—the pride of not knowing one's place—that had driven Mictlantecutli, Neragl, and Ah Puch into such treachery against Mars—and perhaps others yet unknown.

Pride grew when shame was lacking. Shame was brought by defeat. Defeat brought by fear. And it was this that they all lacked—fear. They had lost their fear of the god of war. Of Mars Gradivus! Mars Pater! Mars Augustus!

This would be corrected. Mars cued Michael to carry on.

"You are brought here in disgrace," Michael bellowed. "What say you of your treachery? To your betrayal? To your spurn of the gifts Mars has given you as an Ultimate? Answer for your sins."

Beck dropped to a knee. "O great Mars! The fault is mine."

Mars was unable to hid the shock from his face. "On your feet, Beck. By Jove! What in my father's name are you talking about?"

Beck rose but kept his head dipped. "General, this man was not in his right mind. He was injured on the field of battle against Nergal's forces. The, the—whatchacallit—the bedlam weapon assaulted him, sir. I was warned that the fear weapon could make a human's skin crawl from their skeleton. It had to have damaged him so severely that he was unable to recover. I should have kept him from duty."

Mars's laugh was genuine. It shook the pillars of his palace. The Stalwarts looked uncomfortable, unsure what the god would do next. Good. Every so often it was necessary to keep even them guessing. There was time for a quick lecture. "The Melam of Nergal's chosen is a fearsome weapon, Beck. But it can only cripple someone who holds dark intent. A true Ultimate, one with the pure heart of a warrior, would've recovered. All that Nergal's magic did was reveal the sinner's true self. And in that persistence, this one apparently found a like-minded fool to conspire with. Shut up and step back until I tell you to speak, Beck."

Mars laughed again. Oh, but Beck was amusing! He would try to have the god of war spare the one who not only wanted to foully murder him, but to damage Mars's army in a time of war! There would be a time to instruct him later in the ways of leadership. But Mars's amusement was at an end.

The laughter faded, and the smile went cold and dark. "What have you to say for yourself, Prussian? Speak."

The Viking removed the axe to permit the prisoner to raise his head. He was tongue-tied. Mars shifted impatiently, seeming not to care whether the traitor spoke or not. Just as he raised a finger to cast punishment, the answer came.

"I only wanted to please Mars. Mars is King! How can any but those of higher birth—those of noble blood—lead his army? It was to honor your divine right as a king that we acted to remove one not worthy of your trust."

"And there it is!" Mars laughed again, the frightening swing of emotions that only a god could produce. "Pride. And a false one at that, believing yourself to be noble by birthright rather than by my grace. A grace I had already bestowed upon you in sufficient amount by allowing you to hold the title of Ultimate. What more could a soldier desire? Yet you wanted more. You wanted to command. And you have the audacity to tell me it was for my own benefit that you betrayed me?"

"Great Mars, it is I who bear the blame. It was my responsibility to monitor the candidates closely, and to cull from their midst the unfit." Michael's words were the next source of shock to Mars.

The god rolled his eyes. How had Beck rubbed off on Michael? This nonsense was catching! Time to move on. "Viking! Step back."

Magnus obeyed at once. Mars stood and leveled his spear at the Prussian. "Each carries his own faults. None bear the weight of another's. The well of souls is too good for you. To oblivion, then. Begone from my realm."

And with a flash, the traitor was mist.

The Viking quaked. Mars knew a part of him wanted to throw himself prostrate, but his bearing as a warrior held out over his barbaric childishness, and he locked to attention. Beck and Perrault were rightly impressed as well but kept it together far better than the Viking. Often the up-timers were affected most profoundly by these displays. Such demonstrations conflicted them so drastically, their conception of science and reason challenged in a way they could not fathom.

Mars smiled inwardly at all of this. He could no more consign a soul to oblivion than walk about the Earth of his own free will. The Prussian was gone, of course. Sent on his way to rejoin the path. Mars had merely marked him so that if he came across his spark again, he would know of the deeper defect. Still, the theatrics had the desired effect. The word would go out, and the others would be duly warned.

Betray Mars, and be undone.

"Now onto other matters." Mars looked at his council and settled on Michael. "There's a last matter to attend to before we sound the war horn. Bring the transgressor here."

The council held its peace, but the curiosity over these words was too much to prevent them from casting confused and inquiring looks at one another. What would come next would set the stage for the beginning of a story as grand as that which portended the battle of the Titans.

Even Neton gasped as the rotting corpse that was Ah Puch was brought in.

Mars always judged the wretch weak, but his Stalwarts and Perrault's Ultimates had intercepted the stealthy vanguard making for the royal palace, with Michael himself capturing the Aztec. It was a bold and fearless strategy, showing that Ah Puch was not the coward Mars always judged him, but he was every bit the fool to think such a plan would succeed.

Ah Puch should have known better. Eons of constraint had made memories brittle things and deceived him into boldness—no doubt, fed to flame by Mictlantecutli.

Those who ruled an underworld were always the most grotesque to behold. Ah Puch shed bits of putrid flesh from beneath his coat as he lurched across the polished floor. With restraining hands on shoulders, the Stalwarts didn't retreat from their duty to guard the wreck but could not disguise the disgust for their charge. The wet, lidless eyes set deep in his cavernous skull darted frantically. He knew the deep well of trouble he'd fallen into.

"What could have possessed you to come here, Ah Puch? Did you think to witness my fall yourself? What do you think now? You walking cadaver! Does the God of War appear to be run to ground? And where is Nergal? Trapped here as well without a ride?"

From up on the throne Mars could smell the foul breath that issued with his hisses.

"It wasss you who broke the compact. It isss my right to strike at you in your nest."

Tit for tat was his logic. He'd crawfished Mars more than once: arming his shamblers with disallowed weapons; sending his troops through a gate in advance of the agreed-upon start to lay ambush for the Ultimates; deploying troops in numbers well beyond the negotiated limit. All cheap violations to gain advantage. His violations never bore fruit, but now Mars had his fill of ignominy.

"No, Ah Puch, no." Mars shook my head in mock pity. "Your repeated violations of agreement after agreement made punishment necessary and allowed. You brought this on yourself, you conniving fool! The raid on your domain was but a

light correction. I sent my least capable Ultimates to spank you. Disobedient child!

"I could have purged your domain and all of your sham soldiers, but I did not. And like the fool you are, you confused my mercy with weakness. That was my error; instructing instead of merely punishing. But I will rectify that with a lesson not even an immortal will be capable of forgetting."

Mars glanced Beck's way to see how he reacted to his company being called the least capable. The man must learn that he is not above a little ridicule. Especially if it's undeserved. Beck took it in stride.

Mars nodded to Michael. *"Take the prisoner to his cell to await Mars's judgement."*

"You cannot harm me, Mars-sss!" The corruption sloughed a wet pile on the floor as he raised a fist in defiance. *"The compact requires-sss we all contribute to the churn."*

Mars spat his words. *"Begs the dog who violates the covenants within! Have no fear, you decayed carcass. First, I sort out your ringleader. I have eternity to decide how to deal with you. Enjoy your stay in Aricia as my guest."*

Ah Puch shed a trail of green and black detritus in his wake as he was ushered away.

"It is time to redress this slight. Mictlantecutli knows he has failed. He prepares for a siege as we speak." Mars wiped the loathing from his face and stood. *"What say you to war?"*

Stalwarts brought fists to chest; their spears deafened as they struck the floor as one.

"BELLUM AETERNAM."

"War eternal it is!" Mars raged. Even in the life of an immortal, there were not enough moments such as this. *"Ultimates! It has been long since the universe has witnessed*

Mars Ultor do battle. Are you ready to crest the tide of glory with your general?"

"MARS ULTOR!" Beck, Perrault, and Magnus replied.

"Michael, make ready to sail. We strike before Mick can steal more troops from across the tear to rebuild his army of cockroaches. But it matters not if he has one or a million bugs at his command. Because none can stand against Mars when he leads his army to war once again. WE SAIL!""

All voices shouted. "MARS ULTOR! MARS ULTOR! MARS ULTOR!"

Yes. It was high time that Mars the Avenger returned to do battle.

It's good to be the king.

33

I stood on the open deck while every munition and arm in the realm was brought on board.

"You should know, Beck." Michael tapped an index finger the size of a baseball bat on my chest where the golden rifle was slung. "It was the gift of Gabriel that protected you."

Michael explained how I'd survived the ambush by two Annihilators. The golden death stick I carried had many properties beyond its desirable destructive ones. "It shields its steward as well as providing the hand of your destructive will. You may continue to use the Rod. Teutates will instruct you in what time we have." Michael hailed a particularly large Stalwart carrying a massive crate under each arm as he boarded. "Teutates, come hither."

The demi's crooked nose, thick brow ridge, and folded ears made him the foil to the perfection of a Michael or a Gabriel. At first glance their classical features might lull an unknowing person into a sense of comfort, the deep well of their fearsome power and fury concealed by their beauty. I could never have the same mistaken impression of Teutates; another gold-skinned giant in magnificent glowing armor, but ugly as sin itself. His face reminded me of a Halloween mask. I anticipated a disdain on the level of Neton's to pummel me presently.

But of all the demis—the sometimes paternal Michael, the occasionally sympathetic Hestus—it was only Teutates who'd gifted on me from the first a sense of comradeship. The frightful looking demi dipped his chin and smiled.

"No matter the circumstance, Gabriel would not have entrusted Stellia to any who were not worthy. You must have impressed my brother Gabriel greatly, young Ultimate."

"Stellia?"I asked idiotically, temporarily put off by his friendliness. It was like a drill sergeant offering candy instead of telling you how much you reminded him of something staining the rim of a toilet.

"Gabriel's Rod is named Stellia. Come, little brother, and allow me to introduce you properly. Soon we conjure the spirit of battle to cast spells of fury against Mars's enemies. You are blessed to sail with us, you know. Long have we been held at bay. Today a new chapter will be chiseled in stone, bloody inspiration for the songs of the bards, fierce beauty for the poets to fashion a tale."

"Why is that, Teutates?"

"Why do the demigods of Mars not do battle against the enemies of Mars until today? Because it is the law. But the law has been violated in a way so flagrant, this offense cannot be ignored. The law allows, nay, demands redress by the king of all the gods of war. But do not concern yourself with things beyond your ken, little brother. Instead be joyful to practice your craft in such a grand arena. Now, take Stellia in hand…"

Teutates was a natural teacher. I spent much of the journey learning from him as we sailed. When Mars ordered us to make ready to sail, I thought he was speaking metaphorically. I had in mind some kind of spaceship. You know the sort. Something that *looked* like it could travel through space between worlds unknown.

Instead, we stood on the deck of a massive barge, deep gunwales ready to repel tall waves, thick masts down the center of the deck from which shimmering silver sails sagged overhead. Stalwarts manned the many cannons skirting the deck, and on the stern with spear in hand Mars gazed down at both Ultimate and Stalwart alike, crowded on the quarter and spar decks.

"Michael, cast off! Set course for glory!"

A cheer went out and I joined in. I didn't know what ocean we would sail across to reach Mictlantecutli's domain—perhaps the seas of time itself—but I was certain that at the end of this journey, blood would be spilled. Whatever the color. And we'd be the ones spilling it.

Perrault and I split the remaining Ultimates and found ourselves each with only a handful of soldiers to command—49 in all. If our general was concerned by the paltry number with which we were invading an entire realm, he hid it behind eyes of steel, the countenance of martial determination, and the sublime smile that told me he was enjoying himself. Someday I wanted to be the perfect mimic of what I saw.

Perrault joined my gaze to follow the electric arcs dancing up the masts like Jacob's ladders, giving the sails life as they responded to the push of electrons by billowing fully as though a strong wind filled them. For a moment we were children, not death dealers. As the warship lifted, so slowly and silently as to remind me of a hot air balloon, Perrault spoke with the same wonderment I felt. "Not what I was expecting. You?" He couldn't take his eyes off of the spectacle above and around us.

"Not even close." A radiant aurora like the dawn spread from underneath the ship to surround us, the cloudy glow rising above the gunwales, blotting out my view of Capitoline as it sank out of sight beneath our inertia free climb. The cloud we rode on was so bright that whatever the dark ether we sailed into held, the nature of it was masked by the light of our warship.

"Goshang." I used Perrault's first name, hoping to disarm him. "Before I miss the chance, I wondered if you'd tell me about the future you came from. I'd really like to know what happened after I left Earth. Please."

The elated mood of wonderment we'd experienced was suddenly gone. With my question, I'd killed it as unceremoniously as red paint flung to disturb a white canvas. Perrault was grim. "Can't you already guess?"

I had, but I still wanted to know. "We didn't make it, did we? The NorthAm?" Between Perrault and I was a gulf that I suspected was hundreds of years wide, with no Ultimates filling the gap in time between us. There could be only one reason why.

"To forestall another attempt by you to whip my ass"— he rubbed his jaw—"I'll tell you. But you won't forgive me for it, Ragnar. I know you'll never believe me when I tell you that it'll bring you no peace, but here it is. Almost no one survived your war."

I looked down, and then back up, returning Perrault's gaze. It only made sense.

"The poisons unleashed across Earth were a genie that couldn't be stuffed back in the bottle. The genetic viruses and nano-weapons thrived, mutated, spread, and killed billions—even their creators."

I didn't know if I should feel horrified or elated, but the irony of the Lotus mob being hoisted by their own petard did please me. I didn't interrupt and let Perrault recall for me the history of my future.

"Pockets of humanity survived. Only those genetically endowed with a natural resistance were left after the weapons had done their work. Earth depopulated and fell back into the dark ages for a period. Indonesia and the Nordic countries were the largest groups to remain untouched. The Placker-12 gene gave them the most resistance, though small numbers in other regions survived too. The two became the dominant polity and were the center of science and industry. But a basic conflict started. Not one that led to war again, but a differing worldview for how to rebuild—the Prims versus my ancestors, the Builders. The Prims wanted to keep things simple. They saw science as evil. How hydro-electric dams and antibiotics were evil, I could never understand, but that's how they saw it.

"The planet was probably cleaner than it had been in a thousand years, except for the nuke zones. It was a time of peace, and eventually prosperity returned. But that basic disagreement led my ancestors off old Earth on the first expedition to colonize Mars."

That I hadn't guessed. "Mars!" There was something apropos about the namesake planet being the almost alien-like human's home.

He threw his chest out. "Yup. I come from real pioneer stock. I'm a tenth generation Martian." He tapped his chest with closed fist, then made a sign with his fingers. Some kind of salute, I guess. "My grandfather was a captain in the Explorers and was on the first ship equipped with the Tengku-Sorensen displacement drive. Mars was never going to be terra-formable, so finding hospitable planets to colonize had never stopped being a dream." Then, his mood turned somber again. "My generation was the first to locate another world in the galaxy suitable for human life. But it was already occupied. By the bugs."

During the fight he'd revealed that he knew the enemy we battled against. "The same spiders Mick used against us?"

"Yes. The spiders. I'd just made the jump from Explorer sergeant to lieutenant. The spiders wiped out two research missions investigating LV-277 before the third reported back what they'd found. What they didn't know was that the bugs followed them right back to the Sol system. And for the first time in centuries, we again knew what war was."

My jaw dropped. "The spiders—attacked Earth?" I imagined swarms of spiders crawling over my hometown. I'd once mocked the human robots of the Lotus Hegemony as being little more than carnivorous worker ants. It stabbed me in the heart to think that Earth had almost been snuffed out by one plague of faux insects, only to be attacked by a real one.

"I only know they hit Mars. I assume they eventually found Earth. And if they did, I doubt things went well. Earth was nowhere near as prepared as Mars. Earth remained very pacifistic and anti-tech after her last war, which was part of the schism that led to the split and the settlement of Mars. Mars kept a strong military—we developed just about all the tech you've grown so fond of as an Ultimate. But we'd never fought a battle until the bugs."

The uptimer Perrault—placed over us for our final indoctrination to become Ultimates—was unique among all of the resurrected soldiers. He was the only one to have come here not by dying in battle against the best efforts of his fellow man, but instead giving his all to save the entire human race from a common, dreadful enemy. The ultimate enemy who didn't care what race or country of origin defined them. In that light, perhaps his role as mentor was fitting.

"So now you know the truth about me. I was in one battle. One—where I bought it protecting my home from the bugs. And as far as I know, we failed."

I'd lived with the gnawing doubt that my side had won out after my sacrifice. Perrault wondered if mankind itself had survived after his. I thought I'd been alone in my grief. But there was no way for me to assuage his.

"For what it's worth, Ragnar, I'm glad to have done for you what no one can do for me. The blanks in your future have been filled in whereas mine are still bare. And I suspect they always will be. Because as far as I know, I'm the most uptime Ultimate there is or ever will be—because I died in the last battle of the last war that humanity ever had. So, do you believe me now, Rag? That it does no good to know what I know? Because this is all there is—our Valhalla. And we're lucky to have it."

Even the science-minded, atheistic Perrault had been swayed into thinking of this as some kind of otherworldly reward for a fallen warrior—the Valhalla we called it for lack of a better name. I was no closer to understanding the nature of our existence, but I'd gathered enough to know that whoever the gods were, we weren't here at the whim of their amusement. There was some purpose to our toiling that served the universe. Which meant—

"Goshang, if there's no more humanity because the bugs made us all extinct, then I can't think of a reason why Mars and this churn to drive the force of the universe would keep on. To me, that means that whether we know it or not—buddy, at some point, the bugs got their asses kicked."

Perrault's jaw dropped. "You think there's a chance?" Hope was in his voice.

"I do. Humans are too tough and too stupid to know when they're beat. If there's a cave holding the last man in the galaxy, he's whittling a spear and thinking about how to stab something with it to feed himself or to keep another man from taking what's his. And because we're still here doing this, I think it's proof that he's out there. That means that someday some crazy, hard-luck soldier who died on a one-way mission to the bug home-world will pop up here, ready to prove himself worthy to become an Ultimate. And we'll watch his last battle just like a movie. I'll bring the popcorn."

Perrault seemed to consider this and gave a chuckle. "You know, Beck, for a primitive, you're not a complete orang bodoh."

I remembered the tone if not the words themselves. "Imbecile?"

"See what I mean? If you can learn a proper language, you can't be totally stupid."

※　※　※

Danny and Jess were faced off apart from the others. I left Perrault and made a beeline for my friends. None of us knew what to expect, and in some way it reminded me of our last stand in Panama. I'd spent very little time with the two and felt a little guilty about it. That, and something else.

"Hey, you two."

Both beamed at me. They didn't look like they were worried about, well, about anything. Jess glowed and had a flush to her cheeks.

"Captain." She dipped her head, obviously trying to hide her face from me. Dan grinned. It was a bit incongruous for what I expected from my two best Ultimates as we sailed off to war.

"What's up?"

"I asked Jess to marry me, Rag, and she said yes." Dan stuck a hand out. "How about it, sir? Do we have the blessing of our commander and oldest friend?"

"Of course!" I took his hand and hugged them both.

Jess shrugged. "We figured there's probably not a provision for such a thing here, so if we want to be married, then it means we're married. That's what counts. *We* don't need a ceremony or anyone's permission. We've survived death and made it into the afterlife together. That seems pretty much proof we were meant for each other. And who's to say differently? Only Mars, I guess. And as long as we fight like Ultimates, I doubt he cares."

My gut seized. There was the other source of my guilt. "Guys. I'm happy for you. I really am. I sincerely hoped that you hadn't come to hate me for bringing you both here. I know it's been confusing, and difficult, and that we're not the same—"

Dan stopped me. "Who's to say we wouldn't have ended up here, even if it hadn't been you who named us, Rag? No one named you. We all went down fighting in the manner that gets you optioned for service in Valhalla. However it works, I'm glad it happened the way it has."

"You're not responsible for everything, Ragnar," Jess said. "Not for how we went out in Panama, and not for us being here now. And even if Dan and I aren't together the way we once thought we'd be, at least we're together."

I was relieved. "Thanks, guys." When this was over, I'd speak to Michael. We weren't the same as we'd once been, but we were still human. The qualities that made us human were at the core of why Mars preferred us over constructs for an army. Perhaps there was some way to accommodate Dan and Jess in their desire to be man and woman joined in a bond that I didn't know about. It wouldn't hurt to ask.

"As usual, things are going to happen fast once we hit the ground. But this time, we'll have the Stalwarts fighting with us, and Mars to lead us. Whatever plays out, I'm glad to know you forgive me."

"Ah, it's more than that, Rag. I've got you to thank for everything. I've had the best of two lives now, and in those two lives with you both, I've had the best friends that anyone could ever have. And who's to say if we buy it this time, that we don't wake up in some even crazier dream?"

Jess smirked. "If we do, Danny, the next go around you won't get out of building me a house with a barn and a shooting range like you promised me way back when. This Ultimate will kick the shit out of any god who's got a different plan for us."

"We begin our descent," Michael said, his voice carrying across the deck like a bullhorn.

Mars stepped ahead of the helm where Hestus piloted our barge with focused attention. "Mictlantecutli will be expecting us, but we haven't given him the time to prepare a defense capable of repelling us. What we may lack in numbers, we make up for in audacity and explosive courage. Warriors, what we do now shakes the very pillars of existence itself. Show the gods and their cohorts why Mars is king!"

34

Blossoms of purple fireworks splashed off our hull like soft snowballs coming apart against a red brick wall. The artillery thrown our way was impotent, and if anything, the resistance served only to provoke further proclamations of our general's disdain.

"Is this the best you can do, Mick? Does it make you feel less enfeebled?" Mars nudged Michael, who was working at a fevered pitch at his own floating console. "His feelings of inadequacy stem from his inadequacy."

The chief Stalwart ignored Mars's mirth and maintained his monologue over Hestus's shoulder.

"Be ready to raise the supplemental screen, Hestus. Five hundred meters." The helmsman eased back on the yoke.

Mars roared. "Enough finesse. Get us down, Mike. I want to make quick work of this."

Deck cannons answered the screen of the repelling fire, each burst of lightning rocking the deck with each violent discharge. The faces of the Stalwarts manning the huge guns were locked on the floating images that guided their fire, the virtual images a whirl of icons and shapes that to my untrained eye represented nothing but chaos.

Our descent was marked by guns elevating in unison, the pace of their fire as steady as the sound of hammers striking a hundred anvils. Peeking above the shimmer of our majestic cloud, I caught the first glimpse of our landing zone.

Michael prepared us. "Clear ramps. Ready siege engines. Touchdown."

Beneath my feet a new vibration revved and hummed. A gentle sink, the sigh of coming to rest on strange ground, and the bow and waists opened to reveal between them sparse slices of the new vista as the aurora we'd ridden on faded to a tiny flicker. We'd landed in a massive field, a kilometer wide, ringed by a quadrangle of flat topped step pyramids that surrounded our landing site. It was a murder zone with no cover. We'd set down in the bottom of a dish with high ground all around us.

"I don't think very much of this beachhead, Captain," Jeong said in my ear.

"Stay behind the screens," I ordered. "Don't expose yourself to lay any suppressive fire. Let the gunnery do the heavy lifting."

From the hold rolled the war machines—translucent boxes atop spiked wheels, wavy screens of energy at their front to shield us as we followed in trail like the tank infantry we'd become. A main gun sat atop each riderless engine, the mouth of its cannon protruding through a pocket in the energy screen. They launched thunderous bolts to match the fire from the deck guns as we plodded ahead.

I went with the right flank, Perrault leading his troops left, the Ultimates not busy manning the deck guns taking the bow direction. At the head of the killing floor we'd landed on stood the most massive of all the structures: a pyramid so large it made the others seem inconsequential. A wide rise of stairs beckoned to its peak where sat a multi-faceted crystal sparkling in dazzling brilliance. We fell in to a left and right echelon trailing the lead engines as the autonomous cannons of our machines continued to hammer everything in sight.

I risked a glance around the engine I hid behind. Through the glaze of the shield that buffeted the rare bolt still launching at us, I saw the effect our airborne gunnery had brought to bear against the static defenses of our enemy. No spiders or other forms of hostile life were apparent, just the withering fire from the hidden batteries within the pyramids on our flanks. What was left of them. Most had largely been ruined, the massive casting stones toppled as though Godzilla had waded through a Lego playland.

A bolt passed between the screens of two engines, narrowly missing an Ultimate who'd fallen back to do as I'd done and lookie-loo the scene.

"Yikes!" The harried figure took a determined hop to return to the cover of our war machines.

Magnus scolded. "Smith! Be a gewgaw yahoo on your own time. Hayseed!" My Viking's conversion to hillbilly was advancing to perfection.

From where the bolt had found a chink in our moving wall, all of our turrets loosed on that one spot. Stone turned to gravel, ejecting in a volcanic eruption propelled by a supernova of orange flares from deep within the last of the untouched pyramids. Our fire ceased with the silence of the enemy guns.

Michael's calm voice commanded, "Lead elements, halt advance. Left and right echelon, line formation."

There'd been little to do but march behind the cover of our war machines. I felt the relief of the lull in enemy fire and clicked onto the battlefield view in my HUD. We now stretched on line in a wide front, facing the grand pyramid at the head of the rectangular field a kilometer away. I anticipated a barrage to launch at us from each level of the redoubt, my vision peeling away the layers of the battlements, and I strained to see the defenders doubtless awaiting to pour fire down onto us. The oil-slick sheen of a wall lay at its front, and soon I grasped the tactical situation before us.

Mars rode into the center of our line, impossible to miss, atop a glowing white chariot that matched his armor. A team of monstrously-sized dire wolves, snarling and grunting, pulled the ostentatious carriage. He rolled to a halt.

"If it's a siege he wants, then who is Mars to disappoint? Make ready catapults."

Each of our engines sank into the ground. A beam as translucent as the rest of the engine appeared, slowly extending from the midst of the rectangular block until reaching full length. Stalwarts spread to man each of the machines as Michael shook me from my awe. "Ultimates, form up in gun teams. Follow the direction of the master gunner and prepare for volley."

I tapped those closest on pauldroned shoulders as Stokes and Jeong took over to direct the men to spread out and man the guns. I took position to watch the spectacle as Ultimates in groups of two and three darted into place. Teutates commanded the nearest, and I listened as he instructed.

"We first create our missile, little brothers." He took from a pouch at his waist a small pebble and tossed it on the ground, aimed the tip of his Rod at it, and made a swirling motion that coaxed the tiny mass to grow as he guided. When the missile was a meter in diameter of glowing green, he stood back. "It is not yet armed. Fear not, but hurry. Load the sling."

The two Ultimates bent to lift the magical projectile, and when it sat in its cradle, they too stepped back.

"This is a sight none have seen in all the ages of man," Teutates mused.

"All pieces." Michael spoke and everyone listened. "Degrade setting. Maximum charge."

Stalwarts stepped forward and again touched the radiant projectiles with their golden rifles. The missile took on a menacing deep, dark emerald that signaled their readiness.

"Check deflection. On my command. Fire!"

The long beams circumscribed their arc, the swing of the sling carried with it, and the green orbs hurled away, over our deflection screens, through the air, cast over the bare field toward the imposing stone fortress beyond. It was Charlemagne meets Flash Gordon. My heart soared with the missiles as they careened away. We cheered as they flew.

The barrage struck the all-but-invisible wall, the collisions sending dazzling blazes of power to the surface. Where the missiles struck, an echo of form remained for a brief second. The barrier extended higher than the top of the pyramid by many lengths. None penetrated.

"Sections, reload and await voice command."

Teutates caught my attention. He winked. "Now the siege begins."

I took turns spelling the loading crews as I walked up and down the line. Not for need, but because I wanted to experience the moment as more than spectator. The conjured stones hummed in my arms as we lifted them into place, their electric nature leaving a tingle in my digits after depositing them to take their hurtling course over our shields to crash into the wall of the enemy beyond.

For hours we slung fire at the pyramid. The contemptuous Neton turned his scowl away from me to the wall that buffeted our assault. "This bulwark is strong. Mictlantecutli offered up the other battlements to pay our butcher's bill and left them with naught for defense, saving all for himself. But it will avail him not." The other pyramids had not been shielded as was the lair of Mictlantecutli. "Great Mars's patience wears thin. Our time comes. See?"

I heard the pants and growls of the dire wolves pulling the chariot and took a step back from the course of our general as his team made straight for us. We dropped to a knee.

"Allow me, men." From his carriage Mars touched the broad head of his spear to the glowing projectile and held it there until jets of blue copper ejected from its core to mix among the emerald. "Recover and make ready."

He was off.

Caruthers, the man Stokes had promoted to squad leader, whistled. "The boss crammed Comp B in with the TNT in these warheads. We're in for a show."

Neton bade us stand back. "Soon we'll find out if you're all worth the trouble Mars has dedicated into making you fighting men."

His milk run complete, Mars headed back to the center. As he rode past, he yelled, "Rain hard, men. When we have the outer wall breached, await my order to advance."

Michael's voice returned. "All pieces, on my command. Fire."

I'd become accustomed to the sight of our barrages and the drudgery of it, the wall resisting the buffeting attacks again and again. But even the Stalwarts froze in anticipation of what effect we would see now that Mars had touched our ordnance. The super-charged payloads flew, as had all the previous, and on contact with the barrier, huge holes burned in midair to leave gaps in the defensive screen, the edges of them red as molten steel.

Anticipating Mars, I recovered Stellia from where I'd laid her. That name had made the weapon a "she" in my mind.

Mars's deep, powerful voice boomed his commands. "Engines advance! To towers and breach."

The beams of the catapults retracted, then the siege engines rose off the ground and rolled, picking up speed until we were at a trot behind them. We neared the scintillating perimeter and the engines slowed, grew in height, and eased to a halt beneath the breach above. As the engines settled and sprouted more sections of still-rising towers, the picture that had been the frozen quiet beyond came to a conclusive end.

I saw it just as someone said it: "Spiders on the move!" Through the mirage of the fence, familiar shapes scurried between battlements, and the fusillade of their defense commenced. White bolts launched, aimed at our breaches.

Mars bellowed. "It is a day for us—the bold, the reckless, the fortunate. Stalwart and Ultimate alike, I give you my blessing. Win the day! Assault!"

Neton bounded up the ladder. I jumped, aiming for a deck fifty meters above, and leapfrogged past him. I bypassed the ladder and took another hop, then grabbed the edge of the next platform and swung up onto it. The glowing breach lay just to the side, a double-door width opening that attracted enemy fire like a deluge into a storm drain.

On my belly I crawled over, easing Stellia ahead of me. Now that I knew how, I activated the shield and aimed through my HUD. When the reticle settled on the first battlement to appear through the breach, I let her rip. Good hit! I slid a little further, and after more of the old lather, rinse, repeat, I'd cleared out several tiers.

"Not completely useless," Neton judged behind me. "Though the honor was mine to lead."

"Be my guest." I let him take my spot. From the other siege towers, Stalwarts tunneled through the fatal funnels of our breach points, still magnets for enemy fire. "Pass me a hyper-vel."

From the deck below, hands passed me a missile. I armed it and nudged up to the Stalwart blocking my access to the fight. "Let me give them some of this, Neton."

The huge diamond at the top of the pyramid was too good a target to ignore. I had no idea of its purpose, decorative or functional.

"You may. But be quick about it."

As he pulled back, a white pulse blasted through the hole, close enough I could feel the energy wake as it passed. Things were still very hot. I leaned out, snapped the rocket up, and fired. There was always a pause between mashing the trigger and when the missile deployed, an infinitesimal delay as the drive came to life before the missile uncaged and the parking brake was released. I froze on the glittering gem and held my breath. The top of the pyramid erupted as a giant hand pulled me back.

"But for this one instance I would have thought you useful! A child would have chosen such a target. Such wasted effort!" Apparently Neton didn't think the big crystal was a very strategic target. But in the aftermath of the enormous detonation, a brief respite in the fire coming at us was happening. There was a time to plan, then there was a time to lead from the front. This was that time. I hit my jets and shot through the breach.

Neton watched me with cold rage. "And you again take the honor that is mine to be first through the breach. Dog!"

I ignored him. Speed by itself isn't much of a tactic, but momentum is the only way to achieve superiority over a static defender. I'd had enough trading blows from a standstill. I hit the ground and immediately sprang laterally. A bolt struck where I'd just been. I hopped again, dodged, jagged, skipped, all the while keeping a steady stream of well-aimed blasts heading out wherever I saw a piece of bug body sticking out from behind cover.

I had three hundred meters to cross to reach the base of the pyramid where I had some defilade. Three hundred meters where the entirety of the pyramid could fire down on me like a rat in a burning garbage dump. But as I'd hoped, my solo assault drew another equally predictable response. Predictable, because I knew my Ultimates.

As I drew fire, an avalanche of golden and white blasts rained over the face of the pyramid from behind me. Stalwarts and Ultimates responded with violence unmatched. The dam broke, and bounding figures leaped from on high into the game.

"After him! Follow our captain!" Stokes hollered.

I left each to his task and was now at the foot of the massive pyramid. In powered armor, things could happen quicker than the mind could sometimes plan for. I tucked myself down and stole a glance behind me. A fifty-cal sang its song of death—Denisov carried the favored weapon as it fired—mounted on his shoulder. An M-100 was in his hands allowing him to fill in below with yet more merciless fire. A one-man gun team.

In the air, on the ground, on the bounce, on the run, Ultimates sprang across the plain like a plague of locusts. Purple and red streaks of plasma and accelerated particles blanketed the sky over the battlefield. Stalwarts on the ground behind laid down more fire from their staves, the heavy bolts distinct in their girth and pure rich color. Together they advanced toward the shadow of the giant mountain.

But not without cost. Icons turned red in my HUD with bright flashes on the battleground to tell me men had died. I dashed along the wall of the first level of massive stones, ready to spring up from a new spot, when an Ultimate made touchdown. It was Jakob, firing as he spoke.

"Ragnar, I follow. We alternate upward bounds. Take the next level. Suppressing fire. Move."

"Moving," I was about to say, when from multiple directions Jakob was hammered in succession. He dropped to his knees, arms flung wide.

"Jakob's down! Rain hell above me. I'm making pick-up." In less time than it took me to ask, above me came a volcanic eruption of flowering sparks and flying rocky debris that pinged off my armor. I dashed to where Jakob fell, grabbed his collar, and pulled him backward with me to the cover of the defilade.

Only part of him came with me.

Where legs should have attached to waist, instead was a bloodless nothing. He made no sound. His face raised to meet mine.

"The demons saw me with my head down and thought they had defeated me. But they did not hear me say Amen as I knelt. They do not yet know that I rise to fight them, renewed by faith." He pushed up on his elbows.

"Rest, Jakob." I'd seen many die. Myself included. Jakob was the calmest. "I'll be back for you." I placed a hand on his forehead to ease him down. He ceased resistance and lay back.

"Ragnar, in your struggles, you are not alone. Endure this suffering and your faith will grow. These—even Mars—are lesser. There is but one God. You'll see." And he was gone. Two more Ultimates landed, grenades and bolts unleashing in a hailstorm above us. Another landed, bounced, and walked fire from an M-100 up the pyramid, and down again, landing in the same spot.

"It's clear to the next two tiers. Ready when you are, sir." Their names appeared in my HUD. I gave them Jakob's plan.

"Mohammed, with me. Alternating bounds. Kurtz and Stahl next. Let's go."

I lit out and up. This was a better task for Annie. I traded Stellia to my back, sent a grenade out, and watched the plume of its trail disappear over the next horizontal rise. Moe did the same beside me, and as the explosions of impacts guided, I signaled. "Next bound. Go."

Mohammed scanned around. "Where are they, Captain? We fought thousands of the bugs last time. I thought the foul things would be pouring at us out of a million holes in this nest." Close above us, more explosions.

"Bound," came a voice.

"Good question. Let's go find out." I took a hop. Twenty meters was a tiny jump in armor. I touched down beside our base element and gave another spring up to the next tier. A battlement decorated in grotesque faces caught my eye—fangs and curled tongues taunting in stone—as did the writhing spiders behind it. I sprayed them with a burst from Annie as I landed, then I switched to grenade and launched another salvo upward as I touched down.

The pyramid narrowed with height, and as quickly as we were ascending, we'd soon be crowding into other teams assaulting uphill. I checked the field on my HUD. We covered the pyramid on three sides, and held a rising line now halfway to the top.

Perrault commed me. "Beck, it's going to get crowded up here."

"Flamers and blasters then?" I recommended.

"See you at the top."

I gave the order. Mohammed was already prepared. The terrace we stood on concealed sharp columns jutting into the concourse with deep corners concealing who knew what. With flamer in hand, my companion sprayed around a corner. I pictured a shriveling insect appearing from the other side, but nothing happened. "Check that dead space, Moe."

Mohammed stepped around, then back. "Nothing, sir. If there are entrances into the pyramid, we've not found them yet." The other two Ultimates of our small fireteam landed behind us. Up and down the terrace, more of us touched down.

"Time for grenades. Impact delay. Toss together, wait, and we bounce. Go." We each sent a hand grenade sailing over the next peak. They blew and we jumped. "Dead run to the top, boys."

And it was. We did the same again. Wrecked battlements and pieces of bugs we found as we ascended until finally, we held the top. I landed just as Perrault did from the other side.

"That was a bold move, Beck."

"What?" I asked in earnest innocence.

"Making a one-man charge at the pyramid? Insane. Whatever charm you think is protecting you, caveman, it isn't going to hold out forever."

Hideki's words to his men before dying came back to me. "You can't kill what's already dead."

The giant Teutates hit, sending a splash of dust and debris from where he'd landed. "Save it for someone who's impressed, Beck. No more heroics, Captain."

More Stalwarts followed, the last to reach the top.

"Mars and his escort return for the ship," Teutates informed us. "They will bring down the barrier once and for all. We must continue. Within, our enemy barricades to avoid meeting his justice. Come."

The hyper-vel I'd launched at the top brought the house down, so to speak. The flat deck that held the pointed crystal smashed into a billion clear fragments and collapsed on its columns, sealing the top of the pyramid. "Here will be the entrance." Teutates pointed to a pile of rubble. "Clear our way."

As Ultimates followed his directive to begin the task, Neton's irritable voice rang out. "Aside, weaklings!" He bent and wrapped arms around a jagged slab so large he could barely reach across it. With a heave he lifted, walked to the edge, and dropped the mass. He pointed at me. "I should make *you* clear the way, save that you could not."

"What's he mad about?" Stokes asked.

"Oh, I took the lead away from him. Twice. And I did kind of cause this mess. I thought maybe that big diamond was important. I didn't know it was just decoration. I thought something really cool would happen if I hit it."

Jess consoled me as Neton and the Stalwarts worked. "You never know till you try."

35

"He will not escape," Mars told Michael as they lifted. "Start raking that wall and don't stop till it's down. Then we keep watch. There's nowhere Mick can run. And if he tries, then he gets what's coming to him."

Michael grimaced. "Can he be terminated, Mars? The balance does not—"

Mars anticipated that Michael would argue with him about the compact and was quick to cut him short. "Okay, okay, Mike. But let's just say that if an accident happens, who's the wiser?"

"We are at altitude," Hestus reported behind the yoke.

"Gunnery commencing, Mars." Michael seemed to accept Mars's argument, or at least not press the issue further.

"Thank you, Mike. Just keep eyes peeled. I don't put it past Mick to have another trick up his sleeve. Not that it matters. If he were to make it out of here, the only place he could go would be Nergal's realm. And we do the same for him soon enough."

The deck guns rang out and began to work the base of the wall. It wouldn't hold for much longer. Michael received word that they were starting the search of the oath-breaking god's hold. Which meant soon, Mars would have him in a cage.

"Did you see that madman, Beck?" Mars said aloud but really to himself.

Michael and Hestus worked diligently. Joyless automatons of Mars's kingdom. Too busy to appreciate the pageantry of it all. But not even dull, dependable Michael could dampen this day for Mars.

Beck.

He continued to garner Mars's affection. Such men once received laurels. Mars hadn't thought about a triumph in a very long time. Maybe the citizens would appreciate such a thing. What really mattered was that the fires of the universe were being stoked.

The god of war had chosen well.

⚹　⚹　⚹

"What gives?" Magnus's disgust rivaled that of Neton, though the focus of his derision differed. "Be this some labyrinth?"

Axe in hand, he gingerly probed the wall with its firmness, testing it as part of a reality he understood. There was the Viking I missed beneath the veneer of modernity he'd acquired.

"It's some kind of maze, isn't it?" Jess asked.

Stokes whistled. "That's crazy. What do you say, Rag? You're the expert on these things."

I wasn't so sure about that. The Stalwarts fanned out through the passages, staves at the ready, only to find themselves confusedly converged back at the first intersection of their departure.

The scowl Teutates wore made him even more hideous, the explosion of ruptured gas lines after the earthquake. "Jove! This is dark magic."

"As I thought," Magnus said, looking about for demons as he gave his verdict. "'Tis witchcraft."

Whatever it was, we were at a temporary standstill until we figured it out, and I was content to stay back and let the Stalwarts work the solution. Neton had pushed me back once we'd dropped into the chasm. "This is work for the scions of the gods, not the likes of you. Hold your tiny toy soldiers here."

I swallowed my rage, but I couldn't let the slight go. He wasn't going to intimidate me. "About time you stepped up."

Neton scowled but didn't retaliate. If he wanted to grab some glory, he could be my guest. It had been Ultimates who'd died to get us here, and men like Jakob were more valuable than all the demigods put together. With twenty-nine of us remaining, I was in no hurry to feed my men into the buzzsaw again. But when the Stalwarts collided in the foyer from their differing paths, my resentment at Neton's insults evaporated. This was bad.

"Why do you say such of the captain?" Teutates asked. "How versed is he in these things?"

I spoke up. "I've studied mazes and games, but I'm no help with magic."

Teutates considered. "I curse this place, Beck, but I do not mean sorcery."

"Just put your hand on the right wall as you go and keep turning right. Or left," Stokes offered. "It's always worked for me when I tried your puzzles, Rag."

I frowned. "Nope. That only works if the maze joins the exterior wall at all points." A passage skirted the sloped outer walls of the pyramid where we'd watched Stalwarts disappear, and like the ones who took off down the central passage, all returned to this spot. "This is an island of walls and passages. Besides, I don't think this is a maze, or at least not like you guys are thinking."

"Why do you say such?" Teutates remained interested in my analysis.

I shrugged. "What did you and the Stalwarts find inside?"

"Twisting passages. Nothing more."

"How about it, Captain?" Jeong asked. "One more opportunity to demonstrate again to our exalted demis that mortal man has no better?"

Perrault spoke. "If you can work it out, by all means, Beck. Do it. The delay must end."

I appreciated their faith in me, but just then Gramps's voice was shouting in my head. I'd matured and gained experience in ways he would be amazed by. But what he was reminding me from across the ether of time simply proved that I still needed him. *When the crowd is pushing you to join the majority, just remember, eagles don't flock. A hundred people aren't smarter than one. First be sure you're right, then go ahead.*

Both the Stalwarts' discomfort at their failure to lead the next leg of the fight and the unjustified optimism of my Ultimates in my problem-solving ability grated me.

"This isn't meant to be solved," I said firmly. "Only to confuse and delay—and that it's doing. We're bleeding momentum. There's a hidden route within with a concealed entrance. Has to be. We can waste time searching for it, or we can make the obvious choice."

"Which is?" Denisov had slid into the group.

"Down is where we need to go." I hefted Stellia. "Stand back." I did as I'd been shown and aimed at the floor.

"Stop him," Neton yelled. "The brash ape will bring the walls down on us."

Teutates held out a hand the size of a grizzly's paw. "Hold, Captain. Neton is right, this is rash."

"We're not trying to find our way out. We're trying to find our way in. When Achilles went to kill the Minotaur, if he'd had a staff, he wouldn't have cared about trailing a string to find his way out of the labyrinth."

A Stalwart smacked his head with open palm. "'Twas Theseus who fought the Minotaur."

"Whatever." I dismissed the peanut gallery. "I'm right, Teutates."

The ugly giant sighed. "Michael begs news. Mars grows impatient." He took a step back. "You have the correct task chosen for the staff, yes?"

"I have, thanks to your lesson. I've attenuated the Hand of Hephaestus. We won't bring the house down." I was no longer a blind amateur with the staff. Just an amateur.

"Very well. Proceed."

The red ray expanded to make a neat circle and when it reached several meters across, I stopped its growth and drove it deep into the floor. Rock evaporated like a soldering iron going through ice. I extinguished the ray, and in its place was a bored hole. "Follow me."

Before the objection of Ultimate or Stalwart could deter me, I jumped, and both cautions and curses trailed my departure like a gate closed too late to keep the herd in.

"With you," Magnus said as he followed on my heels.

I landed on solid ground and ducked as winged creatures swarmed past me. Bats and owls in clouds of beating wings swooped through the air, filling the passage. My natural reaction suppressed, I stood erect, pulled a flamer, and sprayed into the torrent. "Magnus, help me cut through this mess."

"Demon consorts, they are," he spat as his own flamer hosed a path through the air, burning volant bodies fleeing and colliding off the walls, the screeches and shrieks deafening. We stood in a wide corridor, quickly filling with more heavy warriors through the tunnel I'd created.

Stokes directed the closest Ultimates. "Three on line. Go." He pushed Ultimates in a direction, shoulder to shoulder, filling the corridor from wall to wall with Annies at the ready. Perrault behind me signaled he would do the same.

"I'll go this way, Beck," he said. "Don't do anything too stupid while I'm gone. Stay in touch." Before I could retort, he pushed ahead, leading the first line, then was down the corridor and turned out of sight.

Smoke filled the air, and Teutates behind me grimaced. "Foul smells for a foul place."

I nodded. "We'll take a brief recon, and if we find no passage, we do the same again." I took off to follow the wave of Ultimates packing the corridor like Play-Doh through a press when a firefight broke out ahead.

White blasts whizzed past and someone yelled, "Spiders." We'd found the party.

"Through the walls! Through the walls!" I yelled, and brought Stellia up to repeat my magic. Stalwarts along the corridor joined in, and soon paths like mine opened on the long unbroken wall. Without pause, armored figures rushed through, gorilla Ultimate and gargantuan Stalwart alike.

"Teutates, have the Stalwarts pierce the 12 o'clock walls only if they must. Otherwise we'll kill our own guys." I had a reconstruction of our path inside the pyramid forming and sent it out. "We can bust right into their strongpoints from behind them. We're not limited to the corridors." With the staves, we had redefined CQB. Need a breachpoint? Make one. Anywhere. Walls no longer mattered. Not even stone ones so thick an atomic blast wouldn't scratch it.

Magnus roared with delight at the carnage. "Indeed, Captain. The spiders are caught unaware. We make progress quickly through the island of the maze."

"Magnus, let's go." I stepped through the new doorway and buzzed Perrault to update him. "We're coming up the middle. Don't worry about trying to push them back, just pile them up in the corridor. We'll hit them from behind." There was no reply. "Perrault?" I checked. His icon pulsed red. One moment your comrade was next to you. The next, he was gone. Like it always was. There was nothing to do but curse and file it away.

"Perrault's down," I said to Magnus as we hurried.

"And more good men with him. Cursed spiders. We find their nest, we find their master, and we end this."

Decisive death had been dealt to the enemy filling the maze. Passages turned left and right. Spider bodies leaking black ichor, awful and twisted in angular death, were stacked so high they blocked passages from floor to ceiling, yet more did not topple them out of the way to push through on endless assault. We hadn't fought them to their last numbers at the Battle of Capitoline until we'd resorted to atomics. It told me that here, the enemy numbers were finite.

We followed where paths had been cut through the walls moments before. Across another cut, through a large room with more insectoid carcasses, I reached the end of a halted train of Ultimates. The rear most pointed ahead. "Sir, through there. Don't know what it is."

I slid past, an icebreaker pushing through the narrow between armored behemoths, until I broke into a concourse curving around a domed room with many arched portals. Through the closest archway, a radiance emanated. In its center, a broad column of light was positioned as though it were a physical buttress. Around it stood the Stalwarts, hesitatingly wary and keeping distance from the thing. Elsewhere the sound of firefights continued.

Teutates hailed me over. "As you predicted, Beck, it is the passage we sought, not concealed on this level of their fortress."

"What are we waiting for? Let's go."

"Hold, Captain. It is locked. Without the key, it would be perilous to enter."

"Locked? So more spiders aren't coming up through that?"

"No. I have examined the enemy, and they do not hold the key. It is locked from the other side."

"So how do we get through?"

Michael's face appeared. "No." He said the single word, apparently the answer to a question I'd missed. "We will not leave Mictlantecutli barricaded in a prison of his own choosing. Mars commands—"

The face of Mars stepped into the picture. "Toots, get me that backstabbing fool. We're not detailing a guard to keep him shut in here forever. He's coming out with us. I want him in chains and in a cage to parade through the streets of Capitoline. We have the wall down, and if need be, we'll drop his rock palace on top of him. But I know you can do better. Get on it."

The image vanished.

"I know the difference between a 'try your best' and 'get it done,'" Stokes said from the corridor. "Mars means for us to do or die trying."

"Teutates, is that what I think it is?" Through the electron mist sat a platform that reminded me of the discs we flew around on in Valhalla. "What would happen if you stepped in? We're shielded from pretty heavy stuff in this armor."

At this point, I was becoming irritable. Which is a polite way of saying pissed. The Stalwarts had proven to me they were all show and no go when it came to being combat leaders. They weren't afraid to fight, but as far as being aggressive leaders? As a lane grader, I flunked them all.

The Stalwart Corotiacus stepped forward. "I am unbeatable in combat, and my armor is impervious compared to yours, yet I could not withstand the passage through the barrier."

"We find another way down. Time to start drilling."

"It will not work," Corotiacus insisted. "The barrier covers all below, much as the exterior wall repelled our attack. It is back to a siege again that we must go. I report to Mars now."

Sometimes, it's the worst quality that makes for what's later called a hero. How many fortresses had been taken just because the guy fighting uphill had become sick and tired and decided he'd had enough? Times when common sense and tactical maturity got choked out by blind rage. I was sure it was plenty.

"No way. You can tell him you don't know how to get the job done. Not me. Time to shit or get off the pot." I stroked Stellia. I'd already experienced the passive protective effect the staff provided when I'd been shot with accelerated plasma at a range that should've turned me into ash. If I tasked her to active protection and hoped for the best, what's the worst that could happen? If I died, at least I'd no longer be standing here debating the dilemma.

I really didn't care anymore. I upped the scale on the shield icon and stepped through.

Denisov pouted. "And *I* am called reckless with lives."

I landed on the disc, and immediately it dropped. Elevator going down.

"No problem with the help of the staff, boys. Up the shield to max and let's go to work. I'm afraid this means Stalwarts only unless I can find the off switch down here." The disc sank, down and down, deeper than I pictured the shaft should be to take me to the next level. "Guys?"

There was no response. The walls of the shafted continued to whiz past. Suddenly I dropped through into a cavern larger than I conceived the base of the pyramid to be.

Spiders, few in number, unarmored and unarmed moved about on the floor still far below. They took no heed of me as the platform continued to sink. Row after row of containers they tended in perfect order. I took a hop off while still descending and aimed myself for a passage between the lines of containers. The path disappeared into the wall, and I made that my destination.

I hit the ground at a trot, ready to demolish anything in my path. Bugs scattered out of my way. Except for causing a temporary detour out of my path, the spiders continued in whatever task they'd been given, oblivious to the presence of an armored juggernaut hurtling down their alley. I focused on the tunnel ahead. Dim light came forth and through it, more of the containers, pushed by eight-legged worker drones out one side, unburdened bugs returning on the other side. I checked up. Standing at the tunnel mouth between opposing lanes of traffic, I saw that the tunnel narrowed and converged at a far horizon where a brighter light beckoned me. I burst into a run.

The tunnel was just wide enough for me to pass between the nauseating things. Somewhere, their militant bug brethren had to be waiting. If it was at the end of this race they waited, then I'd cross the finish line with a bang. I slowed and cast my vision far as I neared the end. Chamber after chamber of spider and containers went about some ghastly business, bloody meat sheared off carcasses in a process no different than any slaughterhouse killing floor. I knew what I was seeing, but it had to wait. If I had hackles, they were raised.

The room beyond was only too familiar to me. A rotunda ringed by columns. Two stone pillars in its center. The sheen between them was of a sickly color. Through it a spider exited, dragging behind it a limp figure in Mark 5 Combat Armor. I fired and swung to the next threat.

Behind the nearby rostrum stood the prize. Atop a blood-spattered skeleton sat a toothy skull, decorated with an owl feather headdress and a necklace of human eyeballs. Dangling from the ears were bones—small but distinctly human—the skeletal remains of more than one child. It wore a coat of webs on which crawled multicolored desert spiders. A cloud of bats circled its head. The thing hissed at me.

"Glad to meet you, Mick."

I tossed a concussion grenade at the god's feet.

"Mars sends his regards."

36

"Down but not out," I thought. Reaching for the restraints on my waist, I plowed at Mick before the dust from my grenade settled. A skeletal foot caught me in the chin and sent me reeling.

Not even down, my inner voice mocked in the most annoying manner possible using Gramps's voice. Stellia was out of my hands. I sprawled to find her when a kick landed in my midsection and sent me flying.

Skeleton or not, a god is a god.

I had no desire to go toe to toe with even a small-g god.

He closed at me like a charging boar, his teeth dripping blood as a banshee howl pierced my skull. Annie came off my back. I mashed the trigger, and before the charge accelerated down the barrel, I thumbed the selector and sent a grenade at Mick's chest. THUNK. The supercharged ball of plasma hit him square on, the grenade landing right behind. I had his attention. For a second. The detonation grew as it was supposed to, increasing the surface area of its impact before discharging with full force, but slowly as though time had been altered. I expected the blast to take us both out. With a scream he swatted the charge aside, and the pace of time resumed. It shot off and impacted against a stack of the black containers like so much spall. The explosion I'd wanted didn't come, but I used the time I'd bought wisely.

Stellia lay close by. I dove and recovered her, rolling to a knee as I brought her glowing tip in front of me as a ward against the evil in front of me. He froze. Here now was something that got his respect. "You know I'm holding back the floodgates of the power of Mars in my staff, don't you, Mick? With just a thought and a touch of my finger, you're done for."

He hissed a whispering wind, the jaw unnaturally motionless, a black maw where tongue should be. The eerie echo of a stolen voice came out. "You are the whisp of what was once a mortal. It is *infamia* for you to touch a vessel of power such as that you hold. And to use it—an insult to the gods! Mars would have no choice but to consign you to hell eternal for breaking the covenant."

Now I knew I had him. "All you so-called gods are liars. But Mars has me convinced of this—you're the one who broke the rules, Mick." I stood, keeping Stellia extended at the ghoulish wreck. "I'm not a cosignatory of any covenant that I know of, so you're barking up the wrong tree if you think that's going to stop me from wasting you. I see I toasted all your little vermin."

The spiders and bats were gone, either dead or they knew to get while the getting was good. Pests knew when the exterminator was in town. He hissed, his vacant eye sockets fixed on Stellia.

The armored body lying in front of the gate told me a tale as sure as if I'd heard it from a living witness. And in the rooms behind him, shells of armor peeled off men lay discarded like trash. Nothing was without the tinge of blood. My vision turned the same red. "Mars said you'd tore into the fabric of the old domain, but even Perrault didn't piece together what that meant. You found the spiders. You helped them reach humanity. And they're bringing you victims to feed on, you sick bastard. If you thought Mars would give you a pass on entering the plane of the living, what do you think he's going to do to you when he finds out about your cannibalism? Why should I even wait for him to punish you?"

"Your kind worshipped at my feet! They begged for the honor to feed me their flesh. They fed of each other to show worship to me. And after so very, very long, I have a new kingdom among the living."

Would Mars be outraged? Would he punish this abomination? Or was this just more feeding the churn? "It's time you go wherever dead gods are supposed to go." I shouldered Stellia and took aim, right between where his nipples would be, if he had such.

"You cannot harm a god! Even if you dared."

"Then you shouldn't be protesting so much, Mick."

"NO!" he recoiled and shrank. "I yield! Do as your god commands you. Mars desires me his prisoner. It is for him to judge me, not you." He tore the necklace away. The glossy eyeballs came off their string and rolled across the floor.

Like a wall crumbling, Teutates spoke in my ear. "Captain Beck! We know your location. We come to your aid now."

I took my finger away from the recessed knot of a trigger. "Where were you and the Stalwarts?"

"Mictlantecutli's trickery prevented us from pursuit," Teutates explained. "The nature of the barrier was transmuted after you passed. Are you in battle?"

"I have Mick. Hurry up before I change my mind and waste him."

I only had to wait a few minutes before I was swarmed with help.

"Beck!" Mars's voice roared. His apparition appeared in the rotunda. "And Mictlantecutli! Mick, you've been a naughty boy. If you're going to strike at the king, you'd best kill him. Stocking up for a long winter I see? Thought to barricade yourself from me until I forgot your treachery? It's going to be a very long time before you get to play again. A very long time. Bring him to me, Stalwarts."

Teutates stood over the cowering monster and produced a scroll as chains were tightened around the hissing, squirming god. "Mictlantecutli, Aztec God of the dead and king of Mictlan, northernmost province of the underworld. I hold a warrant in your name. Come with me now and face judgement by the king."

They led him away.

Mars's disembodied head still floated over us. "Beck, my boy, you did me proud."

I reflexively assumed the position. On knee, eyes down. "Thank you, O great Mars."

"We will have an audience soon, son. Make haste so we can depart."

He was gone.

Magnus exploded forward and hefted me to my feet. "I thought you'd gone alone into the bowels of hell!"

"Pretty much." My armor prevented his bear hug from breaking ribs, but just barely. "Little tight, pal."

He dropped me and gestured to the gore of Perrault's kinsmen who had been pulled through the gates by the spiders—a feast for Mictlantecutli. "What manner of madness is this?"

"I'll explain later. Let's go."

Denisov snapped to attention as I passed and saluted. "Sir. The thing is done. And you have done it."

"No, Ivan Ivanovich. It is not yet done. But we *have* done what Mars commanded, by the courage of our dead. Now it's up to Mars to finish the mission."

No cheers went up. The scene was gruesome, and all I wanted to do was leave.

"We paid a high price," Jeong said. "And these poor souls? What do we do for these men?" The butchered remains spilled on the floor like so much meat made me swoon.

"Our general will know. Our king. Our god." It almost sounded like a prayer. I regretted the words as I said them. Because I knew that our god wouldn't care. "I'm glad Perrault bought it before he learned the truth."

"What truth?" Stokes asked.

"That his future was worse than mine."

✳ ✳ ✳

The lowered waist ramp of the hovering warship rested on the top of the pyramid as the Stalwarts ushered a chained Mictlantecutli forward. Mars beamed down. "Oh, Mick, such grand times we're going to have together, you and me. Ah Puch is already waiting for you. And don't fret, I haven't forgotten about Nergal. I'll be sorting him out presently. It'll be quite the reunion for you three—one that will last for eternity."

The ramp raised, and around me stood the remaining Ultimates. Twenty warriors whose skill and luck had brought them with me to the end of another battle. Were we at that combat ineffective phase that Perrault told me about? A unit with so many losses that Mars mustered the survivors out and started to build again? There were barely enough of us left for two squads. If oblivion was our reward, would what came next be so bad? Living in ignorance in this afterlife had left me apathetic—or at least philosophic—about when my time came to join the fallen.

A cage with bars of vibrating lightning bolts sat on the forecastle. Mars at his command post was still elated and spoke as if he were the emcee of one of those old roasts. "Put him in please, boys. I want him to have the best seat in the house. Michael, close up shop here if you'd be so kind. Hestus, give us a nice racetrack pass so we can all enjoy the view."

We rose once again with same inertia-free ascent, and as Mars had commanded, the ship banked high above the kingdom of Mictlantecutli. The aurora marking the edge of his realm was visible, and beyond, nothingness.

"Very nice piloting, Michael. Turnabout's fair in this case, Mick. You forced me to use atomics on my home turf, I thought to return the favor. Mike, if you please."

A flash. A cloud of atomic fury. And devastation. Where had been the court of the Aztec god of the underworld was a plain of rubble.

Mars threw his head back, his bearded mouth wide, and roared a deep belly so loud it drowned out the fading blast below. "I'd say your kingdom will be fit for you to conjure up some new soldiers about the time you get out of my dungeon. Which is to say, never."

The prisoner shrank and drew the webs of his cowl over him, a wild animal now broken—captive and retreating within itself. I doubted that the bite had gone out of him fully, but Mars seemed satisfied. "Good. The lesson has just begun. Take us home.

"Beck!" I started at Mars's calling my name and trotted across the waist deck to where he commanded from above. He held a palm out to stop me in my tracks before I made obeisance. "There'll be time for an audience later, but I wanted you to know. I've got plans for you, son. I'm gonna make you an offer you can't refuse."

※　※　※

Some soldiers become giddy after a fight. Some become withdrawn. Jess and Danny were the only ones interacting, huddled so closely that armored legs touched, heads bent in quiet conversation, true physical contact prevented by the barrier of their stoic professionalism, even now. I thought about the promise I'd made myself to bargain for a better life for the two.

The rest were like me, alone with our thoughts as we rode the ether back to Valhalla. *An offer I couldn't refuse.* What did Mars mean? I tried not to think about it, or the names and faces of those we'd lost. I tried not to think about the fight that would be next. I tried not to think. Instead, I imaged the glowing aurora around us was the flickering flames of that celebratory fire Danny had once reminded me we neglected to build, the faces of friends from both of my armies around it as we laughed. If I'd ever imagined a heaven, that's what I thought it would look like.

And as Will had told me on day one, Valhalla was not heaven. It was not a place for rest. It was a place to prepare for war. I snapped out of my melancholy. Until Mars told me differently, that's what I would be doing. Nergal was out there, awaiting capture and punishment. That's what Mars would be commanding me to do next. I was now sure of it. The offer would be to command his army again—what remained.

While we'd been gone, the rebuilding had already begun. The citizens of Capitoline labored in the distance of the city I now knew wasn't a Hollywood façade. It was a place of living, breathing people with lives and all that entailed. I wondered who they were. Other, lesser gods? We'd protected them, and that was something to feel good about.

Our Cradle was wrecked. Perrault's stood, and was the logical place to begin to reform my Ultimates. It was there that we returned, and where most of us were finding a new place to rest our heads. I was shown to the deceased commander's quarters, and it reminded me of my own. Barren. Save for the silver diadem on the tiny shelf next to the sleep pallet, there were no personal items. It made me feel interchangeable and common in a way I hadn't felt since I was a private on the first day of basic training, a literal lifetime ago.

How long had it been since I'd placed the silver crown on my head as I prepared for a session of learning while I slept? Mine was gone. Buried in the rubble of our Cradle. I supposed we'd be outfitted with new ones, along with a new complement of gear and weapons. All things to speak to Michael about tomorrow. I lay on my dead friend's bunk, the diadem next to me. Seemed harmless to try. I placed it on, closed my eyes, and drifted off as I wondered if I would dream of how to repair the track of an armored personnel carrier, or how to employ a laser mine defense.

I bolted upright and flipped the crown from my head. These weren't the lucid dreams of any lesson in warfare.

Instead, a pulsing wave of white static, and with it, a feeling of dread. And beneath it all, not a voice, but a message that stayed with me after a night of fitful dreams I couldn't remember.

You are a phantom.

The hall of Mars was no less impressive the next morning than it had been on my first visit. I ascended the stairs and marched ahead to perform my obeisance to a waiting Mars, Michael at his side. A curved seat sat below his dais, and I had an inkling of what was about to occur. Custom completed, Mars commanded me to rise.

"Pull up a chair, son." It was an order, not an option. I sat but remained stiff. "Beck, I'm pleased with you. So much so, I want you to stick around. Perrault told you about his role here. I want you to do the same. You'll be the senior in charge of building a new army for me. But your honorable service to me demands just consideration. I reward loyalty. The choice is yours. You may remain here, or you may take the path of the others."

"Where are they going?"

Michael took up. "Goshang Perrault told you that those who are discharged are sent on their way. It is to the same place that the fallen go. To each his own."

"I barely know where I am now, much less where anywhere else is. Where have our fallen gone? Where do Ultimates go once they've been released from service, Mars? I don't understand."

Mars folded his lips inward. "There's no way you could, but I will try. Mortals have tried to describe the incomprehensible nature of their existence, always with the mind of a child, but one was close when they said that what is done in life will echo in eternity.

"We exist here in all time and at no time. I can reach out at any point in existence and borrow a spark from the thread of the trail that remains from one ascended from their mortal coil. The fallen went to where they were going all along. In fact, their essence, their souls—and yours—are already there.

"Heaven, Nirvana, Paradise, Elysium—where many of my siblings await—all are filled with the eternal souls of all beings who've left the plane of existence for the afterlife. None can interfere with that, not even a god. All I can do is borrow a spark from the fire of those that have the potential to be an Ultimate. It is an echo, pulled from the thread. A ray of light from which a mirror reflects a part of the essence, called by me to burn here for a short while."

I'd felt it for some time. Stokes had stumbled into the truth of it when he said that he wasn't a man anymore, but a ghost. "I am a phantom. What's here is not really me."

Michael gave a solid shake of his head. "You're real, Beck. Do you not possess your memories, your knowledge, your ethos, your drive as a warrior? It is Ragnar Beck who sits before us."

"But I'm also somewhere else in the afterlife? I'm already in—Heaven?"

Michael nodded approvingly as though I'd given indication that the light was going on for me at last. "And so will you rejoin the whole of your being there when your service to Mars is at an end."

"And the well of souls? Oblivion?"

Mars grinned sheepishly but without shame. "If a soldier knew that all he had do was fall, how many would choose to remain here and fight? Even a mortal can see that keeping such knowledge concealed is necessary for the discipline of an army. Would you tell a soldier that he could quit anytime if he so chose? That there was no penalty for leaving service? Duty and honor retain them. But penalties like prison ensure that if they lose heart, they don't desert. Even amongst the fanatical soldiers I pull out of the ether to try out for my army, how many would quit on the spot if they knew? The threat of oblivion or the well of souls is a deception but a necessary one."

"Why us? Why soldiers who've died the way we all did?'

"You know the saying about the general who said that out of every hundred men they send him, there are ten who shouldn't be there, eighty who are only targets, nine who are real fighters—who he's grateful to have—and then there's the one. The true warrior. And it's him who brings the others back. Beck, it's one in a million—billion—who has the right stuff. And it's only those who go out the way you did who leave the trace I can touch."

"So you see that spark and you bring it here. You test it, teach it, and if it makes the cut, you put it to work."

"Not 'it', Beck. You. A man. Remade flesh and blood. When your time here is done, whether you're unsuitable and we send you to the 'well of souls' or you buy the farm in real battle, that spark just rejoins the flame. That's all."

I was following what Mars was saying. I just wasn't sure I believed him. Jakob's final words rested heavily on me. "And the Plains of Eternity? How come we come back from there over and over again?"

"It's a testing ground. It exists as another kind of an echo. It's all construct."

"But why? Why do we fight? What is our purpose here?"

Mars laughed his deep throaty gargle. "Some questions even I don't have answers to. I command an army to keep the churn of the universe swirling, because it is war that makes for the essential fire of existence."

My bearing broke. My head dropped into my hands and I felt dizzy. It was answers I'd wanted, and now, here they were. But it was too much.

Mars gave a slight, almost fatherly smile. "It's okay, son. You're struggling to understand what no mortal ever has. What is reality? What is life and death? It's all a dream. There's only the here and now. Beck, you're not meant to understand. But I thought it was fair to let you try. Can you accept that regardless, the battles waged here are important to the churn of existence? Which means, *you* are important to the churn. I need you here. The time will come for you to go, for that tiny part of the spark of Ragnar Beck that lives here to rejoin with your being in the afterlife of your human existence.

"And while you're here, I'm offering you a position that I've only offered to one other mortal in all of eternity. I'm offering to let you take the place of a Stalwart in this organization. There's a lot to be done. You'll be building my whole army again from scratch. What do you say?"

What could I say? Go sit on a cloud and pluck that harp, or stay here and do the only thing I ever wanted to do since I could remember. Soldier.

Besides, this was all just a mad dream anyway. Why not keep it going a while longer?

"Where do I sign?"

✕　✕　✕

Michael shook his head as Beck departed.

"Whatsa matta, Mike? You don't approve?"

Michael resumed his blank look. "The mortals are an enigma to me, Mars. After an eternity, I am no closer to understanding them. Nor your attachment to them."

"Robots are predictable. They're consistent only in their mediocrity. Humans have flaws, and while some of them have all the worst qualities, some of them have a glimmer of greatness in them. Like Beck."

The anger Mars had put aside returned. "The coup the others attempted caught us off guard. After an eternity, something new has happened. Gabriel's departure for Elysium and the failure of the Stalwarts to carry the fight has made this clear to me: we've gotten complacent. Even I can see that this requires a new paradigm to counter."

Michael took on an almost quizzical look. "Perhaps it is as the churn desires?"

"Change is inevitable, even here. And an iconoclast like Beck may bring us a new advantage. I'm ready to try. Besides, it'll be entertaining! Beck's proven to be that. Oh, come now, Mike, Don't pretend you're not fond of him and the other mortals. Would you prefer our army were constituted of the same clay of animate muck as the others?"

"Hmph. It would be easier. I question, is it certain that there can be no retained memory of his past experiences here? Beck came far in his development this time. If not learning from past mistakes, was it simply luck or astral alignment that's allowed him to advance so well?"

"Luck? Certainly. But each time he leaves my service and rejoins the stream, he takes some residue of his time here with him. Each time I touch the stream of his soul to borrow an-

other spark to use here, some minor amount of that residue returns with it."

Mars had told Beck one in a billion had the right stuff. It was less than that. Such was why he pulled the same sparks over and over. Why he had marked Karl to avoid repeating the mistake of choosing him. *There are too few warriors.*

Michael considered. "Yet it does not explain why some of the others who've been called again and again haven't advanced as he has."

"True. There are mysteries even I cannot solve, Michael. Let's not buy into our own hype."

"Their curiosity is insuppressible. And tiresome."

"Which reminds me, tell S-1 and S-4 to get to work. Get the Cradles rebuilt and restocked, and get Beck a new Diadem of Minerva. He needs to get back to concentrating on matters more important than philosophy. Beck will ponder what I've told him, and fail. With the diadem's help, he'll gradually forget over the next few nights as the educator removes these memories, leaving in their place the purposeful soldier. Ever and always.

"Once you've done that, you can help me plan the Triumph. Nergal's not going anywhere. When Beck gets me a company of Ultimates built back, we'll let him tackle that front. In the meantime, my citizens need to celebrate their king's victory."

"Yes, Mars. Teutates is due his turn to proctor a company. As is Neton. As bristled as he is by the mortals, he too is due a turn at leading. Shall I inform them of their future duties?"

"Not yet, Mike. First, we let Beck get another army built, one company at a time. Then we'll see. Neton, I'll reexamine that when the time comes."

"It's a great trust you place in him, Mars. I need not re-mind you what happened the last time. How long do you think he'll remain for this task?"

"For as long as the fates will it, Mike."

EPILOGUE

Just as Mars promised me, my friends and comrades had met the standards for their discharge. "Home? We're going home? How can that be?" Danny asked with disbelief.

Jess laid a hand on his. "If Rag says it's so, then it is."

"Mars promised me, friends. It was one of the things Perrault told me about that I promised to hold back. An honorable discharge after your term of service is complete."

Michael was there, as was Hestus, manning the rostrum. The gate opened with a pearlescent glow, much different from any of the gates we'd seen before. "Mars has discharged you all after your honorable service to him. He returns you on your way with thanks and honor heaped upon your legacies. Pass through and accept your reward for your faithfulness."

Denisov, Jeong, and the rest stood in kilt and tunic. Without armor, they looked naked. I took my place next to the gate.

Smitty was first to accept my invitation to approach. I stuck out my hand. "Job well done, brother."

He took my hand. "Thank you, sir. I hope to see you around, cousin." Smitty smiled and walked through.

I shook the hand of each man as they departed.

Denisov hesitated. "I always thought that after the grave there was nothing. But I know differently. I do not know what comes next, but I am not afraid. I feel... ready."

"You go on to the place reserved for you before you were even made."

His eyebrows shot up. "I would say it is hard to believe, but I have come to believe anything is possible. Farewell, comrade."

Magnus grunted, then punched me in the chest. "It is to the actual Valhalla I go now. I feel it. Come find me there, brother. You were not meant for rest and peace."

Other than Danny and Jess, Magnus I would miss most. "Somehow I don't think rest and peace will be on the agenda here, buddy."

Danny and Jess were last, side-by-side holding hands. "I had a dream last night, Rag," Jess said in a tiny voice. "A dream about a yellow house with a yard and a fence. And Dan chased children in the yard, and there was a dog, and everything I'd ever dreamed of. It was so real. I woke up crying tears of joy. This is where we're going, isn't it?"

Michael had told me that there wouldn't be any resistance to the news that everyone was being discharged. As I'd long suspected, the diadems did more than just teach us. They conditioned behavior. Which meant it conditioned me too. "That's right, Jess."

"Will you come too, Rag?" Dan asked tearfully.

"Eventually. I'll be along as soon as I can, and we'll all be together. Save a spot by the fire for me."

They each hugged me, and I them. They weren't alone in wiping away tears. Holding hands, they passed through together. The gate closed. I was alone.

I brushed away the last tear and turned back to where the two Stalwarts patiently waited. Michael was the stoic perfection I'd expected. Hestus had a tiny smirk. My two demigods.

"Seems we're stuck with each other a while longer, gents. Mars wants an army built, and we're not getting it done by standing here. What say we get to work?"

※　※　※

I watched the swirl of mists open and a battle scene came into focus. "Is that the one, Michael?"

"It is. His spark is so marked. Observe."

Knee deep in brass and hand grenade pins, the green clad soldier swung an entrenching tool at the heads of the rushing enemy, felling one after another until finally his head snapped back from the impact of a single bullet. He succumbed and collapsed onto the piles of enemy he'd stacked around him.

He seemed an obvious choice. "I'd say he fits the bill of what Mars wants in a candidate. He's as good a place to start as any. Let's bring him back. I'm ready." The training grounds were empty save for Michael and me. But soon there would be a squad, then a platoon, and eventually a company of men on these sands for me to forge into Ultimates.

"Beck. This now belongs to you, by order of Mars." Michael tossed me a bundle. I unfurled it. In my hands was Gabriel's gleaming sword. I was speechless before finally stammering, "I thought Stellia was a great gift. This—" I strapped it around me. "I will use it well."

Michael made the tiniest smile. "Gabriel would approve. Now, make ready."

On the sand appeared the new candidate. I gave him a moment to regain focus, remembering well what it was like to be him. I had my speech well prepared.

"Before man was, war waited for him." I unsheathed Gabriel's sword and marveled as the edges turned to flame. The man I menaced shook himself out of his stupor. The soldier was lean and grizzled with a sharp buzz cut. He took in the sword held by his own hand. His puzzlement faded as he looked at me, then growled. He was ready.

"You've been chosen to try out for the toughest unit that's ever been or ever will be. And if you think you've got what it takes, then you better be ready to prove it. Because anyone who would call themselves a warrior must always be ready to prove themselves worthy.

"So come on, mortal! Show me what you got!"

THE END

To get in touch with Jason Anspach, visit www.JasonAnspach.com. There you can sign up to be notified of his future releases and receive free short stories. He most prefers receiving letters, so please mail him at:

PO BOX 534
Puyallup, WA 98371

Doc Spears is rarely in one place for long. To hear about his next releases, please visit www.WarGateBooks.com and sign up for the WarGate newsletter!

※　※　※